The
Accide
Wife

Rowan Coleman worked in bookselling and then publishing for seven years, during which time she wrote her first novel, *Growing Up Twice*, published in 2002. She left to write her second novel, *After Ever After*, and now lives and writes in Hertfordshire with her husband and daughter.

Praise for Rowan Coleman

'A fresh, warm and hugely enjoyable read . . . truly brilliant. Her captivating style leaps off the page, engrossing you from the first sentence' *Company*

'Brilliant . . . moving, funny – just the tonic every knackered new woman needs!' *New Woman*

'A charming tale' *heat*

'Highly enjoyable . . . Coleman tells her story with bundles of warmth and humour' *Spectator*

'Touching and thought-provoking' *B*

'*Growing Up Twice* was a triumphant first novel and the follow-up is just as impressive' *OK!*

'Emotionally satisfying page-turner' *Closer*

The
Accidental
Wife

Rowan
Coleman

arrow books

Published by Arrow Books 2008

2 4 6 8 10 9 7 5 3 1

Copyright © Rowan Coleman 2008

Rowan Coleman has asserted her right under the Copyright, Designs
and Patents Act 1988 to be identified as the author of this work

This novel is a work of fiction. Names and characters are the product of the author's
imagination and any resemblance to actual persons, living or dead, is entirely coincidental

First published in Great Britain in 2008 by
Arrow Books
Random House, 20 Vauxhall Bridge Road,
London SW1V 2SA

www.rbooks.co.uk

Addresses for companies within The Random House Group Limited can be found at:
www.randomhouse.co.uk/offices.htm

The Random House Group Limited Reg. No. 954009

A CIP catalogue record for this book
is available from the British Library

ISBN 9780099493075

The Random House Group Limited supports The Forest Stewardship Council (FSC),
the leading international forest certification organisation. All our titles that are printed
on Greenpeace approved FSC certified paper carry the FSC logo. Our paper procurement
policy can be found at www.rbooks.co.uk/environment

Typeset by SX Composing DTP, Rayleigh, Essex
Printed and bound in Great Britain by
CPI Bookmarque, Croydon, CR0 4TD

For Erol and Lily, my sunshine

Acknowledgements

I don't think I have ever written a book before that focuses so strongly on female relationships and how crucial they are in a woman's life, and when I began to write these acknowledgements I realised why. So many women are so important to me and to my writing.

Thank you so much to Kate Elton for her unswerving faith in me that means so very much, and to both Kate and Georgina Hawtrey-Woore for the always wonderfully creative and intelligent editorial support they provide. Working with them is always a privilege and a pleasure.

Thank you so much to my agent and good friend Lizzy Kremer, who works tirelessly on my behalf and to whom I have so much to be grateful to.

Also, thank you to my oldest best friends Jenny Matthews, Rosie Wooley, Sarah Darby, Clare Winter and Cathy Carter. You girls have been a part of my life for so long, I never laugh so much as when I am with you and the continued support you give me is key to everything I write.

I could not have written this book without the help of my new best friends Margi Harris, Kirsty Seaman and Catherine Ashley who were always there with offers of help, childcare and occasionally wine! Kirsty and Catherine were kind enough to let me use their names in this book and its only fair to point out that neither one of them is anything like their namesakes!

Thank you to my mum who, I think above everything else, has taught me how to be a good friend.

And finally, thank you to the token man in these acknowledgements, my hsuband Erol who is always there for me, always supporting me and whose love keeps me going. And of course all my love to my daughter Lily who is my sunshine and who makes me feel like spring is here, even on the darkest, wettest day.

Chapter One

Alison James found that her feet could not move.

'Goodbye fireplace; goodbye window; goodbye spider's web; goodbye door knob . . .'

As Alison listened to five-year-old Amy's litany of farewells she thought of her husband in the car, his forefinger drumming against the steering wheel impatiently as he waited for her and Amy to come out and join the rest of the family to go to their new home, their new life. The removal lorry had left almost half an hour ago and Alison knew that Marc was horrified at the thought of his widescreen TV languishing on the damp front lawn while the movers waited for someone to let them in. What he didn't know was that for two of the family, at least, and despite all that had happened here, it was hard to say goodbye.

The car horn sounded, three long bursts that made Amy jump.

'Come on then, sweetheart,' Alison said, taking her daughter's hand. 'It's time to go to our new home. It will be very exciting, won't it? A proper adventure.'

Amy looked up at her mummy. 'But I haven't said goodbye stairs; goodbye loo; goodbye airing cupboard; goodbye . . .'

'How about you just say one big goodbye to the whole house?' Alison prompted her, even though she would be perfectly happy to wait while Amy bade farewell to every brick and board. She knew exactly how her daughter felt about leaving their London home because she was just as reluctant, particularly considering where they were moving to. Everyone else thought they were starting afresh, beginning a new life and turning a clean page. Only Alison understood that they were travelling back into the past, more specifically, her past.

But the decision had been made and now it was impossible to turn back.

'Is Farmington nice, Mama?' Amy asked, closing her fingers tightly around Alison's.

Alison felt an echoing clench of anxiety in her gut. 'Yes, darling, it's lovely. It's the place where Mummy grew up, remember? There's lots of room to play and not so much pollution. And the school will be great. You'll love it. Just think of all the new friends you'll make.'

Alison looked down at Amy's small, quiet face; she could only guess at how terrifying this move must seem to the five-year-old.

What her husband didn't seem to be able to understand was that going home was nearly as terrifying for her.

'Goodbye house,' Amy said on a heavy sigh. 'Be happy with your new family.'

Then finally Alison forced her leaden feet to move and, leading Amy by the hand, she shut the front door on her old life for ever.

'Get a move on, love.' Marc leaned out of the car window. 'I'd like to get us all in before dark!'

Once in the car Alison looked in the rear-view mirror. Fifteen-year-old Dominic was slumped at the very back, his arms crossed, his woollen hat pulled down over his brows so his black hair fanned into his eyes, his beloved electric guitar in its case on the seat next to him. He was plugged into his iPod with his eyes closed, shutting the world out, displaying his disapproval at what was happening with a silent if not peaceful protest. Her middle child, eight-year-old Gemma, was staring happily out of the window, her legs drumming in anticipation of a new adventure, a new world to conquer and hundreds of new friends to make, possibly the only one in the whole family who was truly looking towards the future.

Only Amy, who had her palms pressed against the car window, kept looking back. Only Amy was still saying her goodbyes even as they turned the corner and their old street was out of sight for good. Only Amy, who brushed away a tear with the heel of a hand and then plugged her mouth with her thumb and clung on to her toy for dear life, seemed aware of exactly what they had left behind.

Only Amy and Alison, that is.

'Come on Alison, it's perfect, admit it?' Marc had pressed her only six weeks earlier, when he'd told her he thought they should put the house on the market and that he'd found them the perfect place to move to.

Alison had half looked at the details of the new house he had thrust under her nose the minute he'd walked in the door. That was Marc: he was an all-or-nothing kind of man. Things had to be done right away or not at all. He had made a mistake and now he was taking decisive action to fix it – decisive and drastic. The house in the photo was certainly much bigger than their current house, set in some grounds at the end of what looked like a long driveway.

'There's no way we can afford a house like this near enough to London for you to be able to commute, and if you think that I'm going to be stuck out in the country while you're in town all week then –'

'That's not it at all, Al,' he said. 'I've been thinking, and,

3

well, the dealership in Notting Hill runs itself more or less. It's established. There's no challenge for me there any more and I think we all need a change, a proper fresh start.' Alison waited for the hard sell. Marc took her hand as he sat down next to her. 'You need a change of scenery after everything that happened at Christmas, not to mention what's been going on with Dom. That's twice now he's been brought home by a policeman, Alison. He's already been cautioned for riding in a stolen car. What will happen next? Will we find a knife in his school bag or have the next policeman that turns up on our doorstep telling us our son's been shot for looking at someone the wrong way? You don't want that life for him, do you, Al? This is the prefect solution, and see where the house is.'

Alison had stopped looking at her husband the moment he mentioned Christmas. Only Marc could refer in passing to something so painful and humiliating, as if what had happened was merely an inconvenience that a good holiday would sort out. But when she saw the address of the house, all thoughts of Christmas disappeared.

'This house is in Farmington,' she said slowly, feeling suddenly chilled to the core. 'We're not moving to Farmington.'

'Why not Farmington?' Marc asked her. 'We'll be much closer to your parents once they get back from their grand tour. They only live a few miles from Farmington. Besides, you grew up there. It's the perfect place to bring the kids up. It's surrounded by countryside, it's got good schools and low crime rates . . . and look at what we'd get for our money over there compared to this place. So, why not Farmington?'

'You know why not Farmington,' Alison said, redirecting her gaze at him. 'Marc, you're incredible, you really are.'

Mark stared at her wide-eyed for a moment or two as she waited for him to catch up.

'What? You mean because of . . .? Oh, Al, don't be silly.

That's all in the past now, long gone and forgotten. Nobody cares about that any more, not even your parents!'

'I care!' Alison told him, fighting to temper her tone because the girls were in the next room and Dominic would be home soon. It wasn't so much upsetting him that she worried about, it was more how he would judge her if he found out what his father had planned for them. 'Would you move back to Birmingham, to the place where your foster mother told you she didn't want you living with her any more and that she was putting you back in care?'

Marc removed his hand from hers and she felt the chill of its departure.

'I wouldn't move back to Birmingham because it's a shit-hole,' he said, reacting with anger, as he always did if Alison mentioned his childhood. 'It's not the same, and you know it. I got dragged up through foster care and children's homes, kicked about from pillar to post. You had everything you ever wanted: a nice safe life, in a nice safe town, with nice safe parents. Is it so wrong that I want to give that life to my children, and especially to Dom, before he messes up for good?'

'You don't give him enough credit,' Alison protested. 'If you could have seen him in the school show, you would have realised how talented he is. Maybe if you talked to him every now and again –'

'I have talked to him,' Marc interrupted her impatiently. 'I talked to him for hours after the car incident. I don't know . . . I look at him and I see myself, Al. The boy needs straightening out. I think living in Farmington could be the answer.'

'Look, if you want to move from here then fine, I'm not thrilled to live here any more either. But we don't have to go to Farmington. That is the last place we should have to go,' Alison told him bleakly. 'The night I left there with you I knew I was never going back, I never *could* go back.'

'Who cares now about what happened back then? It's an age ago, Alison, it doesn't mean anything now.'

'Not to you?'

'Of course not to me!' Marc exclaimed. 'Al, the last couple of months have been hard on you, you're not thinking straight. If you were you'd see how perfect this is.'

'Even so,' Alison had looked up wearily at Marc, 'it doesn't have to be Farmington. There are a hundred towns like Farmington, two hundred – a thousand, even. Any one of those would give the children the kind of life you want them to have, but not this one, Marc. It doesn't have to be Farmington. Mum and Dad don't even live there any more!'

Marc bowed his head, his hands folded in his lap as they sat side by side on the sofa. 'When I came to Farmington I was a railway labourer,' he began the story she already knew so well. 'Working nights on the lines, sleeping all day in the park, drinking warm beer in the sun, waiting for some girls to walk by, hoping they'd give me a second glace. I was twenty years old and I was already dead, my life was going nowhere. I looked around that town, at those people and those girls, and I knew that it was a world I couldn't ever belong to. I knew I'd go on drifting from one place to the next until the day I died. I didn't have anything, Alison, until I met you. I didn't even have myself. '

'That's not true,' Alison tried to interrupt him.

'You turned my life around. And now I have you. God knows, I don't deserve you but I still have you and I want to keep you. I want to keep the family I love, with one successful business under my belt and another in the pipeline. I want to go back to Farmington, Ali. I want to go back to the place that rejected me back then and I want to *own* it. Most of all I want to deserve *you*.'

'Tell me,' Alison asked him, feeling suddenly inexplicably

sad, 'is that any better a reason to go back than mine is to stay away?'

'We're going back for you,' he whispered, moving his lips over hers. 'Because that's the place where you and I started. It's the place where we belong and all of the things you're worried about are long dead and buried. I promise you when we're there you and I will be happy again. You'll be happy and I'll be different. I'll have more time to spend with you and the kids. Everything will be different, it will be better.'

He'd kissed her then, his hand sliding from her knee to her thigh, and because Alison wanted so much for this to be the fresh start that Marc talked about she let the discussion slide with it. It was one they would never have again, she knew that. Once Marc had made up his mind about something he stuck to it like glue, which was something she supposed she ought to be grateful for. After all, he'd made up his mind to choose her sixteen years ago.

She just had to hope that he was right, that all her fears and misgivings about going back to Farmington were foolish and irrational. That once she'd got settled back there she would feel as if she had never been away.

The only problem was that it was that eventuality that terrified her the most.

It was dusk as their car finally rolled into the driveway of their new home. Amy and Gemma were both asleep on the back seat, and Dominic was still nodding his head to some barely heard beat.

'Leave them for a second,' Marc whispered. 'I've got something I want you to see.'

Glancing back at her children, Alison got out of the car and waited as Marc asked the removal men to give him another few minutes, slipping them each a twenty-pound note.

'Come on,' he said. 'Hopefully, if all of my plans have worked, then . . .'

Alison walked into the cavernous hallway just as Marc switched on the lights and she saw that it was filled with bouquets of red roses. Twelve of them, Alison counted, arranged on the marble-tiled floor in the shape of a love heart, their sweet scent struggling against that of the new paint but their colour vibrant and bloody against the magnolia walls. It was a dramatic gesture and typical of Marc.

'Happy Valentine's Day, darling,' Marc said, wrapping his arms around her from behind. 'And welcome home.'

Chapter Two

How Catherine Ashley came to be spending Valentine's Day with her almost ex-husband was a story that pretty much summed up her life.

'You don't mind booking Jimmy, do you?' Lois, the PTA chairperson, had asked her at the last meeting, with her own special brand of tact. 'It's not awkward at all booking your ex to play at the Valentine's dance, is it? It's just that I know how you two get on still, and he'll give you a reduced rate. Every penny counts if we're going to raise enough money to pay for the interactive whiteboards.'

Catherine, PTA secretary, had said she didn't mind, and mostly she didn't. It was a fact of life that Jimmy and his band were present at every wedding, christening and even the odd funeral that she had attended, both before and since they had split up as a couple, playing covers for the masses to pay the bills while they waited for the stardom that had so far eluded them. Besides, for the last few months peace had broken out between them, and Jimmy had become almost as much a part of her daily life as he had been when they were living together. Maybe even more so, because the stress and tension that their being together had caused had dissolved at last now that she had stopped waiting for him to leave her and had kicked him out.

Her friend Kirsty said they were the happiest married couple she knew, and she put it all down to the fact that they'd been separated and living apart for two years. Kirsty hadn't been there for the first year, those long and difficult months when they had tried to find a way to be parents without ripping themselves or their children to shreds. But the last year had been OK – good, even. Friendship had finally emerged from the ashes of what they'd once had, and Kirsty was right: for the most part they got on well. One day Catherine knew they'd get divorced properly, but until something happened to push either one of them in that direction she was still officially Mrs Jimmy Ashley, so considering she managed to live quite happily with that on a daily basis, booking her husband's band to play the Valentine's dance was the least of her worries.

The gas bill, the hours her boss wanted her to work, whether or not she'd have the money to get Eloise what she really wanted for her birthday – those were the worries that kept Catherine awake at night. But those were practical problems that Catherine could tackle and fight. It had been the utter paralysing fear of loving Jimmy the way he wanted her to, the way *she* often tried to, that would expose her long-guarded vulnerability. That threat of powerlessness had stalked her throughout her marriage until one day Jimmy proved all her misgivings right and betrayed her, making her thank God that she had never fully committed her heart to him because the shock of what he had done to her and their family was hard enough to bear as it was. If she had allowed herself to love him it would have been intolerable.

It had taken her a long time to readjust her feelings towards him, but she had done it for her girls, for Eloise and Leila, whom she lived for, content to let her life orbit them with the same ordered regularity as the Earth turns around the sun, letting their happiness and beauty warm her, because their love was all that she needed.

And manning the bar at the Valentine's dance with her friend and neighbour, while her ex-husband brandished his guitar like a mammoth outsized phallus on the stage was just one of those things. It was a Jimmy thing. Like talking endlessly about more or less nothing apart from sex was a Kirsty thing.

'On reflection I think I *am* in love with my personal trainer,' Kirsty said thoughtfully for the fourth or fifth time since she had started this one-sided debate. She was holding a plastic cup full of wine and gazing contemplatively at one of the many red cardboard hearts that had been hung from the ceiling and that stirred gently, wafted by warm air created by the dancing crowd below.

Catherine looked at her, crossing her arms. 'No, you are not in love with your personal trainer,' she replied, also for about the fourth or fifth time. 'How can you be in love with him? You hardly know him. You've seen him three or four times for an hour twice a week at most.'

Catherine was grateful that Kirsty had offered to come with her to the dance, as the only other single woman in town without a date, because Catherine wouldn't have come herself if it wasn't for the fact that she was on the committee. But she had been volunteered to run the bar, so having Kirsty by her side did take the edge off the whole Valentine theme and helped to make the evening almost bearable.

Still, if Catherine had known that she was going to be treated to two hours solid of how wonderful Kirsty's personal trainer was, and the varying degree of likelihood that she was in love with him, then on balance she probably would have found standing on her own behind the table like a pariah marginally preferable. She might have looked a bit sad, quietly sipping glass after glass of cheap wine while the town's couples danced happily to '(Everything I Do) I Do It For You', and yes, it would have been more difficult to ignore the four twenty-year-old girl groupies who always seemed to follow her husband and his band around, despite the fact they were all past thirty and would have been has-beens if they had ever been anybody, staring at Jimmy like he was some rock god, but at least she wouldn't be having the same meaningless conversation on a loop *again*.

'So?' Kirsty was questioning her. 'What do you think I should do? It's hard to pull your personal trainer, you know, because, after all, whenever you see him you are fat and red and sweaty. How can you make a man want you when you are fat and red and sweaty? Particularly when, based on the research I've done, I know the kind of women he likes are thin, blonde and have massive tits. Any ideas?'

At six foot exactly, Catherine looked down at her friend, whom she towered above by several inches.

'You are not in love with your trainer,' she repeated firmly, as if she were telling her five-year-old, Leila, that no way was she staying up for the end of *Strictly Come Dancing*, 'so you don't have to try and pull him. You probably don't even fancy him, not really.'

'I think you'll find I do,' Kirsty avowed. 'Have you seen his arms, his chest, his legs, his bum, his . . . oh God, I'm having a hot flush, and not on my neck.'

'That's lust, Kirsty!' Catherine exclaimed, feeling her cheeks colour. A year of knowing Kirsty still had not made her immune to the other woman's insistence on conducting full and frank discussions of a sexual nature in public places. 'Lust is not love, and love isn't even love – it's hormones.'

'It's not lust.' Kirsty was adamant. 'It's so much more than that. We talk and laugh and he *listens* to me. Plus he is the only man in the whole wide world who knows how much I weigh *exactly*. If that's not grounds for marriage then I don't know what is.'

'It's transference,' Catherine went on. 'Like when people fall for their psychiatrists. You are transferring your sexual urges on to the poor man. Remember, you pay him fifty-nine nighty-five an hour to train you. He doesn't turn up out of the goodness of his heart or just so he can get a look at you sweating. And anyway, like you said, he fancies blonde eighteen-year-olds with breast implants.'

'No, no, he *thinks* he fancies blonde eighteen-year-olds with breast implants but that's only because he hasn't met me yet. I mean, he's met me, but he hasn't met *me*. Once he truly knows me, he'll see what love really is. Else there's always plastic surgery.'

'Just listen.' Catherine took a much-needed sip of wine. 'You are not in love with your trainer and he is not in love with you. He is probably in love with himself. Now get over it. Do me a favour and go and ask someone's husband to dance with you. I could do with a laugh.'

Kirsty sighed but allowed the change of subject nevertheless.

'You don't just rush up to a couple and tap the woman on the shoulder and say, "Please can I dance with your husband?"' she told Catherine. 'There's no fun to be had there, and besides, it never works; the married woman is a particularly fierce and protective creature. You have to bide your time, hunt the lone husband. Imagine that you are like a cheetah stalking a gazelle and then, at just the right moment, you pounce when no one's looking and drag your prey off into the bush and devour them whole.'

'On second thoughts maybe you'd better settle for just a dance. Some of those out there are quite scary when they are drunk. You should have seen Lois at the Christmas fair when she found out that Father Christmas had made off with the raffle-prize sherry. She charged like a rhino.'

'Why do you do all this PTA lark?' Kirsty asked her as she scanned the crowd for her prey, regardless of Catherine's warning. 'You should chuck it all in and have a proper grown-up life. After all, you and me – mainly me – we are single women, we should be doing proper single-woman stuff: going on ill-advised dates with men who don't deserve us, setting a terrible example to children and falling out with our estranged husbands, with the emphasis on *strange*, and not inviting them round to Sunday tea! That's what proper single women do.'

'You haven't got an estranged husband,' Catherine remarked.

'Well, there's no need to brag,' Kirsty sighed. 'I could be in the Three Bells right now impressing my trainer with my all-natural if subtle cleavage. You could be with me; maybe he's got a friend, I don't know. The point is that you and I could be out on the town getting noticed.'

Catherine raised a brow. With her statuesque height and red hair, getting noticed had never been her problem. It was blending in that she had found so difficult for most of her life, trying as hard as she could to stay out of the limelight. She always wore black trousers and a black top and flat black boots or shoes. Usually she wore her long hair up, knotted on the top of her head, but she never dyed or cut it, except for every other month, with the kitchen scissors. Beauty and what it meant was something that Catherine had never quite got a handle on, except that she was fairly certain it didn't apply to her. Most men were scared of her, and of the two men she had 'known' in her life, the one she had married had been caught having sex with a groupie in the ladies' loo at The Goat. And what's more, he'd been caught by Catherine. In the end she'd scared him off too. Getting noticed in any way at all was not at the top of Catherine's to-do list.

She watched the crowd dancing for a minute or two, seemingly bobbing up and down just out of step with the music, and suddenly found herself remembering the last Valentine's dance she had been to. It was a bittersweet memory, but this was true of all of her memories before she had got together with Jimmy. Recalling any of them required her to pay a certain price.

Catherine had been fifteen and she had planned a daring escape for the night, telling her parents she was due at a rehearsal at school for the public-speaking team. Instead, she was going to the school disco with Alison.

She and Alison had met outside the church on the high street and got changed together in the public loos outside Tesco, putting on lipstick haphazardly as they peered into the scratched Perspex mirrors screwed to the walls. Alison had brought Catherine a skirt to wear and she tied a piece of black lace into her red hair. She must have looked a sight, but Catherine didn't care then. When she was with Alison she felt invincible.

Of course, none of the boys had asked Catherine to dance, but she was glad of it. She couldn't think of anything worse than turning in a slow deathly circle to 'Love Is All Around' with some boy's hand on her bottom and his nose in her cleavage. Alison had refused to dance with any of the many boys that kept asking her, telling all of them she wanted to dance with Catherine instead, and have a laugh.

When Lee Britton accused her of being a lesbian, she'd grabbed Catherine's hand and kissed it, winking at him.

'You've got that dead right, Lee,' she'd said. 'Imagine that when you're tossing off in bed tonight!' And she had spun Catherine round and round in a circle until the pair of them,

15

dizzy with laughter from the look on Lee's face, had collapsed on the floor.

On the way home that night the two of them had stopped once again in the loos outside Tesco and got changed back into jeans and jumpers – Alison too, even though her parents knew she'd been going to the disco and all she had to hide from them was make-up.

'Your parents are weirdos, babe,' Alison had said as she wiped the lipstick off Catherine's mouth, holding her chin between her thumb and forefinger.

'It's just their way,' Catherine tried to explain, although the older she got the harder she found it to understand them herself. 'They were old when they had me. They still haven't got used to having a kid around.'

'Well, you might not be able to choose your family but at least you've got me, right? And that makes you lucky.'

The pair of them had hugged there in the public loos outside Tesco before going their separate ways. And for a long time, for almost all of her childhood, Catherine had thought that Alison was right: she thought that she was the luckiest girl in the world to have Alison as her best friend, her protector and her confidante. It had seemed like the kind of friendship that would last for ever, a friendship to be relied on.

But Catherine couldn't have been more wrong about that. What was more, when Alison left her she was in the biggest mess of her life with no one to help her out of it.

When she had got home that night her mum was waiting on the other side of the front door for her, her wooden spatula in her hand. Somehow she had found out Catherine's lie. And until tonight Catherine had never been to another Valentine's dance again. She smiled to herself. If her parents could see her now they'd probably still be furious.

'This dance sucks,' Kirsty said, snapping Catherine's

attention back into the room. 'I thought all the best men were supposed to be married. Why are none of them here?'

'I'm sorry, Kirsty, I should have told you that the school PTA Valentine's dance would be no place to meet a man.'

'And *that* is why you are alone,' Kirsty lectured her. 'Everywhere is a place to meet men if you look hard enough – a pub, a club, the gym, the supermarket, even the opticians . . .'

'The opticians?'

'Long story,' Kirsty said. 'What I'm saying is, if you really want to meet a man then you have to try a bit harder.'

'I'm not trying to meet a man,' Catherine said. 'I don't want to meet a man. I'm a happily nearly divorced married wife. '

'Your trouble is that you don't realise what a fox you are. Men would queue up to go out with you if you weren't so uptight and always slightly scary-looking. You know, plucking your eyebrows would make you seem a lot less frowny – I'm just saying.'

'I'm not uptight,' Catherine replied mildly. 'I just don't want to do it again.'

'Do you mean you don't want to have a relationship again, or do you mean you don't want to do *it* again? Because if you are telling me you never want to have sex again I refuse to believe it. You're thirty-two, Catherine. You are at your sexual peak. Why on earth wouldn't you want sex in your life again? Preferably with an eighteen-year-old. I've heard that's the perfect match sexual peak-wise.'

Catherine looked at Kirsty and wondered how to answer that question. By the time she went to bed with Jimmy she more or less qualified as a virgin again, such was the length of time that had passed between her first sexual experience and her second. It had been clumsy and difficult, and she had been embarrassed and awkward, but to her surprise and relief Jimmy hadn't run away as fast as he could afterwards. He treated her sweetly and gently, and gradually the two of them began to work together well, becoming easy and familiar lovers. For a while they brought out the best in each other. Catherine inspired Jimmy's tender and protective side, and he made her laugh and relax, standing tall in a crowd, happy in the knowledge that the man she was holding hands with was two inches taller than she was. But although she had adored him, cared for him, needed him, she had never fallen in love with him the way he always told her she would. In all the years they had been married she had never found the courage to let herself go those few extra degrees it would take to love him, until the night she found him having sex with Donna Clarke in the ladies' loos of The Goat pub. Ironic really that the peak of her passion for Jimmy had manifested itself on the day he decided to cheat on her, the day she knew she would never be able to trust him again.

It was only when Jimmy tried to explain to her why he'd been having sex in the ladies' loo with a total stranger that she understood why their marriage was over.

'It's not that I don't love you,' Jimmy had told her, holding both her wrists so that she wouldn't punch him any more. 'But you don't . . . you don't . . .'

'Don't what – excite you? Is that it? Have you finally realised, after making me marry you, after making me trust you and rely on you, after persuading me to build my life with you and have your children, that I'm not good enough for you?' Catherine had shrieked at him.

'No!' Jimmy protested, letting go of her wrists so that she sprang forward and pushed him to the tiled wall with a thud. 'No,' he repeated as she stepped back hanging her head, her shoulders heaving. 'You don't love me, not really, you can't. You're still waiting for the man you can love to arrive in your life and you want it to be me, but I'm never going to be that person, Cat. I'm never going to change into the kind of man you need.'

'The kind of man I need?' Catherine asked him furiously. 'Tell me, Jimmy, what *is* the kind of man I need?'

'Someone you can really love, someone you can let yourself go with again. I've spent years trying to make you love me and it hasn't worked. You never will love me and why should you?' Jimmy paused, and took a breath as Catherine studied his face, her fury draining away. 'Tonight has proved it to you and to me. I'm never going to deserve you, Catherine, and I can't stand seeing that disappointment in your eyes any more. I'm worn out.'

'You didn't have to do this,' Catherine said, gesturing around her, acutely aware that she hadn't denied anything he said. 'You could have just *told* me.'

'I didn't plan this; I never plan anything, you know I don't. I didn't tell you how I was feeling because I didn't have the guts,' Jimmy had said levelly.

It had taken Catherine a long time to stop being angry about that.

Now at last Catherine's life was a calm ocean and she had some peace. There was no way she could explain to someone as restless and as searching as Kirsty how important peace was in her life, and that she'd take order and regularity over excitement and change any day of the week.

'Look,' she nudged Kirsty in the ribs, 'Lois's husband has been separated from the pack. Go in for the kill now, while he's weak and vulnerable.'

'Right you are,' Kirsty said, her automatic vixen mode revving up, and she was gone.

Catherine couldn't decide what was funnier, Lois's indignation at her husband doing the tango with Kirsty, or Mr

Lois's bright red cheeks and sweaty brow as Kirsty twirled him around the school hall as if they were in Argentina itself. Either way, she kept her mirth to herself, watching on with the implacable mask that she always wore to these functions.

The music changed tempo and Catherine realised that Jimmy's band was taking a break. They'd put a mix tape on instead and the floor filled instantly to the opening strains of 'Dancing Queen'.

As Catherine scanned the crowd she spotted Jimmy fending off one of his groupies, who hung around his neck in a swoon, clearly dying to be kissed. In his clumsy but well-meaning attempt not to embarrass his wife in front of the whole school, Jimmy untangled himself from the girl's advances and smiled at her as she attempted to lunge at him again.

Catherine looked down at the table and counted to twenty in the hope that when she looked up the girl would have stopped pursuing him. It wasn't jealousy she felt, it was more embarrassment and discomfort in knowing that everybody who saw him would be thinking the same thing: Poor old Catherine, all on her own and heartbroken, while her husband snogs another floozie in front of her very eyes.

When she looked up from counting, Jimmy was standing right in front her.

'Hey, babe,' he said, pushing the shades he regularly wore in February up into his long, dark-brown hair. 'Any chance of a beer?'

'I've got white wine, red wine or juice,' Catherine said with a smile. 'I could probably rustle up some Ribena for your girlfriend.'

'Ha, funny,' Jimmy said with an easy grin. 'I'll have two wines then, don't care which colour. You look nice, by the way.'

'I look the same and you know it,' Catherine replied as she handed him a glass.

The girlfriend was loitering a few feet away, uncertain about whether to come over, probably intimidated by the Amazonian ex-wife Catherine thought with some small satisfaction. She did tend to scare off his groupies, probably due to the rumour that persisted that Catherine had punched Donna Clarke so hard she broke her nose that night in the ladies' loo at The Goat. The truth was far more seedy and mundane. Donna Clarke had been so drunk that in her hurry to exit the crime scene she had careered into the toilet door, catching herself right between the eyes. Donna Clarke never told anyone how she got her black eyes and crooked nose (perhaps she couldn't remember), and Catherine never talked about it, full stop. Thus a myth was born. A rather handy myth when it came to keeping Jimmy's fans at arm's length, at least while she was around.

'She looks nice,' Catherine said, nodding at the girl. 'Very . . . firm. What's her name?'

Jimmy shrugged. 'Suzie . . . she is a nice girl but not for me, you know. Nothing much in common.'

'Except for a mutual love of you,' Catherine teased.

'Well, yes, but I have that in common with all women,' Jimmy replied with a grin.

'Are you playing another set?' Catherine asked.

'Yeah, some power ballads to get them going. I was thinking of "The Power of Love" followed by "Move Closer". What do you reckon?'

'I reckon good,' Catherine nodded. 'If you can crow-bar in a bit of Celine Dion then you're laughing.'

Jimmy smiled.

'What will you do with the rest of the weekend?' he asked her. 'Maybe a trip to Paris? Maybe find some handsome Frenchman to French kiss you under the Eiffel Tower?'

'I'm planting up the vegetable patch in the back garden,'

Catherine said. 'We're nearly self-sustainable now, you know. There'll be enough for you too, if you want it.'

'Free veg,' Jimmy said, smiling quietly as he watched Catherine realigning the glasses she had just polished. 'Radical.'

'Hey, mate!' Gazza, the band's bassist, beckoned Jimmy back to the stage. 'We're on!'

'I can drop you home later, if you like. I'm the designated driver tonight,' Jimmy said with an offhand shrug. 'I've got the van until tomorrow and I'm going that way, after all.'

Catherine smiled at her husband. 'Aren't you forgetting something?'

'Just because we're separated doesn't mean I can't drive you places,' Jimmy said defensively. 'I worry about you out on the street at all hours.'

'No, I meant your girlfriend, idiot,' Catherine told him mildly. 'Hadn't you better drop her home, or take her somewhere and do whatever it is you do with them?'

'Oh, yeah,' Jimmy's shoulders drooped as he glanced back at Suzie. 'I might pop round tomorrow then,' he said casually. 'See how you're getting on.'

''Bout lunchtime-ish?' Catherine asked.

'Why, are you cooking?'

'You know I am. You know you're welcome.'

'Cool.' Jimmy broke into a happy grin. 'I haven't eaten hot food in three days.'

Chapter Three

Alison sat on her new bed in her new bedroom in her new house and considered crying. She couldn't allow herself the luxury, she decided. If she started now she'd never stop and then the house would look no better by the time her three children got home from school.

Besides, she wasn't unhappy *exactly*. She was just exhausted and stressed, and it felt strange being in this literally new house with the scent of paint and new carpet still fragrancing the air. And she was worried about the children and about how the three of them would get on this first day at their new schools.

Rooted as she was to the, as yet, unwrapped mattress, she knew that the moment she got up and ventured out of this bedroom she would realise just exactly what remained to be done, and then her no-crying rule would go out of the window.

It was the surreal fact that she was back in Farmington that Alison found nearly impossible to believe. Whenever she looked out of the windows of her bedroom and saw the gentle rise of the hills rolling behind the tree line, she suffered an immediate and unprecedented bout of agoraphobia. You knew where you stood in London, which was largely in the thick of it, shoulder to shoulder with the masses, each of you working through your daily life trying to interact with as few people as possible.

The Farmington of her childhood could not have been a more different place. It was a small rural town where everybody knew everybody else and, what's more, they felt as if they had some form of ownership over the lives of others. That's why her mother especially had suffered so terribly when she and Marc ran away. It had taken Alison a long time – years, actually – to see her parents' side of her unexpected departure. What she had never been able to explain to them was that it wasn't their fault; that they hadn't driven her away before she could take even one of the A levels she'd been studying for. Just as she couldn't make them see that there was nothing either one of them could have said or done differently that would have meant she would have stayed at home and lived the safe, loving life her parents had planned for her.

The simple fact was that her love for Marc eclipsed everything else. Even the fact that she had been pregnant with Dominic on the night she left with Marc had seemed incidental compared to the urgent need she felt to escape with him and make him hers before anything could come between them. She hadn't told him she was pregnant until two weeks after they had left, on an evening when he was drunk and angry and she was tearful and desperate.

'I'm having your baby,' she had screamed at him. 'Are you staying with me or what?' He'd decided to stay with her and he had never gone back on a decision. On that night Alison had been glad she was pregnant, not because she wanted a baby but because she wanted to keep Marc.

At least six years had passed before her mother said something that had finally given Alison an insight into the devastation that her parents must have felt when she left. She and Marc and Dominic had visited them in their new home, in a small village on the other side of the county.

'This is a nice village,' Alison had said as she set out her mum's best china for tea, a sign that at last she and Marc were accepted as a couple.

'It is nice,' her mother had said quietly. 'It's nice living in a place where people don't know everything about you.'

At that moment Alison finally realised how difficult it must have been for her parents to explain to their friends and neighbours just exactly what had happened to their daughter. And now, sitting there on her Cellophane-covered mattress in her brand-new house after returning home to the place where her name had once been the hot topic of gossip, her mother's simple sentence gained a new significance.

It was nice to live in place where people didn't know everything about you.

Alison had taken Dominic to school before the girls, negotiating her way gingerly around the familiar roads and streets as if she half expected her past to leap out from some dark corner and run her off the road. But the town was indifferently busy, caught up as it was in the midst of the school run, and Alison was able to relax as she realised her 4x4 was just one of many on the roads that morning.

As she drove the children along the high street she even felt a surge of affection for the old place, still so pretty with its Victorian shop fronts and medieval church. There was a Costa coffee shop and a Chez Gerard in situ now instead of the All-Day English Breakfast Café and the Italian place her parents always used to take her to on her birthday for a gigantic ice-cream sundae.

On the down side, the grocer's and the butcher's had been replaced with estate agencies, but on the up side there were a number of smart fashion boutiques that looked as if they were brimming with exactly the kind of clothes that Alison had far too many of. The old Co-op had been turned into an exclusive gym, and it was clear that Farmington had continued to go up in the world after she had left it. Alison knew if she looked in the estate agents' windows it would be difficult to find even a modest house priced under five hundred thousand pounds, which made it a place where it was almost impossible for those on an average income to live. It was an exclusive town; you could see that by the cars parked along the side of the road: an Aston Martin, a Porsche, two Mercedes and countless BMWs all lined up nose to tail. The town she had grown up in had been middle-class suburban and staid, where respectability was treasured and flashiness frowned upon. Back then it was a fusty maiden aunt of a town, prim and proper. Now it was a showy trophy wife, with diamonds on its fingers, a pair of gold leather sling-backs on its feet and a year-round fake tan.

But Farmington's apparent face lift offered Alison little comfort. This was not the town that she had once fled, that was true, but it was also not a place that she wanted to come back to. Gentrified or not, this was still the scene of Alison's darkest hour, the place where she had behaved in the most terrible way and betrayed someone she had loved and who had trusted her.

And try as she might to believe Marc's all-too-rational comment that no one would care or even remember what had happened back then, from the moment Marc had begun to move their lives back here it had been hard not to believe that, somewhere amidst the coffee shops and boutiques, her past was still lying in wait for her.

While Alison was putting on a brave face for the children, and Amy had rallied, being bravely stoical about the upheaval, Dom was openly disgusted. The thunderous expression on his face as she drove him to the school gates said it all. He was furious with his parents for bringing him to this place he'd already referred to as 'a dive' and 'a dump' on numerous occasions since they had moved in over the weekend.

'Like your room?' Alison had asked him the first night in the new house. 'Dad had the builder paint it black for you so that it would be just the way you like it.'

'Why are you going along with this?' Dominic had asked her.

'Unpacking?' Alison was deliberately obtuse.

'You know what I mean. I mean this – this poxy house and shitty stuck-up town won't change anything,' her son told her. 'It won't change him and you know it. So why are you making us all go along with it?'

'If I can try, so can you,' Alison had told him, setting down the pile of clothes that she had brought in for him.

'Why should I?' Dominic asked her.

It was a question she had been unable to answer.

'I used to go to this school, can you believe?' Alison said lightly, as she pulled up outside her son's school. She had had to cover the shock of emotion she felt at being confronted with the building that she had spent so many pivotal moments of her life in, forcibly reminding herself that it was just a building, a powerless pile of bricks and mortar. 'It's a good school, Dom. You'll make new friends really quickly here. And there's Rock Club, don't forget? Once you've started there you'll be right at home.'

Alison had been pinning all of her hopes of winning her son over on the flimsy promise of Rock Club. He was a dedicated guitarist – it was one of the few things he openly took pleasure in – and he had worked for two summers without complaint to earn half the two thousand pounds required to buy his dream guitar. When the head teacher had taken them on a tour of the school, the news about Rock Club run by a local music teacher was the only thing Dom had shown any interest in, despite his very best attempts to hide it.

'This sucks,' he told Alison as he opened the car door reluctantly. 'It really sucks that you are making me go through with this.'

Alison knew he was resentful and possibly even a little bit scared about what his new peers would think of him. But she also knew she couldn't reach out and put an arm around his shoulders to comfort him because he'd find that almost as distressing as getting out of the car and walking through the gates.

'Do you want me to come in with you?' she offered impulsively. He looked at her as if she were mentally ill.

'No,' he said, his disgust giving him the impetus to get out of the car and slam the door shut behind him. 'I'm not a kid.'

Alison watched him for a few more minutes as he walked away.

Once they had been so close, always side by side and hand in hand – in step with each other. It hadn't been the birth of Gemma that had changed that, or even his bumpy and painful ascent into manhood. It was the day he realised that Alison was weak and flawed, and incapable of doing anything to change herself. Since then all he had ever seemed to be was angry with her.

'He looks like a right old grump,' Gemma said, leaning forward in her seat to watch Dominic slouch away.

'Will he be all right, Mama?' Amy asked anxiously. 'It looks like a big place to be in on your own. Is our school this big?'

'No, darling, it's little. Remember when you looked round you said it looked like a doll's house? And anyway, Dom won't be alone; he'll be making lots of new friends, just like you will.'

Alison waited for him to go through the gate and head

towards the main entrance. Then, taking her mobile out of her bag, she phoned the school reception.

'Hello, it's Mrs James here. I just want to check that my son is signing in with you like he's supposed to. It's his first day and you know how boys are. He won't let me come in with him to make sure he's OK.'

'Yes, thank you, madam,' the receptionist said in an even tone. 'The delivery has arrived safely. We are dealing with it now.'

'Thank you so much,' Alison said, warmly grateful of the discretion.

'Not at all,' the receptionist said.

It was about two minutes later that she got a text from Dominic saying, 'Stop checking up on me.'

She was a little late getting the girls to St Margaret's First School, but she didn't think it mattered today because she had to see the head anyway before the girls were taken off to their classrooms.

Unlike Dominic's school, which all the children in the town who weren't privately educated went to, Alison had not gone to St Margaret's when she was her daughters' age, and it was something of a relief to be in an unfamiliar and neutral environment. She only wished that both of her daughters felt the same way.

It was a sweet little school, built around an original Victorian schoolhouse, and what it lacked in playing fields because of its town-centre location it made up for in atmosphere. The thing that Alison had liked about it most was the sense of community. The children all seemed to care about each other, the bigger ones looking out for the little ones. Alison thought that this was especially important for Amy.

Dear, precious, uncomplicated Gemma, who could have

little idea how her self-confidence and adaptability kept her mother going, had been chatting happily to her teacher as she had been taken off to her classroom to be introduced to her new classmates. Amy had not gone happily at all. She had cried and cried, clinging to Alison's skirts, begging her mummy to take her home with her. Eventually Alison had had to peel her daughter's fingers from the fabric, desperately trying not to cry herself, and physically hand her to the teacher.

'Come on, darling,' Alison had said, holding her daughter's hand out to the teacher. 'You go with Mrs Pritchard now. You're going to have a lovely time and I bet you'll make a lot of friends, you'll see.'

Amy's sobs had echoed all the way down the corridor.

When Alison had come out of school the playground was empty of parents and pupils and she had been relieved. She wasn't ready to meet anybody just yet, after that dramatic farewell with Amy, which had left her on the verge of tears and on the point of running back into the school to scoop her baby up and rescue her.

She had made the short drive back to her new house with a heavy heart, and once she had pulled into the drive she sat in the 4x4 and looked at the house for quite a long time. It was huge: six bedrooms, third-floor guest suite, an open-plan hallway with a living room, dining room and gigantic kitchen off it. It was twice as big as their London house and ten times as grand. Marc loved it. He loved buying this overstated and opulent palace. He loved the fact that it was brand-spanking-new and slightly tacky, with none of the grace and dignity of some of the other houses they had looked at, the Victorian villas that populated over half the town. He loved the remote-controlled electric gates, the faux Regency pillars that stood proudly either side of the double front doors, and he loved the fact that he was able to buy up the paddock at the back of the house that one day soon he'd promised to occupy with a pony for the girls.

'This says we've arrived,' he'd told Alison on the night they'd moved in, kissing her on the forehead. 'Who'd have thought that you and I would have made it all the way here, hey? We've beaten the odds, Al; we've proved them all wrong.'

Which had made Alison wonder – who did they have anything to prove to now? Except perhaps themselves.

Now, still sitting immobilised on the bed, Alison looked around at her new bedroom, the Cellophane of the mattress squeaking beneath her bottom as she twisted to survey the mountain of boxes that required unpacking.

And she decided she would cry after all. Just then crying seemed about the only thing she was confident she could do.

Chapter Four

Catherine was out of breath when she hit the school gate at three fifteen because she had run the length of the high street from work in order to be there in time. Her job, working as an administrative manager to local PR company Stratham and Shah couldn't exactly be called a career, but the hours fitted perfectly into the school day as long as she was prepared to sprint there and back every morning and afternoon. Apart from the vital if meagre income it provided, it also gave her an interest outside of the house and the girls, and even her unorthodox relationship with Jimmy. Her job was something that was entirely her own. There was not much glamour to be had in binding presentations or managing the online diary for the practice, but Catherine was very good at it. She enjoyed bringing order to the often chaotic and capricious office and garnered quiet satisfaction from the frequency with which the word 'indispensable' was used in connection with her name.

Eloise was already in the playground, hopping randomly, her head bowed in concentration as if each hop was being placed with precision. Catherine stopped just inside the gate to catch her breath and watch her daughter in her one-legged endeavours, her red hair flying in all directions.

'Mum!' Eloise spotted her and raced up to her at full pelt, using her mother's body to break her speed.

'Guess what, it's so exciting!' Eloise hopped onto Catherine's toes. 'I've got a new best friend! She started today and her name is Gemma and she has got a sister in Leila's class. She has just moved to Farmington from London and she has got a bedroom to herself and, Mummy – guess what. Her dad said he'd buy her an *actual* pony! Like, a real one!'

Catherine looked at Eloise, her cheeks glowing hotly on her otherwise pale face, and she felt her heart sink.

'A *pony*?' Catherine repeated. This was bad news. Her daughters begged her for a pet, any kind of pet, on a daily basis, frequently stating that even a gerbil would do. But Eloise's heart's desire, the one thing she longed for more than anything in the world, was a pony. And now here was a girl who was going to have her very own pony. Catherine would never hear the end of it.

'And,' Eloise went on, tugging at Catherine's hand, 'she says I can come round and see it whenever I like, and ride it and play with it and groom it and everything.' Eloise was almost shouting in her excitement. 'So can I go round tonight, Mummy? Can I? Can I? Can I, please?'

'I expect tonight is a little bit too soon,' Catherine said. 'They'll still be unpacking.'

'But please can Gemma come to tea one day soon?' Eloise begged. 'Please!'

'Of course she can, one day,' Catherine said, deliberately noncommittal. 'Let's go round and pick Leila up and then when we get back, if we see Gemma and her mummy, we'll ask her, OK?'

'Yippee!' Eloise called out happily as she skipped along beside Catherine on their way round to Leila's class, catching Catherine's hand and swinging it back and forth.

'I knew being eight was going to be my best age,' she said happily.

33

'How did you know that?' Catherine smiled in antici-pation. While Leila had the light hazel eyes and wavy dark brown hair of her father, she also had the staunch practicality that she could have got only from her mother, as well as, since starting at St Margaret's First School, what appeared to be a quite sincere and devout belief in God.

Eloise, on the other hand, although a carbon copy of Catherine from the ends of her wild red hair to the tips her long skinny legs, was a dreamer and a rebel like her father. Catherine couldn't wait to hear Eloise's theory on why eight was such a great age.

'Because one, two, three, four, five, six and seven are baby years,' Eloise said, gesturing as if she were presenting a new report on TV. 'But eight is halfway to sixteen, halfway to being grown up. When you're eight you start to count in the world; you're not a baby any more.'

'You'll always be my baby,' Catherine said, putting her arms around Eloise and squeezing her tight on impulse.

'I won't, Mummy.' Eloise wriggled free. 'I'm growing up, you know!'

'I know you are,' Catherine said, picking up a strand of her daughter's hair. She remembered the morning when Jimmy had put their first-born in her arms. Her touch, her weight, her smell and the joy of her tiny fingers closing around Catherine's fingers, and the world seemed so much brighter and so sharp, as if she was looking at her life through a new pair of eyes. 'But I'll always love you and your sister just as much as I did from the moment you were born.'

'And now I've met Gemma, and she's getting a pony, and Leila's stopped snoring at night and, well, things are getting better. They are starting to go the right way, aren't they, Mummy?'

Catherine paused and looked down at her daughter. 'Are

they?' she asked tentatively. She knew that although it was Eloise who had suffered the most visibly during the pain and mess of the break-up, that first year after Jimmy had moved out had been raw, confusing and difficult for them all. If she was now beginning to see the separation in a better light, if the work that she and Jimmy had done to restore some stability to their daughters' lives was finally paying off, then Catherine could not have been happier. 'How's that?'

'Well, now you aren't so angry with Daddy any more and he's stopped making you angry. Now you let him come round when he likes, and have dinner and put us to bed. Things are nearly back to the way they were, aren't they, Mummy? It won't be long now.'

'What won't?' Catherine asked, battling the prescient sensation that she knew exactly what Eloise was going to say next.

'Well, soon Daddy will come home for good, won't he?'

Just at that second Leila came tearing out of her classroom, her coat attached to her only by its hood hooked over her head, and her arms filled with several sheets of artwork and some junk models, bits of toilet roll and empty yoghurt cartons flying in her wake.

'Leila, put your coat on properly,' Catherine said automatically, picking the coat off her daughter's head and holding it out for her to put on.

'Look!' Leila said, thrusting out a jumble of what had formerly been food containers of various descriptions. 'It's great, isn't it?'

'It's an amazing . . . car,' Catherine hazarded a guess.

'Is it a car?' Leila scrutinised the object. 'I thought it was an octopus, but anyway, it's good, isn't it?'

'Well?' Eloise asked Leila as she unburdened her sister of her treasure and Catherine helped her on with the coat.

'Well . . .' Leila looked thoughtful. 'I learned about China today, Mummy. Did you know its flag is bright red and there are dragons there, but not real dragons because there aren't really dragons in this world. There are real dragons in Australia, though, and kangaroos, which are true animals because we saw them at the zoo – do you remember? – and they went bounce . . . bounce . . . *bounce* . . . Do you think there were kangaroos on the Ark? Can we look it up when we get in?'

Leila bounced into her sister, dashing her model octopus/car to the floor, where it promptly exploded. Catherine bent down to pick it up, stuffing its various components in her capacious bag.

'Not that, silly,' Eloise said impatiently as Catherine, still on her knees, buttoned up Leila's coat. 'I mean, what about the new girl in your class. Have you made best friends with her? Has she told you she's getting a pony?'

Leila looked blank.

'Did you meet the new little girl that started today?' Catherine interpreted for her younger daughter. 'Did you play with her?'

'Oh, *well*,' Leila said, transformed from complete ignorance to world expert on the subject in an instant. 'The new girl's name is Amy and she cries the *whole* time and Mrs Pritchard didn't even shout at her or put her on the sad face or anything, and we were all nice to her. Ryan didn't even try to chase her, but she cried all day and didn't do any reading because she cried and said she wanted her mummy, which made Isabelle cry for her mummy and then Alfie did and then everyone was crying for a bit. I joined in too, but only pretend because I quite like reading.'

'Everyone in your whole class was crying?' Catherine questioned her.

'Well, Amy and Alfie and Isabelle did,' Leila said with a shrug. 'And when Amy's mummy came to school to pick her up they had to go and talk to Mrs Woodruff. About the crying I 'spect.'

'Typical,' Eloise sighed dramatically. 'Can we wait for them to come out from Mrs Woodruff's office, Mummy? Can we, *please*?'

'No, we can't,' Catherine said firmly, feeling some empathy towards this unknown mother and her attempts to get her children settled in a new school. 'We'll see her tomorrow, I expect, and I'll go and say hello to the mummy then.'

'And you have to make best friends with Amy, OK? Even if she does cry all the time,' Eloise ordered her sister urgently.

'OK,' Leila agreed as she fished a sawn-off washing-up liquid bottle from out of her mother's bag and looked at it. 'Actually, it was pony. It was a good pony model, wasn't it?'

'The best,' Catherine said, but as she shepherded her daughters out of the school gate at last she was thinking only one thing. What if, by trying to make things better with Jimmy for her daughters, she had actually made them worse? How was she ever going to be able to explain to Eloise or Leila that their daddy was never coming home?

As the three of them walked down their street towards their terraced house they could hear music from three houses away.

'Dad's home!' Leila exclaimed.

'And he's written a new song,' Eloise said, listening as they approached the front door. 'It's good, isn't it, Mum?'

Catherine listened for a moment or two to the wail of Jimmy's electric guitar, which was barely muted by the house's four walls.

'It sounds very interesting,' she said diplomatically. This unscheduled appearance at home was exactly the kind of thing that was confusing the situation for the children. But it was also exactly the kind of thing that Catherine had encouraged over the last year. After all, it was still half Jimmy's house; he still paid the mortgage. And he lived on a freezing cold and leaky canal boat, which his dead alcoholic best friend had left him in order that he'd have enough money to do that. And why shouldn't he be there when his children got home from school? She'd have to talk to him; they'd have to find a way to help the children understand the situation.

Just as Catherine opened the front door for the girls, Kirsty came out of hers.

'Any chance you could get him to either shut up or cheer up? Whichever one is likely to happen . . . sooner.' She stopped shouting as Eloise ran in first and Jimmy put down his guitar to greet her.

'Thank the Lord,' Kirsty said, briefly pressing her palms together in an expression of prayer.

'Amen,' Leila said as she followed her big sister inside.

'I'm sorry,' Catherine said. 'He says he can't really hear how it's going to sound unless he plays it loud. Count yourself lucky you didn't live next door when we were still together. Actually that's probably why the neighbour moved . . .'

'So divorce him and then it will be all your house and you won't be a default wife any more. I'd suggest taking him to the cleaners, but in his case I'd mean it literally. Look, I'm glad I caught you, actually. I need you to come out with me on Friday night.'

'Come out with you? What do you mean, come out?' Catherine frowned.

'I mean you coming out of your house – that's the big thing with the bricks and the roof, by the way – and proceeding with me to the pub on a Friday night for a drink. That's another brick thing with a roof on top only it has a licence to sell alcohol too. Now do you understand or would you like me to draw you a diagram?'

'I've told you I don't go to pubs,' Catherine started. 'I'm not normally a pub person.'

'You're not normally a normal person, full stop, but you are going to be this Friday because the kids are away with Bon Jovi in there, aren't they? And because I need you.' Kirsty smiled like Leila in possession of a chocolate-filled doughnut and a DVD of *The Sound of Music*. 'We're going to just *happen* to be in the pub where my trainer drinks. I worked it all out this morning while I was teaching the over-fifties Pilates. He hasn't fallen in love with me yet because he's never seen me at my finest, with my hair done and my push-up bra on, and mascara. So I'm going to *coincidentally* go to the pub where he always is on a Friday night in my new turquoise crocheted dress with the cleavage, and he's going to see me and think, wow, and fall in love with me on the spot for the kind and sensitive person I am. Do you *see*?'

'And you want *me* to come with you,' Catherine said. 'You don't want one of your other friends? You know, the friends that actually like people.'

'Of course I do,' Kirsty sighed. 'But the bastards all have someone. You are all I have left. It's the cross I have to bear. Besides, what you need most in the world is to be brought out of yourself a bit, and if me helping you do that also means that you are somehow helping me in some tiny little way then it's synergy, isn't it? It's cosmic forces in balance. Plus I put up with your husband wailing his head off for hours on end when I'm supposed to be teaching Tantric meditation to Mrs Evans so that she can bring herself to have sex with her husband, so you owe me.'

'He's my *ex*-husband and if you've got a student in there, where is she?' Catherine asked.

'Meditating, obviously. Now what do you say? Yes or no?'

Catherine tried to imagine herself standing in a pub full of Friday night drinkers and couldn't. Then she tried to imagine herself successfully saying 'no' to Kirsty, and that seemed even more unlikely. Perhaps it would be better to just go and try to get the whole thing over and done with as quickly as possible.

'OK,' she relented. 'I'll come for an hour then, tops, just enough for you to pull him. Then I'm going home.'

'Of course you are,' Kirsty said happily. 'That's what I'm counting on.'

Inside Jimmy had thankfully unplugged his electric guitar in favour of his acoustic one and was now strumming his new song, singing to the girls, both of his feet up on the coffee table, an adoring daughter either side of him on the sofa. Seeing the three of them together like that still gave Catherine's heart a wrench. It was impossible not to imagine what their lives could have been like if she and Jimmy had been different people – or not even different, but just the right people for each other. How perfect things could have been if she could have loved him the way he wanted her to, or if she had been enough for him as she was, damaged and incomplete.

But that was a future that had always been impossible, even when they had first got together and for the first time in her life everything seemed possible. They had always been doomed to fail, at least at being together. What they could not allow themselves to fail at was being parents.

'The neighbours hate it when you play that loudly,' Catherine told him, dumping her assortment of bags, drawings and cartons on the dining table.

'Sorry, babe,' Jimmy said, stopping his guitar by placing the flat of his palm against the vibrating strings, before handing it

40

to Eloise and getting up to join Catherine in the kitchen. 'We're laying down a new demo tomorrow and I need to hear how it sounds on the electric. If I tried it on the boat I'd probably sink it.'

'You know I don't mind – it's just that . . . well, if you could think about the volume now and again. I'm sure it doesn't have to be that loud.'

'It's rock and roll, babe,' Jimmy said, looking confused. 'Of course it does.'

He watched her for a few minutes as she crouched and peered in the fridge and began to take out the ingredients for dinner.

'So what are you doing now?' he asked her after a few minutes.

'Chopping an onion,' Catherine said as she sliced into the vegetable.

'No, I don't mean now this second. I mean this evening, generally,' Jimmy explained. 'Do you mind if I hang out, have dinner with you and the girls? Put them to bed – that sort of thing?'

Catherine paused briefly. She needed to talk about what Eloise had said.

'Jimmy, do you ever think it's weird that we still see so much of each other now?' She tested the subject on him.

'No,' Jimmy said firmly, pulling himself up into a seated position on the worktop. 'I think that after everything that happened, the fact we're able to put our children first and be friends means we're well adjusted and like, you know – cool.'

'So why aren't we divorced yet?' Catherine asked him, lowering her voice.

Jimmy didn't answer for a second or two, and then he said, 'Because it costs a lot of money and we haven't got any right now.'

41

'It's just sometimes I wonder . . .' Catherine trailed off.

'Wonder what?'

'Eloise told me today that she thinks you're going to move back in, that we're going to get back together. She's taking you and me getting on and you being here so much as a sign. We can't let them have false hope, Jimmy. We need to talk to them again. Get them to see that this is the way things are for good.'

Jimmy drummed the heels of his cowboy boots against the kitchen cupboards. 'I don't want to do that,' he said.

Catherine turned to look at him, onion tears standing in her eyes. 'But why not? It's the truth.'

Jimmy paused for a moment. 'I know it's the truth, but I don't want to take hope away from an eight-year-old, let alone her kid sister. When you're a kid is practically the only time when hope seems like a real possibility. We might as well tell them Father Christmas isn't real, or that it's been us they've been bankrupting and not the tooth fairy all this time. Next you'll be wanting to tell Leila that Jesus is no more than a historical figure and not the son of God.'

'This is different, Jimmy, and you know it,' Catherine said in a low voice. 'We can't lie to them about *this*. It's their lives we're talking about.'

'We're not lying, we're not doing anything,' Jimmy corrected her. He hopped off the counter, put one hand on each of Catherine's shoulders and looked into her eyes.

'Look, we hurt each other pretty badly. We tore each other up and those two were in the middle of it. And now you don't hate me any more, and that's all right by me, and I'm not messed up by you any more and that's all right by you. Those two girls in there have had enough pain in their lives already. It can't be wrong to let an eight-year-old have hope, it just can't.'

'But it's false hope,' Catherine persisted, wiping the back of her hand under her eyes and feeling an instant sting.

'All hope is false hope – that doesn't make it a bad thing,' Jimmy said. 'Look, if they ask me anything like, "When are you moving back in, Dad?" then I'll tell them I'm not, and you'll do the same, and in a few months they'll stop asking. In a year or two they won't even think about it any more and the way we live will seem normal to them. The hope will fade all by itself, don't you worry.'

'That sounds wrong coming from you, the eternal optimist,' she said, catching a low note in his voice with some concern.

'Oh, don't get me wrong,' Jimmy said, mustering a grin. 'I'm still an optimist. It's just that I'm starting to realise eternity is a very long time. So what do you say – is that a plan?'

Catherine looked into the living room where Eloise was picking out the riff from 'Hotel California' on Jimmy's acoustic guitar, her head bent over the strings while Leila watched her fingers, trying to pick up the notes herself. Just at that moment her children felt safe and happy, and it was a feeling that Catherine was as desperate to preserve as her husband was.

'OK, we'll do that then,' she said. 'We won't lie but we won't say anything either.'

The two of them stood in silence for a moment in the small galley kitchen, sensing another thread of the lives they had once woven together so confidently and hopefully, unravelling and drifting apart. Somehow the closer they got now as individuals, the further away the reality of the couple they once were seemed, and it was a loss that Catherine, at least, still mourned. Not because the relationship they had once shared was right, but because she had wanted it to be so much.

'So are you staying for dinner then?' she asked him finally, breaking the thread in two.

Jimmy's smile was weary. 'I thought you were never going to ask.'

It was past eight when Catherine finally got the girls into bed. It was Jimmy's fault. After his quiet resolve in the kitchen he'd returned to his tall-tale self by the time Catherine served dessert, regaling the girls with stories of what a wonderful life they were going to lead as soon as the band was discovered and he hit the big time – which would be any time soon, now that they had the funds in place to make a new demo. Eloise asked for a pony and Jimmy told her she could have a field full if she wanted, and there was to be an unending supply of sweets for Leila who planned to distribute them to the world's less privileged children.

Jimmy and the girls had still been singing by the time Catherine finally managed to shepherd the little ones up the stairs, and she did have to admit, as they hummed whilst brushing their teeth, that Jimmy's new song had a catchy tune. Jimmy was good at catchy tunes, but somehow they never seemed to fit his rock-and-roll image. Surely a man who wore leather trousers to go to the supermarket shouldn't be writing soppy love songs; he should be writing about mayhem and devil worship and possibly drugs of some description. But Jimmy had never been like that. Yes, he had a skull and crossbones tattooed on his right shoulder, but it was wreathed in roses and once, many years ago, when Catherine had teased him about his rock credentials he'd replied, 'I'm a lover, not a fighter, babe.'

He'd more than proved himself right since then.

When she came down Jimmy was still there strumming on his guitar and humming the now-familiar tune. He'd opened a bottle of wine and poured two glasses out, which meant he wasn't planning on going back to the boat any time soon. Catherine realised that she was glad. They would sit and talk about the girls, and her job and the PTA, and he'd entertain her with stories of the band's latest exploits or whichever kid he was teaching in Rock Club had the most promise, and things would be easy between them, and comfortable. What Catherine missed most about being with him was simply having him in the room on a weekday night sipping a glass of wine and talking. Loving each other had been a trick they had never quite pulled off, but even after everything that had happened they still had the knack of liking each other.

'Do you mind?' Jimmy asked her, nodding at the wine. 'I'll go back to the boat in a mo, but the forecast said frost overnight. I could do with a drink to help keep the cold out.'

'You need a proper home, really,' Catherine said as she sat down, picking up her glass.

'I've got one,' Jimmy said with a shrug. 'It's just that I don't live in it any more.'

Catherine took a sip of wine.

'I mean, you need a proper home for you. You can't go on living in that boat. It's not even a proper boat, just some floating rust bucket that Billy cobbled together when he was half cut and off his face.'

'Don't talk that way about Billy,' Jimmy said mildly. His oldest friend and one-time bandmate had died – some said deliberately, although never in front of Jimmy – from an alcohol and prescription drug overdose almost three years ago. 'If anybody had a good reason to drink it was him. He went from the brightest, best-looking, most talented bloke I've ever known to a shell of himself in less than five years. He could never let go of what he had once been, that's the worst tragedy of schizophrenia. He knew he'd never be that bloke again, never get married and have kids. So he loved that boat instead. He poured every ounce of love and dedication he could have given to a family into it, if only he'd ever got the chance. I miss him.'

'I'm sorry,' Catherine said. 'I know you do. And it's a great boat, but it's not a home, not for you. If paying the mortgage on this place is stopping you getting a flat or something, then we need to think again. I might be able to manage if we cut down a bit.'

'Cut down on what?' Jimmy asked her. 'You haven't got anything to cut down on, Catherine. And it's not a rust bucket. Billy might have been a drunk but he was a master craftsman, a carpenter. He poured his soul into that boat.'

'I just don't think it's fair that you should be freezing to death on a canal boat,' Catherine said.

'It is fair,' Jimmy said. 'The girls need something constant in their lives. They've grown up here, Leila was born here while I played Clapton to her so it would be the first thing she'd ever hear. I want to keep this place for them. And besides, I'm moaning now but you wait. In the summer that boat's a little paradise. The chicks really dig it.'

Catherine found herself laughing. 'It's just that you're getting on now,' she reminded Jimmy playfully. 'You don't want to be getting arthritis in this weather.'

'Hey, lady,' Jimmy warned her with a grin, 'I'm still young. I've still got it all ahead of me.'

'Have you?' Catherine asked him sceptically.

'Course I have, and so have you.'

'Have I? Sometimes I think I don't want anything new in my life. I think that just the way it is now is enough for me. I love the girls, and you and I are friends now, more or less. Everything's ordered and calm. If all I had in front of me was fifty more years of the same I'd be happy enough.'

'Happy enough? Happy enough isn't enough. If it was, then Billy would have kept taking his medication and living a half-life, and I'd have given up my music years ago and become a postman. I've thought I'd quite like the early mornings and the uniform,' Jimmy said, making Catherine smile just as he intended. 'Everybody needs to be loved, everybody needs to love someone.'

'And some people need to love everyone,' Catherine added wryly.

'I don't, though,' Jimmy said, tipping his head back on the sofa and looking at the ceiling. 'I don't love anyone. Not since us. But I know I will love someone again and that someone will love me, because I need that to happen and so do you. It's what makes us human.'

Catherine wanted to disagree with him but she couldn't quite bring herself to do it.

'I'd better get going,' Jimmy said after a while, finishing his glass of wine. 'If I don't get the stove lit now I'll be a block of ice in the morning and frozen corpses hardly ever have number-one hits on iTunes. I'll leave the electric here, if you don't mind. If the damp gets into her she'll be knackered.'

He kissed Catherine briefly on the lips as she stood up to let him out, and then with his hand on the latch of the door he turned round and looked at her.

'Look, I don't know why I'm saying this – but try and remember the last time you were really in love, Catherine, the last time your heart burst out of your chest every time you thought about that person. The nights you spent awake just dreaming about what it would feel like to touch them, longing for their arms around you. He hurt you, I know he did, and she let you down and left you alone to cope with everything. But sometimes I think when you buried the hurt and the pain they left you with, you buried a bit of yourself as well. I know it's none of my business any more but I'm only saying you deserve to be loved, so try and remember what it felt like and then maybe, when the time comes, you'll be able to let it happen again. I just want you to be happy. Really happy.'

Jimmy nodded once and then closed the door carefully behind him so as not to wake the girls.

Catherine tweaked back her curtains and watched him hunched up against the cold as he marched stalwartly towards the canal, his long hair whipped by the wind, clutching his acoustic guitar by its neck.

Despite everything he was still the only person alive who really knew her, who understood her better than she ever understood herself.

Chapter Five

It had been almost unbearably hot the day Catherine had met Marc James.

She been waiting for Alison, of course; a lot of her childhood had been spent sitting in parks, loitering in corridors or sheltering in rainswept bus stops, waiting for her best friend. As the two girls reached the age of seventeen in tandem it was no different. If anything, it took Alison longer to get anywhere, particularly since she had learned that most people, especially boys, would wait for her arrival almost indefinitely. And that summer, even though Alison was nursing her own secret crush, she started getting boyfriends. Not the kind she used to have – some fleeting alliance that would begin at registration and be over by the afternoon break – but dates with real boys to the cinema, McDonald's and sometimes even the pub, where Alison would sip Cinzano Bianco and lemonade.

Catherine had both laughed and listened wide-eyed to her friend's detailed descriptions of her first kiss, the first time a boy put his hand up her top, and how it had taken David Jenkins ages to undo the hook of her bra because his hands had been shaking so much in excitement. It was a development in her friend's life that was as alien as it was fascinating to Catherine. Her imagination simply could not conceive what it would be like to touch a boy, hold his hand or even kiss him, so limited was her experience of the opposite sex. All she knew was that ever since Alison started properly going out with boys, her lateness had increased, and once or twice she hadn't shown at all.

The trouble was, Catherine had thought on that day, as she sat, her back against a tree, feeling its rough bark imprinting her skin through the thin cotton of her dress, she often felt a little bit as if her life wasn't real when Alison wasn't in it. It was like that riddle about the falling tree in an empty forest and whether or not it made any sound as it crashed to the ground because there was no one there to hear it. When Alison wasn't there to see her, Catherine felt entirely invisible.

She closed her eyes briefly and pushed her sunglasses up her nose, tapping her feet as she hummed quietly to herself. And then the sunlight had dimmed behind her eyelids and the skin on her legs cooled as a shadow fell over them.

'Well, about time,' she said easily, pushing her sunglasses into her hair and opening her eyes, expecting to find Alison. Her vision was momentarily dazzled by the bright light. The shape that loomed above in the instant it took her to focus was male. It was boy – no, not a boy. It was a young man.

He was shorter than Catherine, she judged instantly, stocky, with muscular arms and a bare chest. He was holding his T-shirt in one arm and a can of Special Brew in the other. And yet Catherine remembered quite clearly she hadn't felt intimidated by him. Not even then.

She had sat up, pushing her hair off her shoulders, straightening her back a little. She waited.

'Sorry, I didn't mean to make you jump,' he said, even though Catherine hadn't jumped, as he sat down on the grass with bare feet. Catherine noticed the soles of them were surprisingly soft and white. 'I'm just so tired. I'm working nights on the railway line. I should be sleeping right now, but I can't. It's too nice outside to be trying to get some kip in some stinking bedsit. I wanted to come out and sit in the sun for a bit, but every time I relax I fall asleep, and I can't have that. I'll turn the colour of your hair and if I miss the start of my shift I'll get laid off. So I thought I'd talk to you for a bit, if that's all right. At least while you're waiting for your friend . . . boyfriend?'

'Friend,' Catherine had corrected him hastily. For once she was glad Alison was late because she knew that if her golden friend had been here this creature would not be talking to her. He would not have even seen her.

He sat down on a patch of grass just beyond where the shade of the tree's canopy ended, the sunlight reflecting off his amber skin.

Catherine had never seen anything or anyone so beautiful in her whole life before. The sight of him made her heart stop in anticipation.

'My name's Marc,' he said, leaning back on his arms so the muscles in his shoulders and biceps stood out in sharp relief. 'I'm from Birmingham. I go where the work is and this month the work's here. That's pretty much my story. Now it's your turn. Tell me what your name is and why you are sitting under this tree all alone.'

And at his bidding, quiet, shy, awkward Catherine, who up until that point had been unable to hold anything other than the most stilted and awkward conversation with almost anyone other than Alison, started talking. Paralysed with social ineptitude in front of the skinniest spottiest seventeen-year-old, her response to this being, who was so palpably male, could not have been more different. It was as if by the simple act of noticing her he had burst a dam in her. Suddenly hundreds of words poured out of Catherine, thoughts and ideas that must have been building up pressure somewhere inside her for years. They talked about everything and nothing, and she looked at him, drinking him in like a thirsty person stumbling across an oasis in the desert: the light in his eyes as he watched her, the slope of his back as he shifted position, the set of his chin, the line of his nose. She was unable to stop looking at him and telling him about everything: school, her parents, her home life, her favourite books, music and films. Her hopes and dreams that she hadn't even shared with Alison, and he *listened*. Not only could he hear her, he was seeing *her*. For the first time in her short life, Catherine felt like her own person and not just Alison's friend or a neglected daughter. She knew what it was like to be truly seen.

Jimmy had asked her to remember the last time she was in love; looking back, Catherine realised that she was in love with Marc before they had even known each other half an hour. It had taken less than thirty minutes to happen, and how many years to shake off? Catherine wasn't sure she could answer that yet.

'So how about you, how come you've ended up drifting from town to town?' she asked him at last, desperate to know more about him. 'Why did you end up in Farmington?'

'You're here,' he said to her, the roll of his Midlands accent washing over her. 'That's a good reason to come here and it's a better reason than the one I've got. I follow the work. Labouring, railway stuff, mostly. I've not got any skills, see, or exams. I've not got a lot going for me.'

'You have,' Catherine had retorted automatically. 'I mean, you just probably don't know that you have.'

Marc shifted his position once again, crossing his legs, tucking his bare feet underneath each other so that Catherine could see the soft pale soles.

'Girls like me,' he said, with a one-sided smile. 'And I like you, Catherine. You're different.'

'I know,' Catherine replied in dismay.

'It's a good thing,' Marc told her. 'Most girls I try and talk to either won't have anything to do with me, or if they like the look of me they turn themselves into idiots, flirting and pouting and showing themselves off. I'm not saying I don't like it when a pretty girl flirts with me, but well . . . I don't know the last time I really talked to anyone, the last time anyone ever gave a toss about what I'm thinking or feeling.'

'Me neither,' Catherine said, afraid to move in case she caused one second of the remaining time she had with him to fall away before she was ready.

Marc kneeled up and pulled his T-shirt on over his head and then shuffled over on his knees and stopped in front of her.

'I've got to go,' he said. 'Got to get my head down.'

'OK,' Catherine replied.

'Will you be here tomorrow?' he asked her, and Catherine felt as if lightning had just struck the centre of her chest, leaving a gaping burning hole he could see right through.

'Yes,' she said, unable to manage any dissembling.

'Can I meet you here again tomorrow at the same time?' Marc asked, as he reached out and picked up her right hand. Catherine looked at the waxy alabaster of her fingers resting against the deep brown flesh of his.

'Yes,' she said again, her voice low.

He pulled her gently towards his body until she was kneeling opposite him.

'Can I kiss you, Catherine?' he asked her quietly, almost casually.

'I . . .' Catherine froze for a moment, her lips numb and immovable. 'I don't know . . . how to,' she finished painfully, dropping her chin to her chest and closing her eyes.

The next thing she felt was the rough surface of Marc's palms against the skin of her cheeks, drawing her face back up to look at him.

'I do,' he said.

What she felt then was the gentle pressure of his mouth on hers, the sensitive exploration of his tongue between her lips. And then his arm encircling her waist and the heat from his body radiating through the thin cotton of her dress and penetrating her bones. Finally, as Catherine began to echo and return his kiss, she realised that her arms had crept unbidden around his neck, and she felt the muscles of his shoulders contract beneath her fingers as she held him.

It wasn't a long kiss, or a particularly passionate one, but it was perfect. It was a perfect first kiss. A kiss that every other she might receive in her life would have to live up to.

Afterwards, with his arms still around her waist, Marc smiled into her eyes.

'I've never been with a girl like you,' he said almost regretfully. 'And I'm guessing you've probably never been with someone like me. You're different, Catherine, fragile and . . . nice. And I'm not that nice.' He grinned at her. 'I've made a lot of girls angry with me in my time and I don't take things too seriously. I like you, I want to see you again, but I want to be straight with you, make sure you know what you're doing.' Marc sat back on his heels, dropping his arms from her waist, and Catherine felt the chill of their absence.

'I've got to go,' he said. 'If you don't want to come tomorrow, I get it.'

'I'll be here tomorrow,' she told him steadily.

'Will you?' He watched her as he stood up, a faint frown between his brows.

Catherine swallowed and took a breath. 'You said I'm not like the girls you normally go with. You said I'm different, so if I'm different then maybe . . . this will be different. Maybe you'll be different and anyway . . .' she had to force every single tendon in her body to relax sufficiently to allow her to say what she had to, 'I've never had anything like this before, that's mine just for me. I just want to feel like this again – I don't care what happens.'

Marc smiled. 'Someday you'll learn not to wear your heart on your sleeve,' he said, and then he nodded. 'I'll see you tomorrow, Catherine, same place, same time.'

Later that night, while her parents had been watching the ten o'clock news, Alison had crept through Catherine's bedroom window, as she had done every night she could get away with it since they were twelve years old.

'Are you mad at me?' she whispered, easing first one bare leg and then the other through the window.

Catherine, who had been lying on her bed reliving every single moment of her afternoon, had sat up on her elbows and shaken her head.

'No, I'm not, you'll never –'

Alison interrupted her. 'When you hear what happened you'll understand,' she said.

Alison was so used to telling her stories, it would never cross her mind that Catherine might have one to tell in return.

'Go on then, but be quick. Mum'll be up as soon as the news is finished to tell me to turn my light off.'

'I was just leaving to meet you when *Aran Archer* rang me up and asked me if I wanted to watch a video at his. Well, I had to go, didn't I? Samantha Redditch has been after him since Easter. I thought she'll die if she knows I've bagged him.'

'But I thought you like –'

'Yes, of course I like him, I *love* him, but he's never noticed me yet so while I'm waiting, why not go out with Aran

Archer? There'll be parties and I'll get to hang out with my true love more.'

'If you say so,' Catherine said. She'd learned never to question Alison's plans, because Alison did what she wanted to do and worried about the consequences later.

'So I go round to Aran's, and his mum is out, of course. He draws all the curtains in the living room, tells me to sit on the sofa, and gives me a drink of orange *squash!*' Alison shook her head. 'What a saddo! Of course the film hadn't been on five minutes before we were kissing. His tongue was down my throat straight away and his hand was up my top, squeezing them like they were lemons.'

Alison laughed, remembering to cover her mouth with her hand at the last second in case Catherine's parents heard her.

'It was so not sexy,' she said. 'So I pushed him off me and he says, "Oh, go on, Alison, let me see them, please!" And I said to him, "Are we going out or what?" And he says, yeah we are, all sort of desperate and pathetic. So I said, "OK then."

'I couldn't get him off of me for the rest of the afternoon. He wanted to go further but I wasn't having any of that. I'm not losing it to him. Still, he's quite sweet really when he's not with his mates. He said he's fancied me for ages.'

'So you've chucked Ryan, then?'

'Well, I will do,' Alison said, glancing at her watch. 'What about you? What did you do? I would have phoned you here to tell you but I knew you'd rather get out than be stuck in here all afternoon.'

Catherine thought about her kiss with Marc and she thought of how it would sound if she tried to explain to Alison in the way Alison had just described her afternoon with Aran Archer. The moment was too precious for her to share with anyone, even Alison. Especially Alison, because once she knew she'd have questions like, whose hand went where and what did it feel like and when could she meet him? Catherine realised with a sudden lurch she didn't want Alison to meet him. The afternoon she had spent with Marc, the talk they'd had and the kiss was hers. It was perhaps the very first thing that she had properly owned in her entire life, even if it was something as transient as memories and sensations, and Catherine wasn't ready to share them.

'We can do something tomorrow, if you like,' Alison said. 'Aran will be begging me to see him but I don't think I should, do you? I'll be fighting him off again all afternoon and it's such a drag.'

'Actually, I can't tomorrow,' Catherine said quickly.

'Really?' Alison looked surprised and Catherine was sure she'd be caught out in her lie. 'Parents?' Alison asked.

Catherine nodded.

Alison gave her a sympathetic hug. 'Just think, one more year and you'll have A levels and we'll be off to university. Then you'll never have to see them again. One more year and you'll be free.'

'Yes,' Catherine said thoughtfully. 'One more year.'

They heard a footfall on the bottom stairs.

'I'll be back tomorrow,' Alison hissed as she climbed out of the window. 'Same time, same place, OK?'

Hastily Catherine pulled the window shut after her, and glimpsed the silhouette of her friend on the garage roof before scrambling back into bed.

'Lights out now,' her mother said, opening the door.

'Yes, Mum,' Catherine said.

Her mother paused for a moment, looking at the window, the curtain a little askew.

'Have you had the window open?' she asked Catherine.

'Sorry,' Catherine said.

'No windows open at night. Any mad man could get in.'

Her mother had shut the door behind her, snapping the light switch off as she went. Catherine lay back in her bed, stretching from the ends of her fingers to the tips of her toes, knowing. At last she had something to dream about.

Things would have been so different, Catherine thought as she finished her glass of wine, if Marc just hadn't turned up the next day.

She had told her mother she was going to study at the library, taking a big net bag of books and several pens to prove it. Her mother, who didn't like her being around the house anyway, didn't question her. She was glad to see the back of her.

Catherine deliberately walked along the canal towards the park in a bid to avoid meeting anyone she might know, including Alison, on the high street. The spot in the park where Marc had found her was out of the way, beyond the swings and roundabout, under the canal bridge towards the back of the field where the park met the railway embankment. The grass was long, untouched by the council mower. Catherine felt confident that once she was there she would not be spotted by anyone.

Which was reassuring because she didn't expect him to be there at all. She prepared herself for disappointment, relieved that she hadn't told Alison about him because then, when he didn't show, when she didn't see him again, it wouldn't matter as nobody would know about him, and after a few days or weeks, Catherine would stop thinking about him and her life would get back to exactly the way it had been before.

But as she made her way under the bridge she could see that Marc was already there waiting for her, leaning against the trunk of the tree they had met under, the August sun painting his bare chest with patches of gold as it danced through the tree's canopy.

Catherine stopped in her tracks and looked at him. She was seventeen, the most inexperienced girl in her year, if not the whole school. She was thin and flat-chested, with long bony fingers and feet. What did Marc want with her truly? Because he could not want her like *that*. He couldn't look at her the way boys looked at Alison and actually want her. Besides, he wasn't a mere boy. He was a man, more than three years her senior. Seeing him waiting there under the tree for her didn't make any kind of sense.

Instinctively Catherine knew that now was the time she should turn back. It was her chance to heed the warning he had given her yesterday and leave. But even as in her mind's eye she was rotating on her heel and scurrying away to the shelter of the library, her treacherous body was carrying her right to his side.

'I saw you watching me,' he said, smiling up at her, blinking against the bright sunlight. 'Having second thoughts?'

'No,' Catherine said. He reached out, catching her hand and pulled her down onto the grass. 'It's just, I look at you and I . . . I don't know what you want with me.'

Marc laughed. 'Me neither, but it must be something pretty strong because after we said goodbye yesterday I swore blind to myself I wasn't coming here today. But here I am. And now you're here I feel happy. I hardly ever feel happy.'

The two of them watched each other and the anticipation that he might kiss her again made Catherine's insides burn.

'So what do you want to do today?' Catherine asked him.

Applying a very gentle pressure on her shoulders Marc pushed her back into the long grass and lay alongside her, his head propped up on one elbow. 'I want to lie here in the grass, talking and kissing you,' he told her. And that was exactly what they did.

They met every chance that they could, every free hour that Catherine could steal from her mother and explain away to Alison. She would have been content to lie in the long grass with Marc day after day, but on the third day Marc pulled her to her feet and said, 'Let's go somewhere else.'

'Where else?' Catherine was reluctant, afraid of who might see her and afraid to tell Marc that she felt that way, in case she hurt him.

'The pictures,' Marc told her, raising his eyebrows. 'They've got a showing of that film *Ghost* on at the cinema. I've heard it's rubbish, but girls like it, right?'

'You're taking me to *Ghost*?' she said, repressing a laugh because it seemed like such a normal thing for a boy and girl to do and exactly the sort of thing she thought she would never do, especially not with Marc.

'I'm doing better than that.' He grinned, tugging at her hand. 'Come on.'

Never in her life as the tallest thinnest most ginger haired girl in the school had Catherine ever felt as self-conscious as she did that afternoon, walking hand in hand with the shorter, compact, shirtless Marc through the town towards the Rex cinema. She was sure that this would be it, this would be the moment when one of her mother's friends or worse still her mother, caught her in a lie and the daydream she had been living would be over. Amazingly her luck held and as they approached the grand but shabby art deco building, Catherine saw a small queue forming outside its doors.

'This way,' Marc said, leading her not to the entrance but pulling her down a narrow alley that ran along side the building.

'What are we doing?' Catherine asked him, giggling.

'I met this guy in the pub last night, works in the projection room.' He drew her into a doorway with a locked fire door that was marked 'Fire Escape, Keep Clear!'.

'Years ago this old heap was the go-to place for miles around, he reckons. Gold paint on the ceiling, velvet chairs, cocktails brought to your table.'

'Yeah, I've heard that,' Catherine said with an uncertain smile. 'I've seen some of the old photos in the local history books. So?'

'*So*, there were boxes, just like you get in a theatre for the really posh people to sit in. They don't use them now, except for storage but they are still there . . .' He smiled at her and kissed her gently on the lips. 'And the bloke said if I bought him a pint, he'd let us in the side entrance and we could watch the film in a box for free.'

'Really?' Catherine gasped, more delighted that Marc had been thinking of her when he came up with the plan, than the plan itself. *Ghost* was one of Alison's favourite films and they had seen it so many times she was fairly sure she knew the script better than Demi Moore did.

Marc nodded, looking pleased with himself as he banged several times on the door. After a while the door swung open and Marc and the projectionist exchanged a few words.

'Don't get up to anything too energetic in there,' the projectionist told Marc as he pointed them towards the box, chuckling to himself.

'Do you mind,' Marc said, smiling at Catherine as he held the door open for her. 'I'm with a real lady here.'

They sat side by side on upturned boxes, Marc's warm arm around her shoulders.

'This film is crap,' Marc said after about twenty minutes, making Catherine laugh.

'Do you want to leave?' she asked him.

'No,' he said looking into her eyes. 'I want to kiss you.'

*

Almost every night Catherine would hear Alison's latest exploits with Aran, the things he tried to do to her or made her do to him, the things she sometimes let him do and the things she sometimes did.

But it was never like that with Marc; he never tried anything on with her. They sat or lay in the long grass, out of sight of the passers-by, while he stroked her hair and told her about his life, how he'd grown up alone, pushed from one foster home to another. How he'd been kicked out of care at sixteen and had to look after himself, make that choice between finding himself a job or doing one on the local post office with some of the other boys from the home and a sawn-off shotgun one of them said they could get hold of. He'd chosen labouring work because he knew what he was like; he knew he'd mess up and get caught and then that would be his life over. Then suddenly he'd stop talking and Catherine knew he was going to kiss her. She would feel his hand in her hair, or on her waist but never anything more.

She felt safe and when she was talking to him, telling him about her parents, who did not love each other, let alone her, it didn't seem so sad or so desperate any more that she'd grown up in a house without affection or compassion, and that the nearest thing she had to a real family was the girl who lived down the road and climbed in through her bedroom window nearly every night.

Then, on the ninth day, something changed. Marc was kissing her, and it felt just as it always did when suddenly, without warning, something shifted inside her. She found her arms snaking their way around his neck, and she pulled his body hard into hers as she kissed him back, arching the small of her back so that their hips met. Marc stopped kissing her.

'Whoa,' he said, breathless.

'What?' Catherine asked him. 'Did I do something wrong?

'Yes, I mean, no, not wrong but . . .' Marc looked at her. 'I don't think you're ready to . . .'

In the long pause that followed, their bodies relaxed. Catherine felt as if she was backing down from a fight.

'Can I ask you something?' she asked Marc.

'Course you can.' Marc shifted his body weight to create an almost imperceptible but significant space between them.

'Do you want me, Marc? I mean in *that* way. Because we've been seeing each other for a while now and I love talking to you and kissing, and I don't even know what I'm asking you really except that do you *really* like me, or do you just kiss me when you haven't got anything to say any more? Because you feel sorry for me?'

Marc looked dumbstruck. 'What?' he asked her, sitting up and back on his heels.

'You've never tried to . . .' Catherine was at a loss for words to describe what she barely understood, 'do anything but kiss me.'

Marc laughed, flopping back onto the grass. 'Oh Christ,' he said, his hands over his eyes.

'Don't laugh,' she said, punching him lightly on the arm, unable to resist smiling.

Suddenly he grabbed her forearm and pulled her on top of him, the expression in his eyes shifting in a second, all trace of humour gone.

'Of course I want you,' he said, making Catherine catch her breath. 'But I told you, you're different. You're . . . precious. I've never talked to another person in my life the way I've talked to you. You know me, you understand me, and I think I know you. You're pure.'

'So does that mean you don't want to . . . ?' Catherine discovered in that moment that she was becoming very tired of her purity.

'No, it means I want to, I want to a *lot*. But look, Catherine, if we do that – have sex – it will change everything and, I don't know, I like this – the way things are. It doesn't feel real, it feels like a dream, another world where it isn't crazy for me to be in love with you.'

Catherine had lain on top of him, her hair making a curtain for them both as she looked into his eyes.

'You're in love with me?' she asked him on an inward breath.

'I want to be . . . I *am* in love with you,' Marc repeated, unable to look at her this time. 'But I don't know if that is enough. I'm not the sort of bloke who's going to take you away from this or even stick around . . .'

'I don't care,' Catherine said. 'I love you too. And I don't care what happens next week or next month. These have been the best days of my life, Marc.' She paused, nipping sharply at her lip. 'You might as well know I'm a virgin.' She saw Marc hide a smile.

'That obvious?' she asked him happily before looking levelly into his eyes. 'But I want more between us. I want us to do more . . . to do everything.'

'Are you sure about this?' Marc asked.

'You said it yourself. We make each other different, better. This is right, I know it is.'

Marc brushed her hair back from her face. 'It can't be in the park,' he told her, his implicit assent making Catherine want to laugh and scream and cry in one instance.

'No,' she said, blushing only now.

He rolled her off his chest and sat up. 'There's my bedsit, but it's not exactly romantic. You should have somewhere nice, candles and flowers.'

'Marc,' Catherine laughed, pulling him to his feet, 'let's go.'

Marc picked up her hand and kissed the back of it.

'Come on,' he said. And he didn't let her hand go.

The bedsit was small, a single bed against a wall, a sink, a stove, a tiny fridge that burred and hummed in the corner as if it was fighting for its life. The room was neat and clean, and it seemed to Catherine that there was hardly anything of Marc in the room. His fluorescent work jacket hung over the back of the chair. There was a four-pack of Special Brew on the kitchen worktop and nothing at all in the fridge.

'Cup of tea?' Marc asked her as she stood in the centre of the room.

'Um, no, thanks,' Catherine said. 'Can we just . . .'

'Get on with it?' Marc asked her, laughing. 'I'm nervous. I don't know why I'm nervous.'

'Don't you be nervous! I'm far more nervous than you,' Catherine told him.

'We don't have to go the whole way today, you know,' Marc said. 'We can just take it slow. One step at a time.'

'No,' Catherine insisted. 'I'm here now. Let's do it.'

Marc nodded. He took two steps closer to her. Catherine had to refrain from taking the same number backwards.

He pulled his T-shirt over his head, and then Catherine's singlet over hers. She felt the touch of air against her skin raise a legion of goose bumps across her slender pale body, while the sunlight filtered a bloody orange through the bedsit curtains. And then the heat of his hands on her skin as he pulled her into an embrace. He was kissing her neck and shoulders, not the dreamy gentle kisses Catherine knew from the park – these were new, deeper and commanding. In one movement Marc had undone her bra and slid it off her shoulders, pulling her back onto the bed. She heard a moan deep in his throat, she felt herself respond to him, and at last she knew for certain what it felt like to be desired.

'I love you, Catherine,' Marc told her as his hand ascended her thigh. 'Always remember that at this moment I love you more than anything in the world.'

Catherine snapped back into the present, her wine glass in her hand, as she heard a noise on the landing.

'Mummy?' It was Leila.

'Yes, darling?' Catherine called back.

'I went to the toilet on my own!' Leila informed her proudly.

'Good girl. Well, get back into bed then. I'll be up in a minute to kiss you. Don't wake your sister.'

'She already has,' Eloise called out grumpily.

Catherine set the wine glass down on the table.

Jimmy had told her to remember the last time she was in love, and she had, because, despite the huge leap of faith it had taken her to trust her husband with her heart in the twelve years she had known him, she'd never felt the same intensity of emotion for Jimmy as she had during that summer with Marc James. When Marc walked out of her life, just a few weeks later, she felt as if he took with him the part of her that could feel that way again. It frightened Catherine to think that Marc James had been the love of her life, but his was the love that had changed her life – had changed her – for ever.

That afternoon in his bedsit had been the most wonderful, most perfect experience of her life.

At last she'd felt that she belonged to someone.

Amazingly she'd felt that he'd belonged to her.

And then she'd introduced him to Alison.

Chapter Six

Alison looked at the clock on the kitchen wall. It was almost eleven and Marc was not home.

This was to be expected, she told herself as she took a sip from what was her fourth glass of wine, on the grounds that she deserved a drink after the day she had had. It was not unusual for Marc to work late, well into the night without ringing her to tell her what time he would be home. That was just him, or rather that was the way he was now, after fifteen years with Alison. It was the way she had made him.

Alison smiled to herself and tried to imagine that dark and brooding young man she had first set eyes on, on that hot summer's day all those years ago, the heat in his eyes blazing almost as intensely as the sun. He had been the most beautiful thing she had ever seen, like an exotic creature that had somehow wandered into their safe, white middle-class town where everything and everyone looked the same. He was a drifter, without aim or purpose, restless and resentful. The young man he was then didn't look anything like the man who would one day work himself like a dog to make his business a success, keep his family secure and buy himself a life in the very same safe, white middle-class town that Alison had once begged him to run away from with her. He didn't look anything like that person she had fallen so hard for at the age of seventeen, the man she'd left everything behind for, including herself.

Alison stopped that train of thought. She could hardly complain that time had changed him. The intervening years and three children had changed her too, even if she worked hard at the gym to try to slow down time as much as possible. Of course, Marc was still out at the dealership, getting it ready for the grand opening at the weekend. There was a lot to do and he would not leave until everything was perfect. Everything else, including his wife, would have to wait until then. Alison knew that because she had created the man he had become and this, sitting drinking wine alone at eleven o'clock at night, was the price she now paid for her creation.

Topping up her wine, Alison looked at the clock again. The house was quiet at last. Dominic had either turned his music off or plugged his headphones in, and the girls had been asleep for hours, Amy drifting into oblivion the second her head touched the pillow, as if her restless dreams would be a welcome escape from the harrowing day her mother had put her through.

Her two daughters' first day at their new school could not have been more different and Alison was afraid that that was how it was going to be for them for the rest of their lives. Gemma, she didn't have to worry about. Gemma was exactly like Alison had been as a child: she breezed through every social situation, supremely confident and happy, utterly unconcerned by the children who did not like her (and there were a few of those, because Gemma had a knack for rubbing people up the wrong way) and completely adored by those she chose as her friends.

Amy, on the other hand, could have been a changeling. She was not like her father – driven and single-minded, always chased by nameless demons at his heels – and she was not like her mother. Or perhaps that wasn't entirely true. Because Alison had not been the same woman she was when she conceived Gemma as she was when she became pregnant with Amy. During those three years she'd lost a little of her shine, a little of her certainty. Sometimes Alison worried that Amy was a replica of her mother after all, that somehow she had let her younger daughter down by not being the person she used to be, by not being the kind of woman who had daughters like Gemma.

Gemma had been in the playground when Alison had arrived bang on time to pick her girls up, and had come racing up to her mother, full of news and gossip and talk of new best friends whom she simply had to have over to tea at the first possible opportunity. They had been about to go round and find Amy when Mrs Woodruff popped her head out of the reception door and asked Alison to go into her office. Amy and Mrs Pritchard were waiting there for her.

The moment Amy had spotted Alison she had scrambled onto her lap and buried her face in her neck, the child's tiny shoulders shaking as she sobbed silently, her small fingers wound tightly in Alison's hair.

Amy had cried all day. Literally all day, Mrs Woodruff had told Alison kindly, her sympathetic face crumpled with compassion.

'Why, darling?' Alison asked Amy, gently lifting her face from beneath the curtain of her hair by placing her forefinger under her daughter's chin. 'Why did you cry so much?'

'I don't like my new teacher,' Amy sobbed woefully. 'I want Miss Howard, Miss Howard is *beautiful* and *young*.'

'Um, well,' Alison looked apologetically at Mrs Pritchard and was relieved to see a twitch of a smile round her lips.

Amy's face disappeared into Alison's hair again.

'Not coming tomorrow,' she hiccuped miserably. 'Mama, p . . . please don't make me come again. I'm *worried*.'

Alison had encircled her arms more tightly around Amy and set her mouth in a thin line of determination. She knew she had to be firm and force herself not to give in to her daughter's pleas. Her youngest child had been born fragile and full of fear, equipped with the thinnest of skins, and yet Alison knew that of all her children Amy was the bravest, because, despite her fears and her uncertainty, as long as her mother told her everything would be all right, come tomorrow morning she would get up and face the whole terrifying process again.

So now when her tear-stained daughter asked why she had to go to school, even though Alison struggled to find an answer and wanted more than anything to keep her at home and safe by her side, she knew she had to say the right thing. There was no alternative, Amy would have to learn to live her life in this world, as frightening and as harsh as it must seem to her, and all Alison could do for her little girl was to teach her how to cope with it and somehow manage to get through these difficult first few weeks until eventually Amy found the same kind of uneasy peace here as she had done at her old school.

For a second Alison thought of her husband, of his insistence that they move back, and she had to swallow down her bitter anger. They all seemed to be paying the price for his mistakes, even Amy.

'It will take a while for her to adjust,' she told Mrs Woodruff and Mrs Pritchard apologetically. 'I think there'll be a good few tears till then.'

'Of course,' Mrs Pritchard agreed. 'It takes a long time to settle into a new life, no matter how old you are. We'll get there in the end, won't we, Amy?'

'I'll try,' Amy said. 'It's just that I'm so *worried*.'

And then it had been Alison who had to try to stop herself crying.

At least Alison had been able to get the girls home, safe and in one piece, even if one of them was so miserable.

She had made Dominic come out of the gate to meet her before Rock Club because she wanted to go in with him, meet his new tutor and pay for the term. Dominic had flung himself into the car, slapping his body into the seat.

'I've changed my mind,' he said, tucking his chin into his neck as some girls from, Alison guessed, his year strutted past. 'I don't want to go to Rock Club. It's for losers anyway.'

Alison looked at him clutching his guitar by the neck and felt her stomach contract in sympathy. He felt pretty much the same way she had ever since they had arrived here – as if she was waiting to go home to a place where she could relax and be herself, or rather the self she had spent the last fifteen years inventing. That self hardly seemed relevant here.

'Don't be nervous, kiddo,' she told him, putting her arm around him. 'It will be fine. You're a tough kid. Go and rock the joint.'

Dominic's sideways look was one of pure recrimination.

'I'm not nervous,' he countered, shrugging her arm off. 'I just don't want to go in there. It's totally lame, Mum. And anyway how many other kids do you see whose mums made them wait until they arrived to take them in. They're going to slaughter me and it's all *his* fault.'

As if to prove him right, three boys about his age and similarly attired in black combats and printed T-shirts slouched past with that awkward wheeling gait that seemed to be how all boys of a certain age walked, peering at him through the car window as if he were a piece of dirt.

'Look, I have to come in to pay. I promise that after today I'll never come near the place again. I'll even walk ten paces behind you now and pretend I don't know you.'

71

She had been joking but Dom exploded out of the car and took off ahead, taking her at her word.

'Right, well, wait here, girls, then,' Alison said. 'I'll lock you in. Don't open the doors to anyone. I won't be long.'

'Hurry, Mama,' Amy said, her voice quivering, her big brown eyes looking up at the sky as if it might fall in on her at any moment.

'Oh, come on, Muffin,' Alison heard Gemma say as she grabbed her bag. 'Let's play I spy – I'll let you win.'

As she walked back into her old school Alison was unprepared for how the building and its surroundings would make her feel.

It wasn't an especially old building – it had been built in the 1920s – but it was an exact replica of a grand eighteenth-century building, complete with palisades, colonnades and even a chapel. From a distance, set in its own expansive grounds, it looked like a very grand private school, not like the local comprehensive at all.

Close up, though, it was another story. The smell, that slightly musty and acrid combination of disinfectant and damp, was still exactly the same, and, as Alison followed Dominic through the impressive panelled double oak doors that marked the main entrance to the school, she was fairly certain that the interior hadn't been decorated once in the sixteen years since she had last set foot in it. The walls were still that insipid greyish green colour with patches of pink plaster showing through where paint had chipped or peeled away. Even the same framed prints lined the corridors: faded and dusty scenes from Shakespeare, so grimed with dirt that Alison was sure it had been a long time since anyone had looked at them properly or even noticed they were there.

As she looked around her and breathed in, all at once Alison saw her past reflected, bouncing back at her, almost blinding her like sunlight off a mirror. Once this place had been the centre of her universe. There on the stairs she saw where she had made Cathy wait in vain with her for a whole lunch hour just to catch a glimpse of Jimmy Ashley, the hottest boy in school, whom Alison had loved from afar right up until the minute she had met Marc and he had eclipsed everything.

As she walked into the main hall, where her son had already headed, no doubt hoping to dissociate himself from his stalker of a mother, she could see herself up on the hall stage, painting the scenery for the school production of *Grease* and imagining herself as Sandy and Jimmy as Danny, while Cathy scoffed at her and told her she had no idea what anybody could see in Jimmy Ashley.

Alison smiled as she remembered the lower sixth form end-of-year dance. Cathy wasn't allowed to come to the dance, or any dances since that time her mother had caught her sneaking off to the Valentine's disco, which left Alison alone to pluck up the courage to talk to Jimmy. Finally, at the end of the evening, after sneaking several slugs of illicit vodka into her orange juice, she had worked up the courage to ask Jimmy to dance with her. Reluctantly he had consented, holding her waist gingerly as they turned in slow circles to a song by The Cars. Alison had not been able to take her eyes off her feet, certain she would faint clean away if she looked into Jimmy Ashley's eyes. How strange, she thought to herself as she watched Dominic greet a couple of other boys, and a girl in a very short skirt, with studied nonchalance. She had once considered those three minutes, that dance with Jimmy, the pinnacle of her life.

Then only a few weeks later she had found out about Cathy's secret boyfriend, and a few weeks after that she had run away with Marc without giving Jimmy Ashley or Cathy a second thought. The course of her life had changed for ever.

What surprised Alison the most was that these memories, now so vivid and visceral, hadn't crossed her mind in fifteen years. It was as if on the night she'd decided to run away from home, she'd run away from this part of her life for ever, dissecting it from her heart and her head with the kind of bold decisiveness that only a seventeen-year-old in love can have. She had hoped that the detritus of her youth, the wreck of the life she had abandoned so wholly, all those people and the places would be long gone, rotted into the past. It was a doomed optimism that led her to hope that.

Apart from anything else, the school looked as if it had been preserved in aspic. There was even someone over there talking to her son who looked exactly like Jimmy Ashley.

Alison's heart stopped beating for the longest second. That *was* Jimmy Ashley. When it began to beat again it was racing.

Alison felt a blush extend from her ears downwards, and pins and needles in the tips of her fingers. She clapped her hand over her mouth to stifle the burst of hysterical laughter that threatened. She felt just as she had with his hand on her waist at the sixth form dance – dizzy and dazzled. It was the shock, Alison told herself, retreating into a shadowy corner to regain her composure, and the fifteen years that seeing him again had seemed to disintegrate in a second. Thinking about him, the boy she'd once admired so wildly, and then just seeing him standing there in the flesh, tuning her son's guitar, had given her vertigo.

She simply hadn't expected Jimmy to be there looking almost exactly the same as he had the last time she'd seen him. On the other hand, she didn't know where else she expected him to be. He obviously hadn't hit the big time like he'd always said he was going to, so perhaps teaching guitar back at his old school was the obvious location for this living, breathing relic of her youth.

He didn't look like a relic, though. He looked good – better even than he had at eighteen. His shoulders had filled out and his bare arms were toned and muscled. His skin had cleared up and he looked relaxed, at ease with himself. Yes, he looked like a reject from an eighties rock band but if anyone could carry it off, he could. Alison admired his thick long brown wavy hair. Once she had dreamed about tangling her fingers in it.

Biting her lower lip as she hovered in the shadows, Alison was taken aback by how much pleasure seeing him gave her. He still had that hint of a smile on his lips, as if at any second he might start laughing. He still wore jeans so tight that you wondered how he sat down without them ripping apart at the seams. One of the most popular girls at school, Alison had had a boyfriend every other week from the age of fourteen. Other upper sixth formers asked her out, but not Jimmy, never Jimmy. Not the boy she really wanted. Not her son's new guitar teacher.

Desperately she tried to shake off this ridiculous *frisson* of excitement, which had engulfed her the moment she set eyes on him. It made her want to laugh out loud. It was embarrassing, uplifting and foolish all at once. Alison took a deep breath and determined to pull herself together.

Hoping Jimmy wouldn't notice her (and wishing she had put some make-up on and brushed her hair before leaving the house), she edged over to the table where a register book lay open and leaflets about the club and forthcoming events were on display. She found out from a leaflet the amount she owed for Dominic to attend for one term and hurriedly wrote out the cheque, breathlessly expecting that at any moment Jimmy would tap her on the shoulder and say, 'Alison Mitchell, how wonderful to see you!'

But before she could even sign the cheque a sudden burst of electric rock music crackled in the air, making Alison almost jump out of her skin, as if her internal feelings had suddenly transformed themselves into pure noise.

Twelve or fifteen kids were standing around the stage, two playing complete drum kits, three or four (including the short-skirted girl) on microphones and at least seven guitars, which Alison's limited knowledge told her included a couple of bassists. Alison didn't recognise what they were playing and then she realised that was because they weren't playing anything. Jimmy had just got them up on the stage and got them to start making music. The first minute and a half was pretty unbearable, and then suddenly a cohesive tune emerged and Alison saw Jimmy's head go down and his shoulders rock to the rhythm just like he used to when he played at the school dance. And then she looked at Dominic and for the first time since they had arrived he was smiling – no, not just smiling; he was grinning from ear to ear with the pure joy of doing something he loved. Alison knew that neither Jimmy nor her son would notice her now if she cartwheeled the length of the hall and back, which made her feel happy and sad all at once.

She slipped the cheque into the register book and then, caught on a sudden impulse, ran out of the school, narrowly avoiding colliding with the head teacher as she careered out into the car park. Once in the car Alison found herself laughing until the tears rolled down her face, caught up in the moment with the seventeen-year-old girl she once had been. And then as the laughter faded the idea of seeing Jimmy, still living his life out here almost as if nothing had changed since she left, inspired a sobering thought.

Coming back to Farmington wasn't going to be nearly as easy as Marc had promised her, because there were ghosts everywhere. Living, breathing ghosts.

*

Dominic had expressly told Alison that she was not allowed to pick him up from Rock Club, and so even when it had begun to rain, thick grey sheets of water that clattered against the windows in wave after wave, Alison sat tight and waited for him. He was over an hour late when his dark and sodden figure finally emerged out of the torrent of water.

'Where have you been?' Alison asked him as he peeled off his T-shirt and threw it into the laundry basket. She didn't like the shrill tone of her voice any more than he did but somehow, lately, since Christmas, whenever she tried to talk to him normally, that was the voice that came out.

'I got lost,' he told her with a shrug.

'Lost? The school's only down the road.'

'I know. But I wanted to have a look around, and some of the kids said there was this well lame skate park down by the canal that they go to sometimes. I went to have a look and I got lost.'

Alison tried to imagine her son in the canal park, the very same canal park where she had met his father. It seemed like an impossible paradox, as if time had folded back on itself, and not for the first time she got the feeling that her being back here was all wrong. As if somehow Marc was marching her back to the point at which they had met, looking for a way to change a future that was already past.

Alison shivered as she picked up the sodden T-shirt and inhaled deeply. Even in its soaking state it reeked of cigarette smoke.

'Lost with a packet of cigarettes?' she asked him.

'I wasn't smoking, it was the kids I was with,' Dominic retorted automatically. 'They're all at it at that school. I told you, it's a real dump.'

'So you were with local kids who know the area but you got lost?' Alison persisted.

'Just leave it out, Mum, all right?' Dominic's voice rose and Alison knew he was reacting to the look on her face, the expression she could see reflected in the glass door of the eye-level grill. In the dark smoky glass she looked sharp and aged. She looked like the kind of mother who never wanted her teenage son to have any fun, the kind of mother who only wanted to ruin everything for him, the kind of woman who was happy to rule his life but who didn't have the courage to take control of her own. That was who Dominic saw when he looked at her, and at that moment that alien, hard-faced woman was who Alison was.

'You dragged me to this fucking awful place,' Dominic swore at her. 'And now I'm just trying to make some mates – is that such a big deal? It's not as if I'm dealing crack, Mother. I couldn't score any in this place if I wanted to.'

Alison stared at him for a long moment, waiting, waiting for that woman reflected in the glass door to fade away.

'I'm sorry. You're right. I do trust you, Dom,' she told him, lowering her tone with some physical effort. 'It's good that you're making friends . . . so tell me all about your first day then.' Alison squeezed all of the tension out of her voice in a bid to make the question sound purely conversational and not like a declaration of war.

'The same old shit,' he told her, watching her carefully for any sign of reflex to his choice of language. 'Just a different fucking place.'

'But you made some friends?'

'I said, didn't I?' Dominic asked her, lifting a carton of juice out of the fridge and taking a swig from it. Alison considered getting into the 'use a glass' argument with him, but then that bitchy mother would be back again for sure so she let that particular battle go the same way as the 'don't swear in the house' debate had gone, which was out of the window.

Dominic had a lot less respect for her moral qualifications recently, and swilling juice direct from the carton was only one of the ways he chose to show her that. The trouble was, Alison felt that her son was largely right about her so she tried to ignore his challenges, happy to have contact with him at all.

'We can invite your friends over if you like,' she'd told him. 'For tea.'

'Ooh, yes, we can have a tea party and Jammy Dodgers,' he said to her. 'Tally fucking ho.'

He was about to exit the kitchen when he stopped in the door frame for a second, and looked back over his shoulder at her.

'How did Muffin get on?' he asked, using the pet name that he had coined for Amy when she was born because of her two black button eyes that looked like blueberries in a muffin.

'She found it hard,' Alison told him with a sigh. Once, less than two years ago, she and Dominic had always talked like this when he got in from school. He'd been her confidant, her best friend. The struggle with his emergent manhood hadn't got to him then; he hadn't discovered his father's imperfections or his mother's weaknesses. He hadn't been so angry.

'Did she cry?' Dominic asked, his voice gentle now. He'd been with Alison when Amy was born. Marc had not got there in time, caught up with something or someone at work. Dominic was always especially protective of Amy, that was one thing about him that had never changed.

'She cried a lot,' Alison admitted. 'And when you didn't come back she was really worried – you know how she is – so make sure you go in and say hi, OK?'

'I don't know why you made us come here,' Dominic remarked, turning to face her and leaning against the door frame, but without anger now. 'Muffin was pretty happy at home, Gemma was the queen of all her friends. And the stuff

I was into wasn't that bad, Mum, it really wasn't. If you'd told Dad where to go and showed some self-respect you wouldn't have had to worry about what the neighbours thought.'

'The neighbours?' Alison laughed harshly. 'Is that why you think we came here? The month we left London, eight kids around your age were stabbed in less than two weeks. I didn't want you to be one of those kids, Dom.'

Dom shook his head. 'That was never going to happen to me. Don't use me as an excuse for this. You're running away from the wrong thing. It's not houses or areas you need to run away from, Mum, it's him. It's Dad that causes all the trouble, not me.'

'It wasn't Dad sitting in the back of a stolen car, was it?' Alison asked her son, shamelessly changing the subject. 'No fourteen- or fifteen-year-old thinks he's going to walk out of his house and die,' Alison said. 'None of those boys or girls did. But it happened all the same. I want to protect you because, whether you like it or not, I love you.'

'Yeah, you reckon,' Dominic observed sceptically, his implicit disbelief in her feelings for him hurting Alison more than any insult he could dream up, no matter how laced with four-letter words it might be.

'Yes, I do reckon. And anyway, it's better for Gemma and Amy, a better place to grow up in, and Amy will settle in eventually. You know how she hates change.'

'Some things have to change whether you like them or not,' Dominic replied steadily.

'Yes they do,' Alison said firmly. 'Like us moving here. Look, you'll do better out here, and you're going to love Rock Club, and maybe you'll be able to set up your own band like you've always wanted.' Alison gave Dominic the list of all the reasons that Marc had given her when he told her he wanted to move here. All the reasons except for the ones that counted:

because he wanted to. Because he'd made it almost impossible for them to stay in London and because there was still something here in this town that he had to prove to himself.

'And maybe I'll grow up to be a train driver,' Dominic replied, gifting her with a sudden and unexpected smile.

'I miss that smile,' Alison told him.

'Yeah, well, it's hard to smile when you're busy being misunderstood,' he told her. 'Look, all I want is for you to be happy, the way you were when I was Gemma's age. Always laughing. Your smiles were real then.'

'I am happy now,' Alison reassured him. 'Honestly.'

Dominic sighed. 'I'm going to go up and get changed. I'll read the girls a story tonight, if you like.'

Alison smiled at him and longed to give him a hug, even if he did smell like a wet dog.

'Thank you, Dom, that would be a big help.'

'Yeah, well, just as long as you don't expect me to love this shit-hole or speak to him,' he told her as he left the room.

And that was her son, who was just like his father in so many ways but in one way especially: just when you thought you couldn't stand a minute longer of him he'd go and make you fall in love with him all over again.

At least that's what Alison hoped.

Marc's kiss on her cheek woke her, his face looming over hers as she opened her eyes. She must have fallen asleep in front of the late-night film.

'Hello, beautiful,' he said, kissing her lips this time. 'How was your day?'

'Long,' Alison said, struggling to orientate herself. 'And difficult. One child loves everything, the other two aren't so sure, to say the least. How about you?'

Marc clicked on the table lamp next to where Alison had

been sitting, dazzling her temporarily, and dropped a parcel of something heavy into her lap. Alison screwed up her eyes to look at it. It looked like a packet of greeting cards.

'I've had a brilliant idea,' Marc told her. 'We need to make a splash in this town, right? To get ourselves accepted by the locals. There's so much money to be made here, Al – and not just in the town. The whole area's up to its neck in cash – it's better than Notting Hill any day of the week. No Congestion Charge, no one picketing the 4x4s on the road. We want to be part of this community. And the best way to do that is to befriend the community, right?'

'Do you mean send them cards or something?' Alison said, her head still muddled by dreams and memories.

'No, I mean by throwing a party here.' Marc opened the package, pulled out a card and handed it to Alison. 'Half the invites are already sent. I used the guy from the local business forum and some other contacts I have in the area to get the guest list together. Or at least my guest list. I thought you could invite all the teachers, the head – maybe the PTA committee that I suggested you get involved with. Mothers you meet in the playground, anyone you like. Get yourself a social network so you don't feel so isolated. Don't you see? Instead of waiting for things to take off we can kick-start our new lives by throwing them the best party they've seen in years.'

Alison stared at the invitation.

'This date is a week on Saturday,' she said numbly. 'That's less than two weeks away.'

'Yes, it is,' Marc said, brushing the hair from her face. 'No point in letting the grass grow under our feet, is there?'

'Marc, there is no way we'll be ready to throw a big party in time.'

'Well, like I said, half the invites are sent now, so yes we will.' Marc grinned at her, that smile that said he'd made up his mind. 'Come on, love, you've never let me down yet. And the kids will love it. They can invite all their friends. We'll make it a real family event for the young ones too. It might help Amy settle in.'

'Amy doesn't like people, and I know how she feels,' Alison mumbled wearily.

'Well, people love you,' Marc said, watching her face. 'You look beautiful, by the way.'

Alison glanced up at him, the muscles in her shoulders tensing as she caught his look.

'I don't . . .'she protested weakly. 'I haven't even had a shower . . .'

His hand ran down the side of her face, his forefinger tracing the curve of her neck and breast.

'I remember the first time I saw you,' Marc said, unbuttoning her shirt with practised ease to reveal the lace of her bra. 'I wanted you right that minute.' He ran his hands over her breasts and then, lowering his head, nipped at the lace of her bra. 'The second I saw you all I could think about was what you would look like naked.'

'I remember,' Alison said. It was the version of events they had invented over the years, a version that was far more romantic and noble than the reality.

'I was driving through the town today and I saw it – you know, the bedsit – still there. Looks exactly the same. The place where we first –'

'Oh God, Marc,' Alison covered her face. 'Don't remind me.'

'Maybe it wasn't the most romantic place but thinking about it turned me on,' Marc told her. 'And I think it's about time that you and I christened our new house, Mrs James.' He pulled her to the floor, kissing her deeply as she folded onto his lap.

Alison made herself relax into his familiar embrace and waited, waited for that old hunger and need to return to her. As she felt his lips on her throat and breast she found herself thinking back to that day. The day they'd first had sex. It was an easy day to remember because it was also the day they first met.

It was the last week of the summer holidays. And up until that day everything was going in Alison's life more or less just as she had planned and expected it to. She had one more year ahead of her at school. One more year to get the boy she really wanted to want her back, one more year to help Cathy keep sane and get free of her hateful parents from hell, and then she was off, free as a bird to study English at Bristol University. She'd meet a hundred new friends and a hundred new boys, none of whom she'd have a thing to do with because by then she'd have the boyfriend she really wanted and not the one she'd got. Not Aran Archer and his persistent wandering, groping, squeezing, bruising hands. She'd have the boy of her dreams, the boy she'd loved since she first clapped eyes on him.

She'd have Jimmy Ashley. She didn't want him for ever, just for a few years while he was cool and everybody else wanted him, because anyone could see that Jimmy Ashley wasn't the kind of man you married, but he was the perfect boyfriend for any seventeen-year-old girl. Especially now that he had left school and was in a band. It was almost impossible to be more cool than that. On that day fifteen years ago Alison had still been confidently waiting for him to realise that she was the perfect girlfriend for any eighteen-year-old to have. Her affection and desire for him had been unshakeable up until the very second she met Marc and the whole path of her life changed course.

It happened because she knew that Cathy had a secret, which in itself was unprecedented – Cathy never had anything interesting to hide unless it was some exploit that Alison had arranged for her. But even more surprising was that whatever Cathy's secret was, she was also hiding it from Alison. And Alison absolutely had to know what it was, because, after all, the pair of them had been soul mates since they were eight years old on the day Alison started at her new school.

Cathy had been cowering in the centre of the playground, surrounded by a ring of girls, skipping, pointing and chanting, 'Witch, witch, witch!'

'What you doing?' Alison had demanded of them, marching into the centre of the circle. The first thing she noticed about the girl standing next to her was that she was very tall, with the skinniest legs Alison had ever seen. Alison took a step in front of her.

'Her mum's a witch, which makes her a witch too,' one of the other girls had crowed, her soft young face full of hate.

Alison had looked at the tall girl again, a tangle of arms and embarrassment.

'Is your mum a witch?' she asked her conversationally. The girl shook her head.

'Right then, she's not a witch, but I am.' Alison marched up to the ringleader until they were nose to nose. 'And if you say another word to my friend over there I'll put a curse on you that will make you die the most slowest and horrible and disgusting and painful death you can think of. And if you tell anyone I said that then I'll curse you anyway. One more word and you're a corpse.'

The girls had glared at Alison but she had remained silent, turning on her heel with a flash of a ponytail and marching off, chin in the air. Gradually the others drifted off too, whispering amongst themselves about the odd new girl.

'Looks like we're best friends now,' Alison had said, holding out her hand, which Catherine took. 'I'm Alison.'

'Catherine.'

'Right then, Cathy – want to play hopscotch?'

They had been twelve when Alison had got Catherine so drunk on cider that she had thrown up on her mother's feet as soon as she opened the front door to her, and then lay on the floor laughing. Catherine's parents hadn't taken that incident too well and banned Alison from seeing Catherine outside of school for good. Alison remembered her mum going round to Catherine's, certain she'd be able to reason with her, blame it on youthful experimentation, high spirits. But she hadn't bargained for Catherine's mum, the coldest and most unbendable human that had ever existed. But soul mates were soul mates, and a parental ban wasn't about to keep them apart. Alison invented a web of complicated lies that allowed them both to go out sometimes to a school disco or a party for a couple of hours, and best of all she worked out that she could climb out of her own bedroom window and into her friend's in less than ten minutes, if she sprinted in her slippers down the alley behind the houses that separated Catherine's posh estate from her council housing, without either set of parents knowing.

As they got older, their open secret of a friendship fell into an easy pattern. There was Alison and Cathy and Alison and the rest of the world. Alison did her best to be the bridge that Catherine crossed over to the normal lives of their peers. She threatened anyone who wasn't kind to Cathy and let those who were bask in her approval. But their friendship was always a two-way street. She was just Cathy's crusader and protector, her lifeline to normality; Cathy was her heart and soul, keeping her tethered to the ground when otherwise her wilder thoughts and impulses would have had her spinning off into the wild blue yonder, to be lost for ever. Cathy grounded her and kept her safe, and she knew she could tell Cathy what she could never tell her mother. She always thought that Cathy had felt the same, which is why her friend's secret puzzled her. After all, what sort of secret could Cathy have that would require so much guarding?

Alison couldn't imagine it.

Cathy had told her that she wouldn't be around that afternoon. Her mum was making her stay in and study again. But Alison knew it was an excuse, she knew that Catherine's mum worked in the Christian bookshop on Thursdays and wouldn't know if Cathy was studying at home or not. She couldn't go round and knock for Cathy so she waited on the iron railing behind the buddleia just next to the old people's bungalows. It was hot, and Alison was bored after ten minutes so it was lucky really that it didn't take much longer for Catherine to emerge, otherwise she might have gone to find Aran Archer after all.

Alison watched in fascination as her friend walked down the road. Something about Cathy had changed – no, that was wrong – everything had.

She was wearing a long white skirt that flowed around her ankles, a skinny-ribbed green vest top that set off the sway of her long red hair. She had bangles on her wrists and a long beaded necklace that fell between her breasts. Cathy looked beautiful and stylish, sexy even, with a new kind of confidence in the sway of her hips and the way she tossed her waist-length hair over her shoulder.

The way Cathy looked told Alison two things. First of all that Catherine's mother was definitely out, otherwise Catherine would never have dared to leave the house in anything other than the clothes her mother allocated, and secondly, that she was going to meet a male of the species.

Cathy had a boyfriend. Alison marvelled at the new-found information and wondered who it could be. Who at school could possibly have fallen for Cathy Parkin? None of the boys fancied Cathy, but not because she wasn't beautiful, it was easy to see that she was, and Alison had always known it even if she hadn't realised its full extent before. Still, Cathy's beauty was too subtle and oblique for any boy at school to appreciate; she didn't have the yellow hair, obvious breasts or the near-naked thighs that boys in their teens appreciated so much. Alison realised it couldn't be a boy from school that Catherine was going to meet. For a split second the thought that it might be Jimmy Ashley, the boy who had barely spoken two words to Alison and none at all to Catherine as far as she could remember, flashed across her brain, but she dismissed it. Even if Jimmy fancied Cathy, which he never would because she was about as far away from being a rock chick as a girl could be, then Cathy would never be his secret girlfriend. She'd never betray Alison in that way; it just wasn't in her nature.

There were only two ways to find out what was going on. She could either follow her or ask her.

Alison, who was always one to take the fun option, pulled her sunglasses down onto her nose and began trailing her best friend. She giggled as she hopped in and out of bus shelters, cowered behind trees, flattened herself against a shop window. Near to laughing out loud, Alison expected Cathy to turn around at any minute and ask her what she thought she was playing at. But then she realised Cathy was in a world of her own, an exclusive little bubble of her own feelings and thoughts that Alison could not even guess at. For the first time in the nine years she had known Cathy she was on the outside of her head and this boy she was going to meet was on the inside. It took a second or two for Alison to understand that what she was feeling as she slowed to a walk, now only a few feet behind Cathy, was jealousy.

She had to know that instant what exactly was going on in Cathy's life.

'Hi, Cathy, where are you going?' she said, falling into step alongside her friend, making her jump.

'I'm . . . oh, hello!' Cathy smiled, her cheeks colouring. 'I thought you were with Aran. Mum's working so I sneaked out for a walk.'

'Liar,' Alison said lightly. 'Come on, spill. You're on the way to meet a boy, aren't you? You might as well know, if it's Jimmy Ashley then it's over between you and me for good.'

'Jimmy Ashley?' Cathy stopped, wrinkling up her nose. 'It's not him!'

'Aha! So it's someone, then!' Alison grabbed hold of Cathy's wrist and swung it back and forth. 'Come on, tell me! I'm your best friend, aren't I? I tell *you* everything.'

'I was going to tell you,' Cathy said anxiously. 'It's just I wanted to see what would happen. I didn't think it would last longer than one day. But it has.' A slow shy smile crept over Cathy's face. 'We've been seeing each other almost all the holidays.'

'Have you?' Alison asked her. 'That's amazing. Can I meet him, then? The love of your life?'

Alison watched Cathy's face as she thought for a moment, unable to believe that she didn't agree immediately, trying not to take it personally but doing exactly that.

'OK, OK,' Cathy said, taking a deep breath and smiling. 'You can meet him today. He's amazing, Alison. When you see him you just won't believe that he likes me. I know I don't . . . except . . .'

'Except?' Alison prompted.

'He keeps telling me that he does,' Cathy said, her eyes

shining so brightly that Alison almost wanted to slap her then and there and tell her to pull herself together.

'It better be one of Take That,' Alison said as they walked across the high street, down through the canal park and over the railway bridge. 'I'm only going to forgive you if it's one of Take That.'

Finally they stopped at a square-shaped detached house with a yellow sign hanging outside, which read 'Rooms to Let'.

'He's staying here for now,' Cathy said, leading Alison down the overgrown path and through the unkempt garden. A rusted bicycle languished in the seeded grass. 'He's on a contract for the railway. It runs out soon. I don't know what will happen then, but he said he might try and get some more work locally, maybe in a garage or on a building site.'

'So it's not Jason Orange then?' Alison said, wondering just exactly what kind of person Cathy had got herself mixed up with, because if he lived here it wasn't any boy from school.

Cathy pushed the bell and waited, her fingers knotted behind her back.

And as both girls stood there, neither of them could have known that this was it: the fulcrum, the moment, the very second when suddenly their fates would tangle and turn for ever, and from that point on neither one of them would have the life that was meant for her.

'Hi.' Catherine's voice was small when he opened the door. 'Um, this is Alison. Remember I told you about her? She wanted to meet you . . . I thought it would be OK. Do you mind?'

Marc had stopped smiling at Cathy and looked right at Alison and said, 'I don't mind.'

Alison remembered staring at Marc, open-mouthed.

Yes, in her memory she was definitely open-mouthed,

awestruck, as she gawped at him, in his tight black T-shirt and blue jeans, with his skin turned to amber by the sun and his dark eyes taking her in under the sweep of his black brows. The first thing she thought, in the first minute of her new life, was that he was the most beautiful living thing she had ever seen. And the second thing she thought was how on earth did Catherine get him? That couldn't be right.

And then Marc looked into her eyes and Alison knew that he was seeing her in exactly the same way that the boys at school saw her: her breasts first, her short skirt and bare golden thighs, her smooth blonde hair and her soft full mouth. Last of all he'd noticed her eyes, her pretty blue smiling eyes. And she could tell even as Cathy chatted away, introducing them to each other, that he wanted her. She could feel it in every stroke of his gaze.

'All right?' Marc stepped forward and shook her hand lightly, letting his gaze fall from face to her chest and below.

'So I was thinking maybe the three of us could have a picnic instead of . . . you know . . . what we were planning, down in the park. Under our tree?' Catherine suggested sweetly, her happiness so thick that Alison could almost taste it.

Alison did her best to stop looking at Marc. 'You have a tree?' she teased Cathy gently. 'How romantic.'

'It's not really our tree, it's just a tree . . . oh, stop it, Ali,' Cathy said, blushing and laughing all at once.

Alison watched as Marc dropped his arm around Cathy's pale shoulders and kissed her lightly on the cheek. 'We can call it our tree if you like,' he said, challenging Alison with a lazy smile.

The tips of Catherine's ears went pink.

'We could go to the supermarket and get a few things,' Cathy offered. 'Mum won't see us, she's at work, so we should be safe.'

'Good idea,' Marc said, picking her hand up easily as if it was something he had often done. It was the easy intimacy between them that shocked Alison almost as much as it would have done if she'd come across them having sex. Somehow she found it impossible to imagine Cathy and this creature together. It seemed all wrong that it was Cathy who was the confident one, the knowing one, and that it was Alison who was feeling awkward, uncomfortable and out of things. Alison didn't like it one little bit.

She didn't say a single word as she listened to Cathy chatter on the way to the supermarket. She couldn't say anything. The feelings of jealousy and rage and longing that were churning inside her the whole way kept her mouth firmly shut. She was afraid, not of what she might say but of how her voice would sound when she said anything. All she knew was that this was wrong, it was all wrong. Cathy wasn't meant to have someone like *him*. Marc wasn't meant to be with a girl like Cathy.

They had been seeing each other nearly all the summer holidays, Alison thought back. Cathy must have met him that afternoon in the park when she had been waiting for Alison, and Alison had been with Aran Archer. If Alison had shown up that afternoon then there would have been no way that Marc would have looked at Catherine, no *way*. It would be her holding hands with him in the sunshine now, and Catherine walking on her own. And Cathy would have been happy with that, because she would have understood that that was the right thing, that was the way things were.

It must have been about four when Cathy looked at her watch and scrambled to her feet.

'I've got go. Mum'll be back in half an hour. Are you walking back, Ali?' Cathy stood, waiting for her friend. Alison guessed she couldn't wait to hear what she thought of him.

'Um . . . no, I can't. I said I'd drop by Aran's on the way back. I'll see you later, though, OK?'

Cathy nodded and smiled. She looked so happy, as if she felt special for the first time in her life. 'See you at ten,' she said.

Alison watched as Marc got up and, putting his heavy arms over Cathy's fragile shoulder, whispered something in her ear that brought the blood to her cheeks. And then he kissed her, a long slow tender kiss.

Alison didn't know who she hated the most just then, her friend for stealing away her lover, Marc for not seeing he had met the wrong girl, or herself for doing what she knew she was about to do.

After Cathy had gone Marc turned back to Alison and looked at her lying in the sun. He waved a half-hearted hand.

'See you then,' he said, as if he was going to leave.

'Stay and talk to me a bit longer,' Alison said, dropping her shoulder back so that her chest pushed forwards. She patted a patch of grass next to her.

'Thanks, but I should get some sleep before my shift starts,' Marc said, looking at her legs. 'You don't want to be too tired, working on a railway line. I saw this lad get cut in half in Manchester.'

'She was meeting me, you know,' Alison said. 'The afternoon you two met here.'

'Really?' Marc looked over his shoulder at the tunnel that led under the railway line and back to his bedsit. 'So?'

'Well, who do you think you'd have asked out if I'd turned up that afternoon? Who do you think you would have fancied if you met me first?'

Marc looked back at her, his hands on his hips, and he laughed.

'Why do you ask?'

'I'm interested, that's all,' Alison told him, tipping her head to one side, so her hair brushed her bare arm.

'Well, I've never been with anyone like Catherine before,' Marc said. 'So if I'd met you both at the same time I'd have probably made a move on you. But then I would have missed out on knowing her. She's a lovely person.'

'Lovely?' Alison laughed.

'Well,' Marc put his hands in his pockets and looked awkward as he shrugged. 'She is.'

Alison had never been able to believe the words that had come out of her mouth next, only ever able to justify them in later years because for so long she was certain that all she was doing was restoring order to the universe.

'You can make a move on me now if you like,' she offered.

Marc stood still, a slow smile spreading across his face. 'I thought you were her best friend. She talks about you all the time.'

'I am,' Alison said. 'But anyone can see you're not right for her. You two don't fit together. You'll just end up hurting her. She deserves better.'

'And you don't?' Marc sounded sceptical. But he still hadn't walked away.

'I can handle you,' Alison said. 'And anyway, I know that if you'd met me first you'd be with me now. I know it.'

Marc shook his head. 'You're very confident.' He stood still, taking her in.

For what seemed like an age neither of them said anything or moved a muscle. Then suddenly Marc walked decisively over to her and held out a hand.

'Come on then,' he challenged her. 'Come back with me.'

'What, now?' Alison said, scrambling to her feet.

'That's what you want, isn't it?' Marc asked her.

'Yes, yes, it is,' Alison said. And the decision was made.

*

Afterwards she had lain in the tangle of sheets on his single bed and stared at the ceiling.

'Have you done that with her?' she asked him. His eyes were shut, his face perfectly still.

'I've never done anything like that with her,' he said eventually.

Alison found it hard to read the tone of his voice, it was so . . . closed. This moment was not at all like she had expected it to be. She had expected his arms to be around her, for him to be holding her, kissing her, but he hadn't touched her since he'd pulled out of her. Quite a feat in a single bed. Alison fought the urge to cry, telling herself that this was just the beginning. She still had a way to go but she'd get him in the end. She'd make him understand.

Making herself smile, she sat up and leaned over him so that her breasts brushed his chest. He opened his eyes.

'That was my first time,' she told him, careful to erase any trace of vulnerability from her voice.

'I know,' he said, watching her face. 'I'm sorry if I was a bit . . . rough.'

'I liked it,' Alison said steadily. 'It was passionate.'

'You are very sexy,' Marc told her, his voice still unyielding. 'You've got an amazing body.'

'Do you feel bad?' Alison asked him. 'About Cathy?'

'I am a bad person,' he said. 'I told her that the day I met her. I thought I could be better than I am if I was with her, but I can't. This is the way I am.'

'You're not a bad person, you just don't fit with her, that's all,' Alison said, leaning over him. 'If you are with the right person then you don't even have to change.'

Marc didn't move a muscle.

'I don't think anyone can change me,' he said eventually,

and Alison got the feeling that he'd only spoken half a sentence out loud.

'When you finish with her, be kind, OK?' Alison said, sitting up and putting on her bra. A tiny, tender and bruised part of her was still wishing for the hearts and romance and flowers that she'd always dreamed would accompany this event, but still she told herself this was just the beginning. All of that would come when she really had him. 'Don't break her heart. Don't tell her about us. We'll stay a secret for now, until she's over you.'

'What makes you think I'm going to break up with Catherine?' Marc asked her.

Alison looked at him, feeling suddenly out of her depth. 'Well, you have to now, don't you?' she asked him. 'We've had sex.'

'I don't have to do anything,' Marc said, turning his face to the window.

Alison felt she should have some right over him, some extra hold now that she had surrendered to him what Catherine had not. But she had no idea how to play this person. He was nothing like the boys she knew at school, the boys that she could manipulate so easily. Only then did she realise it was he who had a hold over her. He had her in the palm of his hand.

'Are we going to do this again?' she asked him bluntly, because he seemed to like that about her. Marc turned his face back to her, his dark eyes in shadow. One hand reached out and touched her cheek.

'I wish I'd met you first because, you're right, I wouldn't have looked at Catherine, I wouldn't have noticed or known her at all. I'd have gone straight for you. You're very beautiful, you're . . .' His fingers traced a line down her neck to her shoulder. 'You're hard not to touch.'

'So?' Alison pressed him, with a little smile. 'Are we?'

'Yes,' he said simply. 'I think we are.'

Every time they met after that, each secret hour of afternoon they spent together, they grew closer and closer, easier and easier together. Alison knew that Marc still saw Cathy whenever she could get away, that they still went walking in the park, or lay in the grass talking about his past because Cathy would tell her every night, her eyes shining. And somehow Alison could still manage to be happy for her friend because she knew the love that Marc felt for Cathy was entirely different from what he felt for her. He wanted the very bones of her, he wanted to consume her body from the inside out. He couldn't get enough of her body and every single time they saw each other they went straight to bed.

One evening, just as the sun was low in the sky, bathing the room in gold as they were lying in his bed, Alison felt that something was different, something had changed between them. And then she realised: he had his arms around her, her head was resting on his chest, the unfamiliar sound she was hearing was the beating of his heart, slow and steady.

It was then she got a sense, the very first inkling, that eventually, one day, he would love her back.

Now, in the living room of their brand-new house, a lifetime later, Alison felt Marc shift his weight on top of her and she wondered where that desire, that unswerving love for him that she had sustained for so long had gone. He kissed her neck just as passionately as he had always done, his fingers as expert as they had always been in knowing how to please her. But although her body responded to him, her heart was still and silent.

The truth was that Alison was waiting to be in love with Marc again. She'd been waiting now for what seemed like the longest time, and so far this time, the love for him that she had defined her life by had yet to make a return. She felt nothing.

Not for the first time since she found out Marc was bringing her back to Farmington, Alison found herself wondering, whatever had happened to Cathy Parkin after she left her.

What she could not have known was that her husband, still wide awake despite his closed eyes and perfectly composed features, was wondering exactly the same thing.

Chapter Seven

'This is ridiculous,' Catherine said as Kirsty, one palm firmly securing her forehead, plucked her eyebrows.

'Only you would say that,' Kirsty said through gritted teeth as she jerked another hair out of Catherine's tender skin. 'Only *you* would think that having eyebrows that frame your eyes instead of hanging over them is not a good plan.'

'I don't think *anything* about eyebrows. Eyebrows are not important to me,' Catherine said, beginning to regret agreeing to go out with Kirsty at all.

Kirsty paused for a minute, the tweezers hovering menacingly in Catherine's eye line.

'Tell me you shave your legs,' she menaced.

Catherine looked at her sensible shoes and said nothing.

'Good God, Catherine! What's wrong with you?' Kirsty exclaimed.

'What's right with me, you mean,' Catherine retorted. 'I don't feel the need to denude myself in order to be attractive to men, and besides, what's the point of shaving my legs? No one ever sees them.'

Kirsty attacked Catherine's brow with renewed vigour.

'The point of shaving your legs is the same as always wearing sexy underwear, even when you're not on a date. It makes you feel both beautiful and womanly, and then your sexiness exudes from with*in*.' Kirsty yanked hard on a particularly stubborn hair, making Catherine yelp. 'No wonder you are so . . .' Kirsty struggled to find a suitable adjective and failed. 'Look, imagine that you suddenly meet the man of your dreams tonight. There you are, in the pub, I'm in the arms of my personal trainer . . .'

'Out of interest, does your personal trainer have a name?' Catherine asked her, hoping in vain to deflect Kirsty's line of questioning. Ever since she'd let herself think about Marc it had been hard to stop, and for at least three nights this week he had populated her dreams, dreams in which she was seventeen again, before he met Alison, before everything went wrong. She was seventeen and living those few brief weeks when, for the first time in her life, she had been completely happy. Why she had let him back into her head now, Catherine couldn't comprehend. She was crazy to have listened to Jimmy and his rock psychology at all, telling her she'd forgotten how to be in love, as if she hadn't tried to love Jimmy as well as she was able to.

The truth was that after Marc had gone, after Alison had left the way she did, it had taken Catherine a long time to make herself whole again, because she felt as if her guts had been ripped out of her. But Alison abandoning her was a turning point too. It was the beginning of her own life, the life in which her head ruled her heart and every other part of her. It was the time when she first got to know Jimmy, when the two of them became friends, and then finally more, and he gave her the final strength she needed to be able to leave home. It was around that time that Jimmy Ashley had told her he loved her and swore blind that one day she'd love him back in exactly the same way. It was a prediction that she had never been able to fulfil to his satisfaction.

Jimmy had not been back for the rest of week, but if he had

Catherine would have told him. She would have said right to his face that it was he who had hurt her, he who had knocked her for six and ripped up their family. It was Jimmy who had driven her to decide she didn't want another relationship, and if he couldn't live with the consequences then he should just stay away.

And it was probably because he already knew that he had stayed away, because the relationship they had now was one he was determined to preserve.

'Of course my trainer has a name,' Kirsty replied indignantly, pulling Catherine back into the conversation.

'What is it then?'

'Sam,' Kirsty said firmly. 'Or Steve. It's an "S" name and anyway, don't try and get me off the subject. You *know* it takes me a long time to remember names. I was calling you Clara for the first six months we knew each other, and it doesn't mean I love him any less. *Anyway*, there I am, in his arms – kissing him passionately – and up comes this man. He's tall, dark, handsome and he wants you, sexually. He sweeps you off your feet and into his arms. He takes you to his bed –'

'What, in the pub?' Catherine asked.

'Don't be an idiot – unless he's a barman. I had a fling with a Croatian barman once, very convenient for nightcaps. But anyway, he takes you home and *then* to bed and as he goes to run his manly hands along your long lithe limbs he recoils in horror because he's got carpet burns on his palms.'

'If he was the man of my dreams he wouldn't mind,' Catherine said stubbornly, remembering with sudden shocking clarity the pressure of Marc's palms on her thighs. For once she welcomed the distracting pain of Kirsty's attacks on her facial hair.

'If he's any man at all, barring a German one, then trust me, he'll mind,' Kirsty said. 'There are some people that work on the "sod's law" ethos that if you don't shave your legs and you wear your worst pants you are much more likely to pull. I do not think that way. I think that you have to treat pulling as if you were in the SAS. Always be prepared.'

'Isn't that the Boy Scouts?' Catherine asked her. 'Isn't the SAS "Who Dares Wins"?'

'Even better,' Kirsty said, making Catherine's eyes water as she removed three or four hairs at once. 'And that should be your motto, love. It's much better than your current one.'

'OK,' Catherine succumbed to the inevitable with a sigh, 'what's my current one?'

'She who doesn't dare sits about on her arse all day turning herself into a decrepit old woman at the age of thirty-two who is afraid to be happy.'

'That's it,' Catherine said, folding over miserably on the bed, drawing her knees up under chin.

'That's what?' Kirsty asked with some concern, tweezers poised.

'I'm just going to have sex with the first man I meet tonight, whether I like him or not, and then maybe everybody will stop going on at me. Maybe you'll stop telling me I need to have sex to be happy, maybe Jimmy will stop telling me I'm some headcase who's trapped in the past just so he can pretend it wasn't his fault our marriage is over, and maybe . . .' Catherine stopped herself. She had been about to say maybe the images of her and Marc that had been crowding her memory would leave her alone. But she'd never told Kirsty about Marc, Alison and everything that happened. And she wasn't ready to now.

Contrite, Kirsty sat on the bed next to her and patted her shoulder.

'Don't have sex with the first man you meet tonight,' she said gently. 'He might be an old or a fat man, and besides, that's not why I'm taking you out.'

'No, I know why you're taking me out: so I can be the gooseberry when you finally pull Sam.'

'Or Steve,' Kirsty added. 'And that's not why, either. Well, it is, but it's not the only reason.' Kirsty lay on the bed too so that she was facing Catherine, looking into her eyes. 'You don't see yourself, Catherine. You don't see how stunning you are, with your incredible legs and all that hair and those eyes and those cheekbones. And I just thought if I got you dolled up a bit and we went to the pub, you'd see the way men look at you. The way they *turn their heads* to look at you when you walk past. And no, you don't need to have sex to be happy and you're not some headcase who's trapped in the past, whatever the past is. But you are my friend now. And you are fit. And as well as being a mum and an entirely arbitrary wife, you are also a beautiful woman. So don't have sex with any of the men you meet tonight, just come out and stand in a room with your eyebrows plucked, some lippy on and smooth legs, and see what effect you have. Because when you do I bet you'll feel great, I bet you'll feel free.'

'I'd like to feel free,' Catherine said thoughtfully. 'And actually the thought of having sex with the first or any man I meet makes me want to be sick, so I don't mind leaving that part out after all.'

'That's what I thought,' Kirsty said, pulling Catherine into a sitting position. 'We take baby steps, Catherine, baby steps. Right, now, where's your razor?'

When Alison got home from the supermarket, her reluctant son in tow, Marc was in the kitchen with the girls, whose heads were bent over the drawings they were creating, felt-tips fanned out across the marble worktop.

Alison looked at her husband leaning over the girls as they coloured. The last fifteen years hadn't been as kind to him as they had to Jimmy. Marc had filled out too, but it was a slight paunch and not muscle that had materialised underneath his shirt. And his hair had receded quite considerably, not that either of them ever mentioned it.

Of course, the change in his appearance wouldn't matter if she could love him again, it was just that the more she tried, the harder it seemed to be, which wasn't fair because when she loved him, everything else was bearable.

'Mummy!' Amy cried happily, as she caught sight of Alison's arms laden down with bags. 'And Dom, we're all here in our new big house.'

'All right, Muffin.' Dom greeted his little sister with the first hint of a smile that Alison had seen since she announced to him he was helping to get the shopping for the weekend. 'How was school today?'

'It was OK today,' Amy said. 'There's this quite nice girl I like.'

'I had the best time,' Gemma told him, glancing up from her colouring. 'My teacher is lovely and all the girls like me. Eloise is going to be my best friend, though, because she understands me.'

'Oh, does she now?' Marc said, handing Alison a cup of tea. 'Eloise must be a very clever girl.

'She is and she's the tallest in our class,' Gemma said. 'She's tallest and I'm the prettiest and we're both clever, so we can't fail.'

'Except in modesty exams,' Dom said, opening the fridge door, glancing at the bags of shopping at his feet and closing it again.

Alison looked at her entire family gathered under one roof, her successful husband, who made cups of tea unbidden, her musical son and her two smiling daughters. For a few rare minutes during which nobody was shouting, lying or crying she could pretend that she had it all, she had literally every-thing. She even had a waste-disposal unit and hose tap.

'How nice, all of us will be in for dinner tonight!' she said brightly, determined to conjure happiness out of so many good things.

'Ah,' Marc said, his tone immediately dashing her attempt.

Alison looked at him and realised where the cup of tea came from. It was a rather low-rent peace offering. 'You said you'd be in tonight. It's Friday night, Marc. Remember, you said you'd always be home by four every Friday. That was part of our deal. Family time.'

'You sound so surprised,' Dominic said sarcastically.

'I know I did, and it will be usually,' Marc said, ignoring his son's comment completely, causing the boy to slam out of the room, banging the door behind him. 'But it's the lads I've taken on at the showroom. They want to take me out for a drink and I think I need to go. It's a team-building thing, Ali, before we launch this weekend. They're young blokes, they need a bit of direction. It'll just be a few drinks at some local pub. I'll be back by ten at the latest, not much later than ten. It'll give me a chance to schmooze a few locals while I'm at it. Network, that's what it's all about, love. That's what we need to do to make it work for us here.'

'Mum, look at this,' Gemma held up her drawing. 'This is what my pony is going to look like when I get her. Light brown with a yellow mane. I'm going to call her Amber. She's going to be lovely.'

'That's beautiful, darling,' Alison said, not taking her eyes off his face.

'But you're not looking!' Gemma protested, thrusting the picture in front of her eyes. For a second Alison took in the bright blue sky, huge smiling sun and an image of a horse surrounded by happy smiling delirious stick people. That was how Gemma saw her family, like that. Not like this. Why couldn't she be there, Alison wondered, where there was a gaping vacuum between the sky and the grass and where the mother and father always held hands?

'Al,' Marc offered her a conciliatory smile. 'Look, it's a one-off, I promise you. And you know I need to network, meet as many people as I can before the party next week. Which reminds me, have you got your invites out?'

Alison noticed his deft change of subject but wearily decided to ignore it, taking a sip of tea instead. She didn't want the kids to witness another fight. They were so rarely all together that even if it was only for a few minutes she wanted it to be happy, so that when Gemma looked at her drawing she would feel she had captured her family exactly.

'Well, I don't exactly know anyone yet.' She thought of Jimmy Ashley in the school hall. 'So I've left my invites with this woman called Lois at the school and told her to invite the PTA, and I've asked the girls' teachers and the head. Anyway, how many people are coming to this party, Marc?'

'Couple of hundred, give or take,' Marc said, bending over to help Amy colour in the remainder of her smiling and benevolent sun, the symbol that featured in both girls' drawings.

'And when do you have to confirm final numbers for the caterers?' Alison asked.

'The caterers?' Marc looked up at her sharply. 'Fancy another cuppa?'

'You know, the people you found to cater the party at such short notice?'

Marc looked thoughtful and then went back to colouring studiously while Alison felt her insides begin to simmer.

'I sort of thought you'd be doing that,' he said inevitably.

'You thought I'd be making sandwiches for two hundred people?' Alison asked him. 'Me?'

'I sort of thought so,' Marc said, winking at Gemma so she giggled.

'Marc!' Alison exclaimed. 'I just can't believe that after everything . . .' She trailed off, unable to detail exactly what 'everything' was.

'What I *meant*,' Marc added hastily, 'is I thought you'd find the caterers. That's the sort of thing you usually do, isn't it? Find caterers?'

'You said all I had to do was open my house to the whole of Farmington and look glamorous. You didn't say anything about catering. And no, I don't usually organise it, usually your PA organises it, or have you forgotten?'

A brief flash of the Christmas party burned across Alison's eyes and she knew that Marc had seen it too. They stared at each other for a beat of silence.

'Well, look, darling,' Marc said, choosing to brush the moment aside like he always did, 'how about you find a caterer – there's still over a week to go, after all. Don't worry about the cost – however much it takes.'

'It will be "however much it takes" to find a caterer at this short notice, and if I do end up making two hundred egg mayonnaise sandwiches there will never be an upper limit on how much it's going to cost you!'

At last Marc got up and came around the table. He put his arms round her waist and, at almost exactly her height, looked straight into her eyes.

'I messed up,' he said frankly. 'I forgot something huge and big and I tried to pass the buck on to you. Balloons, I remembered, fairy lights and music. I've ordered the champagne, the wine and the beer. But I forgot food and you remembered it. Which is why I need you, Ali. Remember that kid I was when we met? Working nights for the railways? I'd still be doing it now if I hadn't found you. And if you can turn

107

me from that kid into this man – the man who is lucky enough to be your husband – then you can sort out the catering for the party, can't you?'

'Yes, I can,' Alison said, despite herself. The trouble was, he was right. She knew him inside out, just like he knew her. In the end it always came back to this. They'd found each other when they were very young and they had clung on to each other from that moment on, riding their choices with the conviction of those who are determined never to be wrong. She'd made her bed a long time ago, and now who was she to complain that it wasn't comfortable any more?

'You know I love you, don't you?' Marc asked her finally, not because of the catering, but because of the PA who usually did the catering. Alison made herself look at him.

'I do,' she conceded, because he did love her, albeit imperfectly.

'Then that's all that matters right?'

Not all that matters, Alison thought. He never asked her if she loved him back.

'Good, well, I'll be back by ten. Make sure you wait up for me, we've still got a lot of rooms to christen.'

'You're going now?' Alison asked him. 'It's not even six o'clock.'

'There's some curry house they want to take me to first. I'd much rather be eating with you but . . .' Marc shrugged.

'What can he do?' Gemma finished for him with a copycat shrug.

Alison wasn't surprised. It was Marc's favourite phrase, after all.

'I feel so . . . violated,' Catherine said as they approached the Three Bells. 'I can't believe you made me have another shower. I was perfectly clean.'

'There's no point in being clean if you're hairy,' Kirsty said firmly. 'Now, how to do I look?'

Catherine looked down at her friend, who was wearing her best turquoise crocheted dress worn over black underwear and leggings and long boots. She looked like she always looked, well-dressed, stylish and sexy. Whatever it was that transformed a woman from being merely attractive into an out-and-out sex kitten, Kirsty certainly seemed to have it.

'You look spectacular,' Catherine told her, suddenly feeling self-conscious in her black shirt and trousers, despite her newly naked legs being swathed in denim.

'Thought so,' Kirsty said, nodding at the cloud-ridden sky. 'This time I'm going to give the universe a helping hand. It's about time it got something right.'

'Same again?' Marc asked Joel and Craig.

In their early twenties, the pair of them were hungry for money and the kind of success that Marc had already achieved at thirty-six. They admired him and they aspired to be like him one day. It was a kind of recognition that Marc enjoyed. He liked to impress his employees, it meant he could inspire them to achieve greater results.

Ali hadn't been pleased when he'd left her and the kids for a night in the Three Bells but he was sure she'd understand in the end. Ali always understood in the end. That was why they were still together after all this time. She'd understood him from the moment she'd laid eyes on him.

He had known exactly what Alison was feeling when he'd told her that he had to go out. It was the same low-light simmering fury that had been bubbling beneath her skin since Christmas. This time it was taking her a lot longer to forgive him for his indiscretion, but he knew she would, eventually. She always did because, despite everything, she knew that he'd move heaven and earth to make her happy. And because he'd changed his life, changed *himself* to be with her. After all, he'd chosen her all those years ago. He'd chosen Alison and everything that being with her would mean. And that's why she'd come back to him again, because she had to.

What Alison might not understand was that on the night he chose her he had not loved her at all. There had been something there: growing affection and acceptance of the way things were between them. But on the evening after it had all kicked off he'd still been in love with Catherine. If Alison was running away from her parents and her exams, he was running away from Cathy and all the confusing and consuming things he felt for her. He hadn't known that Alison was pregnant, he'd had no idea that leaving with her would not be the simple escape route that he had initially planned. But once it became clear that going with her would change a lot more in life than his postal address, he accepted those changes. Because even loving Catherine as much as he did, he still could not get Alison out of his head.

Alison at seventeen had been a lot like the girls in this pub, glowing with youth and beauty. The sight of her smiling and gleaming at him woke him up from a kind of a dream. Being with Catherine had been like existing in a bubble. The hours he'd spent with her had transformed him into another person entirely – someone as intense and as thoughtful as she was. And she was so intent on keeping him a secret from her puritanical parents that the time they spent together was always alone and always in secret. It was time that felt unreal, as if for those few hours they were trapped together between the pages of a book. It was Alison that had brought him back to his animal senses and the twenty-year-old boy that he was. It was Alison that he had had to have, despite, perhaps even because, he knew how it would hurt Catherine and even himself. It was the only way he could think of at the time to break this hold she had on his heart.

A flash of memory went off behind his eyelids. An image of Cathy, her long white limbs intertwined in his, her green eyes holding his, willing him, daring him to let her down. To say he hadn't thought of Cathy properly in years, not until he announced that he was bringing his family back to Farmington, would not have been true. Often she'd drift into his thoughts, catching him out, but he'd never felt anything but a kind of oblique nostalgia for her. That was, until he decided to come back here. Christmas had happened and he'd sensed that Alison was almost through with him for good. The only thing he could think of doing to stop her going and taking his children with her was to bring her back to the place where they began, the place where the passion that they had for each other had been so strong, they'd given up everything to pursue it.

When he'd been looking at the house and searching for business premises, the thought of Catherine being somewhere in the town hadn't really occurred to him. She'd always said she wanted to leave home as soon as she could, and he was certain that she wouldn't have hung around any longer than she had to once it all came out; her parents would have made her life hell.

But then he made the final journey back with Alison and it was as if the three of them together again in this place, even if one of the triptych was merely a memory, had set his head spinning. Everywhere he looked he expected to see Catherine, almost as if he could feel her somewhere behind him, just out of view.

Marc shook his head, firmly leaning across the bar, his folded twenty-pound note in his hand as he tried to make eye contact with the barman. What would he say to Catherine if

111

he were to see her again, Marc wondered as he gave the barman his order. Would he have the guts to tell her that he'd abandoned her, not because he didn't love her but because he did? And that he was sorry not only for the hurt and humiliation he had caused her, but because of the secret she thought she had kept from him, the secret he had known and, knowing it, had left anyway.

Finally the barman delivered his drinks just as the pub door opened and a gust of cold February air swept through the bar, garlanded with a peal of female laughter. Marc was glad to turn his back on the chill and return to his young employees, feeling the goose bumps rising on his arms as he walked away.

'Has he looked at me yet?' Kirsty asked Catherine in a whisper.

It was remarkable really, Catherine thought. Kirsty had stood right next to Steve or Sam at the bar whilst ordering the drinks, had brushed past him – breasts first – on the way to the ladies and had laughed and tossed her hair at full capacity ever since, in a bid to get his attention, but he hadn't actually looked her way once.

'He might be gay,' Catherine ventured. 'Or maybe have tunnel-vision syndrome and slight deafness in both ears, because that is the only way he would not be able to notice you. You are many things but subtle isn't one of them.'

'He's not gay,' Kirsty said firmly. 'He used to go out with a pole dancer, and anyway, Catherine, I'm ashamed of you conforming to such an obvious stereotype. Just because he's well turned out and takes care of himself doesn't make him gay.'

'OK then,' Catherine said. 'Maybe he's just really, *really* interested in what his friend has to say.' Steve or Sam was certainly deep in conversation with his friend, a tallish, fair-haired and pleasant-looking man of about her age, Catherine guessed. This was the friend that Kirsty had deemed it her destiny to distract when she went in for the kill. She studied him covertly. She had no idea how to distract anybody, let alone a man, other than point at some unnamed object over his shoulder and shout, 'It's behind you!'

If Kirsty ever did get to talk to her trainer Catherine was fairly sure that she would mess up the friend-distraction bit. But there was an *if*, because what Kirsty hadn't thought of, and what Catherine didn't want to point out, was that if her personal trainer wasn't gay and didn't have a sight and hearing problem then the alternative was that he was ignoring her because he didn't want to have anything to do with her. It didn't seem to be a conclusion that Kirsty was likely to reach on her own, and Catherine didn't want to be the one to bring it up.

'What about him?' Kirsty nudged her quite hard in the ribs, throwing her a little off balance even in her flat boots.

'What about who?' Catherine was confused. Surely Kirsty hadn't moved on to the next love of her life already.

'Him over there.' Kirsty nodded to Catherine's left and when she looked she caught the eye of a fair-haired man, perhaps a little younger than she was, who smiled at her fleetingly before dropping his gaze back to his drink.

'What about him?' Catherine asked her.

'He was totally checking you out like a motherfucker!' Kirsty exclaimed quite loudly so that one or two people (but not her trainer) looked over at them.

'Was he?' Catherine said drily. 'I had no idea that one could be checked out in such a way.'

'Well, one can, smart-arse, and he was. He's been looking at you all night. And him.' This time Kirsty nodded none too discreetly just over Catherine's left shoulder.

'Don't look!' she shrieked when Catherine automatically began to turn her head slowly. Kirsty stared at the point over her shoulder. 'Wait . . . wait . . . – OK, now look.'

Catherine looked and this time shared a brief moment with a man with a goatee beard.

'Loves you,' Kirsty confirmed, with a nod.

'Or alternatively he might just wonder why that short woman and that tall redhead keep staring at him and screaming,' Catherine suggested. 'Anyway, can we get back to you? What's *your* plan?'

'To be gorgeous, but so far it doesn't seem to be working out too well. Have you got any ideas?'

Catherine thought for a moment. 'Well, why don't you go up to him, tap him on the shoulder and say hi?' she ventured.

Kirsty shook her head. 'Oh, you are so naïve,' she said. 'Where were you during your teens? Didn't you learn anything from *Grange Hill*?'

'Why not just talk to him?' Catherine asked her with a bemused shrug.

'Because then he'll think I fancy him,' Kirsty replied as if she was stating the obvious. 'I don't want him to know that. I want him to think that I, his beautiful and very bendy client, is merely flitting by him like a beautiful but unobtainable butterfly that he longs to capture . . . a woman who can only be – oh, hi, Steve.'

Kirsty went bright red as her trainer appeared at her shoulder.

'Kirsty, I *thought* that was you.' He smiled at her. 'And it's Sam, by the way.'

'I knew it was an "S" name,' Kirsty beamed at him. 'Can I buy you a drink? I mean, water for me because, obviously, I don't really drink, apart from this gin and tonic, and honestly it's a lot more tonic than gin, gin-flavoured tonic really . . .'

Catherine unconsciously took a step back as Kirsty focused all her attention on Sam. He was nice-looking, Catherine had to concede, but not her type at all, although to be fair to Sam she'd never really established what that was. He was tallish, with friendly eyes and very nice arms. She could see why Kirsty would be smitten with him, even if he was completely bald. She smiled to herself. If Jimmy was here he'd be tossing his hair around and squaring up his shoulders the way he always did when he met a man who was so overtly masculine. Catherine wished very much that he was there right then. At least she could always talk to Jimmy. Tentatively, she glanced in the direction of the fair-haired man across the bar. He smiled at her; she didn't look that way again.

'So that's your friend chatting up my friend then?'

Catherine started as Sam's friend appeared at her side, a little of her drink splashing onto the back of her hand.

'Sorry, didn't mean to make you jump. Just thought you might like some company. Looks like your friend's got mine monopolised for the evening. I'm Dave, by the way.'

He held out his hand and hesitantly Catherine took it. She hadn't talked to a man she didn't know and wasn't somebody's husband, including hers, in . . . well, it was certainly months and might even be years.

'Hello,' Catherine said. 'I'm Catherine and I'm sure Kirsty won't keep him all evening.' She looked over at her friend in full flirt mode. 'Actually, she might.'

'Oh, *that's* Kirsty,' Dave said with a grin. 'No wonder he was trying so hard not to notice her all evening. He digs her big time.'

'Does he dig her big time?' Catherine said, noticing Dave smile as she repeated his phrase. 'That's nice, because she digs him big time too. Like seriously a lot. I'm probably not meant to tell you that, but she never shuts up about him.'

'I won't tell if you don't,' Dave said, taking a step closer to her. 'So, anyway, enough about them, tell me about you.'

'Me?' Catherine tried to think of something, anything but the truth, which always sounded much worse when spoken out loud than in her head. This time was no exception. 'I've got two kids and a sort of a husband, who I'm married to but don't live with any more since he slept with another woman more or less right in front of my eyes, and I work in a local PR company. Oh, and I like growing my own vegetables. That's about it.'

'OK,' Dave laughed. 'Right, well – just an everyday kind of girl then.'

'That's me,' Catherine said with a smile. She quite liked talking to Dave, as it happened.

'So it looks like we've been abandoned then,' Dave said, nodding at Kirsty and Sam, who in the blink of an eye had gone from chatting to deep, deep kissing.

'I expected it,' Catherine told him.

'Well, why don't we head off somewhere else then, somewhere a bit quieter. We can get a drink and talk, what do you think?'

Catherine looked at him. She was fairly sure he was chatting her up. Either that or he just wanted to hang out for a chat with a still-married yet single mother of two who was two inches taller than he was.

'I . . . look, I have to go,' she lied. 'I've got kids, two under eight. The babysitter goes mad if I'm late back.'

'But it's only just past ten,' Dave said, seemingly unfazed by her children. 'Have one more drink with me.'

'I'm sorry,' Catherine said. 'I can't.'

And she raced out of the pub and back home as fast as she could until she was safe, back behind her own front door, where she could grow the hair on her legs, cook dinner for her ex and where she could be safe and shut off and never have to worry about what to say to mildly attractive men in pubs or, worse still, what they might say to her.

'Women,' Dave muttered, perplexed, as the pub door slammed shut behind Catherine.

'Girlfriend giving you grief?' Marc asked him as he tried to edge his way past. 'I know how you feel. I'm late and if I don't get home in the next half-hour the wife's going to kill me.'

Dave took a step to one side to allow him to pass.

'Beautiful women –' Dave told Marc, glancing bitterly at Sam and his conquest –'all the same, all think they're too good for anyone normal.'

'That's true,' Marc said, clapping him on the back in a conciliatory gesture. 'And that's why they're the only ones worth chasing.'

Chapter Eight

'Mum,' Eloise said through a mouthful of toast on Monday morning, 'can I ask Gemma to tea this week, can I, please? She said she might be getting her pony this weekend, so can I, *please*?'

Catherine looked at her daughter, who had twisted her long hair into her best approximation of a ballerina-style bun and secured it with some froufrou nonsense that Jimmy's mother had probably inflicted on her during the girls' last visit there. Catherine knew the scrunchie was a silent protest against what her daughter saw as a violation of her human rights, in that if she was not allowed to have ballet lessons on a Monday afternoon, she would do her best to look like the girls who were.

'Don't talk while you're chewing,' Catherine told her. 'And, anyway, if you are so keen to see her pony you should be visiting her house. It's not as if she can bring it round here.'

Catherine knew something that Eloise didn't, but just for the moment she was refraining from telling her because she liked to be able to eat her breakfast in relative peace.

'But she's the new girl, like a guest at a party, and I am sort of the host. So I have to ask her first and then she'll ask me back and I'll get to see her pony. *Please*, Mum. You never let us do *anything*!'

The oblique reference to lack of ballet lessons again thus

118

reinforced how meagre her request was to have one paltry friend back to tea in the hope that it would elicit a return invitation and the chance to visit a pony, another treasured wish that Catherine was not able to fulfil for her daughter. Feeling inadequate and depressed, Catherine rather wished she had told Eloise what she had known before this conversation had even started.

The new family were having a house-warming party, and Catherine and her daughters were both invited. Lois had rung her yesterday evening just after the girls got back, telling her that all of the PTA and their families had been invited to attend on the following Saturday. Lois told her it was a shameful bid on the part of the mysterious new mother to buy her way onto the PTA committee, despite the fact that new applicants weren't normally considered until September. Still, Lois had pointed out, it would be an excuse to nose round her house. She'd being dying to look round one of those new builds for months – she'd heard they were terribly vulgar inside. Gold-effect taps. Then Lois told Catherine she had already RSVP'd on behalf of the whole committee.

A huge party like that thrown only a couple of weeks after they had arrived meant that Gemma's family must have a lot of money. Catherine was as proud of her daughters as any woman could be, and she loved the ramshackle cut-price charm of her terraced cottage. But it was difficult not to wonder what some of the other parents thought of her when they brought their children to one of the smallest houses in Farmington, with its second-hand sofa and only one loo. What did they really think of the thirty-two-year-old with a philandering, long-haired, largely unemployed, estranged husband, and vegetable patch in the back garden? Did they call each other at night and discuss the chipped enamel on her bath?

Catherine never craved normality in the sense that she wanted *things*. She didn't want things. She would just like sometimes not to feel self-conscious about who she was and the life that she had chosen, or rather the life that had chosen her when she wasn't really paying attention. She supposed when she was a girl she had the same expectations as everybody else, that, as plain and as awkward as she was, one day somebody would love her and then hand in hand they would lead a normal life, married in her twenties, children, a nice home, a steady but modest income. When she married Jimmy she'd hoped for it, the kind of simple life that seemed to be the right of other people. Jimmy had been her friend and her lover but also her escape route, lending her the extra strength she needed to leave home and a place to go to once she had left. Eventually she would have had the courage to leave her childhood behind on her own, but Jimmy made it happen faster and she was grateful for that, even if the first thing she ever saw in him was a way out. But their marriage, though often wonderful and occasionally painful, had never been normal, because, Catherine felt, they hadn't begun it the normal way. There had been hope and expectation but certainty had never been present, and only twelve years later did Catherine realise she had always expected it to fail somehow. She just hadn't been able to pin down when.

Farmington normality was a three-car family and a five-bedroom house. Catherine, with her part-time job and reliance on tax credits, was not anything like the norm. Even so, she couldn't deny Eloise a new friend with a pony because of her own insecurities. Besides, Eloise was right about one thing: she was one of the few girls at her school who didn't take ballet, or do gymnastics, or have riding lessons at weekends after stage school. After the mortgage and the bills had been paid the money for those things simply wasn't there, and guitar lessons for free from your dad didn't have quite the same cachet. Catherine was forced to deny her daughters those things, and she knew they didn't really understand why, no matter how often she talked through money with them (if you haven't got very much, Leila would say, just go to the bank and get some more. It's easy!), so she would not deny them their friends.

'Well, actually,' she said, bracing herself for the squeals of excitement that were sure to follow her announcement, 'you *are* going to be Gemma's guest, because her mum and dad have invited us all, and just about everyone else in Farmington, to a party at her house next Saturday night!'

'A party! A party at Gemma's! Oh, thank you thank you thank you, Mum!' Eloise jumped up and planted a buttery kiss on Catherine's cheek, before scowling. 'We are going, aren't we?'

'Of course we are going,' Catherine said.

'Is all of us going, me too?' Leila asked her from the other end of the table, reserving her excitement until she had clarified that point.

'Yes, of course,' Catherine smiled.

'And do we get to stay up late?' Leila asked happily.

'A little bit later than normal,' Catherine said.

'Thank you, God!' Leila grinned at the ceiling as the girls sprung up from the table and clung on to each other as they jumped up and down.

'It's going to be great,' Eloise told Leila, her eyes wide. 'We'll be able to play with Gemma and Amy as much as we like!'

'Will it be dark, though?' Leila asked.

'Pitch-black,' Eloise replied.

'Ooooh, goody, goody, goody!' Leila shrieked.

'What's going on?' Jimmy asked as he appeared through the

back door. 'I've never seen them this keen to go to school on a Monday morning. I'll have to brush up on their antiestablishment training.'

'No, silly, we not being anti-dish-table-is-went, we're all going to a party!' Leila said, flinging herself at her dad's legs, nearly knocking him off balance.

'Are we?' Jimmy asked, steadying himself against the door frame and smiling at Catherine. 'Cool. Any chance of a quick shower? I'm laying down that demo today and then Mick's going to take some photos after to put on the CD cover and I have to look my best. When's this party?'

'Help yourself to the shower,' Catherine told him. 'There are fresh towels in the cupboard and the thing is I don't think you are exactly invited to the party. At least, not on my invitation. It's for PTA members and their families.'

'But Daddy is our family,' Eloise said.

'Yes, he's our *daddy*,' Leila added, as if Catherine was being a bit thick. ''Member? Plus mankind is one big family, Mummy.'

'I know, darling, but . . .' Catherine looked at Jimmy, who clearly wasn't going to help her out if it meant forging an invitation to a party where there would be free booze, not to mention free food, two of his most favourite things.

'I'm just saying I don't think you were specifically invited. It was an open invitation to the PTA and you are not on the PTA.'

'Well, I might as well be, the amount of discount I give your lot for my services. Look, if it's an open invitation, how do you know if I was invited or not? Even the people who are doing the inviting don't know who they've invited in that case.'

'It's Gemma's mum and dad,' Eloise told him with an air of pride. 'She's my new best friend and she's getting a pony.'

'And, Daddy, we're going to stay up late in the dark!' Leila told him, making a spooky face.

'Are we?' Jimmy grinned down at his daughter as he disengaged her and headed up to the bathroom. 'Cool. Give me five minutes and I'll walk with you to school.'

'Mummy, why does Daddy come here for a shower?' Leila asked as Jimmy's heavy footsteps sounded on the bathroom floor above their heads.

'Because Daddy doesn't have a shower on the boat,' Catherine said absently, distracted by the sound of his feet on the floorboards.

'Daddy practically doesn't even have a *roof* on the boat, it's so leaky,' Eloise mumbled.

'Yes,' Catherine looked thoughtful, 'Daddy really needs somewhere better to live.'

'Like here?' Eloise asked hopefully.

'Like a house or a flat with a decent roof,' Catherine replied. 'And some form of heating.'

'Like here then,' Eloise added, and Catherine remembered her agreement with Jimmy.

'Somewhere like here, but either he'll have to sign a record deal or I'll have to win the lottery because at the moment we can't afford it.'

'We could afford it, if he lived here,' Eloise said, and Catherine decided it was impossible to argue with her because, after all, she was right.

'No,' Catherine said again as the four of them walked briskly to school, running a good five minutes late because Jimmy wanted to blow-dry his hair so it didn't go all frizzy, and the girls would not leave without him.

'But do you really mean no?' Jimmy asked her, striding along beside her. 'Think of what an experience it will be for them, how much great music they will hear live.'

'No, Jimmy, no, you are not combining your tour of

Oxfordshire with your turn to take the girls on holiday. You are not going to drive them around unsecured in the back of a van, make them stay up all night in pubs while you perforate their eardrums and then put them God knows where while you do what you . . . whatever you do.'

'*Nothing*. I do *nothing* after gigs. I have a pint or two and then go to bed *alone* in whichever B & B we're staying,' Jimmy said, obviously offended.

'Well, even if that's true, you can't do that with a five- and an eight-year-old!' Catherine protested, flinging out her hand in exasperation.

'But the van's just passed its MOT and I'd put car seats in the front for them to sit on. I'd even throw in a seat belt.'

'No,' Catherine repeated, throwing him her warrior queen look. 'End of. It's not going to happen.'

'But why, Mum?' Eloise asked her. 'We could be roadies. Please, it will be fun.'

'Daddy said we could be backing singers,' Leila urged her. 'Plus the van's just passed its PMT!'

Catherine narrowed her eyes at Jimmy. 'I will never forgive you for bringing this up in front of them.'

'I'll add that to the list then,' Jimmy said in exasperation.

'That's not fair, Jim, and you know it. I cook for you; wives do not cook for husbands if they still give a damn about . . . well, you know what. Anyway, this isn't about us. It's about our two *little* girls. Sometimes I think you forget that you are their father and not just their friend.'

'I know that,' Jimmy replied, hurrying to keep up with Catherine's long strides. 'That's the one thing I definitely do know. Look, OK, you're probably right, taking them gigging isn't my best plan. I suppose I thought it would be economical, like killing two birds with one stone. Multi-tasking – I know you dig that, right?'

Catherine scowled.

'OK, so how about I take them to the Donnington Monsters of Rock Festival, because you never know who on the line-up might be dead this time next year. I'd be taking them to see history in the making.'

'No.' Catherine had to raise her voice to be heard over the chorus of pleases that followed Jimmy's suggestion. 'Take them somewhere rife with drunkards and drug addicts, where it will probably be raining and cold – are you insane?'

'You're the one who's always saying modern children are too pampered, and that they need exposure to bacteria and germs to toughen them up,' Jimmy countered.

'To bacteria, yes; to subzero temperatures and crack cocaine, no,' Catherine said. She suddenly stopped dead, which meant her disparate little family overshot her by a few steps before coming to a juddering halt.

'Jim, please, think about what you are suggesting,' she said, looking up into his eyes. Jimmy held her gaze for a moment or two and then dropped his eyes to his cowboy boots.

'It's probably not a good idea, after all, girls,' he said, his comment greeted by a selection of groans. 'Mum's right. When you're a bit older I'm definitely going to take you, but right now you *are* too young. We'll think of something else to do. We could go and visit Nana Pam.'

Catherine glanced at him before walking on at speed, giving him that look of hers, her speciality, the look that said that as her husband he was more of a burden than a partner. It had become a frequent expression of hers during the last year or so they were living together. That constant unspoken disappointment was partly what had driven him to go with Donna Clarke to the ladies' loos.

'Look,' Catherine said as she charged along at double-quick pace. 'I know you love the girls, I know you do your best for them. But I just wish sometimes that you'd think further ahead than five seconds. You never seem to plan anything.'

'I'm more of an instinctive kind of guy,' Jimmy said with a half-smile. 'Like a Ninja.'

Catherine's exasperation bloomed into a reluctant smile and Jimmy found to his immense surprise that he had been holding his breath until it appeared.

Neither Gemma nor her younger sister were in the playground when the bell rang, which infuriated Eloise, who was determined to firm up a tea arrangement, party or no.

'Where *is* she?' she asked, holding on until the last second as her classmates filed in around her. 'I want you to meet her, Daddy. She's really nice.'

'Just chill, babe,' Jimmy said. Catherine had left him to wait with Eloise while she took Leila round to her class, a feat she normally had to juggle on her own, and one that was only just about manageable if she arrived ten minutes earlier than they had today. 'You'll see this Gemma in class, won't you?'

'But I want to go in with her,' Eloise said, pawing the ground like an impatient colt. 'So everyone will see we're best friends.'

Jimmy looked down at his flame-haired girl. 'You are everyone's best friend, Ellie. Look, you've got to go in now otherwise I'll have to sign the late book and your mum will be even more cross with me than she already is.'

'Sorry Mummy's angry with you, Dad,' Eloise said, hugging Jimmy around his waist.

'She wasn't angry as such, just direct, and that's never a bad thing,' Jimmy said, edging both of them towards the school entrance, which was now deserted. 'Besides, she was right. It's an irritating habit she has.'

'I was thinking on the way here,' Eloise added, 'if you got a cold or got sick or something, and were *really* poorly and you couldn't stay on the boat any more because you might *die*, then you'd have to come and stay with us until you got better, wouldn't you? And then maybe if you liked it, and Mummy liked it, you could stay for ever. And you wouldn't have to worry about the stinky boat or finding more money to rent a flat.' Eloise looked up at him, her expression serious. 'It's a good idea, isn't it, Daddy?'

Jimmy took a breath. 'But I never get sick,' he said. 'I'm as strong as an ox, and I love that stinking old boat, so don't you worry about me, darling. In you go.'

Eloise looked disappointed but nevertheless she raced into class, her bright hair flying behind her, calling out over her shoulder, 'Gemma's got blonde hair and a blue shiny coat and she usually has some sparkly clips in her hair. If you see her with her mum, will you ask her about tea, please?'

'Deffo,' Jimmy called after her, although he had no intention of doing any such thing.

All these year-round tanned women, with their smart hairdos and high heels just to have coffee in, did his head in, even more than the groupies that hung around at his gigs. At least he knew what those women wanted with him, and all it required to deal with them was basic evasive techniques.

He thought of Janine Seymour, who had cornered him in the pub last night. When it had come to chucking-out time she had thrust him up against a wall and put his hand up her top. But while Janine Seymour had a lot of the qualities required for the CV of a real woman, particularly with her curves and enthusiasm, she still didn't match up to Jimmy's exacting standards. Many a young woman, her eyes glittering with vodka and bristling with self-assurance, had pounced on Jimmy after a gig like Janine had, but in the end Jimmy always

127

declined because, despite his reputation as a ladies' man, fifteen minutes in the ladies' loo at The Goat pub with Donna Clarke was really all it was based on.

So making small talk with whatever the name for the posh wives was – glamour mamas, or something – wasn't on Jimmy's agenda. He didn't have the stomach for those women, as brown and as shiny as they might be. He liked real women. Women you could have a laugh with.

Jimmy had really only ever met one real woman in his life, and he'd married her. Married her, had children with her and then saw himself settling into a life that wasn't meant for him. Husband, father, even a wage slave. He'd seen his dream slipping away and the more settled he and Catherine became, the less chance he thought he ever had of hearing her tell him she loved him. When he'd gone to the loo holding Donna Clarke's hand he had wanted to escape Catherine and make her want him all at once.

Two years later, he realised that somehow he'd failed to do either.

The story of my bloody life, he thought, his head down.

'My God, Jimmy Ashley!' Jimmy stopped dead and looked at the blonde woman standing in front of him. Good-looking, nice shiny hair, a long white mac and high-heeled boots under some faded jeans. She was unquestionably one of them, so how on earth did she know his name? He couldn't see her at one of his gigs somehow, unless she had a thing for slumming it, and besides, he was fairly sure he'd remember sleeping with her and her orthodontist-whitened teeth.

'Run in, love, you'll just about make it,' she said to a blonde little girl in a shiny blue coat. 'Don't want to sign that book again!'

Another little kid, one about Leila's age, was clutching her arm.

'Right then,' Jimmy said, preparing to leave, but the woman just looked at him expectantly.

'It's great to see you again after all this time,' the woman gushed, her face flushing. Jimmy was confused but intrigued.

'Is it?' he said. 'I mean, it's good to see you too . . .' There was a long gap where the absence of a name flashed like a neon sign.

'Alison,' the woman said, her smile fading just a fraction. 'You don't remember me, do you?'

Jimmy gazed at her. She looked nice for one of them, though he was fairly certain he had never seen her before in his life. It seemed wrong to offend her right out. He smiled at her, interested to note her blush deepen.

'Honestly I don't, but I can't think why. It must have been that serious water-skiing accident that I don't remember having last year, because only serious amnesia would be a good enough reason not to remember you.'

To his amazement the woman giggled like a sixteen-year-old, and then there was something about her that seemed familiar.

'I'm *Alison*,' she told him as if her name was sure to remind him. 'Alison James. When you knew me I was Alison –'

'Mrs James?' The woman looked up as the head teacher popped her head out of the reception door. 'Any chance of a quick word before you take Amy in? I know you are already running late.'

'Of course,' Alison said, looking disappointed as she smiled at Jimmy. 'Time-keeping is not my strong point.' She reached into her bag and handed Jimmy an invitation. 'We're having a house-warming party on Saturday – can you come?'

'Oh, you're Gemma's mum,' Jimmy said, as if that should be reason enough to know who she was. 'I'm already coming with my wife, well, ex-wife sort of, and my daughters. My Eloise is very keen on your Gemma.'

'You're Ellie's dad?' Alison looked surprised. 'I'd never pictured you as a dad. I don't know why, maybe because you look the same. You teach my son guitar – he's just started at the school? Dominic.'

'Oh, yeah.' Jimmy began to relax. 'He's a talented kid. When he's not sulking. A lot of them sulk these days. They think if they're not depressed they've got no cred. Only thing is, most of them haven't got anything decent to be depressed about.'

'Mrs James?' The head appeared again and this time there was a definite edge to her voice.

'Do you know what, Jimmy? It's been really good to see you,' Alison said, laying her hand on his arm.

'You too, Alison,' Jimmy said, because although he still couldn't place exactly who she was, it was always good to see a good-looking woman who was pleased to see him.

Alison flashed him another dazzling smile as she trotted towards the head, her smaller girl lingering a step or two behind her.

It was just as she went into the building that Catherine appeared around the corner at full pelt, running right into Jimmy.

'Jimmy! Why are you still here? Please tell me you haven't had to sign Eloise into the late book, have you? I'm only still here because Lois would not stop going on about the sodding Easter Fayre. You don't fancy dressing up in a bunny costume, do you?'

'I bumped into this woman who thought she knew me,' Jimmy began to tell her, 'but I don't know how because she's this Gemma's mum, the one whose party we're all going to.'

'Oh, was she nice?' Catherine asked, although she clearly didn't want a reply as she was walking backwards towards the gate as she talked. 'Anyway, I've got to get to work. I have three minutes to make it down the high street. I'll measure you up for that suit, OK?'

'I'm off to work too,' Jimmy called after her as she sprinted off at full pelt. 'Laying down a demo today,' he added in a lower voice as the playground had now entirely emptied of all people with purpose and direction. 'Today's the day. This is the day that's going to change my life. This is the one.'

Alison practically skipped her way to the gym to take up the new membership.

It was foolish, she knew, literally idiotic, to feel so happy about bumping into a man who clearly had no idea who she was. But he'd had no idea who she was with some serious charm and a sexy smile. So what if he didn't remember that she was the girl who used to lean forward on the edge of the stage in the hope he'd look right down her top? He'd never noticed that girl anyway. But he'd noticed her now, a grown woman. He noticed her and she was fairly sure he had flirted with her too. It might have been the first time a man had actually flirted with her since the early 1990s.

That, coupled with the tentative smile on Amy's face as Mrs Woodruff had led her by the hand into class, put her in exactly the right mood for her one-on-one Pilates class with her new teacher.

'Hello there,' a woman about her age smiled at her and held out her hand as she walked into the private studio she had booked. 'Mrs James, is it? I'm Kirsty Robinson. I'm going to be teaching you Pilates.'

'Right,' Kirsty said. 'From that position step one foot forward and we'll stretch out your hip flexors.'

'So?' Alison asked her with some effort as she stretched her left leg behind her. 'Are you going to see him again?' Her new teacher had been regaling her with the details of her love life for the last half an hour, something that Alison found most entertaining, not to mention diverting.

'I think so,' Kirsty considered. 'We had a nice time in the pub, and he is a great kisser. I let him walk me home and everything, and he didn't even *try* to invite himself in for sex, which I was slightly disappointed by, even though I would have definitely said no because I hardly ever do sex on the first date with men I like. But he didn't call me over the weekend and today when I saw him he was playing it cool as if we hadn't spent half an hour with our tongues down each other's throat on Friday night. I still think he likes me, though. And if he doesn't then I'll just revert to Plan A until I've got over him.'

'Ignore him and pretend nothing happened,' Alison confirmed as she followed Kirsty's movements in the mirror.

'Exactly.' Kirsty grinned at her. 'OK, relax into child pose and then roll yourself slowly and carefully up into a standing position, working each vertebra.' She and Alison rose in unison in front of the full-length mirror.

'Shake yourself out and you're done,' Kirsty told her.

'Thanks, I really enjoyed that,' Alison said warmly.

'Me too. It's good to have a client that's nice and not some stuffy old cow who thinks I'm one of her servants.'

'I really hope you get things sorted with Sam and that he asks you out again.'

'Well, he will or he won't,' Kirsty said with a sigh, catching sight of herself in the mirror and giving herself an admiring glance. 'It's not the end of the world if he doesn't. Yes, I'm in love with him. But look at me: I'm gorgeous and still young. I'll love again.'

Alison laughed. 'And it's better to shop around than buy the first thing you see and find out fifteen years later you don't really want it any more,' she said completely out of the blue, then paused for a moment as she heard the words that she had just said out loud for the first time.

'You are so right,' Kirsty smiled. 'You should meet my neighbour. She got married in her twenties to some guy she went to *school* with, and course it didn't work, and now it's like she's stuck in a time warp. Can't go back, can't go forwards. I'm trying to crowbar her out of it, but it's a challenge, let me tell you. So how long have you been married?'

Alison pursed her lips and looked down at her painted toenails.

'Married fourteen, together nearly sixteen years,' she said sheepishly.

'So you bought the first thing you saw in the shop then?' Kirsty laughed.

'More like shoplifted him out from under my best friend's nose,' Alison said. 'But you know, when you're seventeen you don't really think.'

'Well, it's obviously worked out for you,' Kirsty said. 'So tell me, what's your secret?'

'I don't know,' Alison said with a shrug. 'We implement Plan A a lot.'

As she picked up her bag she pulled out her last few remaining invitations. 'Listen, we're having a house-warming party and –'

'Oh, I already know about that,' Kirsty said. 'All the sports centre staff are coming. Even Sam.'

'Well, maybe while you're not ignoring him you'll have a drink with me. I don't know anyone in the town yet and the thought of having two hundred strangers in my new house is slightly intimidating.'

'I'd love to,' Kirsty said. 'And I'll introduce you to my

neighbour. She's a bit like a young Miss Marple but once you get to know her she's pretty cool, and then you'll have two friends and I'll know two people to lead astray instead of one.'

Alison grinned at her. 'I'm perfectly capable of leading myself astray, thank you very much. I've lived my life by it.'

Chapter Nine

'Are you sure that you can plug all of those fairy lights into my house and it won't explode?' Alison asked the Fairy Light Man as he plugged yet another extension into yet another extension on the morning of the party.

He scowled at her. 'Yes, I'm completely sure,' he said, his voice a weary monotone.

Maybe it was because in his daily life he was commonly referred to as the Fairy Light Man, Alison thought. Maybe that gave him a complex, challenged his masculinity, perhaps that was why he was so surly and ungrateful for the several hundred pounds they was paying him to plug in a few lights. Very charitably, she decided to give him the benefit of the doubt.

'OK, well, I'll leave it up to you then,' she said, trying to get back into his good books in case he shorted the fuses just to spite her. 'You're the professional. I don't know anything, me!'

He turned his back on her and resumed plugging more things into more things, which Alison took as a sign that he agreed with her self-assessment. In a flash of Fairy Light Man insight she could picture just exactly what he thought of her: a spoiled rich housewife who treated all tradesmen like servants and still believed that the working classes were born to serve her. Maybe that *was* what she was like, a little bit now, even if her upbringing on the immaculately kept but down-to-earth council estate couldn't have been more different. Her life had transformed with Marc, and Alison supposed that it was inevitable that she would change too, because now she was new money and that was the way she often sounded and acted, even if she didn't *truly* feel that way.

Sometimes she just couldn't stop herself. She'd hear her own voice, and even as she was talking she'd be thinking, who *is* that stuck-up stupid cow? That's not really me, is it? Invariably she was disappointed to find out that it was.

It had been a challenging week to get to this point and Alison had had a hard time keeping up the good mood her Pilates class had left her in on Monday. The first set of caterers she thought she'd miraculously managed to book for Saturday let her down, citing some lame excuse like a death in the family and referring her on to a friend's brand-new only-just-started family-run business called Home Hearths.

From that moment Alison had felt that luck was not on her side. She had been well aware that *any* caterer available for booking a scant five days before an event was not exactly going to be top of the range, but by that time she had very little choice but to go with the family company. She'd even booked them blind without any tasting or menu discussion. Alison had told them she wanted canapés for two hundred people and they told her they'd provide the waiting staff. That, as far as Alison was concerned, was as good as it was likely to get.

Marc had not been around for almost the whole week. He'd been at the office until past eleven every night, working on getting the new showroom up and running. If Alison wasn't asleep by the time he got in then she found she was in too bad a mood to make small talk with him, something he always annoyingly wanted to do, regardless of the hour, because he'd be as high as a kite and wouldn't care that the children and the low-level bone-splintering radioactive stress of her day had drilled her into the ground. But it wasn't just the contrast in their days that infuriated her: him high-flying and go-getting, making things happen and living the dream he seemed to be able to believe in so entirely, despite considerable evidence to the contrary; and she, who literally ran just to stand still, putting in thirty minutes on the treadmill at the gym because she was determined not to let her body look one second older than it absolutely had to, arguing with her children over yoghurt vs. fromage frais, withstanding the barrage of passive aggression that radiated out from her son whenever he was in a room, a feat that was only just eclipsed by the constant nagging fear about what he was doing whenever he wasn't.

It wasn't the unjust disparity in their lives, even though Alison knew that her lifestyle was privileged and rare. No, it was her husband's sheer bloody thoughtless optimism that had infected him ever since they decided to come back to Farmington that nearly drove her to murder him.

She'd never imagined that Marc's determination to change himself to adapt to her dreams would have brought them quite this far. It was as if he was on a quest that would never be satisfied. A three-bedroom semi in Kennington would have made Alison happy once. But she had a feeling that no such comforting middle ground was available to her and Marc now. For them the only way was either up, up and away or a very, very fast journey back down. It all depended on Marc. Everything had always depended on Marc.

At least the week was over, the weekend was here and, even if the house was about to razed to the ground by an entire town, at least she had two whole days when she didn't have to worry about getting into school so late that she had to sign the late book, something she had done for four days in a row.

Usually the playground at St Margaret's was empty when she and her two girls charged in through the gates at full pelt, after Alison had performed her daily miracle of raising Dominic from his bed and delivering him a mutually agreed distance from the school gates. Gemma would be laughing and dancing, enjoying the thrill of the race, and Amy clutching on to her wrist with both hands as if her mother was about to toss her into a pool of piranhas. The only time in the girls' second week at the school she had managed to escape the ignominy of the dreaded late book was when she had bumped into Jimmy Ashley in the playground and the head had called her in.

Alison felt a foolish little flutter in her chest when she thought of the conversation she and Jimmy had had. There was maybe a very small part of her that was deliberately trying to recreate the circumstances of that meeting by turning up to school at almost the same time every day, even if it did mean her daughters were late to class; the same part of her that used to be accidentally outside the Civic Centre just around the time his judo class finished, or happened to be walking down his street for an hour and half in the rain on the off chance he would either leave or return to his house while she was there, and give her a second glance. But in the year and a half she'd been mad about him he'd never even given her a first glance, let alone a second one. Alison laughed to herself. All those hours she'd spent deciding what to wear or where to be to attract his attention had all been for nothing. She'd left too soon for him even to be able to remember who she was.

But now she had the chance to rectify that, Alison reminded herself as the Marquee Men began to set up in the drizzly back garden. She didn't have to try to engineer encounters with

Jimmy Ashley any more. Because Jimmy Ashley would be at her house this very weekend. She'd even be able to flirt with him a little bit, if she could just remember how.

Alison caught her train of thought slipping from flirtation into something much more radical and largely naked, and found herself saying out loud, 'Get a grip woman – good God, act your age!'

'Forty-seven.' Alison spun round to find Amy standing behind her decked out in her Cinderella outfit.

'Pardon, sweetie?' Alison kneeled down to her daughter's level. She loved to see Amy dress up. It was one of her few moments of self-expressiveness, and even then she seemed only to be able to manage it if she was pretending to be a Disney princess.

'You said act your age and I said forty-seven. That's your age, isn't it, Mama?'

'Thirty-two, darling,' Alison said, unoffended. 'But I feel forty-seven a lot of the time, so you're spot on really.'

'You *look* beautiful,' Amy told her wrapping her arms around Alison and whispering in her ear, 'Love you, Mama,' as if it was their little secret, which Alison sometimes felt that it was.

'Love you too, precious,' Alison whispered back.

'You're welcome,' Amy said, releasing Alison from her embrace. They had been learning manners at her old school and she had been responding arbitrarily to any comment with that phrase ever since. 'Dominic said I had to tell you there was some "old minger unloading what looks like sandwiches from a clapped-out Volvo estate out the front and that you might want to go and check the tax disc because . . ." I forgot the rest.'

Alison gave Amy a little hug. 'Thank you for being so helpful, darling, but don't use that word. Don't say "minger". It's not a nice word for little girls, OK?'

'You're welcome,' Amy replied.

Alison was in a dilemma. She wasn't sure whether to check if indeed the caterer had arrived in an untaxed Volvo or go and strangle her son about his cavalier use of language in front of his sisters first. Panic and emptiness won out over her violent thoughts in the end, and she made her way out to the drive.

'Hello there, Mrs James?' A surprisingly mature lady in a green body-warmer and red tartan pleated skirt waved at her. 'I'm Home Hearth Caterers, at your service! It's all gone swimmingly well considering it's our first party. I think you'll be pleased.'

Alison looked at Home Hearth Caterers' mud-caked Wellington boots and wondered what 'considering it was our first party' meant.

'Mind grabbing a couple of quiches?' Home Hearth Caterers said, piling platters into Alison's arms. 'This way, is it? Don't worry, I'll follow my nose!'

Alison watched powerless as the old minger tracked mud all across her hallway, and she wondered where the hell her husband was when she needed him to blame.

'You can't wear *that*,' Kirsty said, looking Catherine up and down.

'I think you'll find I can,' Catherine said firmly. 'Look, there's only so many times I can take you coming round my house and insulting me. You've made me shave my legs, now leave me alone.'

'You do realise that leg shaving is something you have to repeat, don't you?' Kirsty asked her. 'Tell me you've done it for tonight, I beg you!'

'Yes, I have,' Catherine lied for a quiet life, looking sulkily at the outfit of a black chiffon shirt with jet-effect beading down the front that she had got from Oxfam last year, and a pair of straight-legged black trousers with a stay-press pleat ironed down the front that actually reached her ankles.

What Kirsty did not know was that this was her best outfit. This was, in actual fact, also her most daring outfit because it required her to wear it over a black camisole to prevent her bra from showing. (She was determined to wear a bra although Kirsty argued that one as flat-chested as she should go commando and let her nipples do the talking, a comment that practically made Catherine reach for her thermal vest, and certainly cling on to her firm support 32B.)

That was *partly* why Catherine had never worn it before; the whole see-through element threw her a bit. The other reason was because although she manned many a bar at many a PTA event, she hardly ever went to parties where she was actually invited as a guest and not simply required to pour drinks.

'I *like* my outfit,' she said, looking at Kirsty whose idea it had been to come over three hours before the party was due to start to have a girly getting-ready session.

'Three hours? Catherine had asked her when she suggested it earlier that morning whilst having breakfast with her and the girls. 'Do you mean three actual hours? It doesn't take that long to get ready for *anything*, does it?'

'Yes, it does if you are a proper girl, doesn't it, ladies?' Kirsty asked Eloise and Leila. 'Tell your mum why.'

'Well, you have to have a shower, hair wash, hair style and hair dry,' Eloise listed, ticking off each item on her fingers.

'*And*,' Leila added, 'there's choosing what to wear, access-or-eees, see, Mummy? That means like earrings and necklaces and nail varnish – ooh, can I wear nail varnish? Nana Pam gave us some in secret that we are never to tell you about.'

'*Also*,' Eloise said, quickly attempting to cover her sister's slip, 'there's eye make-up, putting on mascara and lip gloss. Can I wear lip gloss, Mum? Kirsty might lend me some.'

'Or we could use the stuff that Nana Pam gave us . . .'

'Shhhh!' This time Eloise prevented her sister from saying any more by clamping her hand over her mouth. Catherine chose to let the revelations go uncommented on only because she had found their secret stash of play cosmetics long ago and thought that everyone, even very small girls, deserved some secrets as long as their mother secretly knew what they were.

'How do they know all this stuff?' Catherine had asked Kirsty in amazement. 'Are you creeping into their room at night and whispering it in their ears?'

'No, I shout it over the garden fence when you've got them out digging potatoes in the bleak midwinter,' Kirsty said, rolling her eyes at the girls and making them giggle. 'They know all that stuff because it is ingrained in their DNA. It is the primal urge to make yourself look beautiful. Since the dawn of time, soon after woman invented the wheel and discovered fire, she also realised how much fun it was to paint herself with bright colours.' Kirsty had clapped a hand on Catherine's shoulder. 'You too were born with it once, my friend, but somehow you have lost your feminine way and need to be brought back to the one true path that leads to uncomfortable shoes and exfoliation. Follow the lead of your daughters, follow me, for we have the key to the world of womanhood.'

Catherine had been unable to resist a smile, particularly when all three of the other females at the table started fluttering their eyelashes at each other, hands arranged under their chin like Botticelli's angels.

It *was* a sort of club, feeling feminine and pretty, and if Kirsty was in it then maybe she wasn't too old to feel that way too, at least sometimes. Besides, she knew it would make her daughters happy to have a mum that made a bit more of an effort. ('Did you see Isabelle Jackman's mum this morning?'

142

Eloise would often say to her. 'She wears high shoes and it's only a Wednesday. Isabelle says that's because she's not letting herself go. That's good, isn't it, Mummy?' And Catherine would give her a talk about looks not being everything and Leila would say something like, 'Maria von Trapp is pretty and good of heart and you can be both. Look at the Virgin Mary,' at which point Catherine would change the subject.) So, in short, in a moment of weakness, she had agreed to the three-hour pre-party preparation party.

It was a decision she regretted the minute she realised that Kirsty had engineered the whole thing, first so that she could drink the bottle of Cava that Catherine had had in the fridge since Christmas, and secondly so that she could try to get her to wear something that she had brought with her.

'For one thing,' Catherine said when Kirsty held up a short black denim skirt that belonged to her, 'I am six foot tall. You are five foot two. If I put that on it will barely reach below my bum.'

'I *know*,' Kirsty said. 'That's the advantage of not having one. You'll look great.'

'I'll look like a *tart*!' Catherine exclaimed, lowering her voice on the last word lest her daughters stop screaming with excitement for long enough to hear her.

'And looking like a tart is the first of many steps you will need to take to have sex. That's when a man and a woman who like each other very much have a special cuddle and the man puts his –'

'You don't need to look like a tart to have sex,' Catherine admonished her neighbour. 'If I were ever to have sex again, I'd want it to be with someone who respected and cared about me.'

'Interesting.' Kirsty tipped her head to one side so her sleek brown bob fell at an angle. 'You are now not entirely ruling

143

out the possibility of ever having sex again. And OK, you don't *have* to look like a tart to have sex, but it can help. It's sort of the express checkout to shagging, if you like. Ten items of clothing or less gets you laid much faster.'

'God, you're crass, and I'm *not* wearing that skirt.' Catherine pushed the bedroom door shut as if to limit the contamination of Kirsty's filthy mind to her own bedroom.

'I knew you'd say that,' Kirsty said. 'I only brought it to push your boundaries because what you are actually going to wear is this . . . tad-dah!' She pulled out a Primark bag. 'I picked you up this knee-length pencil skirt for a few quid today. Please just try it. I promise you, you'll still have that harbinger-of-doom-at-a-funeral look you like so much, only with your foxy long legs on display.'

Catherine said nothing as she looked at the skirt. She hadn't worn a skirt in two years. That wasn't a joke, she actually hadn't. Not since the night she caught Jimmy in the ladies with someone whose skirt was wrapped around her neck at the time. Whether the two facts were related in some way she didn't know; she didn't want to think about it.

'Please try it for me, Catherine,' Kirsty pleaded. 'After all, what other friend have you got who is prepared to narrow down her own chances of pulling at this party by helping her insanely gorgeous neighbour realise her full potential? That's love, that is. Any other woman would be drawing your eyebrows on, not trying to prune them back.'

Kirsty tried her best encouraging 'you can do it' smile on Catherine.

The smile in itself didn't work. What did work was not only that Kirsty *was* Catherine's only friend who was prepared to try to get her out of her rut and into a short skirt, she was really more or less her only friend, full stop. More than that, Kirsty was the only real female friend she'd had since she was seventeen.

'I'll *try* the skirt,' Catherine said, unable not to sound begrudging. 'But that's all.'

The minute she had it on, along with her chiffon shirt, Kirsty called the girls into her bedroom. Having got themselves ready by digging out all the secret and largely glittery contraband that Nana Pam smuggled into their lives, and covering more or less every inch of themselves in netting, shiny nylon satin and glittery bits of lace, the minute they saw Catherine in a simple skirt they ooohed and ahhhed as if it were she who was dressed up like a psychotic ballerina.

Kirsty, Catherine realised, had pulled off a tactical stroke of genius. If she took the skirt off now her girls would be disappointed, and if there was one thing Catherine could not stand to do it was to disappoint her girls when it was in her power not to. It was something that happened all too rarely.

'I'm wearing it with opaque tights then,' she said, and Kirsty, clearly feeling she had won the war if not the battle, cheered.

'Well, you'll have to as you lied about shaving your forests . . . I mean legs,' Kirsty added.

'And flat shoes,' Catherine added, looking at Eloise's clear plastic play heels. That was one secret Nana Pam item she had not discovered. She'd have to start looking harder.

'Well, of *course* flat shoes. We don't want you to tower over all the men, do we?' Kirsty replied glibly. 'Actually, put on your long boots – they are like cleavage for the knees, you know – plus they make you look a bit kinky.'

'I'll put them on if you stop saying words in front of my children that will get repeated in class,' Catherine warned her.

Kirsty nodded in satisfaction at the final effect.

'You are a fox,' she said. 'You must be the last woman on the planet who doesn't realise what a fox she is.'

'Mummy isn't a fox,' Leila said, looking perplexed. 'She's a human bean, aren't you, Mummy?'

'Well, my darling,' Kirsty said, putting an arm around the five-year-old and hugging her, 'there is a rumour going round to that effect, it's true.'

Catherine was brushing out the backcombing that Kirsty had tried out on her hair when the doorbell sounded.

'I'll get it,' Kirsty said. 'It'll be Jimmy.'

'Dad's here, Mum!' Leila said, scrambling into her bedroom and grabbing her by the wrist, dragging her out of the bedroom before she could twist her mass of hair into its customary ponytail. 'Come and show him your legs!'

'Leila, I . . .' Catherine felt herself freeze on the stairs. For some bizarre reason, although she had come to terms with half of Farmington seeing her legs from the knee down, albeit beneath seventy deniers of nylon protection, the thought of her almost ex-husband seeing her made her panic.

'Come on, Mummy,' Leila said, tugging her down the last few steps. 'Look, Daddy, Mummy's got legs!' Leila exclaimed.

Jimmy's charmed chuckle at his daughter's comment faded when he caught sight of Catherine, her head bowed, her hair obscuring half her face. But even though Jimmy knew how much she hated to be looked at, he seemed to spend an inordinately long time, at least two seconds longer than was acceptable, looking at her long and thin legs.

Catherine felt her cheeks grow hot and herself grow cross. This was all Kirsty's fault. She didn't need to know that Jimmy found her effort at dressing up ridiculous. Her life was so much easier when she was in neutral, when he didn't notice her or what she was looking like at all.

'You look . . .' Jimmy struggled to find a compliment.

'What?' Catherine asked him, with a wince.

'You scrub up all right, don't you?' Jimmy said with a shrug. 'You've pushed the boat out. Good for you.'

146

'Oh, how erudite! And they say the art of the compliment is lost,' Kirsty observed.

'I'm sorry,' Jimmy shrugged. 'I mean, you look nice. Whatever.'

'Are you really thirty-three or are you just an extremely old-looking fourteen-year-old?' Kirsty asked Jimmy, hooking her arm through his and leading him out of the front door before Catherine had to suffer any more embarrassment under his ham-fisted scrutiny.

'Right.' Catherine looked at her two children. Every part of them that was dressed was covered in nylon satin and fake silk, and every part of them that was not was adorned in glitter, including their hair. 'I have never seen two such beautiful girls in my life,' she told them, her heart glued into every word. 'So come on then, let's go to this party and see what the rest of Gemma's family are like.'

'They'll be perfect,' Eloise told her, taking the hand she proffered. 'They are bound to be perfect, because Gemma is.'

Chapter Ten

'Bloody hell,' Jimmy said as the five of them walked through the wrought-iron electric gate, which swung open on their approach.

'Magic gate!' Leila said with a little hop as they walked down the drive leading to the floodlit house situated in a little dip at its foot.

'Electric gate,' Eloise told her, suddenly seeming a little more subdued.

'Nice place,' Jimmy said, nodding at the double-fronted faux-Georgian palace.

'Big place,' Eloise said quietly. 'Much bigger than our house.'

'I'd say they paid at least one point two mil,' Kirsty added, turning to Catherine. 'What do you think?

'I think that all of those fairy lights are a wanton waste of energy,' Catherine said. 'And that just because you have money to burn it doesn't mean that you should.'

'And I think I hope there's plenty of booze,' Jimmy said, whisking Leila up onto his shoulders and out of the way of a Mercedes SLK as it swept by, leaving a ricochet of gravel in its wake. 'I'm going to need it.'

The house was already filled with people; everywhere Catherine looked she saw someone she knew at least by sight.

Half the PTA were instantly visible, as well as three or four teachers from the school, including Mrs Woodruff and the optician from Boots. It must have been *the* optician, because as soon as he saw Kirsty his eyes lit up, and as soon as she saw him she vanished. The massive hallway alone had to be accommodating fifty or sixty people talking, sipping champagne and taking sandwiches from a passing teenager with a tray. Catherine looked for someone new, who might be one of Gemma's parents, but so far she already knew everyone she saw.

'What do we do now?' Jimmy asked Catherine. The pair of them stood there side by side, one daughter hanging off each of them as they manoeuvred their little party towards the relative safety of a sheltering wall.

'We get a drink, I suppose, and mingle,' Catherine answered as if she were just suggesting they smeared themselves in ketchup and jumped into a den full of starving lions. 'Make small talk and all that stuff.'

'Right,' Jimmy said. 'Or we could just take the girls to Harvester, get off our faces on the house white and forget about it. What do you reckon?'

Catherine looked at Jimmy and felt a sudden rush of warmth towards him. At that exact moment in her life she could think of nothing that she would like to do more than run away with Jimmy and the girls, and yes, maybe even get a little bit tipsy with him over an onion relish dip. But before she could accept, Catherine found herself engulfed in squeals and yelps as her daughters were embraced by a blonde girl who must surely be the mythical Gemma.

'Mum, this is her, this is Gemma,' Eloise said, tugging dangerously hard on Catherine's chiffon sleeve. 'This is my best friend!'

Catherine looked down at the pretty blonde little girl

standing next to her daughter and suddenly she got a vivid flashback. She and Alison, standing side by side at Siobhan Murphy's tenth birthday party, admiring the pink Miss Piggy cake. Edward Stone had come up to Catherine and told her that he didn't want to be her boyfriend any more because she was too ugly. Alison had punched Edward Stone quite hard in the stomach, making him double over in pain and throw up iced rings on the carpet.

Catherine blinked, and suddenly the moment had passed and she was looking at her own little girl again, standing next to Gemma. For a moment Catherine got the feeling that it was not the past she was looking back on but the future she was touching. Gemma looked exactly like Alison – *exactly* like her – but she couldn't be hers . . . because it would just be too . . . Alison wouldn't come *here* after . . .

She stared at the plump little girl with her big blue eyes and smiled at her.

'Hello, Gemma. Nice to meet you,' she said, hoping she was the only one who noticed the tremble in her voice. 'Eloise has talked about you a lot.'

'Hello, Mrs Ashley. Nice to meet you too.' Gemma smiled prettily at her. 'Eloise has been so kind to me since I started at the school. I feel like I fit right in now.'

'That's great, Gemma. By the way, where's your mummy? I'd like to meet her.' Catherine glanced quickly round the room, her heart in her mouth, afraid of whom she might see, constantly telling herself that there must be a hundred blonde little girls in this town who bore a passing resemblance to Alison, this was purely a coincidence. That's what Catherine told herself, yet at exactly the same time she knew with complete certainty what the truth was. Alison was back.

'I think Mummy's in the kitchen being cross about the sandwiches,' Gemma told her, before saying to Eloise, 'And

150

Amy's in the tent being Beauty from *Beauty and the Beast*, dancing to the disco. Want to dance?'

'Yes, yes, yes!' Eloise said. 'Can we, Mum, please?'

Catherine paused. 'OK then,' she agreed reluctantly because she would rather have kept them close to her just in case she needed to make a quick exit. 'But don't go out of the house, OK? Don't talk to anyone you don't know . . . or some people you do know, and when I say it's time to go it's . . .' but the three girls had disappeared.

'I guess that's the Harvester idea canned then,' Jimmy said regretfully. 'We definitely can't go without them . . . can we?'

'Jimmy, what's the name of the people whose party this is?' Catherine asked him urgently.

Jimmy looked perplexed. 'I don't know, Cat. I never exactly saw the invitation. I met the woman, the mother, though in the playground, do you remember? She said her name was . . .' Jimmy trailed off, unaware that Catherine was hanging on every nuance of his silence.

'It's gone,' he said, shaking his head and shrugging.

'What did she look like, the mother?' Catherine pressed him.

'What's up, Cat?' Jimmy asked her. 'I didn't crack on to her, if that's what you're worried about, even if she did fancy the arse off me.'

Catherine's stomach dropped ten storeys.

'Just tell me, what did she look like?'

'Blonde, money all over her, you know, the usual. Great teeth, nice smile. Said we used to know each other but I couldn't think how I'd know a chick like that . . .'

'Oh my God,' Catherine said, looking around her with wide-eyed horror. 'Oh. My. God.'

'What?' Jimmy exclaimed.

'It's Alison.'

'You're right!' Jimmy clicked his fingers. 'Alison, that was her name. How did you . . .? Oh Christ. It's *that* Alison. The actual Alison.'

The two of them stared at each other. Catherine nodded, unable to move.

'How do we feel about that?' he asked her, his hand steadying her arm.

'I don't know,' Catherine told him. 'I don't – it shouldn't matter after all these years, should it? So what if she's come back and my daughter is her daughter's new best friend? It's all in the past, water under the bridge, it doesn't matter any more, right? Right?'

Jimmy didn't say anything for a moment, as he watched Catherine's wide-eyed face drain of any colour.

'We're upset about it then,' he confirmed.

'I don't know how else to be,' Catherine admitted. 'I feel sick, Jimmy. Why did she have to come back here, that's what I don't get. Why now?'

'Look,' Jimmy felt now was the time to be decisive and take control, 'I'll get the girls and we'll go, OK? You don't need to deal with this now. You need to go home, have a think about it. Let it sink in.'

'She can't have known I was still here. If she'd known she wouldn't have come back,' Catherine said, her voice low and dark. 'She wouldn't want to see me.'

'Maybe, maybe not – but the point is, you don't need to see her tonight. Wait there, I'll get the girls. We'll go home and talk this through. OK?'

Catherine gripped his hand hard in hers. 'OK,' she said. 'And thank you. Thank you for not thinking I'm stupid and irrational and delusional.'

'You forget, Cat,' Jimmy said, placing the palm of his hand briefly on her now blazing cheek. 'I know.'

Catherine waited, standing in the hot and busy room, with all the good people of Farmington chatting and laughing around her, and she was glad for once that she had developed the talent to fade into the background, folding in on herself until she became near invisible.

Even so, her heart was racing, her skin was pulsating with the blood that was careering around her body. She felt light-headed and hot, as if she had a fever, as if she'd suddenly been stuck down by the flu.

'She was just a girl you once knew, a girl you fell out with over a boy,' she told herself, braced against any eventuality. 'It doesn't matter, why should it matter now?' An answering thought slowly descended, slotting into place with exacting care. Alison hadn't come back to Farmington alone. She'd come back with two girls and a teenage son and her husband.

Her husband. The day after Alison had gone it was as if she had disappeared into a parallel universe. Catherine's parents had banned any discussion about her, the boy she had run off with and what might have become of them. Catherine gleaned snippets of rumours, whispered in hushed tones behind half-closed doors, but since her parents had taken her out of school she had been unable to find out what had really happened with Alison and Marc. After her mother found out about what had happened between her and Marc, she had been a virtual prisoner in the house for almost a year while her parents sought to purge her of the evil she had become tainted with, and it took exactly the same amount of time for Catherine finally to learn to let them think that they had. Only when Catherine began to show them outwardly, at least, that she was calm and obedient did they let her have any freedom. A little bit more each week until eventually she had begun to lead her own life in secret, for the first time without

Alison to tell her what to do, climbing in and out through her own bedroom window when her parents were both asleep.

Catherine had never known what became of Alison and Marc, but maybe it was possible that she had married him and if she had . . .

Once again Catherine's eyes swept the room, but this time she was looking for something different and the sight that stopped her heart was the back of a man's head, dark hair cut short into the nape of his neck. That in itself was unremarkable, but the shape of the head and the angle it was set on those shoulders was not. She was looking at her living, breathing past.

And then, as if he sensed the touch of a gaze on his skin, slowly and uncertainly the man turned round and looked right at her, and recognised her.

In that one second it seemed as if time was standing still and Catherine found it so hard to breathe that for a second she wondered if that thin layer of atmosphere that came between her and the magnitude of space had evaporated, collapsing her lungs and halting the pounding of her blood in her ears.

It was Marc. She hadn't seen him for nearly sixteen years and then suddenly there he was. He was smiling at her. He looked happy to see her.

It was Lois's scything voice that brought her back to her senses, shocking her into living again.

'And you must meet our Catherine,' Lois said, bringing Marc over to where Catherine was standing, dumbstruck. 'She is an absolute treasure. I simply do not know what we would do without her.' She looked from Catherine to Marc again and, when neither spoke, filled in the void. 'I was telling Marc about the PTA, Catherine?' Silence. 'Catherine, are you quite well?'

Catherine tore her eyes away from Marc's face and looked at Lois as if she was the one who was the complete stranger.

'Lois, I'm afraid that Catherine is in shock because of me,' Marc said with an easy smile. Catherine was surprised to hear that his voice wasn't the same. It was refined now. He had lost his Midlands accent and picked up some 'h's and 't's along the way. 'She and I know each other, you see, although we haven't seen each other for a long time. She has probably been struck dumb by how old and fat I've got, and she's got every right to be. She doesn't look a day older than the last time I saw her, only more beautiful.'

'Oh? Well, how unusual,' Lois said, clearly deflated by Marc turning his attention from her. 'Well, I'll leave you to catch up then. You can tell me all later, Catherine.'

'I knew it,' Marc said a second or two after Lois had left them alone. 'I didn't even know that I knew, but I did. I knew I'd find you here.'

'At your party?' Catherine asked him, banally.

'In Farmington,' Marc replied. 'I think you're the reason I came back. You might even be the reason for this party. I've been looking for you and I didn't know it until I saw you.'

'What?' Catherine asked him. 'What are you talking about?'

'Just recently you've been on my mind a lot,' Marc took a step closer to her, causing Catherine's heels to graze against the skirting board. He smiled. 'I thought about the way I . . . we . . . left and how it must have hurt you back then. Maybe it doesn't matter any more but I want you to know I didn't plan anything to happen the way it did. I didn't plan, full stop. I didn't plan to get involved with you or Alison, and I didn't know I was leaving with her until the minute she told me I was. I let things happen to me back then, Cathy, and I didn't care about the consequences. But that doesn't mean I don't regret them now.' Marc shook his head and laughed. 'You know, I didn't expect to have this conversation tonight either,

155

but I'm glad that I am having it. I'm glad I've got the chance to say that I'm sorry. I'm sorry for hurting you, Cathy.'

Catherine looked into his black eyes, at him standing here in the flesh right in front of her, and felt the ground shift a little beneath her feet. A few minutes ago he was a part of her history, a time past that could never be recaptured. Now it seemed as if he had never been gone.

He had no idea, she told herself steadily.

'You are not having this conversation tonight,' she told him, making herself smile, shrugging so that her loose hair fell over one shoulder. 'When my husband gets back with my daughters we are leaving.'

Marc let go of her arm, leaving a residue heat of a summer sixteen years old where his fingertips had been.

'You don't have to go,' he said. 'It must be a shock, I know, but please don't go. Stay and wait for the shock to wear off. Alison will be here somewhere. I know she'd be so pleased to see you. Catherine, please.'

Before Catherine knew it he was embracing her, hugging her thin frame against his. It wasn't the hard, toned body she had once known that she felt graze against her ribs now, but it was still his body, and at his touch a tiny spark of memory ignited in her belly and made her muscles contract.

She was relieved when he released her, and she glanced over her shoulder, looking for Jimmy and the girls. They were nowhere to be seen.

Alison decided that she had spent long enough in the kitchen waiting for her husband to come and tell her what to do about the fact that the food had run out about half an hour ago. Why she was waiting for him she didn't know. There was nothing they could do about it now anyway. It was just that if he was here, if he had come like she had asked him to, then she would be able to show him the empty platters that were scattered across the kitchen and say, 'I told you so.' And that would make her feel better. Still, at least they had plenty of champagne. Champagne that Alison had not had nearly enough of. Something she was keen to remedy.

'Right, well,' she said to the waiting staff, who were hovering about. 'Just make sure everyone gets drinks, OK?'

'Can't we have a drink?' one boy asked. 'This is a cool party.'

Alison looked at him and crossed her arms. If she spent one more minute in her expensive dress in this expensive kitchen, as stone-cold sober as the Italian granite work surfaces, with incompetent teenagers, then she would literally implode.

'Just one,' she told the boy, 'but if I catch any of you getting drunk there will be trouble, OK?' She watched in relief as the teenagers filed sedately out of the kitchen, trays laden with champagne.

Alison peered into the hallway where many guests were still congregating, and searched the crowd for the familiar shape of her husband, who was, no doubt, working the room somewhere in the house. She stood on her tiptoes and craned her neck, but she couldn't see him out there and if he wasn't out there then she didn't want to brave the crowd without him, at least not until she'd had two more glasses of champagne. Retreating back into the safety of the kitchen she reapplied her lip gloss reflected in the stainless-steel oven door and then, taking a bottle out of the fridge, poured herself first one and then another glass. When both glasses were finished and she could feel the bubbles in the wine popping behind her eyes she decided to go and see if Jimmy Ashley had turned up at her party.

She found him in the marquee, trying to persuade his daughters to come off the dance floor, but he wasn't having much luck. The disco lights turned the mêlée of children green, red and blue, making them look like multicoloured fairies flitting across the floor, but there was something familiar about the tall girl, the one that had to be Gemma's much-loved Ellie. She must take after her father, Alison thought, smiling warmly at Jimmy as he tried to catch his smaller girl and failed.

Tipping the rest of the bottle of champagne she had brought with her into her glass and immediately emptying it, Alison thought she might as well be at the sixth form dance again, trying to pluck up the courage to get Jimmy Ashley to dance with her because that was exactly what she was about to do now. Alison waited as the room tilted and swayed for a moment before setting itself right and she heard a sane little voice inside her head telling her that this was not at all the right way to make a good impression as a wife and mother and the hostess of the party. But unfortunately for the sane little voice, Alison couldn't give a stuff. And besides, it was largely because her husband had not introduced her to anyone that she felt fairly safe that most people here wouldn't even know that she was the hostess.

Jimmy had not noticed her coming until she was standing right next to him.

'Hi, Jimmy!' she said, quite loudly, right in the shell of his ear, making him jump. 'Come with me and have another drink.'

'Alison,' Jimmy said, stepping aside so that his daughters could race away from him unhindered.

'Oh, you remembered me.' Alison was thrilled. 'Yay! Jimmy remembered me at last!'

'Alison from school,' Jimmy said. 'That's how I knew you. You hung about at band practice a lot. You were Catherine Parkin's best friend.'

'Yes,' Alison said, a little more hesitantly this time. 'Yes, that was me. I used to know Cathy.'

'She got married, Cathy Parkin,' Jimmy said. 'Her name's Catherine Ashley now.'

'Oh,' Alison said, her eyes widening. 'Oh shit.'

'We need to talk,' Jimmy told her.

A few minutes later, as his eyes adjusted to the light, Jimmy saw Alison perched on what looked like an upturned box with a bottle of champagne in her hand, her bare legs crossed, showing a little upper thigh. She had led him outside to a sort of a copse situated in a dip just behind the marquee.

As he'd allowed her to lead him out into the darkness Jimmy had got the distinct feeing that he shouldn't be following any woman, never mind this woman in particular, into any kind of woods and that he should really be taking the girls back to Catherine and getting her out of there like he'd promised. But he told himself that by talking to her he was trying to make things easier for Catherine. Alison had no idea about what had happened to Catherine after she ran away – Catherine had never had the chance to tell her – and now the only people in the world who knew about her were Catherine's parents, Catherine and him. Jimmy clearly remembered the night she had told him. It was the same night that he'd first asked her to marry him. As she'd told him what had happened and how she would always feel about it, he was convinced that she was using it as a reason to say no to him, but then he realised it was her way of showing him she trusted him. It was her way of saying yes, maybe. If he kept asking her, even after knowing everything about her, then maybe one day she would say yes.

Jimmy was afraid that there was every chance that Alison would treat the whole thing as if it were a joke, like something they could look back on and laugh over, but Jimmy knew that wasn't the case. He felt he had to warn her, but not for her sake, for Catherine's.

'Well, talk then,' Alison said, retrieving another bottle from one of the boxes next to where she was sitting. Marc had instructed the spare crates of champagne to be left there so they would keep cool. She twisted off the cork, unbalancing herself a little, and took a swig from the bottle. 'Sooner or later my husband is going to find out that there isn't anyone passing out drinks any more because the waiters have drunk it all and he'll send someone down here to get some more. In fact he'll probably want to send me, but he won't be able to because I'll be here with you! Jimmy Ashley Who Married Cathy Parkin. That's poetic justice for you, isn't it?' She tipped her head back and laughed like a little girl, which made Jimmy smile, despite himself.

She took a long draught from the bottle and then, wiping the back of her hand across her mouth, she handed it to Jimmy. 'I'm a bit drunk, actually. Which is a good job because when Cathy sees me she's going kill me.'

'Catherine's not like that,' Jimmy told her as he took the bottle and a swig. 'But you should know it's going to be hard for her. When you went you left her in a real mess. A real mess.'

'I know it must have hurt her losing him, Jimmy, but she got over it otherwise she wouldn't have married you. You know, I bet she married you to get back at me.'

'What?' Jimmy asked her.

'I fancied you at school for years, Jimmy – did you really not notice? God, that is so depressing. I still do fancy you, actually. You're a very sexy man, bringing me out here to talk about your lady wife.' Jimmy took a couple of steps away and glanced back at the lights of the house twinkling in the distance. Suddenly he felt very out of his depth.

'But, Jimmy,' Alison went on, 'he might have loved her but he never would have been any good for her, not in a million years. Trust me, I *know*.' Alison's laugh was entirely mirthless. 'Funny, really. I got her life and she got mine. All of this is your fault. If you had noticed me throwing myself at you back then, then I would have let her mess herself up with Marc and I would have had you. And we'd be happy.'

'I'm sorry,' Jimmy said for want of anything else to say, 'but the truth was I didn't actually discover women until I was in my twenties. I was too much into my music to get serious with anyone. I never had girlfriends at school, never had anything serious until I met Catherine. I didn't even know I'd gone to school with her for years. That's how blind I was. And if I didn't even notice the stunning tall girl with the bright red hair, how would I have noticed you?'

'Mmmmphf,' Alison said, pouting. 'I have decided not to take offence.'

'Look,' Jimmy said, trying to get back to why he was here in the wood with her, 'the fact is that you're here now –' he looked up at the house laden with a million twinkling lights – 'and it looks as if you're here to stay – but you're going to have to be . . . sensitive with her, Alison. Allow for what she went through, give her time to adjust. She's never had anyone to talk about it all to except for me. She still cries about it sometimes, Alison. That's how much the whole thing hurt her. It damaged her.'

'She still cries about Marc and me running off together?' Alison's laugh was harsh. 'Seriously? As her husband, doesn't that piss you off?'

Jimmy looked at her. 'She still cries about the abortion. The abortion her parents made her have when she found out that Marc had made her pregnant.'

There was a long silence punctuated by a hiccup as Alison

stared at Jimmy, the defiant smile on her face faltering and then finally fading.

'You've got that wrong,' Alison insisted. 'What are you talking about, Jimmy? There *was* no abortion. *She* wasn't the one who he got pregnant, it was me. I know because he never had sex with her – he told me that at the time. He never felt that way about her; they didn't have the passion we had, have.'

Alison swayed a little on her perch as she took another drink.

'Where did you get the story of an abortion from anyway?' she asked Jimmy defensively. 'I had him, I had Marc's baby – he's in there now, probably secretly drinking and skulking around the waitresses.'

Jimmy sighed. How it had fallen on him to break this news to Catherine's archenemy was beyond him, but he felt it demanded some tact, some diplomacy – qualities that had never featured highly in what he considered his most obvious attributes.

'Look, Alison, I don't know what Marc told you back then. I expect he told you a lot of things that weren't true. Men usually lie when they are sleeping with two women at once. What I do know for certain is that Catherine was pregnant when you left.' Jimmy's hot breath made his words visible, a mist in the chill of the air. 'She was pregnant with Marc's baby too, only she didn't get to keep hers. Her parents saw to that.'

Jimmy watched as Alison's glassy eyes brightened and filled with tears that glittered in the reflected glory of the decorated house.

'She was having his baby?' Alison asked, her voice a whisper. 'She was having his baby too?'

'Yes, she was going to tell him – she wanted to tell you but in the end she decided she couldn't . . .'

'No, you see, that's not right.' Alison was determined. 'Because it was *me* he wanted, *me* he needed. He played around with her, strung her along, but he didn't do *that* with her. He told me. He told me that *I* was the one he couldn't keep his hands off. That was what made us special and what made her and him nothing more than a childish fling. She bored him, he told me that. Jimmy, I'm sorry but Cathy's made the whole thing up. I don't know why – maybe to get you to feel sorry for her – but anyway, it's a lie.'

Jimmy's face darkened as he took a step or two nearer to Alison. 'Catherine doesn't lie,' he told her. 'Does Marc?'

'No!' Alison stood up abruptly. 'He doesn't lie, he doesn't . . . and anyway, don't you see, Jimmy? I can't not have known about that. I *would* have known. We knew everything about each other, Cathy and me.'

'Not everything,' Jimmy said. 'Not this. I'm sorry, Alison, but it happened. Marc got Catherine pregnant, she had an abortion.'

Without warning Alison flung her arms around Jimmy, buried her face in his neck and wept. At a loss as to how to react, Jimmy kept his arms stiffly held out at a steady ninety-degree angle, her shoulders shook and he felt her hot breath against his neck.

'This is too much,' she said, into his neck. 'This is one lie too many, and it's not fair because it was the first lie, and if I'd known about the first lie then maybe I wouldn't have stuck around for the second or the third or the hundredth or the millionth lie.' She paused and looked up at Jimmy, her face very close to his, and Jimmy couldn't help but notice that despite the drinking and the tears she still looked beautiful. 'It must have been hard for Cathy.'

'I think that is a bit of an understatement,' Jimmy said, swiftly disentangling himself from her embrace and stepping away from her. 'Like I said before, it damaged her and that's why I'm asking you to back off, to take it easy.'

'I'm going to kill him,' Alison said, having to steady herself without Jimmy to lean on. 'He fucked us both up and now I'm going to kill him.'

'Look,' Jimmy said, suddenly feeling uneasy. 'I suppose it's an obvious question, but Marc? He is here somewhere, isn't he? And sooner or later he'll find Catherine. She's kind of hard to miss.'

Alison's head snapped up and before Jimmy realised what was happening she was marching past him back towards the house. He had to jog to keep up with her.

'Are you OK?' Marc asked Catherine.

'I'm fine, really. Go and talk to your guests, please. I'm waiting for my husband,' Catherine said, but Marc stood stock-still.

'I don't want to leave you like this,' he said.

Catherine bit her lip, repressing the obvious retort. She shook her head and conjured an approximation of a smile, 'Go, I'll be fine.'

Catherine watched him watching her, his dark eyes intense. He'd looked at her in exactly that way on the day when they had first met and he'd kissed her. For one heady petrifying second Catherine got the feeling he might do exactly the same thing now. He took a step closer to her, his hand grazed her shoulder, striking sparks as it passed.

'Liar!' Suddenly Alison was in between them, causing Catherine to stagger backwards and into Jimmy, who was following at her heels.

'What?' she asked him.

'Thing is . . .' Jimmy began, but it was then that Alison slapped her husband hard around the face. The whole room stopped and looked.

164

'Ouch, darling.' Marc smiled at his wife. 'The caterers weren't that bad.'

'Liar!' Alison repeated, and was about to slap him again, but this time he caught her wrist.

'Let's take this outside, shall we?' he said in a low voice as he gripped her wrist. 'Remember our guests?'

'You told me you never had sex with her,' Alison accused him. 'You were sleeping with both of us the whole time.'

'Look, Alison,' Marc pulled her closer to him, trying desperately to keep the conversation between themselves. 'Please, we'll talk about this later.'

'You've lied to me for fifteen years,' Alison said, her voice hard and cold. 'After everything we've been through and all the promises you made, you've kept on lying. You're still lying now. I used to think it would end one day, but it won't ever end, will it, Marc? It comes as naturally to you as breathing.'

She jerked her wrist out of his grasp and looked around at the crowd of guests.

'Ladies and gentlemen, this party is now over due to the unforeseen circumstance of my husband being a disgusting lying pig. Please collect your coats and make an orderly exit.'

Spinning on her heel she came face to face with Catherine. The two women stared at each other, aware that not one guest had made an attempt to leave yet.

'Cathy,' Alison said quietly, carefully avoiding looking at her husband because she was afraid of how he would react to what she was about to say. 'I didn't know. I didn't know about the baby.'

'Would it have changed anything?' Catherine asked her, and Alison knew she was avoiding looking at Marc too. 'If you'd known?'

'It might have,' Alison said. 'It would have changed something.'

Catherine felt the scrutiny of all of those around her and knew that she had to be out of it within the next five seconds.

'I have to go,' she said. She looked at Jimmy. 'We'll find the girls and go, OK?' He nodded.

'Thank you for coming,' Alison said to her foolishly. 'Will you believe me if I say that it's really good to see you again?'

Catherine nodded, tears standing in her eyes. 'I do.'

'Perhaps I'll see you in the school playground. Perhaps we can talk, sort things out, put things . . . to rest.'

Catherine paused to look directly at Alison. 'Why did you come back?'

'To rescue my family,' Alison said. 'I don't think it's working out quite as we planned.'

Catherine nodded and then without saying another word she turned on her heel and, slotting her hand into Jimmy's, walked out of the room as the crowd parted before her.

The cool air soothed Catherine's hot face as they began their walk back home, Leila asleep on her shoulder and Eloise in Jimmy's arms.

'You handled that amazingly well,' Jimmy said. 'I was so proud of you, Cat. You were so serene and dignified. Even with him, the bastard. You were brilliant.'

'I can't believe you told her,' Catherine replied. 'I can't believe it.'

They were silent for the rest of the walk home.

Chapter Eleven

Alison lay on her bed, staring at the ceiling. The room lights were out but the thousand or so fairy lights outside her bedroom window illuminated the room in pulsating glittering bursts of radiance.

Much to her deep irritation the party had not finished when she had declared that it was over. Far from it. That had been a good hour ago, and the chatter of Marc's guests still rose in the hallway as if nothing had happened. After Cathy had made her exit, splitting the party crowd like Moses parting the Red Sea, with Jimmy Ashley loyally following in her wake, the room had fallen silent save for the background thrum of the disco in the marquee.

Glancing about, Marc had laughed, then put his arm around her and kissed her hard on the cheek.

'May I introduce you all to my wonderful, fiery, impetuous and amazing wife, Alison James, a woman who certainly knows how to make an entrance almost as well as she does an exit.'

And somehow Alison had found herself standing side by side with Marc, her arm linked through his, smiling graciously while she received a round of applause from the good people of Farmington. Only Marc could have done this; only Marc could have the front and magic to turn a marital brawl into a social nicety, something that was even romantic, and, still reeling from the news that Jimmy had given her, Alison could quite happily have slapped him again for doing it.

However, with everyone's eyes on her and the buzz of the champagne having eroded into a head-churning fuzz, not to mention the sight of her two daughters come to find her, Alison realised she didn't have any choice but to go along with the illusion that Marc had created.

She put her arms around his neck and kissed him on the lips.

'Anyone for more champagne?' Marc asked the crowd in general the second the kiss was broken, leaving Alison's side to go and arrange it before anyone could answer.

'I'm tired, Mama,' Amy said, putting her arms around Alison's waist and resting her chin on her tummy. 'When are all these people going home?'

'Ellie's mummy came and made her and Leila go home. She looked really cross,' Gemma said. 'I'm not tired, by the way. Can I stay up some more? You could come and dance with us, Mummy. And Daddy and Dominic – we could all dance together.'

'I don't think so,' Alison said, crouching down so that her youngest could hook her arms around her neck, then hefting Amy onto her hip. 'I think you two girls have had a good run and now it's time for bed, OK?'

''K,' Amy said, resting her head on Alison's shoulder, her thumb in her mouth.

''Spose,' Gemma sighed. 'Although I could dance for at least another hour without getting tired.'

And Alison was finally able to make her escape, leading her two girls to bed, both of them falling asleep as soon as their heads touched the pillow. She briefly peered over the banister to the throng of people below. Marc was the centre of attention, talking, throwing his head back with laughter, gesturing like a hypnotist who had a whole room in his thrall. He was rescuing the situation, turning it around, making it happen, recreating the façade of their lives from scratch yet again, doing all the things he was so good at – except he hadn't seemed to notice that she was up here on her own and he was down there running all of their lives single-handed as if he hadn't lied to her for fifteen years. As if he hadn't been sleeping with them both.

Alison closed her eyes, but the lights still twinkled cheerfully behind her lids, so she pulled the duvet over her head to blot them out, breathing in the scent of her relationship, her life, that was embedded in the sheets.

Of course he had been sleeping with them both, of course he had. If she had any kind of knowledge or experience of men back then other than trying to fend off the wandering hands of the boys from school she would have realised it was inevitable. She and Cathy were still girls – almost women but only just, and only in body. They were still making the choices and decisions that girls made when it felt as if there would be no consequences and no tomorrow.

And Marc had been a man – just a young man, that was for sure – but he had had to grow up fast, thrown out of the children's home at the age of sixteen and left to fend for himself in a world of brutal and unsympathetic adults. At the age of seventeen Alison had believed that she had a sexual power over him. She had the breasts and the legs and the heat between them that he really wanted. But she was wrong. Cathy had it too, it was just that with Cathy it was much less obvious.

'Have you ever done this with her?' she'd asked him.

'I've never done anything like *that* with her,' he'd replied. He hadn't lied; he couldn't have been more blunt. Alison had chosen to believe what she wanted to.

Alison pressed the heels of her hands against her pounding forehead. Cathy had been pregnant. She had been pregnant with Marc's baby, a baby that would only have been conceived a week or two apart from Dominic, maybe even on the same day as her son – it was quite possible. Looking back, Alison realised Jimmy was right: Cathy had tried to tell her, after it all came out. After she found out that Alison had been sleeping with Marc and everything started to disintegrate around her. Alison remembered she felt as if she was standing in the eye of a storm, perfectly calm, absolutely determined, while the rest of the world was whipped into chaos around her.

She remembered her last conversation with Cathy before she left.

It had been raining; thick rivulets of water blended with her friend's tears as she stood on Alison's doorstep and pleaded with her.

'Please don't do this, Alison,' she'd begged her. 'You don't love him, not really. You only want him because I've got him. Please, you don't understand what you're doing to me!'

'It's no good,' her seventeen-year-old self had replied. 'He loves *me*, Cathy, he wants *me* – not you. You have to realise that. And besides, I need him now. I *really* need him.'

'But what about us?' Catherine had wept. 'You and me? Who will I have if I don't have you? If I lose him I lose you too. I don't know what I'll do, Alison. You don't know what you're doing to me. I need you, I'm –'

'Look, I'm pregnant,' Alison had hissed, taking a few steps forward into the rain and drawing the front door almost to a close behind her so that her parents would not hear. 'Nobody knows yet, not even him, but I'm having his *baby*, Cathy. And I *love* him. I love him and he loves me, and that's the way we've felt about each other since the minute we met because it

170

was me that he should have met in the park, and not you. If it wasn't for bloody Aran Archer, it would have been me. He's angry now with both of us, but tonight I'm going to find him and I'm going to ask him to leave Farmington with me and he will. I'll make him come with me because I know that he wants me more than anything else in the world. You were never anything important to him, you have to see that, Cathy. I mean, look at you – can you really picture the two of you together? Now I have to put myself and my baby first and if you can't get used to that then . . .' Alison had shrugged.

Catherine hadn't said a word. She'd just stood there in the pouring rain, as if her whole body was melting into the salt water, her mouth open, speechless as she tried to understand what Alison was telling her. Alison had stepped back under the shelter of her porch and waited.

'But you're my best friend,' Catherine had begun. 'The only person in the world I could talk to and trust . . .'

'Not any more,' Alison had said. 'Not any more. I'm sorry, Catherine. You'll just have to get used to it. Marc belongs to me now.'

Now Alison tried her hardest to get back into the head of the girl she was then, and she asked herself what she would have done differently if she had known that her friend was pregnant too. And she couldn't say that she wouldn't have still left Cathy behind. Back then she didn't know any better. She didn't want to know anything except that she was meant to be with Marc and that he belonged to her.

Another nagging uneasy thought was tugging away at her as she lay in bed and that was the memory of her husband standing behind her downstairs at the party when she had told Cathy she didn't know about the baby. It should have been news to Marc too, but there was nothing. Not a gasp, not a movement – there was no reaction at all. He was perfectly still.

171

Did that mean that he knew about the baby when he ran away with Alison? It could have been that, or it could just have been Marc maintaining appearances no matter what sledgehammer came swinging out of the past to floor him. It was impossible to know and, Alison decidedly wearily, she didn't want to know. Not yet, at least. She was growing weary of discovering secrets.

There was a knock at the door. Alison composed herself for Marc, and then she realised he would never knock.

'It's me,' Dominic called. He opened the door a crack, the blaze of the hall light momentarily blinding Alison as she peered over the covers. 'Are you OK?'

'I'm fine,' Alison told him, mustering a smile. 'I've just got a headache. What's the time?'

Dominic shrugged, he didn't wear a watch. Alison glanced at the clock. It was almost midnight.

'You should be thinking about bed,' she told him as he came in the room, shutting the door behind him.

'What was all that about, Mum?' Dominic asked her. 'You shouting at him, and slapping him. You looked proper angry. It was mental, well cool.'

Alison frowned. She didn't know how to feel about impressing her son with an act of violence, but it was hard not to feel pleased because he was so rarely impressed by her these days.

'You should have arrived fifteen seconds earlier, he was all over that woman, the tall scary-looking one. Is she why you slapped him? Has he gone and done it again already?'

Alison, who had been rubbing her eyes, froze for a second. She hated that Dominic knew about Marc. She hated the fact that her son's expectation of his father, of both of his parents, was now so low.

She sat up and turned on the bedside lamp.

'Don't be silly, Dom. Dad hasn't done anything,' she told her son, as he sat on the edge of the bed. She ventured out a hand and touched his soft as yet unshaven cheek with the back of it. 'You know Dad: he's a charmer and a flirt, all touchy-feely. But it doesn't mean anything.'

'I call fucking some tart a bit more than being touchy-feely, Mum,' Dominic said, his words but not his tone brutal. 'Look, I'm not a kid any more. I see things, I hear things. We both know that everyone was talking about him before we left London, and you – they talked about you too. About what kind of woman you must be to put up with what he did. I know you like to tell everyone including yourselves that we moved because I'm such a dead loss and on the verge of becoming a hardened criminal. I don't even care if that's what people think about me, but we both know that's not the real reason. We left London because you finally found out Dad was fucking that tart at the showroom. But not because of the actual fucking, because you've put up with that in the past and it didn't seem to bother you. No, this time we had to leave because you realised that everybody, all your friends, all his slimy mates, knew about it for months and you didn't.' Dominic shrugged. 'Dad did what he always does and promised that it would never happen again and you did what you always do and believed him. Only this time you couldn't stand living in the same street, going to the same gym and the same school where everybody knew what he'd done to you, and what a fool you were. So you made us move back here and blamed it on me.'

'Dominic,' Alison said steadily, reeling from the so nearly accurate portrayal of her life her son had just related to her, 'you can always talk to me, but please don't use that language. It doesn't shock me, it doesn't mean anything. Talk to me like an adult, not some foul-mouthed kid who hasn't got the brains to know better.'

'Oh, come on, Mum,' Dominic said. 'Don't do that. Don't do the middle-aged parent thing with me. That's not who you are. Not with me.'

'That's not true,' Alison said, about to deny all of it, but then, weary of deceit, choosing only to deny the inaccurate parts of her son's interpretation. 'I didn't want to come back here. You father wanted to come here.'

'Why?' Dominic asked her, his confusion framing her own.

'Because . . .' Alison remembered Marc's reasons but none of them seemed very plausible any more. 'He said it's a nice place. It's the place where we started and the place where he still has something to prove. And as much as you'd like to deny it, moving here had got plenty to do with you. You of all people shouldn't listen to gossip, Dom. People say things that aren't true . . . maybe that was part of the reason for leaving, but it wasn't all of it. Both your dad and I wanted a fresh start.'

'A fresh start?' Dominic looked disgusted with her. 'Mum, I don't know what was going on back there with that woman, but this isn't a fresh start. It's an . . . old ending. Are you sure Dad didn't just come here for that. For her?'

Alison stared at her son, the boy who might have been conceived on the same day as Cathy's baby, Cathy's long-gone child.

'You don't have to worry about any of this . . .' she began, reaching out to pat his hand.

Dominic snatched it away. 'Yes I do,' he told her, making some effort to keep his voice down. 'Of course I bloody do. Do you think your shit marriage only happens to you two? Do you think the rest of us aren't involved? And it's not just me. Gemma puts on a front but before we moved away she came and asked me to go to her school and beat up this boy who'd been saying things about Dad . . .'

'You didn't, did you?' Alison asked him, horrified on all fronts.

'Of course I didn't. I'm not a psycho. I told her to tell him I would if he ever talked about it again and it seemed to shut him up. And do you think Amy would really be so shit-scared of everything if it wasn't for the fear of you and Dad busting it all wide open? You think that everyone else looks at us and sees a perfect family, living in a nice house, with a perfect life. But you're wrong. Everyone in London knew the truth about us and before long everyone in this dump will too.'

Alison didn't say anything for a moment. She just stared at her hands on the bed covers, flat and immobile.

'You'd be better off without him.' Dominic said.

'I . . . you can't say that, Dom,' Alison reacted at last. 'You don't understand. You don't know what we went through to be together and how hard we've fought for everything, we were only a little bit older than you when we met. No one thought we'd make it, and look at us. Grown-up life isn't pretty, it isn't easy. You do your best, you keep going, you wait for things to even out.'

'Me,' Dom said matter-of-factly.

'What?'

'What you two had to go through to be together was me. I can do maths, Mum. I know he got you pregnant with me when you were seventeen. You two got together because you had to, because of me, and you've been stuck together ever since, even though you don't fit.'

'No, no,' Alison said firmly, leaning forward and holding his wrists. 'You're a clever boy, Dom, but you've got that bit wrong. I loved your father so much. I wanted him so much. I was mad for him. When I realised I was having you it was a bit of shock. I was frightened and it was hard to know how to cope. But when your dad and I got together it was because we thought we could make a go of it, not because we had to. Not because of you, even though you would be the best reason in the world. We loved each other.'

'But not any more,' Dom stated.

'That's not . . . stop it, Dom, stop saying all of these things, just because you are angry with us. This is your father you are talking about and no matter what you say about him he loves you and you love him.'

'I don't,' Dom said simply.

'You do,' Alison insisted.

'Mum, I don't even know him. I never see him except when he wants to bollock me. I never speak to him. He never even looks at me when we're in the same room together. At least you shout at me sometimes – he doesn't even do that. It's because he resents me, because it was me in your belly that got him tied up in this family he's so keen on wrecking.'

'Now you're just being silly,' Alison said. 'You and Dad talk and spend time together. Look at . . . well, what about when . . .?' Alison trailed off. She couldn't remember the two of them talking in the last month, let alone the last week. 'He's very busy at the moment,' she said instead.

Dominic dropped his head so that his dark hair fell over his face and Alison wondered if he was crying.

'Look, I maybe haven't been the best mum in the world. You and I grew up together, and I'm still growing up, still wondering how to be your mum even now, especially now you are turning into a man. But I love you, Dom. I love you.'

Dominic looked up at her and his eyes were bright with tears.

'Leave him, then,' he said. It was the first time he'd asked her.

'I can't just . . .' Alison began.

'Leave him. We'd be all right on our own. I'd help look after you and the girls, and you could be you again. You say I don't understand what life for an adult is like but even I know that if your life is shit and if you are unhappy then you have to change it, because you are the only one who can. Sometimes, Mum, you have to be brave.'

'I can't just leave him,' Alison said, with some surprise because, despite everything, the thought had never once occurred to her until then.

'You could,' Dominic said. 'If you wanted to.'

'But I don't want to,' Alison said automatically. 'Look, Dom, I'm glad we've talked, I really am, and the things you feel are so important, but you've got everything muddled. Dad and I are having a rough patch and it will be over soon. We're not going to split up because, well, we're just not. We are meant to be together. In the morning I'll talk to him about you, about how you're feeling. We'll sort out some time for you two to spend together – how about that?'

'Whatever,' Dominic said, standing. Alison sensed the connection between them had gone.

'I promise you everything will be fine,' Alison told him just as he closed the door on her.

After Dom had gone Alison lay back on the bed and covered her eyes with her hands.

Of course it was easy for Dominic to imagine that she could just walk away from this life, her marriage with Marc. That it was simply a question of making a choice and abiding by it. After all, she'd believed exactly the same thing at almost his age. She'd made the choice to be with Marc, to leave behind her home, her parents, her exams, her future, and it had been a simple choice to make. At the time it hadn't even felt like a choice. It was simply something she had to do.

Now, though, she was living with the consequences of that decision, and at thirty-two it wasn't that easy simply to overturn a lifetime of consequences. You don't just pack your bags, dump your old life and take off. It was impossible to imagine living without Marc and all the complications he created. Trying to picture it made Alison's head hurt. Then she remembered something, or more accurately someone, that she had met only briefly last year but whose story kept coming back to her again and again.

Every Tuesday evening Alison had gone to aerobics at her local gym. She could have done it during the day much more easily but she liked the evening class better, she liked the female instructor who took it, and the energetic women who had worked all day but were still prepared to jump around for an hour just to justify the takeaway they were going to buy on the way home. Alison had made a few friends there, but especially a woman called Christina she used to giggle with in the back row, and who made Alison laugh because whenever the instructor wasn't looking she'd stop with her hands on her hips for a breather.

Just before Christmas, Christina had invited Alison out for a drink with her and some of the others from the class and Alison had accepted gladly. Even then, before she had found out about Marc's latest affair, Alison had been able to sense the barely tangible build-up of tension at home. At the time she put it down to the approach of Christmas, which always wound her daughters up, Dominic's erratic behaviour and the fact that Marc was under so much pressure at work. The period of calm and contentment that Marc went through when he first met another woman must have passed by then because he was becomingly increasing terse and short-tempered with her. How Alison hadn't guessed what was really going on she didn't know. Perhaps she just hadn't wanted to know. On the evening she went to meet Christina, though, she felt that she needed a drink.

Everyone else had already arrived when Alison got there,

over an hour late and flustered because Marc had not got back from the office when he said he would and she'd had to wait, sitting on the bottom step in her make-up and going-out shoes, watching the clock until his key finally turned in the latch.

Christina had not been sitting with the other women from the class but was at the bar, deep in conversation with a blonde woman that Alison didn't recognise. Pretty, with waist-length poker-straight hair, she was laughing with Christina about something.

'Alison!' Christina said finally, catching her eye as she hovered on the periphery of the occasion. 'Come here. Come and meet my friend Sophie. She's turned up this evening completely unannounced on a whirlwind visit back to London from her new life in the country, didn't you, Soph?'

'Well, I was going to stay in and be a good daughter but then my mum started getting her dogs to sing in harmony to the *EastEnders* theme tune and I thought a quick drink out couldn't hurt.'

Alison laughed. 'Hi, I'm Alison James.'

'Sophie Mills,' the woman had smiled at her. Alison guessed they were probably about the same age but Sophie looked, not younger than her exactly, but lighter, as if her life hardly weighed her down at all.

'A new life in the country sounds exciting,' Alison had observed politely.

'Exciting! That's an understatement,' Christina jumped in as her friend rolled her eyes. 'Listen to this. One minute Sophie here was über careerwoman, living for her job and nailing a massive promotion, and then out of the blue guess what happened.'

'Um,' Alison said. 'Redundancy?'

'No, she got custody of her dead best friend's children. Two little girls, six and three, isn't it, Soph?'

'Oh!' Alison gasped, thinking immediately of her own daughters. 'Poor little things.'

Sophie nodded. 'It was a difficult time. It's still hard for them to get used to. They miss her.'

'And Sophie dropped everything to look after them,' Christina said.

'Well, it wasn't that big a deal . . .' Sophie said. 'Anyone would have done the same.'

'Of course it was a big deal. It was massive,' Christina insisted. 'You'd only ever looked after your cat before those children came along. Anyway, it all kicked off, the kids' dad came back, Sophie got offered this promotion at work and then the dad moved back down to Cornwall with the children and we all thought that normal service had resumed. Sophie the ice queen was back. But guess what happened then.'

'Christina,' Sophie crossed her arms and raised a brow, 'Alison doesn't want to know all about my life.'

'Oh, give me a break, Sophie, of course she does. I never get bored of telling people this story. Maybe one day I'll meet the love of my life and all I'll be able to talk about will be me, me, me, but right now you are far more interesting.'

'What happened?' Alison had asked Sophie directly, laughing. 'I have to know now!'

'Well, I missed the children. I'd got to know them and I fell in love with them, I guess. I missed them – it took me by surprise how much. But then a good friend told me that if I was so unhappy without them it was simple enough to put right. I should go and move closer to them. So I did!'

'I think you're missing out something quite crucial,' Christina observed, raising a brow.

'No I haven't,' Sophie said, an air of challenge in her voice. 'I've pretty much talked about myself all night. Let's talk about *you* now, Christina.'

'What's she missing out is that it wasn't only those darling little girls she fell in love with,' Christina told Alison, despite Sophie's warning frown. 'It was their dad. The tall, dark and handsome Louis. He turned up after being away for years, and as he bonded with his children he and Sophie fell for each other.' Christina sighed theatrically and fluttered her lashes. 'The only man ever to melt the ice queen here. Many have tried and failed, but it was Louis that Sophie fell for, and it wasn't just those girls she moved for, it was Louis too.'

'That's a big step to make,' Alison had said, not sure if she was impressed or terrified by the impetuous decision Sophie had taken.

'I'm not exactly the world's most impulsive person,' Sophie told her. 'I like to plan for everything, but then sometimes you realise that you just have to do what is going to make you happy, even if on paper it seems completely crazy.' She smiled a small, but joy-filled smile. 'So far it's working out pretty well.'

'And now you're a family?' Alison questioned her.

'Well, I'm not officially living with them or him. I'm not even officially his girlfriend as such. I live in a B & B down the road and we've been dating for a while now and . . . it's nice.'

'You left everything you had and moved hundreds of miles to *date* a man?' Alison asked her.

'And to be in Bella and Izzy's lives too,' Sophie said happily. 'But yes, partly to date their dad. I know, I'm insane!'

'Not insane,' Christina said. 'I think you've got balls. I think you're the bravest woman I know, which is ironic because you used to be such an uptight old cow.'

'I just can't imagine my life without those children now,' Sophie said with a shrug. 'No matter what works out between me and Louis I'll always be there for them.'

'Oh, stop being coy,' Christina told her. 'You so totally love him.'

'I'm sorry, are you twelve?' Sophie had asked her with an arched brow. 'Only I thought I was friends with a grown woman. I could have got better conversation out of my mother's Labradoodle.'

'Hey,' Christina said, deciding it was time to change the subject, 'whatever happened to that handsome American you used to know? Is he still on the market?'

But Alison had not been listening after that. All she had been able to think about for the rest of the evening and on her way home was the idea of a woman more or less her age just leaving it all behind to do what she wanted, to follow her heart. Taking that risk simply on the off chance it would result in happiness.

Now, as the noise from downstairs gradually began to ebb and fade away, Alison realised something. She had never thought it would be possible for her to be happy without Marc in her life. The key to happiness, she was sure, lay in finding the way to make their life together work once and for all, as she wanted it, with him at her side, no other women in his bed, and the children happy and secure in their family.

Only now, only after the party tonight and Cathy coming back into her life and taking her back to the point when she'd made her own reckless choice, could Alison start to glimpse that that resolution might not be possible. Only now did she begin to see that she might never be happy as long as she was married to Marc James.

Chapter Twelve

Jimmy looked out from between the drawn living-room curtains at the cold misty early morning and he wondered what exactly had changed last night. The street outside looked the same as it always did, except the pavements were gilded in dew and shimmered under the threat of the rising sun. The trees stood like sentinels along both sides of the road, standing guard over the same row of cars parked nose to tail, in exactly the same order as they always were. Other people still asleep in their houses, still – as far as Jimmy knew – living their lives exactly as they had yesterday.

Yet in the space of one night everything had changed for him completely, he just couldn't quite put his finger yet on how. He knew only that for some reason he felt as if this dirty February dawn, so far removed from any promise of spring, was a new start for him. Apart from anything else this had been the first night he had spent in his home for two years. Yes, it had been almost exactly two years since Catherine, ignited like a solar flare, had thrown his second-best acoustic guitar out of an upstairs window. She had thought it was his favourite one, and he'd never told her otherwise.

His wife had not spoken to him once on the way home from the party. He'd walked a step or two behind her, weighed down by Eloise, who was actually much heavier than she looked, as Catherine marched on, carrying Leila like she was bag of feathers. Jimmy decided he wouldn't even attempt any conversation. He couldn't imagine what she was thinking or feeling, and he had no idea how to approach her, or if he even should. It wasn't just Alison and that Marc showing up that had rattled her so; he'd pissed her off too. He'd shared her confidences without seeking her permission, which Jimmy thought on reflection, knowing Catherine as he supposedly did, possibly wasn't the best idea he'd had.

But that's what happens, he'd thought a tad sullenly, as he trudged along behind Catherine, when you plan to go to a party, have a few beers, a laugh with your wife and kids, and end up dealing with your ex's major personal crisis instead. He was unprepared for mediating between his wife and her evil archnemesis, not to mention that twat of a git who quite clearly still had the hots for her, judging by the way he was leering at her. He didn't have time to think things through, he had to go on his instinct, follow his gut. Unfortunately for Jimmy, to this day he couldn't think of one decision based on his gut feeling that had worked out well for him or anyone.

Even if he hadn't pissed Catherine off he wouldn't exactly know where he stood in this new situation in her life. The last year between them had been mostly good. It was almost like the first phases of a new relationship, treading so carefully around each other, so keen not to give the wrong impression or to scare the other one off as they tried to adjust to each other as something other than lovers and to establish a new kind of intimacy. He'd thought they'd created an even keel now, found a place where they could be together without either feeling the pressure or absence of love so keenly. It had been a difficult journey, much harder for him than he would ever admit to Catherine, but even so, who was he to her now?

Was he her friend? Was he someone she could really talk to? Perhaps about the children or work or the PTA, but not about this; he didn't think she'd talk to him about this.

When they had finally got home, Jimmy had followed Catherine up the narrow stairs and helped her to get the girls undressed and into their beds. Her voice was low and calm as she murmured to the half-asleep children, buttoned their pyjamas, and tucked them in, and as he watched, Jimmy thought how nice it must be to feel as safe and as warm as his two girls must have felt just then.

After kissing his girls good night he'd walked downstairs and found Catherine standing in the living room, her long arms wrapped around her slender body, her head bowed as she stood in front of the cold grate.

'Will you make a fire?' she asked him before he could excuse himself. 'We never have a real fire any more. I can never get it to light. And I feel cold, I feel cold in my bones.'

Jimmy hesitated. So he wasn't leaving right away and she was talking to him.

'Sure,' he said, attempting to mask his surprise at her request.

'I'll make tea,' Catherine told him, lifting her head as he walked through to the kitchen and the back door. 'Or would you prefer something else?'

'Tea, thanks,' Jimmy said, pausing by the back door. 'Look, just so I'm clear here, you want me to stick around for a bit, yeah?'

Catherine went into the kitchen and picked up the kettle.

'Would you?' she asked him. 'I'd like it if you'd stay.'

And the feeling that Jimmy had got in the pit of his stomach, as he headed out into the freezing midnight air to fetch some logs from the shed, frightened him to death.

*

Once the fire was lit Catherine sat on the rug in front of it, chin resting on her knees as she hugged her mug of tea, watching the flames.

Jimmy sat in the armchair, holding his own drink. He wondered what to say to her. He wondered if he could take his cowboy boots off because his toes were cramping and the hole in the bottom on the right one meant his foot was soggy and chilled. He didn't know what the protocol was. Could you take your shoes off in front of your ex-wife if you knew that you had odd socks on and one of them would be damp and possibly a bit musty?

The two of them sat like that for a long time and then finally Jimmy pulled off first one boot and then the other.

Catherine looked at him.

'My feet hurt,' he explained. 'It's the pointy toes.'

She nodded and stared at the fire again.

'Look,' Jimmy said after a while, because it somehow felt that Catherine was waiting for him to talk. 'OK, she's back, he's back, it's weird because they were so important in the early part of your life, but, well, it doesn't really matter any more, does it? You came through all of that business with your parents and the . . . you know. And you made yourself into an amazing woman, a great mother. So, yes, they are here and it's weird, but once you've got over the weirdness, do you really care?'

Catherine thought for a moment. 'When I saw him my heart just lurched,' she said. 'It was just like I was seventeen again, going to meet him in the park. He doesn't look the same, he's older and fatter and he's got a lot less hair, but it was still him. Still that face I've been waiting to see for all of these years.'

Jimmy sat up a little in his chair, trying to hide just how much her words had winded him. The pain surprised him, but he smothered it quickly.

'Well, yeah – because it was a shock. It'd be like me bumping into Alice Cooper in Tesco – not that I used to be in love with him or anything, well, not in that way – but anyway, what I'm saying is that just because you felt that way when you saw him it doesn't mean that you still have feelings for him . . . does it?'

'I don't know,' Catherine said. It was not the answer that Jimmy had discovered he'd been hoping for. His gut clenched and his heart contracted. This was hurting him. Catherine was causing him pain and she had no idea.

'Right,' he said, concentrating on sounding neutral. You're supposed to be here for her, he reminded himself sternly, helping her to get things into perspective. This was not the time to open the old wounds that had caused the end of his marriage, wounds it had taken almost two years to heal. But Jimmy couldn't help the uneasy churning of his stomach that he felt when Catherine talked that way about Marc. He felt sick with jealousy, because he knew Catherine had never felt about him the way she once had – maybe even still did – about Marc.

'Obviously I'm not in love with him – I mean, I'm not insane,' Catherine said, perhaps reading some expression on Jimmy's face that even he wasn't sure of. 'It's just that I saw him and even all these years later I felt like that girl I was. I felt drawn to him. I suppose I remembered all these powerful feelings and what it was like to love him. What it was like to love like that, so deeply and so much.'

'Heavy shit,' Jimmy said idiotically, to cover the sting her words unwittingly inflicted on him. In all the years they had been married she had never once talked about him that way. She'd known this Marc for barely two months and she still remembered exactly how it felt to be with him. Jimmy dragged himself back to Catherine, trying hard to regain

187

control of the situation, to keep the atmosphere light and easy between them. 'But I mean, you wouldn't crack on to him now, because he's, like, married. Plus, I think we've established that he's a heartless wanker, right?'

Catherine smiled. 'He can't be that bad. He stayed with Alison when she was pregnant, and they are still together but even so, I wouldn't crack on to him now, no,' she said with less conviction than her words suggested. 'I'm just saying that's how I felt when I saw him, all jangled up.'

'Good. I mean, good for you, not about being jangled up, good about not cracking on to him because I don't think that would help anything . . .' Jimmy stalled. 'Just ignore him, I reckon. Like, when you see someone you've slept with and don't really like any more, the best thing to do is to ignore them.'

'Oh, Jimmy, you are such a kid,' Catherine laughed.

'I'm not a kid, Cat,' he replied. 'I am a man, this is what men do. And if you doubt me then wait and see. I bet you Marc, or whatever his name is, ignores you from now on. I bet he acts like he never knew you.'

'I hope so,' Catherine said, returning her gaze to the fire with a wistful tone that belied her words.

'And what about her? What do you feel about her?' he asked, referring to Alison.

Catherine set down her tea cup.

'The morning after they'd left Alison's mum came round to our house. Banging on the door at seven in the morning. She'd gone to take Alison her tea in bed and found her daughter had gone. All she'd left was a note: "Mum, I've run away with the man I love. We have to be together. Love, Alison." Alison's mum was clutching it when she came round. They all thought I would know where she had gone. My mum dragged me down the stairs to see them but I could see she was pleased that Alison's parents were going through this. It was proof of what kind of daughter they had. What sort of parents they were. My mum was enjoying it.

'I told them I didn't know where they'd gone. I could see that Mum was itching to slap me around the face. She told me now was not the time to be protecting my friend. I said, I'm not protecting her, I hate her. That shut them all up.

'"What do you mean you hate her?" Alison's mum asked me.

'So I told them: because she stole my boyfriend from me, I said. She took the one good, one happy thing I had in my life and she's run away with him. I don't know where. Mum hit me then. I told them his name and where he worked, where he had been staying. And I waited for Alison's parents to go because I knew that the moment they had, my mum would really wallop me. I would have just taken it normally, wouldn't have said a word, never did. But now there was the baby. I was worried about the baby, so I begged her to stop hitting me. I told her I was pregnant.

'She stopped in mid-strike, her fist raised. I closed my eyes, because I expected her to really lay into me but she didn't. She just stood there, staring at me. She shut the door and went downstairs. It was this thing that Mum used to do if she was really angry with me. She wouldn't punish me then and there, get it over with. She'd go all quiet and go away, just to let me know that she was thinking about how to really hurt me. Just to let me know that when the punishment came it would be especially bad.

'What I should have done then was what Alison did. I should have climbed out of my bedroom window and never come back. I was seventeen, nearly a grown woman. If I'd had the guts I would have gone out of that window. But I didn't. I just lay on the bed waiting for her to come back. I was scared.

189

I had no idea where to go or how to look after myself on my own and pregnant. And the one person I could have trusted, the one person I could have relied on had gone. Not Marc – I knew from the minute I had him that I was going to lose him – but Alison.

'It was dark by the time Mum opened the door again. "You do nothing but bring shame and disgrace on this family," she said, her voice was cold as ice. "Fortunately now I've uncovered your lie nobody needs to know. We'll sort this out between ourselves. Get rid of it and get back to life as normal."

' "Can I keep it?" I asked her. I remember my voice sounded like a child's in the darkness. "I want to keep it."

' "Don't be so ridiculous," she said, and that was it: the decision was made.

'I should have fought it, fought for myself and the baby, but I didn't. I let everything happen around me and all I could think about was how much I hated Alison. I felt like she'd run away with my life, almost as if she'd run away with my baby. She had everything. She had Marc, her baby, she had her freedom. I didn't even have the guts to fight them, Jim. I didn't even have the guts to protect my baby. I didn't know how to. I lay there in the dark and I hated Alison, I hated her with every single cell in my body.

'In the clinic, with my parents sitting either side of me like prison guards while I gave the doctor my consent to abort, I hated her, because it was her fault that I was there alone with no one to stand up for me. And when the baby had gone, and when I felt so empty and used up and lost, I hated her more than anything.

'It was like an energy, like a power source. It was hating her that finally got me away from home. I was hating Alison that night I slapped my mother back, whacked her hard around the face so that her head snapped round on her neck like a whip.

That was the night I told her about you. I hated Alison when I walked out of home to live with you and told them I was never coming back. Even on the day that Eloise was born, even at the moment they put my baby in my arms and I was so full of joy and love, I hated Alison . . .

'And then I saw her yesterday out of the blue after all these years and I . . .' Catherine trailed off, gazing into the fire.

'What?' Jimmy asked.

'I missed her,' Catherine said, perplexed. 'I looked at her and the first thing I wanted to say was, "Oh, hello, it's you. I've missed you."'

'And then the hate came back?' Jimmy asked her.

'No,' Catherine frowned. 'Just sadness, a lot of sadness. And some bitterness and anger, but not hate. I didn't hate her.'

'What does that mean?' Jimmy asked her, leaning forward in his seat.

'I don't know,' Catherine said. 'All I know is that she's here now and I don't think they are going anywhere. How I'll cope with it I don't know. I don't know anything, Jimmy. I'm a mess. You'd think that in all of these years I'd have grown up, got stronger. I'm a mother now, and a wife . . . I've been a wife. I've had a life since they left. A whole huge, massive, wonderful, painful, important life. But I'm still that silly little girl, I'm still that child who couldn't do a thing to stop her parents from aborting her baby.'

Jimmy had got up from the chair and down onto the rug, kneeling next to his wife before he realised what he was doing. The moment he put an arm around Catherine he felt certain she would bat it away. But she didn't. Instead he felt her body relax and mould into his.

'You are the strongest person I know,' he told her. 'Courageous, brave, fierce, loyal. You grew up with a woman

191

who beat you, who hated you, and yet look at you. You are a wonderful mother to two girls. To be able to be the parent that you are after having grown up like that makes you incredible. What happened when you were seventeen wasn't your fault, Catherine. You can't go back in the past and change the person you used to be. It's the person you used to be that's made you how you are now. You were a child, with evil fuckers for parents and no one in the world to turn to. I just wish . . . I just wish . . .'

'What?' Catherine tipped her face to look up at him.

'I wished I'd found you earlier,' Jimmy told her, dropping his gaze from hers. 'Before Marc did, before Alison left, before your mum could do what she did to you. I would have protected you. I'd have battered that old bag.'

Catherine smiled, her head dropping onto Jimmy's shoulder, causing him to hold his breath in case the slightest movement from him would make her move away.

'I can't imagine you battering anyone,' she said.

'Only because I've never had to batter anyone yet,' Jimmy told her. 'But I will if the need comes. I'm like a tightly coiled spring. Ready for action at any minute.'

Catherine moved and sat up away from him, brushing her hair behind her ear.

'Jimmy, I've known you a long time now; you've never once been tightly coiled in your life.'

'How long is it?' Jimmy asked her, even though he knew exactly. 'Not counting all those years we were at school together. It must be almost twelve years. I remember the first time I saw you. The first time I really noticed you, that is. You were at that party where the band were playing, some bird's twenty-first. We were on a break and I was at the bar getting a drink. You were standing at one end of it looking a bit lost, dressed all in black like you'd come to a funeral. I remember

192

thinking to myself, that chick is *tall*.' Catherine laughed and rolled her eyes. 'You were looking like you'd rather be anywhere else but there, and then the girl whose party it was – what was her name? – Denise something, came over and hugged you and she said something to you that made you laugh. And you lit up, Cat, sort of from the inside out, like a lantern. I wanted to get to know you then. You didn't make it easy.'

'Because the whole of the town was queuing up to go out with you, I couldn't think why you'd want me,' Catherine said.

'I wanted to be the one to make you laugh,' Jimmy said. 'I wanted to be the one who lit you up every day. I blew that. I blew it big time.'

He'd blown it because he'd cheated on Catherine exactly like Marc had, Jimmy thought bitterly to himself. He'd behaved no better than the other man. In fact, his act of betrayal was far worse than Marc's because Marc never loved Catherine and Jimmy did. He'd hurt her because he loved her, and what kind of coward does that?

'No, you didn't blow it,' Catherine said. 'I mean, you did, but it wasn't just you. It was me too . . .' She sat up, pushing her fingers through her hair, shaking it from her shoulders as if she were trying to wake herself up from a dream. 'Look, Jimmy, let's not rake all this over now. Not now when we are friends at last, OK? Let's just agree that we both did things wrong. That we're better suited to being friends than husband and wife. Now that Alison and Marc are here, well, I don't know what's going to happen but I know I'm going to need you to be my friend. And I don't want us to run the risk of falling out again.'

'That's not what I was trying to do,' Jimmy said awkwardly. 'All I was trying to do was to . . . I don't know actually; make you see that you have changed, you're not the same kid you were at seventeen. You might feel like it tonight, but it's temporary, I swear.'

'Look, will you stay here tonight?' Catherine asked him. Jimmy felt his chest tighten. 'The sofa's quite comfy.'

'Yeah? I mean yeah, course. If you like.'

'I would,' Catherine said. 'Do you want some more tea?'

'Second thoughts, got any whisky?' Jimmy had asked her and they'd found the bottle that had been in the understairs cupboard for two years since Catherine won it on a tombola at the school fair.

Catherine had had perhaps two or three sips from her glass before she had fallen asleep upright on the sofa. Gently, Jimmy had taken the glass from her hand and then with infinite care had lifted her legs up onto the sofa and eased her shoulders down, placing a cushion beneath her head and drawing her crocheted throw over her. That had been about four hours ago and she still lay there now, her hair trailing over her face, one hand clenched around the corner of the cushion as if it were the last straw.

Jimmy had tried to sleep in the chair, but sleep had not come. Every time he closed his eyes, fireworks went off behind his lids, his brain hummed and his body ached. At some point during the course of this day something had changed inside him because, whenever he looked over at Catherine sleeping on the sofa, he felt as if his whole body had been cleaved in half by the sight of her.

And then as the morning sun rose in the sky and burned the mist away, the realisation that had been nudging at his thoughts all night suddenly dawned. Nothing had changed, nothing was different. For the last twelve years he had always felt like this, only recently he'd managed to tell himself that he didn't. But now when she needed him that pretence had fallen away like a sandcastle disintegrating under the incoming tide.

194

Jimmy still loved Catherine; he felt as if he always had.

He bit his lip and rested his head against the back of the chair. As he closed his eyes, he felt a stray tear trickle down his cheek and into the corner of his mouth, and he tasted the salt on his tongue.

The fact that he loved his wife was not in question.

Whether or not he'd have the guts to try to do anything about it was another story entirely.

Chapter Thirteen

Alison opened her eyes and waited for the second or two it took for her to remember her life. She had been dreaming about being with Cathy. Not about any event in particular, but just about her and Cathy when they were around Gemma's age, running along the canal towpath in the sunlight, the heat of the sun on their shoulders as Alison chased after Cathy, whose hair was made amber by the sunshine. That was all; nothing else had happened in the dream except that Alison had felt light inside, she had felt free like she thought Christina's friend Sophie had looked that night in that bar in London.

Now that her eyes were open and she had reabsorbed her daily life back into her bones, she felt the weight of reality sinking into her skin. She truly had seen Cathy last night; she hadn't dreamed that.

Marc was not in bed next to her. She rolled over and looked at his side of the bed. The pillow was plumped and smooth, the duvet unruffled. He had not come to bed at all. Briefly Alison wondered if he had followed Cathy home and was with her right now and some ember of jealousy flickered in her throat, but she swallowed it down.

Pushing herself up onto her elbows, Alison made herself get out of bed. Her legs were heavy, her arms ached and she felt as if her brain was somehow insulated by one or two layers from reality. Everything seemed just a little bit further away than it normally did.

It couldn't be a hangover, she told herself. Yes, she had drunk quite a bit of champagne very quickly, but not *that* much. If she was hungover from anything it was not alcohol, it was her life and its culmination the previous night. The choices she had made that had somehow brought her life to this point had finally caught up with her. There was nowhere to hide any more.

In the bathroom Alison dunked her face in a bowlful of cold water once or twice and then rubbed some more on her neck and between her breasts with a sponge, feeling the cold water trickle down over her belly. Roughly rubbing herself dry, she took a deep breath and looked in the mirror. Her reflection looked tired, dark shadows under her eyes, her skin thin and frail. The trouble, Alison thought, was that when she never saw Cathy, it was easy not to think about her or about the kind of person that she herself had been. It was easy not to have to face up to that selfish spoiled little brat, the thoughtless girl that would wreck half a dozen lives just to get what she wanted.

But now Alison had seen Cathy face to face it was inevitable: she had to acknowledge the truth.

This person, the woman looking back out of the mirror at her was the very same girl who had abandoned Cathy, alone and in the hands of her parents. Of course Alison hadn't known that Cathy was pregnant. But in the cold light of day, as she looked at her reflection in the mirror, she knew that even if Cathy had told her she would have left anyway. She would have done anything to be with the man she loved.

Tired of looking at her tired self, Alison padded barefoot out of the bathroom and went to check on her children.

Dominic was sprawled face down diagonally across his bed, one arm flung over his guitar, his iPod still plugged into his ears. He looked fifteen again and nothing like the enraged and passionate young man that had visited her in her bedroom last night. Alison tiptoed carefully through the detritus of his teenage life smeared across the floor and gently pulled the earplug from his right ear. When she realised she couldn't reach the left one she carefully located the iPod and switched it off.

Dominic mumbled something, brushing one hand outward in a spasm as if he were attempting to swot a fly, before settling back into sleep, and then he didn't even look fifteen any more but five, his face relaxing into that little boy that had once been her guide and beacon. Alison looked at those dark lashes and that soft mouth that used to tremble whenever he was sad, frightened and furious, and, unable to resist, bent and kissed him lightly on the head.

He wanted her to leave Marc, to strike out on her own. But he was young and angry and full of fire. For the first time, last night Alison tried to think of a life without her husband and found she couldn't imagine it. Perhaps she had created Marc, but he had made her too. He'd made her a mother and a wife, a woman who lived for her family or at least who told herself she did. But did she?

Alison dragged Dominic's duvet cover over both boy and guitar and crept back out of the room to check on her daughters.

Gemma was arranged as neatly as always, the back of one hand resting demurely against her cheek, the other tucked neatly under the cover, like a true sleeping princess. She always looked so ordered and so tidy. For the first time Alison wondered if that was right, if it was natural for an eight-year-old always to be in such control of herself, even in sleep.

Amy, on the other hand, looked as if she had wrestled a crocodile in her dreams, which wasn't past the realms of possibility, Alison thought, as she looked at her youngest child, one leg hanging out of bed, soft vulnerable toes touching the floor, her quilt flung to one end of the bed, her head twisted awkwardly to one side and her pillow on the floor. Although Amy had slept through the night since the age of two she seldom seemed to have a peaceful sleep, except for those rare occasions when she shared a room with Gemma on holiday or when she was allowed to creep in bed with her mum, which was only ever when Marc was away.

Alison crept over to the bed and, kneeling, tenderly lifted Amy's leg back onto the mattress and covered her with the duvet again. She might have been imagining it but she thought she saw her daughter's face relax as she became dimly aware that she was not alone any more.

Perhaps Dominic was right, perhaps she had been so busy creating and recreating this perfect family life for her children that she didn't noticed how the stress and tension between her and Marc was affecting them. Gemma was so easy – that's how Alison always described her middle child. She assumed that Gemma's confidence was due to happiness but perhaps it was like armour, hiding away her anxieties. Maybe her eight-year-old was trying to protect her. And Amy's fears weren't nameless or imaginary, not if she sensed that the fairy-tale castle her parents had built for her to live in might crumble away to nothing. If that was true then no wonder she only ever relaxed when the whole family was in one room.

Alison sat on the pink wicker chair opposite Amy's bed and put her face in her hands.

Her life had come full circle back here to her home town. It was ironic that she had had to walk back into her past to finally face her future. The trick was going to be trying to

199

work out exactly how to face it, how to face Cathy and Jimmy, and especially her husband. How to make sense of the accidental life she had forced herself into, and of the accidental wife she had become.

It was impossible to shake the feeling that she was not meant for this life, that she was the interloper, the impostor. And for the sake of the children, herself and even Marc, she had to try finally to make some sense of that, make sense of the person she had become since the day she ran away from Cathy.

The house smelled of stale alcohol and egg and cress sandwiches, some of which were trodden into the stair carpet or ground into the hall tiles. Abandoned glasses were everywhere, filled with various liquids to varying degrees, giving Alison the almost irresistible urge to pick up her son's drumsticks and play them.

Marc was not in the kitchen, or any of the downstairs rooms, and from the look of things he hadn't even slept on the sofa.

Alison walked gingerly over broken crisps to the french windows.

The sun was almost up, burning mist off the lawn, which spiralled up into the air like magician's smoke. Marc was in the garden, huddled up in his wool coat, sitting on the white wrought-iron garden furniture he had bought in a job lot from the show home on the development. He had his back to the house and was looking at hills that swelled and rolled across the valley, lush green and gold in the early morning, the horizon garlanded with trees. Above the mist, the sky looked bright blue and clear. Alison thought that this might be the first sunny day of the year.

The grass was wet and cold under her bare feet, slick with

dew, but she didn't go in to find shoes or slippers, sensing that if she turned back she might not return, and this moment, this clear new day, might be lost in the routine of their lives again.

As she approached Marc, he looked up and smiled at her.

'Good morning, beautiful,' he said. 'You really should have something on your feet. It's a bit nippy out here. Thought I'd take the morning air and survey my kingdom. Have a bit of a think.'

Alison sat down on one of the wrought-iron chairs. Drawing her feet up onto its seat and tucking her knees beneath her chin, she felt the cold of the dew seep through her nightdress.

They smiled at each other for a moment, like two old cohorts who were finally realising the game was up.

'Well, I certainly didn't picture this when we came back,' Marc said. 'I just didn't think Cathy Parkin would still be here. That was a turn-up, wasn't it?'

'Didn't you?' Alison asked him. He looked at her. His nose and cheeks were red from the chill and his eyes looked puffy and sore. Briefly Alison wondered if Marc had been crying, but in all the years she had been with him she'd never seen him shed a tear.

'I didn't plan it,' Marc said. 'I swear to you.'

'I'm sorry I slapped you,' Alison said, hugging her knees, the thin cotton of her nightgown proving inefficient at protecting her from the ice in the air.

'I deserved it,' Marc said.

'Maybe fifteen years ago you did. I mean, of course you were sleeping with her,' Alison said. 'I don't know why I hadn't worked that out years ago. I don't even think that was why I slapped you. Or the fact that you'd got her pregnant too. It was seeing her there in front of me. I saw her and I

201

missed her, and blamed you. So I slapped you. And I shouldn't have. It must have been very embarrassing.'

'I carried it off, though,' Marc said. 'And anyway, I understand, because I felt the same way.'

'Embarrassed?' Alison asked him, tucking the hem of her nightgown under her toes.

'No, when I saw her, I missed her. Missed the way she used to make me feel back then . . . missed who I was when I was with her.'

They sat in silence and Alison tried to work out if the burning she felt in her chest was caused by hurt or relief. Because although Marc's comments were painful, at least he was being honest with her.

'What would you have done,' Alison asked him, 'if you'd known she was pregnant too? Would you have stood by her as well? That would have given the town something to talk about. Man fathers two children born within a week of each other.'

Marc's laugh surprised Alison. Mirthless and sharp as it was, it seemed inappropriate.

'I knew she was pregnant,' he explained. 'I think I knew long before she did. I was waiting for her to tell me that we couldn't go to bed because her period had come. I waited for three weeks, four weeks, five weeks and the subject never came up. I knew we couldn't carry on for ever then. I knew there would be a crunch and I wanted to leave before it arrived. '

'You knew she was pregnant and you still chose me?' Alison asked him. Once she would have left it at that, let herself believe that that one action fifteen years ago stood as a testament to how much she had meant to Marc, but not today. Because for once in his life he was being honest and she needed to know the truth, so she asked him another question. 'Why?'

Marc didn't answer for a moment, as he looked out towards the horizon. Then, taking a breath, he began to talk.

'You told Catherine about us. I knew you would sooner or later,' he said. 'I'd been expecting it since that first afternoon. It must have been a schoolday because Catherine turned up at the bedsit in her uniform. I'll never forget it, seeing her there in her blue checked kilt and school sweater. She was crying. She asked me if it was true that I'd been sleeping with you and I said that it was. And she asked me if that meant me and her were over. I was shocked, upset for her even if I didn't show it. She should have told me it was over, not asked me. She should have been stronger than she was. But she wasn't strong, I knew that when I got involved with her. I warned her. So I told her that it was; it was over.

'I braced myself, waiting for her to tell me she was pregnant, but she didn't. She must have known by then but she didn't mention it. She just turned on her heel and walked away.' Marc looked up at the clear sky. 'It was pouring with rain.'

'She was coming to see me,' Alison said, more to herself than to Marc. 'She tried to tell me about the baby. But I wouldn't let her.'

'I went to the pub that night, my first night off in ages. I wanted to get bladdered, really out of it. I didn't want to think about anything. The work in Farmington was coming to an end; I heard there was some work coming up near Croyden. Not that far away, but on that night it seemed like a welcome refuge. And then suddenly you appeared. I don't know how you found me . . .'

'I looked in every single pub.'

'Well, you found me. You walked in and all the blokes looked at you, your hair all wet, your top soaked through. All that eyeliner you used to wear running down your cheeks. I saw you and my heart sank. I thought, here we go again. Ding,

ding, round two. But I was ready to take whatever you wanted to dish out. I thought I deserved it.'

'I asked you to go outside with me,' Alison remembered. 'Told you I needed to talk to you. I had no idea what I was going to do if you didn't come, but you did come.'

'We stood outside in the rain,' Marc went on. 'I had both my hands in my pockets and I was staring at my work boots. I couldn't look at you, because you were the one thing I hadn't been able to resist, like a bloody greedy kid in a sweet shop. You were the one thing that made me mess up again.'

'I said, I'm running away from home. I've done it already. I'm going anyway, whatever. But I want you to come with me. Will you come with me? And I felt like screaming because I was so frightened,' Alison recalled.

'I just kept on staring at my boots, I heard you talking but the words weren't going in. And then you said, I want to be with you more than anything, I have to be with you and you have to be with me because I know that we are meant to be together. Come with me and I'll be your family. I'll stand by you, I'll help you. I'll look after you. That's what you said: I'll look after you.'

The two sat in silence for a moment, each separately remembering the same event.

'I could see that you were shaking from nerves,' Marc said, 'and the cold probably, I don't know, but I just stood there with my hands in my pockets looking at my boots and . . .'

'. . . thinking.' Alison completed the sentence for him. 'Deciding whether or not to come or go back in the pub and finish your pint. I remember. I couldn't even believe that you were thinking about it. I mean, I knew that you wanted me, I knew we had this physical thing but, even as naïve as I was, I didn't think you'd run away with me, not really. I think, even if I didn't admit it, it was really just some grand crazy gesture.

Something I had to prove to myself. I think if you'd gone back in for the pint, like I thought you were going to, I'd have gone back home and gone to bed and my mum would never have known I'd run away at all.'

'But you said you'd look after me,' Marc said. 'And I knew that there was no way a seventeen-year-old girl would be able to look after *me*, but nobody had ever said that to me before. Not anyone. I didn't realise how much I wanted to hear it.'

'And is that why?' Alison prompted him. 'Is that why you came with me?'

Marc shook his head, taking a deep breath.

'It was one reason, but there was another one. A stronger one.' He looked Alison in the eyes. 'I was in love with Cathy, Alison. Back then at that very moment, standing outside of the pub in the rain, when you asked me to run away with you like I was some kid in a play and not a twenty-year-old railway labourer, I was in love with Catherine. I loved her, but I couldn't be a better person for her. I couldn't make myself be good enough to deserve her. She was the first person I had ever loved and even though I knew how important and how special that was I still went to bed with you, and I kept on going to bed with you because I couldn't stop. Because for most of my life I'd had nothing. When I got the chance to have everything I took it. But I loved *her*. If I hadn't have met you then she would have been enough. She would have been enough until I met the next girl I couldn't keep my hands off. I loved her, and I knew she was having my baby and I knew I couldn't be there for her or her kid. I knew I'd mess it up sooner or later. And there you were, standing in the rain, shivering, asking me to run away with you, telling me you'd take care of me. And that meant a lot to me. I didn't love you, but I knew you loved me. I needed to be loved, I needed to *change*. So I took my hands out my pockets and put my arms around you and held

205

you until you stopped shivering and I said, "OK then." I said, "OK, come on, let's go."

'I didn't run away with you, Al. I ran away from her.'

Alison, still with her chin on her knees, rubbed her toes.

'So when I told you about my baby, why didn't you leave me then?' she asked.

Marc stood up and shrugged his coat off. Underneath it he was still wearing the shirt and trousers he'd worn to the party. He draped the coat around Alison's shoulders and she gathered the edges close over her.

'You had the most balls of anyone I'd ever seen,' Marc told her. 'Fronting it out in that shitty flea-ridden hostel when I knew you wanted to go home about a million times a day. You stuck it out, you didn't cave in. The longer you did that, the more I respected you. The more I believed you meant what you said. And then you told me. You said, "Well, I'm having a baby, so there. You know about it now. I'm keeping it, it's up to you what you do – stay or go, I don't care."'

'I was scared shitless,' Alison said. 'I wanted my mum, I wanted Cathy.'

'I know,' Marc told her. 'I looked at you, seventeen, run away from home with some bloke you hardly knew and bollocks all clue about how to look after yourself, let alone my baby in your belly, and I knew I couldn't leave you. You needed me, and I liked you needing me. I started to need you. Looking after you made me get things done. Made me look for regular work and a decent place to live. Why I couldn't do that for the girl I loved I don't know, but I could do it for you. You made it easy.'

'But you say you love me now,' Alison said. 'You are always saying that you love me. Is that a lie too?'

'Dominic was born and we got the flat, I got the job in the garage. Your dad came round a few times and threatened to kill me. Those first couple of years seemed like a blur and I didn't have time to think about Catherine, I didn't have time to think about what had happened to her and the baby. Before I knew it Dominic was four and I'd got the promotion at the garage, remember?'

Alison smiled. 'Yes, they said they'd put you on sales because all the ladies loved you.'

'And we'd taken that flat. The two-bed on Seven Sisters Road. I came home from work and you were sitting on the living-room floor with Dominic, playing with Lego or something. You had the window open, and it was a sunny evening. It sort of lit up the back of your hair like a halo. I looked at you and my son sitting on the floor and I felt as if I'd been kicked in the chest by a mule. I realised I loved you both more than anything. I don't know when it happened exactly, but it was then that I realised. I loved you. I love you. I still do.'

Alison looked out across the horizon. A horse in a field on the hillside opposite was galloping through the wet grass, mane and tail flying, tossing its head in sheer abandon. Alison shut her eyes and tried with all her might to will herself onto that hillside with that horse. But when she opened them again Marc was still sitting on the white-painted wrought-iron garden furniture watching her.

'Everything's changed now that we've moved back here,' she said. 'Now that we've found Cathy again. Things can't go on as they are.'

'Yes they can,' Marc insisted. 'Yes they can. I know it's weird seeing Cathy again, I know we put her through a lot, but we can come through it, Al, like we always do. We've had our problems, and coming back here has stirred up old memories and opened up old wounds, but maybe that is a good thing. Because maybe now we can clean them and let them heal for good. And I love you, I love you so much, Alison.'

Alison looked at him, shielding her eyes against the advancing sun so that she could see his face clearly. He was watching her intently, waiting for her to smile and acquiesce like she always did.

'The trouble is, Marc,' she said after a long pause, 'I'm not sure that I love you any more.'

Chapter Fourteen

'Are you sure you don't mind?' Catherine asked Jimmy again as he stood at the door with the girls.

'Of course I don't mind,' Jimmy said. 'Why would I mind taking my own daughters to school? I've done it loads of times before.'

'I just feel so . . .' Catherine looked at her two girls kicking at pebbles in the front garden, Leila with her coat hanging off her shoulders as always, and Eloise pointing her toes like a dancer. 'I can't see her today. Or anyone. I'm not ready. I'll probably never be ready actually, so while you're out I'll be checking property prices in the Outer Hebrides.'

'That seems like a long way to go to visit,' Jimmy said.

'Well, obviously you'd have to come too,' Catherine said, lifting Jimmy's heart for a fraction of a second. 'You could buy the house next door.'

'Right, well,' he said. 'I've got this thing up in London later.'

'What thing? Don't tell me you've been discovered at last?'

'No, well, not exactly. Maybe some session work coming up. I'm going to a sort of informal audition. Pays well, so if I can land it I could maybe get a deposit together on a flat, couple of months' rent to get me sorted.'

'That would be fantastic, Jimmy.' Catherine's face lit up.

'Yeah, I'd probably have to stay up in London for a few weeks . . . you know how these musicians are. Sometimes it's a twenty-four-hour job.'

'Well, if that's what it takes to get you off that boat,' Catherine said, without hesitation. 'And it's not as if we're that far away. There'll be weekends.'

'Maybe,' Jimmy said slowly. 'It's not really a nine-to-five sort of gig. But anyway, I haven't got it yet. Let's wait and see. Might not have to worry about it at all.'

'Good luck,' Catherine said, kissing him briefly on the lips. 'Oh, and . . .'

Jimmy waited.

'If she's there, if you see her, just . . . don't tell her anything we talked about, OK? I don't know what's going to happen between us. I'm just not ready to face up to it all yet.'

'OK,' Jimmy said. 'Probably won't see her, probably wouldn't say anything to her even if I did see her.'

'She used to have the major hots for you, you know,' Catherine said. 'In all the years we've been married I've never told you that. Didn't want to. But she was mental about you, to basic stalker level.'

'Well,' Jimmy said lightly, 'she's only human, right?'

Catherine looked at the girls, who were peering rather nosily into Kirsty's front-room window.

'She probably *still* fancies you,' she added, lowering her voice.

'Cat,' Jimmy looked offended as he thought about Alison's arms around his neck at the party. 'She's a married woman.'

'Yes,' Catherine said, 'and you're a married man, but that's never stopped you before.'

Catherine's smile faltered when she saw the stricken look on Jimmy's face.

'I'm sorry, I was only joking,' she said. 'What you get up to is your business. I was trying to lighten the mood, you know, after the whole depressing, soul-searching, mortifying week-end of doom. I didn't mean to make you feel bad.'

'I know,' Jimmy told her. 'But it was only once. I only did it once.'

The two looked at each other for a moment, but just as Catherine was about to speak she heard the girls burst into excited laughter as Kirsty slammed her front door shut and climbed over the low brick wall, still wearing her red checked flannel pyjamas and pink fluffy slippers.

'Bloody men,' she said, staring hard at Jimmy. 'Bloody bastard men. And by the way, where did you go to at that party?'

'Not up to scratch then?' Catherine asked Kirsty as she opened the door to her friend. 'Not the love of your life after all? All those steroids shrunk his man parts away to nothing?'

Kirsty wandered into the front room and sat heavily on the sofa.

'No, his man parts were all present and erect,' she said sulkily, staring at the carpet. 'Everything went *great*. He was funny, charming and gorgeous, and so was I. At the party we were chatting away, getting on like a house on fire one minute, and then the next we were in the downstairs loo, going at it like a pair of freight trains. I thought, this is it; this is the end of my life as a single philandering hussy and the beginning of my life with the *love* of my life, with Steve.'

'Sam, and doing it with a man you hardly know in a loo was your perfect scenario for true love?'

'It wasn't where we did it, it was how. It was so sexy, Cat. And the sink was pretty sturdy too, so that was a bonus. Anyway, we made ourselves presentable and came out, and you'd gone. I couldn't find you anywhere. So I let Sam walk me home. And I let him come in and I let him stay for the whole weekend. It was wonderful. The whole weekend, just the two of us in bed. Getting up to make bacon sandwiches, or uncork a bottle of wine, but mainly just us in bed doing it and laughing and talking and sometimes sleeping. It was *lovely.*'

'So?' Catherine pressed her, sitting down beside her on the sofa. Sooner or later she'd fill Kirsty in on the Alison débâcle, but Kirsty's love life was a more than welcome diversion. 'If it was all so wonderful why are you so down? Wait – was the "doing it" bit not up to scratch? Was he funny, charming, handsome and willing but a narcissistic and selfish lover? After all that build-up did you have to endure a weekend of anticlimactic sex?'

Kirsty sat up and straightened her shoulders. 'No, my dear, the sex was perfect. It was multiclimactic. He was attentive, generous and very well hung. God, can that man ever fuck.'

'Right – so why are you here looking all cross and fed up?' Catherine was perplexed. 'Did he snore or talk in his sleep? Has he unwittingly revealed he has a thing for ladies' underwear?'

'None of those would necessarily be a deal breaker,' Kirsty said on a heavy sigh. 'I'm here because he's gone. I woke up, and it was so nice, Catherine, to be all achy and sore in all the right places, the sort of feeling you only ever have after a great night of sex, and I thought I was about ready for some more, so I rolled over to wake him up and . . . he was gone.' She shrugged, dropping her chin onto her chest.

'To the loo?' Catherine asked her, optimistically.

'Nope, gone out of the house. Left. Not a goodbye, not a note, not a nothing. After that whole lovely long weekend he just got up before dawn and went home. I don't even have his number.'

'Well, he probably knows he'll see you at the gym later,' Catherine said.

'Yes, he probably does,' Kirsty said miserably. 'But after a whole weekend of sex and talking and laughing and kissing, Catherine, you don't just get up and leave without saying goodbye. It's not done. It isn't sex etiquette. It's not sexiquette.' She sniffed loudly. 'I really thought he liked me.'

'Are you going to cry?' Catherine asked her nervously.

'No,' Kirsty said, promptly bursting into tears.

'I'll make tea,' Catherine said.

'I'm fine really,' Kirsty said, sometime and several tissues later. 'I mean, yes, he was handsome and funny and great at sex – but he wasn't really my type, not really.'

'I didn't think he was,' Catherine said with a wry smile. 'I always thought you were more into the ugly, dull and impotent men myself.'

'Catherine, this is no time to be teasing me. I know you're rusty at this best-friend lark but this part is where you give me a pep talk and say something to make me feel better, OK?'

'OK,' Catherine said. She had never considered herself to be Kirsty's best friend but now that she mentioned the idea it made her feel quite pleased. The old best friend had stalked back into town all high and mighty and married to her first love, but it was OK because Catherine had a new best friend. One she was fairly sure would not run off with her husband. She thought for a moment.

'There are plenty more fish in the sea,' she said.

'That is a bollocks pep talk,' Kirsty said, sniffing. 'You're so right, you know. I never thought I'd say it but you, Catherine Ashley, are absolutely right about everything. I take it all back.'

'Good,' Catherine said. 'What am I right about?'

'Men. Men are shit, and you and me, we're old, we're past thirty. Boys in petrol stations calls us "madam", men don't look at us when we walk by any more. Our bosoms – or at least those of us who have bosoms – are collapsing. The wrinkle creams don't work. The hair dye doesn't cover all greys. We've had it. All we can do is what you're doing, give up on love and sex and hope and life and all that bollocks completely, because it's horrible out here, Catherine. It's horrible being single and old.'

'And you think *I'm* bad at pep talks,' Catherine said mildly. 'Look, you are nothing like me. First of all you are not old, and second of all men love you, Kirsty. You're pretty and funny and fit and have hardly any wrinkles, and have really nice shiny hair that always goes into a style. You go out there and grab life and look for happiness instead of just waiting for it to somehow find you, tucked away in a terraced two-bedroom house, trimming your split ends with a pair of nail scissors. And probably Sam was just being an idiot man, a stupid idiot man who doesn't know the rules of – what did you call it? – sexiquette, and thinks he'll see you later at the gym to get your number off you and arrange a date. He's a personal trainer, Kirsty. He probably had to go for a fifty-mile run before breakfast or something.'

Kirsty smiled at Catherine. 'Now that was a pep talk,' she said. 'But still, how will I know if he really loves me? How will I know?'

'Well, when you see him today go up to him and say, hi there, great weekend – let's hook up again, how about tonight? And if he says yes then he likes you, and if he says no then he might be busy tonight so suggest another date, and if he still says no then he probably doesn't like you, but it's best to be clear, so if he says no then ask him outright if he doesn't like you and he'll tell you and . . . that's how you'll know if he really loves you.'

Kirsty stared at her. 'That seems an awfully *literal* way of finding out.'

'Well, what else can you do? Employ a psychic?'

'Oh, you are so naïve,' Kirsty said. She rubbed her eyes with the heel of her hands, completing the panda look. 'Never mind all this asking business – what I'll do is implement Universal Plan A.'

'What's Plan A?' Catherine asked her, perplexed because Kirsty sounded as if she was quoting from a well-known textbook called *How to Deal with Men: A User's Guide*.

'Catherine, where have you *been* all of your life?' Kirsty exclaimed. 'Universal Plan A is act as if nothing has happened. You meet a boy, you like a boy, you and boy have sex, boy disappears into the night but you still have an appointment with boy to work on your buttocks on Monday at eleven fifteen. You attend the aforementioned appointment. You act as if none of the above has happened. Either the mystery of it will do boy's head in and he'll be forced to asked me if I'm still into him, or he'll be so grateful I don't want to pursue it any more that he'll act as if nothing happened and we'll be able to put it behind us for ever. And then I'll know. I'll know if he really loves me.' Kirsty looked resolute. 'That's a much better way of sorting things out. Never mind asking him straight questions and expecting straight answers. That would blow all his circuits for sure!'

'I don't know.' Catherine sounded unconvinced by Universal Plan A. 'Would it not be better to perhaps try to talk to him about last night – clear the air, at least? Find out what happened so you don't drive yourself mad thinking about it?'

Kirsty looked at her friend, her face an expression of pure pity.

'Oh, my dear,' she said, 'for one so old you have so very much to learn. Rarely in the history of humanity has a woman actually talking to a man about anything ever got her anywhere. You have to manipulate them, Catherine. It's the only language they understand. But don't worry, I actually feel better now that I've talked to you. So tell me, where did you go to at the party? If you tell me that you went home and had sex with your husband you owe me five hundred pounds because I bet you months ago that that would eventually happen.'

'No you didn't!' Catherine exclaimed.

'I did, I just didn't tell you.'

'Well, anyway, I didn't have sex with Jimmy, of course I didn't. We are well past all of that now. No, what happened was far more weird and strange and . . . I don't know what I'm going to do about it, Kirsty. I have no idea how to handle it at all . . .'

'So tell me then!' Kirsty shouted. 'I've got hours to kill before I have to go to the gym to ignore Sam.'

Catherine looked at Kirsty's empty mug. 'I'd better make another cup of tea first,' she said.

'Da-ad,' Eloise said, stretching out the word, swinging Jimmy's hand as they walked to school. Jimmy with his rucksack on his back and his guitar, in its case, slung over one shoulder.

'Yes, love,' Jimmy said. He was watching Leila, who had run a few feet ahead and was mid-performance in her latest staging of Leila –The Musical as she danced and sang her way along the high street.

'Litter bin! Litter bin!' she sang as she stopped to do star jumps in front of a rubbish bin. 'People put litter in you and that is goooooooooood! Yeah!'

One thing Jimmy could say about his younger daughter was she was never afraid to use a jazz hand. He wasn't sure if that was a good or a bad thing.

'Well . . . is Mum OK? I know you stayed up all of the night after the party talking, and you've stayed in the house all weekend. What does it mean, Dad? Does it mean you're moving back home for good?'

Jimmy was very careful not to let the question break the rhythm of his stride at all.

'No, love,' he said. 'No, I'm not moving back in. Mum just needed a friend around this weekend to talk to and I'm her friend now.'

'Kirsty next door is her *friend*,' Eloise said. 'You're her husband and she wanted you around all weekend so that might mean she wants you to move back in, mightn't it, Dad? It might mean that it's nearly time?' Eloise hopped a little, tugging on Jimmy's hand.

'Ellie,' Jimmy began purposefully, 'I don't think I am going to be moving back home at all. In fact, I might get this job soon. That means –'

'But you would, wouldn't you?' Eloise interrupted him, dropping his hand. 'If Mummy said you could move back home for good, you would, right?'

Jimmy sighed inwardly. He'd promised Catherine never to lie when it came to questions like this one, that he'd never gloss over the truth or give the girls false hope. Yet how could he, a grown man – a parent – confide in his eight-year-old daughter everything that he was still struggling to come to terms with? Of course he'd move back in if Catherine asked him to, he'd move back in like a shot. But she wasn't going to, and the nearest he was ever going to get to her now was being her friend, her children's father, and soon enough even that would be nothing more than a periphery character on the edge of her life as she blossomed and grew and found her own way in life, which she was bound to do. Jimmy knew that Catherine was really only at the beginning of herself, even if she didn't realise

217

it yet. But how could he explain all of that to Eloise, who just wanted to hear that her daddy would come home if he could?

'I don't know,' Jimmy tried to explain uncomfortably. 'I live on the boat now . . .'

'Yes, I know, but if Mummy says you can come home you will, won't you?' Eloise persisted.

'No, I mean, I would but . . .' Jimmy got the distinct feeling he'd said something that he shouldn't.

'But what?' Eloise asked him. 'You do want to come home, don't you, Daddy? You do miss us, you've just said so. So, but what?'

'But Mummy doesn't want me to move back home,' Jimmy blurted out before he really knew it. He grabbed Leila's hand as they came to the zebra crossing and for a few awkward moments Leila performed her self-taught version of Irish dancing over the black and white stripes while Eloise was silent as she walked next to him. Once on the other side Jimmy released Leila again and watched her gallop off through the school gate and into the playground, where she immediately commenced skipping around in a circle, an activity that soon attracted four other participants. Those were the days, Jimmy thought, the days when all you had to do to feel good was skip in a circle.

He looked down at Eloise, whose face was filled with thunderclouds. She was so like her mother, his breath stalled in his chest.

'Look, it's not really Mummy's fault,' he attempted to explain, resorting guiltily to trotting out the standard speech. 'These things happen. Sometimes grown-ups who still care about each other just can't live together, and it doesn't mean they don't love their children . . .'

'I hate her,' Eloise said quietly as they followed Leila into the playground.

'Now, listen.' Jimmy stopped and put his hand on his daughter's shoulders, bending to look in her green eyes. 'You don't hate your mummy, you love your mummy.'

'But you've said you are sorry and you want to come back, and me and Leila want you to come back. And anyway, in assembly Mrs Pritchard said that when someone's done something bad you should try to forgive them.'

'That *is* what Jesus would do,' Leila counselled as she skipped by.

'Right . . .' Jimmy paused, it was hard to argue with the son of God. 'Well, I expect he would but the thing is, when you're grown up it's not always as simple as saying sorry and forgiving people and stuff . . . like that.'

'Why isn't it?' Eloise asked him, pinning him to the spot with her mother's eyes.

Jimmy couldn't answer her for a moment. 'Because when you're grown up and you do something wrong, more people get affected. More people get hurt and it's very complicated.'

'But what about me and her?' Eloise asked him baldly, nodding at her sister. 'We're people, we got hurt – why doesn't what we think matter? We think you should come home.'

As Jimmy looked at his daughters he felt the crushing weight of failure on his shoulders. He'd let them down. He'd done this to them and he couldn't bear to admit it.

'Sometimes,' he repeated finally, heavily, 'even though grown-ups love their children very much they just can't live together any more . . .'

He watched his daughter as her eyes darkened like a stormy sea.

'You shouldn't have got married and had kids if you couldn't keep loving each other properly. It's not fair!'

The bell rang and Eloise snatched her school bag from

Jimmy's hand and ran into her classroom, along with most of the rest of her class.

'That didn't go quite the way I planned,' Jimmy said, watching her go, feeling her words stinging like slaps on his skin. She was right, of course. According to all the songs ever written, many of them by him, it was impossible to make somebody love you just because you wanted them to. And yet with Catherine he had truly believed that he would be able to make it happen, because he loved her so much. You couldn't love a person as much as he loved her and not inspire something similar in them, you just couldn't. At least that is what he had always believed, and it was hard to let that kind of faith go, even when the facts had discounted it long ago.

Life had been very simple before Jimmy Ashley got to know Catherine Parkin. There had been the band, music, the band, his friends, the band, a few girls here and there and the band. Jimmy hadn't needed or wanted anything else. At the time he put his single-mindedness down to his ambition, but just recently he wondered if it wasn't more to do with his dad dying when he was seventeen. Knowing that his dad wasn't at home meant he didn't want to be there either.

So when his mum told him she was moving away to Aylesbury just as Jimmy was approaching his nineteenth birthday it was with some relief that he told her he was going to be staying in Farmington, sharing a place with the rest of the band. Jimmy liked the feeling of being rootless, he liked the freedom it brought him, the idea that at any moment he could pack a bag and be gone – not that he ever did. But it didn't matter that he hadn't done that; what mattered was that he could. He was ready, poised for life.

And then he met Catherine. No, not exactly met her because she'd always been around on the periphery of his life, the skinny ginger girl who hung out with the blonde bombshell, but it was when he was twenty-one and Catherine was twenty that he first truly saw her. And once he started looking at her he couldn't stop. She wasn't good-looking in the traditional sense of the word, the sense in which he and Billy always defined an attractive woman, by her hair, breasts and general availability for sex. Catherine had plenty of hair, that was true, but her body was long and thin, with skin that seemed almost translucent. Jimmy remembered that Catherine reminded him of his mum's best bone china, the set that, if you held a piece up to the light, you could see your fingers through it.

He had known that something had happened with Catherine and her friend with the short skirts a few years before he first noticed her properly. He knew that she had dropped out of her A levels and never made it to university and that she still lived at home and worked in the Christian bookshop. But until he saw her smiling at that twenty-first birthday party he hadn't wanted to know or even thought about knowing any more than that.

It had started with a conversation – his love for Catherine – a conversation that had begun with Catherine glancing over her shoulder as Jimmy approached her, unable to understand why he wanted to talk to her. There had been a lot of conversations after that. Jimmy became a regular visitor to the Christian bookshop on the days that Catherine worked there and her mother did not. Eventually he managed to persuade her to come to a gig, made her promise that she would try to come so he could show her what he did best. He was proud of his music, but, more than that, he'd hoped that when she saw him up on stage she'd fancy him. It seemed to work on a lot of girls that way, and he'd hoped that, seeing as simply showing an interest in her had won her over this far, then maybe Catherine would be the same.

Jimmy remembered scanning the crowd at the gig until he caught sight of her, a good head taller than most people there, and then he'd played all night to her, never taking his eyes off her.

'What is it with you and that skinny chick?' Billy had asked him after he'd tried and failed to get Catherine to stay and have a drink with him after the gig.

'I like her, that's all,' Jimmy said, disappointed that he'd played his very best and she still hadn't let him buy her a drink, let alone fallen into bed with him.

'Don't go falling in love, mate,' Billy had warned him. 'We can't conquer the world with our music if one of us is in bastard love.'

'Not me,' Jimmy had told his friend. 'Never me.'

But it was already too late. Before he'd ever kissed her he loved her.

Actually, getting to kiss her had been a lengthy process that had taken almost four months.

'I can walk you to your door, if you like,' Jimmy had offered one warm spring evening as he walked her home after a gig she had stayed at long enough to have one drink. 'I'm also available for coffee and the full range of hot drinks.'

Catherine had laughed at his joke, standing underneath a cherry tree in full blossom, the scent of it ever after mingling with his memories. The sound of her laughter made him happy.

'You can't walk me home,' Catherine told him. 'My mum doesn't know I went out to a gig in a pub with a man. She thinks I went to a book group. And she can't know about you because if she did it would spoil everything. I'm not supposed to listen to rock music.'

'What?' Jimmy exclaimed. 'Am I in *Footloose*? You're twenty, you can do what you like.'

'I do do what I like,' Catherine had replied defiantly. 'Which is why I have to keep things secrets from her. She's very hard to live with.'

'Then leave home,' Jimmy told her.

'It's harder than you think,' Catherine said, and suddenly she looked hopeless. 'I don't know how to.'

On impulse and after weeks of being too afraid to touch her, Jimmy put his arms around Catherine and held her close to him. He'd waited for a long time in the moonlight, the night silent and still, until her rigid body, which had stiffened instantly at his touch, relaxed and softened. He felt her bones against his.

'I like you, Catherine,' he said, holding her, her chin resting on his shoulder. He found it was much easier to talk to her when he didn't have to look at her.

'I'd worked that out,' Catherine replied. 'I don't get it – why *you* would like *me*, of all people – but I know that you do.'

'Do you like me at all?' Jimmy asked her nervously, because in the four months they had spent together he had no idea what she felt about him other than that she tolerated him with a certain degree of fondness.

'I like you . . .' Catherine had begun. 'I don't know about anything else, Jimmy. I don't know if I can do anything else. I'm not sure I know how to love someone.'

Jimmy pulled back from the embrace just as a warm breeze disturbed the branches of the cherry tree, causing its blossom to waft lightly into her hair, glowing silver in the moonlight.

'Listen,' he said softly. 'I don't know what's happened to you to make you feel like you can't love someone, but you can. You of all people could love better than any of those half-asleep idiots in their houses, who think they've got it all. You just need to believe that you can be free to grow, and go to gigs and invite blokes in for coffee whenever you like, especially if they are me because I am so in love with you. But anyway, you can do it. You just need someone to show you how.'

'What did you say?' Catherine asked.

Puzzled, Jimmy started ticking off most of the major points in his speech on his fingers.

'I said you can find love, grow . . . er . . . go to gigs and, um, oh, yeah invite guys in –'

'You said you were in love with me,' Catherine interrupted, and Jimmy realised she was angry. 'You shouldn't go around telling girls that you love them just because you want to sleep with them.' She pushed herself out of his arms. 'I'm not that naïve, Jimmy.'

'Huh?' Jimmy was confused. 'Did I say that? I never meant to say it out loud, at least not yet. I haven't spent four months getting you to let me walk you home to freak you out now. But you might as well know I do love you, which is pretty weird considering all we've ever done together is talk and have a laugh. But I do love you and I'm not even trying to get you into bed, talking about extreme weirdness. I just want to be near you. Obviously I'd like to have sex with you too, but not until you're ready. I can wait for as long as it takes, and for the record, I actually mean that. I love you, Cat.'

Catherine was silent for a long time before she said anything.

'Cat?' she asked.

'Yeah, sorry,' Jimmy said, shrugging. 'It's your eyes, cat's eyes. I won't call you that again.'

'I like it,' she said. 'It's new. And I like you, Jimmy, a lot, but maybe not like you want me to, and I don't know why because you are a great guy.'

Jimmy took one of her hands. 'Plus way sexy too,' he added.

'Yes,' Catherine had smiled, slowly. 'I suppose so.'

'Never thought I'd be trying to get a girl to like me,' Jimmy said. 'Normally it's the other way round.'

'Perhaps it's the thrill of the chase you can't give up,' Catherine suggested. 'Maybe once you've got me you won't want me any more. I'm not very experienced at sex, for example.'

Jimmy had had to take a minute to think about that.

'Are you implying that I may have a chance of "getting you", as you put it?' he asked her. Catherine took a step closer to him.

'What if I don't fall in love with you?' she asked him.

'I'm Jimmy Ashley,' he told her. 'Of course you are going to fall in love with me.'

And then, as the cherry blossom drifted down, he had kissed Catherine for the very first time, completely certain that he was right.

Only now, with the benefit of hindsight, could he finally accept that he had been wrong. Because no matter how much Catherine cared for him, desired him, protected him and relied on him, she had never once looked him in the eyes and told him she loved him.

Which meant that Eloise and the pantheon of rock was right. He never should have believed that he could make the impossible happen.

Jimmy pulled himself back into the present as his younger daughter, seeing him hanging his head, hopped over.

'Did Ellie be mean to you, because never mind, because she's mean to me all the time and she doesn't mean it really.'

'Right oh,' Jimmy said. 'Come on, love, I'll take you round to your classroom.'

'Mind if we join you?' Jimmy turned round to find Alison at his side, her hair brushed and smooth, just the right amount of make-up on, a pristine white wool coat and caramel-coloured boots. It seemed as if the night of the party hadn't impacted on her at all. Nevertheless, when he looked at her he was conscious of his fifteen-year-old leather jacket creaking at every movement.

'So that was some party,' he said, not knowing exactly what he should say to this woman, the other woman. Yes, she had betrayed his wife, but if she hadn't betrayed Cat then there was a good chance he would never have got together with her, which, despite everything, was something he couldn't regret.

'Yeah, I'm sorry about that. Weird or what?' Alison said, making Jimmy smile because she sounded about fifteen instead of thirty-two.

'Weird is one way of saying it,' Jimmy said. 'Definite proof of a small world and all that bollocks.'

'Is she OK?' Alison asked him. 'Not too totally freaked?'

'She is too totally freaked,' Jimmy said, unable not to smile again. 'Her head is completely done in.'

'Heavy, man,' Alison replied, and the pair of them chuckled. Once again Jimmy wondered if he should be trying harder not to like her as they reached the younger girls' classroom door. Catherine hadn't explicitly said he was not to like her, but Jimmy felt on balance it was probably more honourable not to.

'Come on then,' Leila said, offering her hand to Amy, who was half hidden in the skirts of her mother's coat. 'You can come in with me if you like and sit next to me at snack time. Hopefully we won't have raisins today because I can't eat them because they look like dead flies with their arms and wings pulled off, don't they?'

Hesitantly Amy took Leila's hand, and with one last glance at her mother, followed Leila into school.

'That's the first time since she's started that she's gone in without a fuss,' Alison said, suddenly reaching out and holding Jimmy's forearm. He looked at her perfectly mani-cured hand on the arm of his leather jacket and noticed she was not wearing her wedding rings. Both her painted nails and bare fingers made him feel anxious, he couldn't exactly pin down why.

'It would be so great if Amy and Leila would make friends.'

'Would it?' Jimmy asked her. 'Or would it be seriously complicated and difficult?'

Alison looked at her watch as if she had anywhere particular to be.

'Can you come for a coffee with me?' she asked Jimmy.

Jimmy looked at his watch as if he had anywhere particular to be, and for once he did; he had a train to catch up to town, but not for another half-hour, when the cheap rate started. He could go for a coffee with her but whether or not he should was another matter entirely.

'I don't know . . .' he began.

'Why? Don't want to fraternise with the enemy?' Alison asked him. She laughed but there was no humour in it. 'Please, Jimmy, I think we have a lot in common in all of this, you and I.'

'But I'm on Cat's side,' Jimmy said.

'Oh God, Jimmy, we're not at school!' Alison exclaimed, which for a second made Jimmy feel exactly like he was.

She smiled at him, tucked her arm through his and dragged him in the direction of the coffee shop, tossing her hair over her shoulder.

Jimmy put up no resistance as he went with her, telling himself he wasn't fraternising with the enemy, he was going undercover.

'So you, like, slapped your husband,' Jimmy said conversationally once Alison had ensconced them on the sofa at the back of the coffee shop. The location was a little too clandestine to make Jimmy feel entirely comfortable. It was a little bit too much as if they were meeting in secret, behind people's backs, and he felt bad for feeling relieved about it. 'How did that go down?'

'He dealt with it,' Alison said, loading her skinny latte with sugar. 'Just like he deals with everything. He's a master at it. It's funny really, because the man I met, the man Cathy met back then, isn't there now. I don't know where he is. I don't even know when he disappeared. But when I . . . we fell in love with him he was tough and dangerous but sort of vulnerable and gentle too. Every teen girl's – no, every woman's – idea of heaven. Then he changed, and he changed because of me, because I made him change. But he changed the good bits, the bits I loved, and kept the bad bits. The bits that sleep around with other women right under my nose.'

Jimmy thought about the ladies' loos in The Goat pub.

'Well, nobody's perfect,' he said. Alison looked up at him over the rim of her coffee cup with her tranquil blue eyes.

'Did you cheat on Cathy?' she asked him 'Is that why you two aren't living together any more?'

Jimmy shrugged and nodded. The whole town knew about him and Cat – there was no point in trying to cover it up. 'It was only ever once, though.'

He waited for Alison to pass judgement but she didn't. She just watched him through the steam from her drink and said finally, 'Have you noticed that all of us have been unfaithful to Cathy in some way? We've all betrayed her.'

'Yeah, but me and Cat don't have anything to do with you and him and her,' Jimmy said, shifting in his seat and glancing at his watch again. 'We're not part of that.'

'I think you are,' Alison said. 'I think the mistakes we all made back then affected your chances of making it work with Cathy. I think I stole her life and she got mine by mistake.'

'What?' Jimmy leaned forward in his seat. 'Alison, *what* are you talking about?'

'I don't love Marc any more,' Alison said, finding that once she said it out loud it was oddly liberating. 'I'm thinking of leaving him, which is a freaky and terrifying thought, but if I can get myself together and find the guts I need to be on my own for the first time ever in my life, maybe it might be the right thing to do. What really worries me is that I haven't ever loved him, not from the beginning. I wanted him, yes, I was jealous of Cathy having him right from the moment I set eyes on him. I was obsessed with him, to the point that nothing else mattered but finding a way to be with him. Not my mum and dad, not Cathy, even the risk I was taking having unprotected sex with him – I'd do anything just to have those few minutes of his attention . . .'

'OK,' Jimmy said, tapping the table. 'Slightly too much info there.'

'Well, Cathy did it too,' Alison said, looking slightly hurt.

Jimmy was silent. He didn't want to think about that.

'Anyway,' Alison went on, 'what's been driving me mad ever since I saw Cathy again and you is this – what if I never loved him? What if I've conducted the last fifteen years of my life, had his children, put up with what I did based on the false idea that I loved him more than anything, when really I didn't? When really I tricked myself into thinking I was having feelings I wasn't to justify what I did?'

Jimmy looked over his shoulder as if he were hopeful of making a quick exit through the unisex toilets.

'Look,' he said after a while, 'I'm not really qualified for all this chick stuff, this "what if" bullshit. Want to discuss who'd win in a riff-off between Hendrix and Clapton then I'm your man. Hendrix, by the way, every time. But chick stuff – do I love him, does he love me – not really my field of expertise.'

That wasn't exactly true. In fact, Jimmy spent quite a lot of his many lonely nights on the boat thinking about exactly that, but he didn't want anyone, least of all Alison, to know.

'But this is important to you too,' Alison said.

'Er, how exactly?' Jimmy asked.

'I stole Marc from Cathy, like a jealous child snatching a toy. I stole him and I think I might have stolen her life too. Maybe if he'd stayed with her things would have been different, right? Maybe he would have been different. If he'd stayed with her he might have changed for her, but the right way. By dropping all the bad bits and keeping all the good. He might have been a whole man for her. She might have been able to keep her baby.'

'And what about your baby?' Jimmy asked her. 'What would have happened to Dominic?'

Alison thought of her son, whom she had delivered half asleep to the school gate earlier that morning, his tousled hair pulled over his eyes in a bid to try to hide the eyeliner he had applied that morning. She thought about him, his bravery and determination, and her heart ached. She'd like to think she would have kept him whatever happened, but she remembered the terror that had engulfed her the second she realised what was happening to her body. And the absolute total determination she had to have Marc by her side while she had his baby, no matter what. If Marc had not yielded to her persuasions and her demands then she couldn't be sure she wouldn't have done the same as hundreds of other lonely and frightened seventeen-year-olds, the same as Cathy had done. All that mattered, she told herself, was that he was here now and that she loved him.

'Dominic exists and I love him,' Alison said. 'He's a fact.'

'All right then,' Jimmy said. 'So what's the point of the "what ifs"? We've all got a long list of what ifs, not just you and me but everyone in this coffee shop, in the entire bloody world. What if Marc Bolan never wrapped his Mini round a tree . . . what if Mark Chapman hadn't shot Lennon in the back of the head . . . what if I hadn't let my wife find me with another woman? But you can't dwell on them, it would drive you mental.'

'You can try to put things right, though,' Alison said.

'What?' Jimmy asked her. 'Is it coffee you've got there or vodka?'

'If Cathy had stayed with Marc and I'd stayed in Farmington then maybe, maybe when you finally looked up from your guitar and noticed girls, you would have noticed me. I'd had a crush on you for the longest time. All I could think about was you. If I'd never met Marc I would have still been hanging around waiting for you to notice me. I'd have been standing right in front of you when the right moment came.'

'Yeah, but,' Jimmy started, tapping his fingers restlessly on the arm of the leather sofa, 'I didn't fall for Cat because she was right in front of me. I fell for her because she's her, beautiful and brave and funny and clever and sexy and . . . look, no offence. You're a nice-looking girl and everything, but you're not her.'

'I know that, but maybe you should have just had a teenage fling with me and we both would have moved on with our lives, found the right path instead of getting caught up with them. I think those two should have been together.' Alison paused and leaned a little closer to Jimmy. 'And I think we need to put it right.'

'What?' Jimmy leaned backward as far as the sofa's plump cushions would allow. 'You think *what*?'

'I know my husband,' Alison said urgently. 'I know that sooner or later his curiosity is going to take him back to Cathy. He is going to want to see how he feels around her, if he can recapture anything that he's lost. He's going to want to know how he makes her feel. And I'm going to let that happen. If he wants to try and get back anything of what he once had with her then I won't stand in his way because I want that too; I want her back too.'

'Look, if you want to be Cat's friend again then that's cool. I actually think she might go for it,' Jimmy said. 'But there is no way, no way at all, that I'm letting that creep into my wife's life to mess with her all over again.'

'But she's not your wife any more, is she? Not really,' Alison said.

'She's . . . look, I know that, but I still care about her,' Jimmy answered, stung from the slap of reality that Alison had dealt him.

'I just want to know,' Alison said. 'To know if somehow we ended up with each other's lives. And to ask you if . . .'

'What?' Jimmy asked her.

'If you'd like to have that teenage fling with me now,' Alison said, with a small dangerous smile.

'I've got to go,' Jimmy said, getting up quickly.

'Look, I'm sorry.' Alison reached out and held his wrist. 'I didn't mean to embarrass you but I just had to say it. I still fancy you like mad, Jimmy.'

'You say you want to be friends with Cat again,' Jimmy said. 'Sleeping with me isn't going to help.'

'I know that,' Alison said. 'And I knew how you'd react but I had to ask you because I had to know. And now I do. See? That's one "what if" that won't drive me crazy any more.'

'I have to go.' Jimmy broke her grip and left.

As Jimmy's train rolled into the station he hesitated. Maybe he shouldn't get on the train after all, maybe he should go straight back round to the house and see how Cat was. Alison might be right and Marc might be heading round there now.

He had no idea how his wife would react to seeing her first love again, no idea what would happen. But given that he'd only just worked out that he had never stopped loving her, not even for the fifteen minutes in the ladies' loo in The Goat pub, he wasn't quite ready for her to move on yet. He wasn't quite ready to deal with her being in love with someone else. If he was there at home with her, then nothing could happen. He'd be able to preserve this precious non-relationship they had for a little longer. The train squealed to a halt alongside the platform and a handful of people got out, walking past Jimmy as he stared at the carriage.

He'd just told Alison that dwelling on 'what ifs' would drive you mental, but wasn't that exactly what he was doing now? In the scheme of things, in the big picture, it didn't matter if he loved Catherine or not. What mattered was that she did not love him, she never had. He'd thought he had a choice, but he hadn't.

With a sense of finality Jimmy got on the train and swung himself into a seat by the window. As he watched Farmington slip out of view he clutched the neck of his guitar as if it were a life jacket. He knew there was nothing that he could do now.

Chapter Fifteen

Alison looked at herself in the wall of mirrors in the private exercise room as she waited for Kirsty. Her cheeks were pink, her eyes were hot and glittering and she hadn't done a stroke of exercise yet.

Not twenty minutes ago she had asked Jimmy Ashley to have sex with her! She'd just gone and blurted it out as if she'd planned it. One minute he'd been telling her how much he loved Catherine, how Catherine was everything that she wasn't, and the next, for some reason, she thought it would be a good idea to ask Jimmy if he wanted to have a teenage fling with her. No, that wasn't true, she hadn't been thinking at all.

It was as if she were going a little bit more mad as each minute passed. As if after fifteen years of keeping herself on track, suddenly she'd derailed and was careering out of control downhill. Alison had no idea what was happening with her and Marc because since they'd talked on the lawn in the morning mist they hadn't spoken at all. She had barely even seen him. He'd spent the rest of the weekend at the dealership and when he came home he went to sleep in one of the guest bedrooms.

Somehow it was hard to believe that this was the beginning of the end of them, the start of unravelling her life from his. Then she had to go and do something stupid like ask Jimmy

Ashley if he wanted to have sex with her, and she realised that everything was changing, including her, except she wasn't changing into something new, but something old. It was as if returning to Farmington had restored her default factory settings. She felt stupid, crazy, impulsive and confused.

She felt seventeen years old again.

The door swung open and Kirsty walked in. Alison smiled at her. Kirsty didn't smile back.

'You might as well know I'm Catherine's best friend,' she said, crossing her arms under her chest. 'I had no idea who you were when I started teaching you. But if it's a question of sides then I'm on hers and don't try and make it any different. Got it?'

Alison looked at her. 'God, it's knackering always being the villain,' she said, and she sat down on the floor and wept.

'Well,' Kirsty said, handing her a tissue she had retrieved from her handbag, 'I didn't expect you to cry. That's kind of thrown me a bit.'

'All this is happening to me too, you know,' Alison sobbed into a tissue. 'I don't want you to take sides. I don't want there to be sides. It's just that I'm breaking up with my husband and I've just come face to face with my best friend again after fifteen years and it's very confusing. I'm not evil, you know. I'm not some crazy scheming witch. I'm just trying to sort out this whole mess and put things right again.'

'I didn't know you and him were breaking up,' Kirsty said. 'Catherine doesn't know that.'

'No, well, I didn't know it until I saw Cathy. Until I realised there was an alternative to being miserable married to him. I don't love him any more and when I saw how he looked at her I don't know if the way he loves me will ever be enough. And now my only friend is a fifteen-year-old boy who wears eyeliner and periodically despises me.'

'Catherine doesn't hate you, you know,' Kirsty said after a while. 'She's extremely freaked out that you are back. But when we talked about it, about how she felt when she saw you, hate was not a word that cropped up.'

'I miss her,' Alison said, drying her tears. 'Especially now. I feel like I've been in suspended animation for fifteen years, playing at being a grown-up but really I haven't matured by one second. I even just asked Jimmy Ashley to have sex with me.'

'You did *what*?' Kirsty exclaimed. 'You asked Catherine's husband to have sex with you? I'm not judging you or anything, but are you *mental*? I just don't think that is necessarily the best way to get back into her good books, given that the last time she saw you you were running off with the love of her life.'

'They've split up, haven't they?' Alison challenged her weakly.

'Technically, yes, but in my book splitting up means burning photos and never speaking to one another again, it doesn't include sharing meals, taking long country walks and always living in each other's pocket, which is pretty much what they do. There's something unfinished going on there and if you want a hope of being Catherine's friend I suggest you stay well out of it, at least until they've worked out how to finish it.'

'Well, don't worry,' Alison sniffed. 'He politely declined. But that's what I'm talking about. I'm a mess. I'm a big fat useless pointless mess. I've got two little girls who don't know their lives are about to fall apart, a son who holds me in contempt for about ninety-five per cent of the time, and a husband who . . . who I don't love any more.'

'Right, well, I didn't know any of that either,' Kirsty said. 'You are in a pickle, aren't you?'

'That's one way of looking at it.' Alison said, stifling a sob.

'I tell you what,' Kirsty said. 'How about we sack the Pilates and go for a cup of coffee instead? Maybe between you and me we can work something out.'

'I don't know,' Alison said with a watery smile. 'The last time I went for a coffee I starting making random offers of sex to men who patently aren't interested in me.'

'Oh, honey,' Kirsty told Alison as she pulled her up onto her feet, 'welcome to my world.'

Catherine lay on the sofa and stretched her toes. It was almost lunchtime and she had lain on the sofa all morning. Almost since the moment Kirsty had left to go and ignore Sam she had stayed there, a now cool cup of tea resting on her chest as the hours slipped past.

For the first time ever in three years of employment at the Stratham and Shah agency Catherine had phoned in sick. Her boss had been sympathetic but had not sounded surprised, a fact which in itself was surprising, given Catherine's previously spotless attendance record.

For the first time it occurred to Catherine that other people must have seen what had happened between her and Marc and Alison on Saturday night. Certainly everybody had seen Alison slapping her husband, just as many must have witnessed Catherine and Alison's brief but taut conversation. Every single person in that room knew who Catherine was. It probably wouldn't have taken long for those in the know to work out that Mrs Alison James was *the* Alison, and that her husband must be that young railway labourer she ran off with in her teens, devastating her mother and scandalising Farmington.

People were talking about her, Catherine realised, feeling discomfort and anxiety grip her belly like a vice. She hated to be noticed and known, and the thought that other people were discussing her private life appalled her. But as disturbing as that was, it wasn't the reason that she had lain down on the sofa in her pyjamas and had not moved.

Seeing Marc and Alison again had taken her by surprise, but somehow the way she felt about seeing them again surprised her more than the actual event. It was almost as if on some level she had always been expecting this moment, knowing that one day it would come. Now they were back she felt curiously complete, as if a missing part of her life had been returned to her. Knowing where they were and what they were doing released the pressure of the past that had been building inside her, like a dam that had burst, and she could feel it flowing free out of her fingers and toes.

As she looked into the face of her old friend she'd felt happy and sad simultaneously, but the bitterness and anger she had expected were not there at all. Alison looked almost exactly the same, only in the brief moment Catherine had talked to her she hadn't seen Alison's fearlessness, that passion for life that had propelled Catherine through most of her teens, connecting her to the world outside of her parents' house. Seeing Alison as she was now, the real woman and not some imagined paragon leading a perfect stolen life, Catherine found herself wondering what had changed her friend so much over the years. She found herself wondering how Alison was.

Being confronted with Marc was altogether different. Jimmy asked her how seeing Marc again had made her feel, and she hadn't exactly lied, but had edited the truth because she couldn't tell anyone, especially not Jimmy, how it made her feel to look into his eyes again. There was no evolution of emotion, no surprise reaction as there had been with Alison. When she looked at Marc it was as if the last fifteen years had been contracted into a single second and she was sitting in the sunshine in the park once again, her eyes closed, her lips parted, waiting for him to kiss her.

The whole town might be gossiping about her, her oldest ally and enemy might be back in town, but it was that feeling, that troubling heavy feeling of unresolved longing that kept Catherine pinned to the sofa for all of the morning, staring at the ceiling wondering what on earth Alison and Marc's return meant and what in God's name she was supposed to do about it.

Early that morning, still restless and unable to sleep because every time she closed her eyes her mind was flooded with sunshine and memories, Catherine had got up early and come downstairs to find Jimmy stretched out on this very sofa, his forearm across his forehead, his mouth open slightly as if he were on the verge of smiling.

Jimmy had stayed all weekend because she asked him to, because she knew that having him around was like having a buffer zone, an insulation between herself and the chaotic feelings that Marc had stirred up in her.

Jimmy was the only person who Catherine had ever allowed herself to be truly angry with. The only man she'd ever screamed and shouted at, hit and even hated, and now all of that rage had receded she found that he was the only person who could calm her. As angry with him as she had been for telling Alison about the baby, at exactly the same moment she had known she needed him around to keep her anchored.

Just having Jimmy listen to her, trying not to fall asleep as she talked the night away, had made her feel safe and sort of complete. With him around she was Catherine the woman, steady, reliable and strong. Without him she could have been that frenzied teenager again. That foolish girl who would have done anything to have a few more minutes with the boy she loved. Catherine didn't want to be that girl again. That girl, with all her raw emotion and her heart pulsating on her sleeve, frightened her. That girl was all too easily crushed.

Sunday with Jimmy at home had been a perfect, happy, simple day, the four of them enclosed within the walls of their house from morning until night as if together they had the power to take themselves outside of time just for a little while.

But Catherine knew she couldn't keep asking Jimmy to stay, even if she was sure that he would in his own affable whyever-not, go-with-the-flow way. It would confuse the girls; it would confuse *her*. As frightening as the thought of him not being around to come between her and her fears was, she had to face whatever came next on her own. After all, her problems were not Jimmy's problems any more.

Just before Jimmy had taken the girls to school he'd found her in the kitchen, her bare feet cooling on the tiles, looking at a packet of cereal.

'I don't have to go to London,' he'd offered.

'Yes you do,' Catherine had said, setting the cereal packet down. 'You need that job. Deposit on a flat, remember?'

'Yeah, but if I get it I'll be away for a few weeks . . . Will you be OK?' Jimmy asked her. 'Without me, like.'

Catherine had turned round and made herself smile at him. 'Of course I'll be OK. I've been OK on my own for the last two years, I don't need you to stick around now, honestly.'

It had been a total lie. Of course, more than anything she wanted him to stick around and be the magic ingredient that brought back a sense of rhythm to her life. But she needed to let him have his own life now, find his own way and be free of her.

The thought of him going to London hadn't helped her move her body from the sofa, though.

Stretching her arms out over her head, Catherine sat up and looked at the clock. It was almost two. She had to get up, shower, get dressed and go to get the girls in just over an hour.

The knock at the front door made Catherine jump, and she put her feet on the floor, sitting forward on the sofa. She looked at the door for a few long seconds and considered the possibility of not opening it because she knew who was standing on the other side.

She was still in her pyjamas, at two in the afternoon, with her hair unbrushed and her face unwashed, and the very last person in the whole world she wanted to see was on the other side of that door. But Catherine didn't seem to have any control over her own limbs. Just as she was thinking about sneaking out of the back door and taking refuge in Kirsty's shed, her body had got up and opened the door.

And there he was. There was Marc.

And with the cooling insulation of her husband gone, all she could feel was how he burned with heat, as if he had somehow captured all the sunshine from that distant summer in his eyes.

'Afternoon,' Marc said, looking at her pyjamas and then looking away. 'I looked you up in the phone book. I was going to phone but the address was there and I just got this feeling I should call round, see for myself how you were after the party. Maybe talk a bit about . . . everything.'

He gestured at her attire. 'Are you ill?' he asked.

'No,' Catherine said, her rebellious body stepping aside to allow him in even though her head was shouting at her to slam the door in his face. 'Just tired.'

She held her breath as Marc walked into her tiny living room. She saw her home through new eyes, through his eyes: the tiny room, the shabby sofa, the grubby carpet and breakfast things still piled on the dining table. She wondered if it would have been possible for their lives to take more divergent paths than they had.

Marc turned and looked at her where she was still standing by the front door. He was wearing a camel coat over a suit and he held a pair of black leather gloves in his hand. The living-room light that had been burning all morning reflected in the leather of his shoes. She could still feel the heat of him, even from three or four feet away.

'Drink?' she asked him, unable to think of anything else to say.

'Coffee?' Marc suggested. 'I tell you what, I'll make it, you go and get dressed, OK?'

'Sorry,' Catherine said, dropping her head so that her hair fell over her face.

'What for?' Marc asked her.

'For being in my pyjamas.'

'Don't apologise,' he said, walking into the kitchen. 'Just get dressed. You look far too appealing that way.'

Catherine practically ran up the stairs and set the shower to freezing cold.

Twenty minutes later, when she came down in her black trousers and black long-sleeved top, with her skin still rosy from the cold water, Marc was sitting at the table and the breakfast dishes had been cleared.

'I could only find instant,' he said, gesturing to a mug he had set on a coaster that Catherine had forgotten she'd ever had.

'I've only got instant,' Catherine said.

She sat down at the table and took a sip of the coffee. All the time she was trying to adjust to this new reality. Marc James, *the* Marc James, the man that had stalked her dreams for so long, was sitting at her table in her house drinking instant coffee. He'd even cleared away her breakfast things. It was as if by somehow allowing her to think about him again, to dream about him, she had conjured him up out of thin air, like letting a genie loose from its lantern.

'This is all a bit odd, isn't it?' Marc said finally.

'Yes,' Catherine agreed. 'I sort of can't believe that you're here.'

'Do you hate me?' Marc asked, glancing briefly sideways at her.

'I don't think I ever hated you,' Catherine said. 'But even if I did, all of that business was a long time ago. I've got married, had children, moved on.'

Catherine wasn't sure if she was lying or not, but it seemed like a sensible thing to say. It was a way to put distance between herself and him, even across this three-foot-wide table.

He looked at her, his sudden smile causing her to grip the sides of her chair beneath the table.

'You haven't changed,' he said.

'I have,' Catherine replied. 'And so have you.' Marc laughed once and nodded.

'I think about the kid I was back then, and wonder if I am the same person. I mean, I can't understand how I turned from him into me. It doesn't seem possible.'

'Alison made it possible, I suppose,' Catherine said carefully. 'It looks as if you two were meant to be together after all.'

'I didn't want to let her down,' Marc said. 'But I have. I never learned to resist that urge to spoil things that were good for me. You were good for me, you made me feel human. I couldn't wait to ruin that.'

Catherine didn't say anything for a long time.

'We were all young,' she replied eventually. 'How many twenty-year-old men would turn down the chance to have two teenage girls on the go? I was naïve and you were you. I was

243

passive. Alison fought for you, she won you. She deserved you.'

'Some would say she got what she deserved,' Marc said. 'You do realise I only left with her because I didn't love her? It seemed easier to be with a girl I didn't love than to be with one I did.'

Catherine looked out of the back window, down her long thin garden where the grass was overgrown and the vegetable patch was covered in polythene sheeting to protect the seedlings from the frost.

She had absolutely no idea where the next few minutes would take her, and knowing that made her feel dizzy, as if she were balancing on a knife edge.

'Why are you here, Marc?' she asked. 'Not why are you back in Farmington, although I could ask you that too, I mean why are you here now, sitting at my table, drinking instant coffee?'

'For the same reason I'm back in Farmington,' Marc said, sitting very still. 'To find you.' Catherine heard the sound of her own indrawn breath, and she knew that Marc must have heard it too.

'I don't suppose I expected to actually find you standing in my hallway at a party. I honestly thought you'd be long gone. But I wanted to find the *memory* of you. I wanted to get close to that person I was for those few weeks I was with you. I've never been like him before or since then, Catherine. That person was the best I've ever been. Almost since the day Alison and I left I keep letting people down. I keep hurting them even when I don't want to. It just seems to happen around me. I thought in this place I might find you and I might find the man I was when I was with you. I thought that you, the memory of you at least, might heal me and make me whole.' Marc smiled and looked at his hands. 'And then there you were, the living, breathing you, standing right in front of me in the hallway and now I don't know what to do.'

'There is nothing to do, is there?' Catherine asked.

'Isn't there?' he said, looking up at her. 'Look, on Sunday morning Alison told me she didn't love me any more. It's been like a set of scales over the years: the more I loved her, the more I hurt her and the less she loved me. I love her, Catherine, but I've used up all the love she had for me at last.'

'What, and now you want me to make things better?' Catherine asked, frowning.

'No, I just want you,' Marc said. 'I want you.'

Catherine made herself look at him and they held each other's gaze for what felt like an age. He had just walked back into her life after fifteen years and told her that he wanted her back even though he was still in love with his wife, who was leaving him. She should be furious. She should be incandescent with rage, but all she could feel was the pull in her guts when he told her he wanted her.

She needed to put distance between her and him right now.

'I have to pick up my daughters,' Catherine said eventually, scuffing the chair on the carpet as she stood up.

Marc stood up too.

'Are you happy?' he asked her, reaching out and catching her hand. His fingers felt hot on hers.

'Yes, thank you,' Catherine said, unable quite to muster the energy required to withdraw her hand from his.

Marc drew her hand closer to him, and her treacherous body followed.

'Wouldn't you like to know,' he asked her, his voice diminishing to a whisper, 'if our kiss would still feel the same?'

He drew her body flush to his and brought his lips to within a whisper of hers.

'I . . .' Catherine had no idea what she was about to say

and just as her lips formed a nameless word the back door opened.

She sprung away from Marc as if he had given her an electric shock.

Jimmy stood in the kitchen doorway and looked from Catherine to Marc. Catherine discovered that she could not look at her husband.

'I came back,' Jimmy said flatly. Marc turned and smiled at Jimmy, holding out his hand.

'We meet again!' he said pleasantly.

At last Catherine made herself look up at Jimmy. His jaw was set, his hazel eyes clouded and dark.

'What are you doing here?' he asked Marc. Catherine rubbed her hands over her face, trying to wake herself from the stupor she'd been lulled into.

'He just popped in to say hello, to catch up,' she said, as guilty as Marc was of acting as if nothing had happened but desperate to diffuse the tension in the room. 'Anyway, why aren't you in London?'

Jimmy did not take his eyes off Marc, the fury he felt illustrated quite clearly by the tension that pulled back his shoulders. 'I got to Euston and I changed my mind. I don't want work that's going to take me away from . . . the girls. It's not worth it. I came by to tell you I'd pick them up, if you liked. Now I'm here I think we should pick our children up together.'

Catherine could not hide her surprise at his vehemence. Was Jimmy concerned about her welfare or had he decided to get territorial about two years too late?

Marc hadn't budged.

'Well,' Catherine said, looking at Marc, 'you'd better go.'

'OK,' Marc said. 'It was so good to see you again, Catherine.'

'And you,' she replied automatically.

She watched him walk out of the front door and suddenly felt as if all the air had rushed back into the room and she could breathe again. She sat down on the dining chair with a bump.

'What was going on?' Jimmy demanded. Catherine looked up at him; she'd only ever seen him actually angry once and that was when she vandalised his amplifier soon after Donna Clarke.

'Nothing,' she said, not sure why she wanted to push his anger a little further. 'He just came round, that's all. I didn't even know he was coming.'

'You were about to kiss him!' Jimmy shouted, catching his voice as it rose and struggling to contain it. 'You were going to *kiss* him, Cat!'

'Jimmy, back off,' Catherine told him. 'It was nothing . . . we just got nostalgic and, OK, maybe things were getting out of hand, but you came back and saved the day. Nothing happened.'

'Is that what you really want?' Jimmy asked. 'To let something like that happen so easily between you and him, you just felt like giving it away?'

'Jimmy!' Catherine gasped. 'I didn't plan it, I don't know if I wanted it. Maybe it would have been one way to finish things . . . or start something.'

She had no idea why she was being so antagonistic, it was just that Marc had left, she felt furious and Jimmy was the only one here to turn her anger on.

'He is a married man!' Jimmy blurted out.

'Yes, I know that, Jimmy, but it's funny, I thought you'd be the last one to judge what a married man should or should not do.'

'He messed you up, Cat. For years and years he blighted

247

you, blighted our marriage, even the birth of our children. He made it almost impossible for me to keep loving you and impossible for you to love me. *Him*, that . . . shit of a man did that. And you let him breeze back in here, and what? You were about to climb back into bed with him?'

'Why do I have to tell you *anything*?' Catherine shouted at him, her fury giving her the strength to stand. 'And who says Marc was the reason I didn't love you? Maybe I just couldn't love *you*. And anyway, none of this has got anything to do with you.'

The instant the words were out of her mouth Catherine regretted them, but they were out there now and she knew they had hit Jimmy hard.

'This has got everything to do with me,' Jimmy told her darkly, his anger making him tremble. 'I'm the one who sat up all night listening to you talk about how confused you were. I'm the father of your kids. I'm the man who . . . the man who really cares about what happens to you, despite what you may think about me. I'm the one who is always here for you.' Jimmy stood firm. 'Whether you like it or not this has got everything to do with me. So you tell me right now – were you going to kiss him back?'

Catherine flung her hands in the air as she slammed past Jimmy, causing the chair she had been sitting on to sway and topple on the carpet.

'Leave me alone, Jimmy,' she told him as she marched to the front door. 'Go back to London and make some money for a change.'

'Were you going to *kiss* him?' Jimmy demanded once more.

'Why do you care?' Catherine turned and asked him. 'Really, what difference does it make to you?'

'I need to know, Catherine.' His voice caught, making her pause and take a breath.

'I'm fine,' Catherine replied. 'Nothing happened and everything's fine.'

'Would you have kissed him?' Jimmy repeated, frustration inhabiting every word.

Catherine took her hand off the door latch. 'Yes.' She threw the word at him with full force. 'Yes, I think I would have kissed him. But you came in and I didn't and I'm glad I didn't. Because it would have been a terrible idea; it would have been the biggest mistake I'd ever made. But, yes, I would have kissed him. I wanted to kiss him.'

'Right.' Jimmy seemed to deflate in front of Catherine's eyes, the tension draining out of his muscles. 'You would have kissed him.'

'Look,' Catherine said, 'nothing happened and I'm glad nothing happened. Let's just leave it at that, OK? I appreciate your concern and everything but, really, we're arguing over nothing.'

'What about the next time you see him?' Jimmy asked her. 'Will you kiss him then?'

'I don't know!' Catherine exclaimed before catching hold of her tattered nerves. 'No, probably not, and anyway, now he's gone I don't know what on earth I was thinking. I just got caught up in the moment.' She chanced a half-smile. 'Jimmy, I get that you are worried about me, and I appreciate that, but I don't need you to march in here and start laying down the law. I've got to handle this my way and you should have stayed in London. This mess shouldn't stop you from getting on with your life.'

'But you are my life,' Jimmy said almost to himself. He looked up and caught Catherine's expression. 'I mean, you and the girls. Like it or not, you are a big part of my life. Whether we are together or not I have to make sure you are OK. You'd do the same for me, right?'

Catherine thought for a moment and then, dropping her bag, she walked across the small room and put her arms around him, and held him. His heart was still racing.

'Of course I'd do the same for you,' she said. 'I needed you at the weekend and you were there for me, but now . . . I've got to sort this out my own way, Jimmy. I've got to work out how to handle this. I've never really had to stand on my own two feet. I always had Alison or my mother telling me what to do, and then there was you, rescuing me, taking me away to safety. But I can't let you rescue me this time – it's not your place to even try any more. I have to sort this out for myself. You understand that, right?'

'I understand that,' Jimmy said, hugging her briefly back before stepping out of the embrace.

'Coming to get the girls then?' Catherine asked him.

Jimmy shook his head. 'I need some air,' he said. 'Unpack my rucksack, that sort of stuff.'

'See you later then?' Catherine offered.

'Maybe,' Jimmy said. 'I don't know.'

'OK.' Catherine shut the front door behind her, leaving Jimmy standing alone in what had once been his living room.

He knew he couldn't rescue Catherine this time. He'd understood that long before he'd seen her on the brink of so carelessly kissing the man that had once ripped her life to shreds. What Catherine didn't know, what she could not understand, was that Jimmy was still hoping against hope, still believing with that same unshakeable ill-founded faith, that one day it would be Catherine that rescued him.

Chapter Sixteen

'Do you ever think,' Kirsty asked Catherine later that night as they sat in her back garden with a cup of tea each, after Kirsty had knocked on Catherine's living-room window at just after ten, 'that there is anything out there? You know, like a higher force or something. God sort of thing?'

Catherine looked up at the dark and crisp March night sky. The evening was chilly and the sky was perfectly clear so that the stars glittered with a particular brightness and a kind of intensity that made Catherine catch her breath to think that just a tiny bubble of atmosphere was keeping her here on the earth instead of wheeling out there lost in the magnitude of space. Only a couple of miles away from where she was sitting now, a huge sucking gaping, gulping universe waited to swallow her up, and after the last few days' events there was a little part of her that couldn't quite extinguish the desire to find a pin big enough to burst the bubble so she could go sailing out amongst the stars.

'No,' she said to Kirsty, her voice perfectly level, despite all the coincidences and consequences that had suddenly beset her, making her feel exactly like a rather panicky chesspiece on some cosmic board. 'Not really.'

'I do,' Kirsty said, as Catherine knew she would. 'I think there has to be. Because otherwise why are we here?'

'Because this planet happened to be the right distance from the sun to allow the production of water and to facilitate life. Probably a billion- or even a trillion-in-one occurrence. Our existence is completely random,' Catherine told her, because that was what she wanted to believe. It was easier to accept the tangled and chaotic mess her life had snowballed into if it was an accident. If some sentient being had thrust all this upon her then she was not only confused, she was extremely pissed off.

'Now *that's* madness; of course that is madness. You don't get all of this . . . you and me, your children and love and heartbreak and happiness and music and *orgasms* from a freak random occurrence. You just don't. There's something else out there.'

Catherine sipped her tea, tasting the sweetness of the sugar on the back of her tongue.

'There are probably aliens,' Catherine conceded. 'Given the vastness of the universe it would be insane to think that we lived on the only planet capable of sustaining life in some form. Probably on some planet far away from here male aliens are messing up the lives of female aliens with a wanton disregard for manners or decency.'

'You say you didn't actually kiss him,' Kirsty said thoughtfully.

Catherine had filled her in on Marc's unscheduled visit that afternoon, about five minutes after she had climbed over the back fence for a cup of tea, and unusually Kirsty had not said a word about it until now. For the first time in their friendship, Catherine realised uneasily, she was waiting to find out what Kirsty was thinking, which meant that what had happened was probably very, very, *very* bad, as opposed to just really bad, which is what Catherine had been hoping for.

'No, I didn't actually kiss him,' she gushed, relieved that

Kirsty had broken her unusually sagacious silence. 'But if Jimmy hadn't turned up when he did I think I would have kissed him. And what then? What would have happened then?'

'Well, based on my experience, probably foreplay followed by sex, possibly on the living-room floor,' Kirsty remarked flatly, before adding a touch wistfully. 'Do you know one of the saddest things about being over thirty is that you never get to just kiss any more. A kiss is always followed by sex these days. Kiss, sex, kiss, sex, kiss sex. Whatever happened to just making out?'

'But what if I had slept with him?' Catherine went on. 'What would it have proved? Would it have changed anything except to make a really complicated situation worse? What was I trying to do, steal him back, get revenge? Why would I kiss him?'

'Because you wanted to get your rocks off?' Kirsty suggested, tipping her head to one side. 'Not quite as emotionally delving as your reasons why, but the most likely one. It's like you're a bottle of milk of magnesia . . .'

'A *what*?' Catherine scowled at her friend.

'And you've been sitting on the shelf in the back of the bathroom cabinet since nineteen ninety-four, well past your sell-by date, just going a bit stagnant and mouldy and then *suddenly* along comes this great big fuck-off complicated situation and shakes you right up. Kick-starts your natural womanly urges. You got turned on by seeing Marc again. He is quite hot in a sort of paunchy, suited way, so I don't totally blame you. You experienced a physical reaction, not some deep psychological one. Seriously, Catherine, think about it – it's not rocket science. This whole situation is actually extremely interesting. Beats *Desperate Housewives* into a cocked hat any day of the week . . .'

'Oh, I'm so glad that you find my messed-up life interesting,' Catherine said. 'At last I'm the interesting one!'

'I wouldn't go quite that far,' Kirsty said, with a little smile. She took a sip of her tea, feeling the steam curling out of the mug cool on her cheeks. 'What is interesting, though, is that you, "Catherine the Nun" as I like to call you sometimes . . .'

'I've never heard you call me that,' Catherine said.

'Not to your face, obviously. Anyway, *you*, the world's most cautious, uptight and sexually stunted woman, nearly threw caution and your pants to the wind over this particular man. You weren't thinking about consequences and implications. You weren't thinking at all. Your lady parts were doing all the thinking, and that's interesting because that is not you. Or maybe it is you, but a you you never knew you were until now.'

Catherine set down her tea and looked utterly appalled.

'Promise me something,' she said.

'Anything,' Kirsty offered.

'Never give up Pilates to become a psychiatrist. The suicide rates would soar.'

'God, you're ungrateful,' Kirsty said mildly, gazing up at the sky, her feet up on the bench seat, her knees tucked beneath her chin. 'I believe in fate, I believe things happen for a reason, like a sort of cosmic symphony. Maybe it's the stars, or God or . . . aliens. The two people who were a big part of making you into who you are today are back here for a reason. You can't just go along pretending that nothing's changed and go around all day going, "La-de-da-de dah, I nearly snogged the face off my married ex after about five minutes, but everything's still normal and fine!" You can't. You have to face up to it all. Face up to fancying him and wanting to shag him, if that's what it takes.'

'But if anything happened between me and Marc it would

be a terrible, terrible mistake,' Catherine moaned, leaning forward and dropping her forehead to her knees, so that the ends of her hair grazed the patio stones.

'Yes, I *know*,' Kirsty said with some emphasis. 'You are talking to the queen of terrible, terrible mistakes here. But you have to crack a few eggs to make an omelette, right? Whole and grown-up people are made up of all the terrible, terrible mistakes they've made and learned from. If you are too afraid to take chances, if you're too cautious, then you're bound to get stuck in one great big fat boring motherfucking bastard of a rut.'

Catherine turned her head sideways and one eye glinted in the reflected light from the kitchen window as she peered at Kirsty.

'I must be going mad because you are starting to sound quite sane,' she said, straightening her back and sitting up. 'Even slightly wise.'

'I have hidden depths,' Kirsty told her. 'That's why I'm so popular with men.'

'So, are you telling me to seek Marc out and have sex with him?' Catherine asked her. 'Behind Alison's back, behind Jimmy's back, no matter what the consequences are?'

'No, I'm telling you to follow your instincts for a bit. Find out why you felt the way you did around Marc, explore the way you're reacting to him and Alison being back in your life. Perhaps,' she added carefully, 'you should see Alison too, see how that goes.'

'I can't,' Catherine said. 'I think I would have but then I almost got off with her husband. Funny, I can stand her stealing him off me much better than I can stand the reverse, it seems. And anyway, while I'm off following my instincts and exploring my feelings, what about Jimmy?' Catherine felt anxiety well in her chest when she thought of the expression on Jimmy's face when he'd seen her and Marc together. Since that moment, whenever she thought about her husband, she felt jangled and disconnected, and she couldn't quite work out why, except that it was something more than the embarrassment and discomfort she had felt at being found in such an unorthodox situation.

'You should have seen him; he was so angry when he came back.'

'Why do you care?' Kirsty asked her flatly. 'He has all the half-witted women in the county after him and you still make him Sunday dinner. You nearly snog the only other man you've slept with in your entire life and he goes nuclear. What a hypocrite! Ignore it, Catherine. He's just getting all male and territorial when he had no business to be and, frankly, considering he wears his hair in a scrunchy, he should know better. Don't feel bad about him. You're not together any more, remember?'

Catherine nodded. 'I know, but he's such a big part of my life, and the girls', and I don't want to fall out with him.'

'You don't fall out with him over his girlfriends, do you?' Kirsty reminded her. 'Why should you fall out with him over what you do?'

Catherine didn't answer because she could not think of any.

'If I ask you a full and frank question will you give me a full and frank answer?' Kirsty asked her, leaning a little closer and peering at Catherine in the darkness.

'Suppose,' Catherine replied cautiously.

Kirsty smirked. 'That's not exactly the affirmative I was hoping for, but nevertheless it will have to do.' She sat up straight. 'Are you, Catherine Elizabeth Ashley, still in love with your sham of an ex-husband, the spandex-wearing Jimmy . . . er . . . Hendrix Ashley?'

'No!' Catherine said immediately. 'No, don't be stupid. Of

course I'm not still in love with him. If I was still in love with him would I have been tempted to kiss Marc? No I wouldn't. It was hard for me to get everything under control after he did what he did, but I have done that. And we've got a relationship now that I care about. But I don't love him. Of course I don't love him.'

'Well, then,' Kirsty said. 'All I'm saying is that at some point you will have to make a choice between what you want for you, and being Jimmy's friend. And if, when it comes to it, you put Jimmy's friendship first then maybe you'll want to rethink your answer.'

'What does this mean?' Catherine asked the sky, standing up suddenly. 'If I still have one type of feeling for Jimmy and another altogether for Marc – what does that mean?'

The two women were quiet for a moment as if both of them hoped for a reply, but the night was silent, except for the distant sound of traffic.

'I don't know what to do,' Catherine groaned. 'I don't know how to be, or how to feel about anything!'

Kirsty stood up and put an arm around her friend. 'This is actually all good,' she said.

'How is this good?' Catherine asked her, her voice small.

'Because you are awake and *feeling*, Catherine,' Kirsty told her. 'Your heart is racing, your blood is pumping, you're scared and confused, and you have no idea what is going to happen to you. You're alive, my friend, you're alive!'

Catherine looked up at the star-spangled sky. 'I'm not sure I like it.'

She glanced up at the window of her daughters' bedroom, where the night-light behind the pink curtain glowed steadily. Eloise would be sucking her thumb, even though she vehemently denied she did any such thing, and Leila would have wound her finger so tightly into her hair that in the morning it would take Catherine minutes to extricate it. Catherine smiled and shivered in one instant. They were so small, her girls, and so fragile. It seemed wrong somehow that all that stood between them and the freezing fathomless universe was a thin stretch of atmosphere and their mother, who was only now waking up after one hundred years of slumber, with no idea what was still a dream and what could be a reality.

'Something's going to happen,' Kirsty said after a little while with the confident air of an oracle.

'Yes, piles, if we stay out here much longer,' Catherine said, grimacing as she shifted on the seat.

'No, I mean something big is going to happen to help you decide how you feel, and you'll have an epiphany and everything will be fine.'

'I moan at you,' Catherine said, hugging Kirsty and resting her hot cheek against her friend's cool one for a moment. 'But I think you are actually the best friend I've ever had.'

'Including Alison?' Kirsty asked her. 'Before she turned to the dark side, I mean.'

Catherine thought for a moment. 'She was so important to me. I don't know what my childhood would have been without her. She was my lifeline.'

'I've got an idea,' Kirsty said. 'The girls are off with part-man part-poodle this weekend, right?'

'Yes,' Catherine said. 'He's taking them to his mother's on the boat.'

'Come over to mine, we'll have girly night in. I'll cook, we'll drink a load of wine, we won't talk about any type of man or male thing, not your love interests, not even mine, principally because mine seems to have dumped me as he hasn't spoken to me *once* even though we've seen each other loads today, so now I've got to retrospectively dump him, which is going to be tough, as first of all I'm ignoring him and second of all we weren't going out and third of all I really bloody liked him, the bastard arsehole, and I thought he liked me and in eight years' time I'll be forty! I haven't got time any more to go around falling in love with people who don't love me back . . .' Kirsty paused for breath and smiled sheepishly at Catherine. 'Sorry, it's just it's been you, you, you all bloody night. Anyway, we'll have a proper girls' night in and it will be lovely. You can stay over.'

'Are you sure?' Catherine asked her. 'I mean, I know you hate cooking, and cleaning your house so that it's fit for visitors.'

'For you, my love, I'll get in a takeaway and push things under the sofa.'

'It's a lovely idea, but we could always do it here, if you like,' Catherine offered.

'No.' Kirsty was quite firm. 'You'd only be looking at your table and thinking about Marc bending you backwards over it all the time. No, my place it is. I've decided.'

'Thank you, Kirsty,' Catherine said, picking up both of the tea mugs and heading indoors. 'I couldn't have a better friend than you.'

'Possibly,' Kirsty said under her breath as she paused to look up at the sky, nipping at her bottom lip. 'And then again, possibly not.'

Chapter Seventeen

Alison had signed the late book four more times that week, and on Friday morning the secretary asked if she could spare five minutes to talk to the head. Alison sat on a chair that was far too small for her outside of Mrs Woodruff's office, feeling as if she was about to be given detention.

'The thing is,' Mrs Woodruff said when Alison had taken a seat opposite her on a full-sized chair in her office, which somehow didn't make her feel any more grown up, 'you've only been here a few weeks and you've signed that book more often than not. I've made allowances, Mrs James, for the settling-in period. I know young Amy has found it hard, and I know that moving your family to a new house, a new town can be chaotic. But there are rules, procedures. There is the school-parent contract. If this carries on I'll have it put on your children's attendance record and you wouldn't want that, would you?'

'Of course I wouldn't. It's just . . .' Alison paused and wondered exactly how she could explain that the reason she and her children were late every morning was because she was desperate to avoid the friend she had once long ago betrayed, and the friend's husband, whom she had recently offered to have sex with. Alison decided there was no way to explain *that*.

'It's just things at home . . . we have family problems. And I know I shouldn't let it affect the girls at all, let alone getting them to school on time, but hopefully, after this weekend, it will be a lot less . . . *difficult.*'

Mrs Woodruff looked concerned, but chose not to pry any further, for which Alison was silently grateful.

'Can you give me your word that the girls will be on time for the remainder of this half term?' she asked Alison.

'Probably,' Alison said and, seeing Mrs Woodruff's frown deepen, added hastily, 'I mean definitely. Whatever happens on Saturday I promise they'll be here on time.'

'Good, because I've been watching Amy this week in assembly and in the playground. She seems to have formed an attachment to Leila Ashley. Leila's a bubbly little girl, full of fun and mischief. I think she'll bring Amy out of herself.'

'Really?' Alison could not have sounded less enthusiastic and she was aware of what a terrible mother and terrible person she must appear to be. She forced herself to sit up straighter. 'I mean, that's great! It's great. Leila Ashley, great, because Gemma's already fond of Eloise Ashley so that is just perfect.'

Mrs Woodruff said nothing but Alison suspected that the head teacher was examining her and searching for traces of drunkenness or madness or both.

Pull your socks up and concentrate, Alison warned herself inwardly. She knew she had to drag herself back out of her seventeen-year-old self and into the real world, the world where she was a parent and wife. Where she had children to care for and a husband to . . . to deal with. She'd been so good at it for so long, that it came as something of a shock that letting go of that role for even just one reckless moment was like pulling the thread on a sweater; she was watching the entire fabric of her adult life disintegrate into nothing before her eyes, and the more she tried to get a grip on it the faster it unravelled.

'Well, then, if you ever need to talk,' Mrs Woodruff said, gesturing at the door, 'I could always put you in touch with a family counsellor.'

Feeling like the epitome of a failure, Alison got up and walked out into the empty playground.

This had to be it, she thought to herself, the rock bottom that people are so fond of talking about. Surely things have to take an upward turn from here?

Saturday night, Alison hoped, would change everything one way or another. After Saturday she'd know what to do. Because tomorrow night she and Cathy were meeting at Kirsty's for dinner. The very fact that Cathy had agreed to go gave Alison hope that something good would come out of their move to Farmington, because now more than ever she longed to see her friend again. To hug her and laugh with her and ask her, 'What should I do?'

For the rest of the day Alison had gone through the motions of walking around the supermarket and picking up the girls from school, all in preparation for this moment. This hour, four o'clock on Friday afternoon, was family time, the afternoon when Marc was supposed to come home early and they were all supposed to eat dinner together.

Gemma and Amy were sitting at the table already in anticipation of the roast chicken Mummy was cooking, even though it was a good half-hour away from being ready. The men of the household were nowhere to be seen, though, and Alison wasn't surprised. Dominic made it his business to be late for everything, and if Marc arrived back at all before the entire family had gone to bed Alison would be stunned. In a way she was relieved that he wouldn't turn up, just as she had been relieved that he'd been avoiding her all week, because she had no idea that he'd react to her revelation in the way that he had. And so far she had no idea how to deal with it.

They had sat in the cold on the white wrought-iron chairs and she had told him that she didn't love him. And he had cried. Not sobbed or anything, but he'd shut his eyes and two tears had rolled down, followed by two more and then two more, until the water ran in rivulets over his cheeks, meeting in the corners of his mouth. They were the first tears she had ever seen him cry.

'I'm sorry,' Alison had said. 'I didn't expect you to . . . I didn't think you'd really care.'

Marc had looked at her, rubbing the tears away with the heels of his hand.

'Of course I care. I'm not made of stone, Alison. I *love* you, I love my children. I love this family. I don't want us to end.' He dropped his chin and took a deep breath, exhaled a plume of warm air in the chill of the morning.

'I've done my best to give you and the children the life you wanted, but I expect I've never really fitted into it, never really felt comfortable. Maybe that was why I did the things I did. Or maybe it's just because that's what I'm like. I'm just half a man who can never quite love anyone enough to be true to them. I don't know, Alison, but I must love you as much I possibly can love anyone, because right now . . . I feel pain.'

Alison looked at him, the tears falling, and she wondered why on earth she wasn't going to him, putting her arms around him and hugging him and kissing the salt off his face, and promising that everything would be all right between them, that everything would be fine. It was what she wanted, *longed* to be able to do. To set things the right side up again, settle back into the routine of happy families.

263

But she couldn't, because as much as the sanctuary of appearances appealed to her, when she looked at her husband crying she didn't feel anything, except remorse that she had made him sad.

'I'm going in,' Marc had said, sniffing and getting up. 'I think I'll go into the dealership. The weekend's a busy time. They'll need me.' He paused and turned round. 'You're not . . . you're not going to go anywhere? I mean, you're not going to leave me today? You'll be here with the children when I get back?'

'I'm not going to leave today,' Alison told him. Their affair might be over but she had no idea how to end their marriage. He nodded and shoved his hands in his pockets, walking back up to the house slowly, as if he were very tired.

Alison had barely seen him since.

Perhaps he was giving her space, or perhaps he thought if she didn't have to see him there was more chance of her staying.

Alison didn't know, but in any event she didn't expect to see him tonight.

'Mummy, it's nearly quarter past four, where is everyone?' Gemma asked her primly. 'Where is Daddy?'

'Well, the thing is, Daddy . . .' Alison was just about to conjure up some explanation when she heard the front door close.

'Here's Dom, anyway,' she said brightly, winking at the girls and calling out, 'Count yourself lucky that you've showed up more or less on time, young man. Ten more minutes and your dinner would have been in the . . . dog. Oh, hello, darling.'

Alison masked her surprise with a smile for Marc as he walked into the kitchen and kissed her lightly on the cheek. He'd shaved that morning, and his skin was cool, soft and smooth against the heat of hers.

They held each other's gaze for a moment but Marc did not return her smile.

'Daddy!' Amy exclaimed, running to hug him around his legs. 'I had the best day today, Daddy. We saw an actual play at the school, actual real people came and did a play and it wasn't on the TV or anything, and I sat next to Leila Ashley, who is my new friend. She let me eat her carrots at snack, which her mummy grew in the *ground*.'

'Did she, darling?' Marc said, ruffling her hair and sitting her on his knee as the two of them joined Gemma at the table. 'Well, it's great that you two are friends with the Ashley sisters. It's sort of like history repeating itself, right, Al?'

'I suppose so,' Alison said uneasily, as she peered into the oven. Having tested one leg, she took the chicken out to rest, covering it with foil. Marc had come to eat dinner at 'family time' to make a point, and it was clear what it was.

'What do you mean, Daddy?' Gemma asked as he shifted Amy off his knee and unbuttoned his shirt collar. 'How can the past repeat itself. Is it like *Dr Who*?'

'Not like *Dr Who*. You know, don't you,' Marc asked his daughters, 'that once, a long time ago, when Mummy was a little girl, she used to live in Farmington?'

'Yes,' the girls chorused at once.

'Well, Mummy used to be best friends with Leila and Eloise's mummy, didn't you, darling?'

Alison felt her shoulders tense. Her back to her family, she strained her supermarket-bought carrots, tipping the water into the pan to make gravy. There was an edge of anger to Marc's voice that unnerved her.

'Yes,' she said, over her shoulder. 'A long time ago now, though. Practically a lifetime.'

'Does Eloise's mummy know that you are you?' Gemma asked her excitedly. 'I bet she'll be so pleased to see you,

Mummy! Then all of us can be friends and we can all go round to teas and things. Won't it be great, Mummy?'

'Well,' Alison said. 'Maybe, we'll see.'

'Pleeeaasssse,' Gemma pleaded, which was her stock response to the phrase 'We'll see'.

'The thing is that Mummy and Eloise and Leila's mummy fell out and they've never made up since.'

'Why, Mama?' Leila asked her. 'Didn't you do make up, make up, never, never break up?'

'Anyway, why did you fall out?' Gemma asked her. 'Was it over sharing?'

'Sort of,' Marc said before Alison could answer. 'Your mummy and Eloise's mummy fell out over me.' He grinned and a waggled his eyebrows, making the girls giggle.

'Don't be silly, Daddy,' Amy said. 'Mama didn't even know you when she was little.'

'Well, Mummy wasn't quite as little as you when she fell out with Eloise's mum,' Marc explained. Alison shot him a glance across the kitchen as she stirred the gravy but he ignored her.

'I'm not little, actually,' Gemma interjected primly.

'Or me. I'm not little either,' Amy added. 'Much.'

'Well, Mummy was only a little bit older than Dom is now when she met me and fell madly in love with me, and who can blame her?'

'Because you are handsome,' Amy agreed. 'Like the prince in *Cinderella*.'

'Only fatter,' Gemma added. 'And sometimes you can see the skin on the back of your head through your hair.'

'Well, anyway,' Marc said. 'The trouble was that Eloise's mummy had met me first. And she was already in love with me.'

'Ooooooh,' Gemma said, wide-eyed. 'What happened?'

'I chose your mummy, of course,' Marc said. 'I gave up

266

everything to choose your mummy, and Dom and you two girls, and I worked very, very hard to make you all as happy and as secure as I could.'

'Was Eloise's mummy sad?' Gemma asked, frowning slightly.

'I think she was sad,' Marc said. 'And a bit cross.'

'And are they still not friends even now?' Gemma asked him. 'That's a long time not to be friends. I wasn't friends with Emily Shawcross once for two weeks at our old school. That was the longest time I've never not been friends with someone.' She looked concerned as a thought suddenly occurred to her.

'Mummy, this doesn't mean I won't be able to be friends with Ellie, does it?'

'No, of course not.' Alison looked crossly at Marc but he only winked at her. Dominic was not here, the food was spoiling and Marc was doing his level best to rattle her, for what purpose she could not imagine except to try to exert some power over her. Well, she had some news she knew would shut him up.

'Everything will be fine because I'm going to see Eloise's mum, and hopefully after we've had a good talk about things, we'll make up then.'

'When?' Marc sat up in his chair. 'When are you seeing her?'

'Tomorrow,' Alison said. 'Amazingly the one friend I've made since we moved here is her next-door neighbour. She's invited us both round to dinner. You don't mind babysitting, do you?'

'And Catherine's fine about that?' Marc asked her, his brow furrowed.

'Yes, clearly she is, otherwise Kirsty would have told me by now,' Alison replied, smiling at the girls. 'So by Sunday morning everything will be straightened out. It will be nice, actually, after all these years.' She looked at Marc. 'After all, I knew her before I knew your dad. I miss her.'

'You can do make up, make up, never, never break up, Mama,' Amy suggested.

'And things will go back to how they were before you knew me,' Marc said, his face closed.

'I doubt that very much,' Alison said, keeping her voice light as she watched him.

'Where's Dom?' Amy said, looking anxiously out at the cloud-heavy sky.

'I'm here,' Dom said, sauntering in through the back door. The smell of stale cigarette smoke drifted in with him along with a girl, as thin as a blade, with a curtain of black hair that revealed only one kohl-blackened eye and an ear that had been pierced several times. She seemed to be holding Dominic's hand, although Alison couldn't conclusively tell because her sleeves were pulled well past the tips of her fingers, as were his.

'This is Ciara,' Dom announced. 'I've brought her home for dinner, like you said, Mum.'

Alison pressed her lips together, balancing her irritation with the need to get through this dinner unscathed. Yes, she had told Dominic to bring his friends home, but she had foolishly hoped that he might give her some notice. At least a guest would diffuse some of the tension, Alison hoped. Marc was always at his most charming in front of strangers.

'Hello, Ciara,' Alison said, still coming to terms with the sight of her son possibly holding hands with a girl. 'How lovely that Dom's brought you home. Have you told your parents? Would you like me to ring them?'

'I've told them, thanks, Mrs James,' Ciara said, producing a mobile from her pocket and waving it, with one fingerless gloved hand. 'Thank you very much for having me.'

'My pleasure.' Alison smiled warmly at the girl, who sounded much nicer than she looked. 'Gemma, set another place at the table, please.'

'So, Ciara,' Marc smiled at the young girl as she sat down next to Dom. 'Do you go to Rock Club too?'

'Yes,' Ciara said, tossing her hair back off her shoulder and revealing quite a pretty face. 'I do vocal, mainly, but I'm learning to play the bass too because Mr Ashley says that versatility is key in the industry. You've got to have a USP.'

'Everybody needs a USP,' Marc agreed. 'Dom loves his guitar, don't you, Dom? Sometimes he actually sleeps with it.'

Ciara looked at the table and smiled, raising her finely plucked brows.

'I don't sleep with it,' Dominic said, glowering at his father. 'Sometimes I fall asleep playing it, because I'm always playing it. It's the only fucking thing to do in this shit-hole of a town.'

Ciara breathed in sharply, this time her eyes wide with awe.

'Dominic.' Alison slammed a pan down and stared at her son.

Dominic returned her gaze.

'You never ever use those words in front of your sisters,' she said, her voice low, noting how Marc was doing nothing. Marc always did nothing about his son until a situation reached crisis point. 'I treat you like an adult when you behave like one. So don't show off just because you've got a friend here. Don't make me embarrass you.'

'Which words were bad words, Mummy?' Amy asked as Alison set two plates of food in front of Gemma and Amy.

'Never you mind,' Alison said. 'I'm sure Ciara doesn't use that kind of language, do you, Ciara?'

'I don't, actually,' Ciara said. 'I think the use of swearwords demeans and cheapens one. It makes us look weak and ineffectual.'

Marc laughed out loud, making the girls giggle too.

Dominic sat perfectly still in his chair, his hands on the table, tapping his chipped black nails on the surface.

'So are you two an item then?' Marc asked Ciara as Alison gave them each a plate of food. Dominic chewed the inside of his cheek furiously.

'We've hooked up a few times,' Ciara said quite calmly.

'Young love is so sweet,' Marc said, causing Alison to shoot him a warning glance that he deflected with a shrug. 'Well, it is, at your age. It's nice, uncomplicated.'

'We're not in love, right?' Dom said, looking at Ciara, who merely shrugged in agreement. 'Look, Mum, I thought I'd bring a friend home for dinner. I thought you'd like that. I didn't think she'd get the third degree. From *him*.' He jabbed a nod in the direction of his father.

'I don't mind actually,' Ciara told him. 'I'm quite good with parents.'

'I mind. It's none of his business,' Dom said. He got up and went to the fridge. 'Do you want a drink?' he asked Ciara.

'Please,' she said. When Dom sat back down he set two bottles of beer in front of him and the girl.

'Cool,' Ciara said, picking hers up and taking a swig straight out of the bottle.

'I don't think so.' Alison reached over and picked up the bottles. 'Look, Ciara, I'm sorry, but we don't let Dom drink alcohol at home. I know he's probably trying to impress you but I'm not sending you home to your mother with beer on your breath. I don't condone underage drinking.'

'That's OK, Mrs James,' Ciara said politely. 'Although actually once you're fifteen you can legally drink in the home, if your parents allow it. My parents let me have a glass of wine with Sunday lunch because they feel that if I am familiar with alcohol I'm less likely to go overboard and binge on it when I'm unsupervised.'

'Really,' Alison said, sitting back down with a jug of orange juice. 'Well, if you'd like to give me your mother's number I'll ring her and ask her if she minds if you have a glass of wine with your meal.'

'That's OK, Mrs James,' Ciara said. 'Juice is fine by me.'

All, bar the three girls, who fought the tension bravely with chatter, were silent at the table. Gemma asked Ciara about all of her earrings, and Amy quizzed her on her make-up. Alison felt surprisingly grateful for the girl, who fielded her daughters' questions with good grace and didn't seem to mind that the boy who had invited her over was silent and sullen. Perhaps that was what she liked about him, Alison found herself wondering. Perhaps to her he seemed mysterious and misunderstood.

She was deep in thought, trying to imagine how her son must appear to teenage eyes that she was completely unprepared for what happened next.

'This is fucking joke,' Dominic said under his breath.

It took Alison a second to register what he had said. 'Dom,' she warned him, 'one more word and you'll go to your room, and Ciara will have to go home.'

'Oh, come on, Mum,' Dominic said, shoving his untouched plate away from him. 'Admit it. We're sitting round the table on so-called "family night" and it means nothing, there's no family here. It's a fucking joke and you know it. This isn't a family, it's a sham.'

'Dom! Stop it, stop it! Mummy, make him stop!' Amy said, covering her ears, her face crumpling.

'Go to your room, now,' Alison told him, her voice shaking.

'No!' Dominic stood up abruptly and, leaning across the table, shouted the word so that his hot breath and spittle collided with her face. 'I will not go to my fucking room. Admit it, admit that all of this is bollocks and that this whole family is just one big fucking mess that's falling to pieces. I won't move until you tell me that he –' he stabbed a finger at his father – 'is a useless, lying, cheating waste of space and we'd all be better off without him!'

'GET OUT OF HERE!' Suddenly Marc sprung up from the table and hauled Dominic away from it by the collar of his school shirt, slamming him back hard against the kitchen wall. Dominic, his cheeks flushed and his eyes glittering, laughed in his father's face.

'Yeah, that's it, hit me. Show your true colours, Marc. Show us what you really are. Just a navvy thug, who can't keep his dick in his trousers, that's the real you, isn't it, Dad? Might as well knock your kids around too!'

Before Alison could move she saw Marc grab Dominic with his left and draw back his right fist.

'DADDY, DON'T!' Gemma screamed over her sister, who was wailing uncontrollably. 'Don't hit him, don't hit him!'

Marc paused, and Alison saw that his arm was trembling.

He released Dominic, taking a step back, staring at the boy as if he had no idea who he was.

Shrugging his ripped shirt back on his shoulders, Dominic pulled himself off the wall and, looking Marc right in the eye, spat in his face. Picking up one of the opened beer bottles Alison had left on the side, he slammed out of the back door.

Able to move at last, Alison gathered Amy up onto her lap and put her arms around Gemma.

'Never mind, never mind,' she whispered. 'Silly old Dom and Daddy. They didn't mean it . . . never mind . . .'

Ciara looked regretfully at the plate of food that was still steaming in front of her.

'I'll go after him, Mrs James,' she said, standing up. 'He's been wound up all week, really angry about something but he wouldn't say what. I didn't know he was going to do that or I would have tried to stop him.' Ciara paused, not quite sure how to exit. 'Don't worry, I'll make sure he's OK. And thanks very much for dinner.'

She edged quite calmly past Marc, who was still standing facing the wall, his fists clenched.

'I'm going out,' Marc said, once the girl had gone.

'Marc,' Alison said as evenly as she could, 'don't go. Wait, please. We need to talk about this.'

'Do we?' Marc said. 'It's quite clear who you talk to in this family and it isn't me. You didn't have to do that, Alison. You didn't have to turn my own son against me.'

'I didn't,' Alison reacted coldly. 'I didn't say a word to him. You did that all by yourself.'

'I'm going out,' Marc repeated without looking at her, and he left without his jacket, picking up his wallet and keys on the way.

Alison sat with her two crying girls and she rocked them, all three, back and forth until all she could hear was the ticking of the kitchen clock.

When her husband and her son had come in tonight they had both planned to hurt her. They'd both wanted, for very different reasons, to show her what she was doing to their family.

Marc wanted things back the way they once were and Dom wanted everything to change. Strange then, given that, both had gone about it in exactly the same way.

They were more alike than either of them would ever admit to.

It took Alison a long time to get the girls to sleep, and only once she allowed Amy to climb into bed with Gemma had they eventually drifted off, after insisting that Alison sat by them until they were asleep. Gemma had been brave and resilient, promising Amy that it was a big fuss about nothing but still she had not wanted Alison to leave them. Amy was still crying when she finally surrendered to sleep, the tears drying on her cheeks.

As Amy slept Gemma looked at her mum from the bed. 'Will you and Daddy split up, Mummy?' she asked.

Alison closed her eyes, feeling as if she were crumbling and collapsing from the inside out.

'No,' she said, because she wanted her eight-year-old to be able to go to sleep without being afraid. 'It was just a silly row, that's all, between Daddy and Dom.'

'But Daddy and you don't like each other as much as you used to,' Gemma said. 'You pretend to, but I can tell. You're all . . . far apart.'

'It's all just a bit funny at the moment because we've moved house, and we're both a bit tired and grumpy, that's all. You'll see, when things calm down everything will be fine.' Alison fought to maintain the soft, calm timbre in her voice.

'Do you promise, Mummy?' Gemma asked her. Alison bent over and kissed Gemma on her smooth round cheek.

'I promise you,' she said.

And as she walked out of the room she didn't care what she had to do or give up to keep that promise, she just knew she had to make it true. So what if other people like Christina's friend Sophie risked failure to be happy? Perhaps happiness wasn't as important as the world kept on insisting that it was. Perhaps it didn't matter if she didn't love Marc the way she used to, and if she stuck with him then maybe the feeling would come back. Dominic thought he knew what was best for her but he was just a boy. He had no idea what it really meant to be married, committed to a relationship, come what may. Marc had behaved badly in the past, and almost unforgivably tonight, but like he said, he cared about her, he loved her the very most that he could, and perhaps she would just have to learn to live with that.

As Alison walked down the stairs in the dark she told herself again and again that she could make it work. Maybe after tomorrow she and Cathy would be friends again and perhaps, in time, good friends. If she had Cathy to lean on she thought she could manage it; she thought she could do anything for her daughters. Anything that would prevent Gemma from knowing that her mother was a liar.

At just gone eleven Alison was trying to work out exactly who it was she was waiting up for.

She'd called Dominic several times, but of course his phone wasn't switched on.

At one point she almost phoned Marc, to tell him that Dom was wrong and he was right, that the family was worth staying together for, no matter how difficult it would be. But her thumb hovered over the call button and eventually she set the phone down undialled. She had to see his face when she told him that; she had to see the way he looked so she could be sure she was doing the right thing.

Leaning her head back against the sofa, Alison closed her hot dry eyes for a moment and tried to imagine Marc's face. She'd wait up until he got in and then she'd tell him every-thing was going to be all right, and when she woke up in the morning the sun would be out and order would be restored. Marc and the girls would be happy and Dom would come round eventually, once she explained everything to him.

Because in the end, Alison decided hazily, as her thoughts and feelings swirled like the coloured patterns behind her lids, there wasn't any other choice for her to make. She'd made her choice long ago and all that remained was for her to see it out.

*

She sprang awake when she heard the front door latch close. Sitting up, she saw Dominic appear from the hallway.

'Is he here?' he asked.

'He stormed out too,' Alison said. 'The two of you are so alike.'

'Don't say that,' Dom said, but his voice was low, drained of all aggression.

Alison held out a hand to him and reluctantly he came and sat down next to her.

'Why did you do that?' Alison asked him. 'Why do that to your sisters? They were so upset.'

'They are going to be upset sooner or later,' Dom said. 'Divorce is hard on the kids, but if you're upfront with them they'll take it better.'

'No,' Alison said. 'No, they won't . . .'

'Honestly, Mum, I'm so sorry,' Dom told her as if he hadn't heard her. 'I just lost it this afternoon. I didn't mean to do it, I didn't even plan it. I just couldn't stand him being at the table with us. Acting as if he cared, acting as if this family meant anything to him. And you're wrong, Gemma and Amy will be able to handle you and Dad breaking up. In fact, probably once it's out in the open they'll be fine, because they'll know where they stand and they won't be worrying so much.'

'They already know where they stand,' Alison said, bracing herself.

'You talked to them?'

'Yes.' Alison picked up her son's hand. 'Dom, I told them that everything was going to be all right between me and your dad. I told them we weren't going to split up. They won't have to deal with anything . . . I'm going to fix things.'

'Mum . . .' Dominic shook his head. 'Mum, wait, listen –'

'No, Dom, I've decided. I'm not leaving your dad. I know

276

things aren't perfect, but, well, your dad and I talked. I've made my feelings really clear, and it's shocked him. It's hurt him and I don't think he really understood before what was at stake, what he risked losing. I think that if I . . . if *we* make an effort now, then we can really come through. We can stick together. I think this time your dad really listened to me and understood how I felt. I think he'll change, Dom. I think he'll do his best to keep us all together. It's what he wants and it's what the girls want, and so then it's what I want too. And I need you to understand that and to support me. Who knows, perhaps once things have calmed down you'll start to get on better with Dad.'

'You've talked and he's changed,' Dominic said, shaking his head as if he hadn't heard half of what Alison said. 'When did you talk? Tonight, after I'd gone? Tell me, Mum, when did you talk?'

'Last Sunday after the party,' Alison said. 'He's been really good since. I think he's tried to be considerate. He's given me space, he hasn't tried to change my mind, even though that's what he really wants, even though that is why he got so angry with you tonight. I thought he would do this one thing that I expected him to do right away. But he hasn't done it, Dom. I'd know this time if he had been with . . . someone else. He gets sort of calm and still for a while. Peaceful. Not at all like he was tonight. He was that way because he is fighting to keep us. He's going about it all wrong but still he's trying, and after fifteen years I have to let that mean something. Dom, I'm not saying we're all just going to be a happy family again. But when I saw how upset the girls were tonight I just knew I had to try, and if your father is prepared to try too then, who knows, we might just make it.'

Alison felt a surge of hope bubble in her chest as she finished her speech, realising that she had been attempting to convince herself as much as her son.

'Last Sunday,' Dom said. 'That's funny, because on Monday I saw with him with another woman.'

'What?' Alison was stunned into silence for a few minutes. 'What do you mean? How – you were supposed to be in school?'

'We had a free period and it was almost the end of school so I went down the canal with some of the other kids,' Dominic said.

'You saw your Dad in the park with another woman?' Alison laughed. The image was so absurd, it was as if Dominic had somehow glimpsed into the past.

'No, I was walking on the road down the bridge and I saw him at the door of a house. I was going to sneak by because I didn't want him to see me but then the door opened, and it was that woman. The woman that was at the party, Mum. Tall, with red hair. She only had PJs on and it was gone two. She let him in and closed the door.'

'He was at Cathy's,' Alison whispered, almost to herself. 'I knew he'd go there. I knew he would . . .'

'That's not all,' Dom said. Alison looked up at him. 'He was in there for a while, so I thought I'd hang about, you know, see if he came out, ask him what he was doing. But he was ages so I crept up and looked through the window. She'd got dressed by then. They were holding each other; it was pretty obvious what was going to happen next. What had probably already happened. I didn't want to see that so I legged it. I didn't know how to tell you, Mum. I hoped I wouldn't have to tell you but then you said all of that stuff about trying and hope, and I had to.'

'I really thought I'd know if he'd been with Cathy,' Alison said bleakly. 'I really thought I would.'

'I'm sorry,' Dom said. 'But I'm not lying.'

'I know,' Alison told him. 'I know.'

She felt something flare in her chest, a reignited spark of those old passions, fury and jealousy, which had driven her to take Marc from Cathy fifteen years ago. That's what had been between her and Marc at the beginning. And after any love they might have managed to conjure up between them had finally vanished for good, that was all that remained: fury and jealousy.

'So when you thought he was hurt and worried and upset he was already trying to get off with someone else,' Dominic said triumphantly. 'Don't you see that's why we can't go on like this? You have to end it.'

Alison was silent.

'I'm going to bed, before he gets in,' Dom said, kissing her on the head as he got up. 'I'm sorry I had to tell you, Mum, but can you see now why I got so angry?'

Alison nodded. 'I see,' she said.

Once her son had gone up she found that she was crying. But not because Marc had betrayed her. Because her friend had. And for the first time in sixteen years Alison knew what that felt like.

Chapter Eighteen

Catherine lay in bed and listened to her empty house. When it was her weekend to have the girls they would be downstairs by now, bashing about in the kitchen making themselves cereals, slopping milk onto the floor and sloshing juice into cups. And then they'd eat, sitting on the carpet in front of the TV because it was the only day of the week their mother would let them get away with it.

But this weekend they were away with Jimmy and the house was quiet. No, it was more than quiet, it was hollow. It echoed with their absence.

Catherine stretched her fingers above her head and her toes towards the bottom of the bed, sat up and paused, not for the first time, to reflect on how her absent family had been thrown off balance by everything that had happened. The return of Marc and Alison hadn't just pitched her into turmoil, but the feelings and thoughts of those around her too, including her children, and she couldn't stand that.

It frightened Catherine to death when she thought about the sane and steady life that she had worked so hard to shore up over the last couple of years being threatened, and she knew she would do whatever she could to try to protect the makeshift harmony that she had created for her daughters. But, just as she was resolved to do that at any cost, a stealthy image of Marc and the remembrance of the heat of his touch intervened, so that her heart beat a little faster and she felt the blood pumping in her veins, and for a few terrifying seconds she had the impulse to throw everything away just to feel like that again, and hang the consequences. She had felt like that once before and it hadn't ended well.

Catherine got out of bed and pulled the curtain back. It was cold outside, a sharp blue sky promising chilly sunshine. She pressed the heat of her cheeks against the cool glass for a moment until the thought of what might have happened next if Marc had kissed her faded to a bearable level.

It was all very well for Kirsty to tell her to rejoice in being fully alive, but when you weren't used to it, it wasn't that easy. It was like waking up one hundred years in the future; everything seemed louder, faster and a whole lot more frightening, a world full of terrifying possibilities.

Despite what had happened on Monday Jimmy had still been around for most of the week. He had picked up the girls and taken them to school every other day, and on Tuesday he'd walked with Catherine to work because he knew she was dreading it, even if she didn't say so. He'd had dinner with them on Wednesday night and on Thursday had come round to replace the rotting floorboard in the bathroom, a job he'd been promising to do for at least three months. He'd been there, but at the same time he'd been absent too.

On Friday afternoon, he'd come round to pick up the girls' luggage before he collected them from school to take them straight off to his mother's. He'd stood there in silence, holding up the rucksack while Catherine folded in changes of clothes for each of them and then carefully stowed favourite toys and books.

They hadn't talked about what Jimmy had seen on Monday since then, but Catherine felt that she should be talking about

281

something, because it just wasn't like the two of them to be silent and polite, so she'd asked him a question.

'Are you sorry you missed the audition for session work? I feel so bad that you missed it because of me. Maybe if you called them now it wouldn't be too late.'

Jimmy shook his head, bending to scoop one of Leila's soft toys from the floor where Catherine had dropped it. He picked it up and squeezed it tenderly before dropping it into the bag.

'No,' he said. 'I was in two minds about it anyway, and besides, I'm needed here right now.'

By his usual standards he was being singularly uncommunicative and although Catherine could understand that walking in on her and Marc had made him angry, territorial even, and unusually macho, she couldn't work out why he'd seemed so sad. Catherine hated to see him sad.

'I just don't like to think about you missing out, because of me,' she said. 'Because of my stupid mess. I can manage without you, if you want to go.'

'I know,' Jimmy said with a shrug, staring at the toes of his cowboy boots. 'Session work is for losers anyway. I've got the band to think about. Right now the band need me. We're at a crucial writing stage. Plus we've got that wedding at the Holiday Inn, week after next.'

'Jimmy?' Catherine had asked him uncertainly, afraid that his sadness was a symptom of regret. 'Do you ever wish you'd never met me, that we'd never got together and you'd never become a dad so young? Because then you wouldn't feel obliged to hang around me now and make sure I don't make a total idiot of myself.'

Jimmy had looked at her for a long time.

'I felt like that once, on one night for about half an hour, and that was enough to end our marriage.' He'd shrugged and, as Catherine put the last toy in the rucksack, bent to strap it up. 'But I've never felt that way for one moment before or since. Why do you ask? Is it because you think if you didn't have me or the children in your life *you'd* be free now? Free to run off with arse-face.'

Catherine had known her laugh at the insult was probably ill advised, but it escaped before she could repress it. Jimmy glowered at her.

'I'm sorry,' she said, composing her features. 'It's just – look, I know you think I'm an idiot and possibly some kind of slut for getting as close to him as I did after seeing him again for about five seconds, but you know me, Jim. You know that in the last twelve years you're the only person I've . . . I'm not the kind of woman that jumps into bed with people for the sake of it. I got swept away in the moment, in the past. I know what's at stake and besides, I've never stolen another woman's husband yet and I'm not going to start now. Please don't be angry with me, please don't be so . . . disappointed in me. For one thing, I can't take it. I need you to like me because what you think of me matters to me more than what anyone else thinks, and for another, Kirsty says you are being a right royal hypocrite and that I should punch you for being so up your own arse.'

This time Jimmy's mouth twitched a little, but only a little.

'Maybe it's just hitting me now,' he said. 'Maybe that's why I'm so . . . down.'

'What is hitting you? Marc and Alison turning up?'

'No, us, breaking up. The end of our marriage.' Jimmy sighed and looked at the ceiling. 'Look, I've got a reputation, girls hang around me a lot of the time. I don't really blame them: I am Jimmy Ashley, after all. But for what it's worth I want you to know that I haven't been with anyone else in twelve years either. Apart from Donna Clarke in the ladies' loos of The Goat. At first I let you think I did go with other women because I was angry at you for not forgiving me, and I wanted to hurt you even more. And then I did it because I thought I actually might meet someone new and sometimes, recently, just because it seems easier to pretend that I'm something I'm not. That version of me is a lot easier to live with, the version that doesn't give a bollock about what he's messed up.' Jimmy shrugged. 'I know you have every right to see other men and move on, even arse-face, if you really want to – I know that – but when I saw you with him then it hit me. We're over. We're really over, and sooner or later everything will change for ever because we can't go on like this and live our lives.'

Catherine had been silent for a moment, listening to the radiators rumbling against the cold and the whoosh of the traffic splattering through the puddles outside the window, and to her astonishment, as Jimmy's words sank in, she found she had to fight the well of tears in her eyes and blink them away.

'You'd better get the children,' she said, dipping her head to use her hair as a curtain as she composed herself. 'Got all their stuff?'

Jimmy picked up a big and battered old backpack, the same one he'd had when he left home at the age of nineteen.

'Right here,' he said, mustering a smile. 'Although why they need this much stuff for a weekend at my mother's I don't know.'

'Especially when she'll send them home with a whole new wardrobe of pink anyway,' Catherine said, grateful for his smile. 'Never could get her head round redheads and hot pink.'

The pair stood up and eyed each other cautiously.

'Have a good weekend,' Jimmy said, hugging her briefly. 'And take care of yourself.'

'I will,' Catherine promised him. 'And you make sure you keep the girls warm and dry. I want them on that rust bucket for the least amount of time possible. Give my love to your mother.'

'Seriously?' Jimmy asked her wryly. 'She won't send you any back, you know.'

'Well, give her my regards, then,' Catherine told him with a smile. 'I can be magnanimous.'

And then on impulse she had thrown her arms around him and hugged him until his arms had encircled her waist and he'd held her.

'No matter what has to change you'll always mean the world to me,' she told him.

'Same,' Jimmy said, looking briefly into her eyes. 'And all of that bollocks.'

Eloise had not been sad but she had been angry. She had been silently, resolutely furious with Catherine since Monday afternoon when it became clear that Jimmy was not moving back in for good.

The eight-year-old had made a point of not holding Catherine's hand on the way home, and pretending she was asleep before Catherine could even kiss her good night.

At breakfast the following day she had been surly and rude, and on Thursday Leila had watched open-mouthed as Eloise told her mother to mind her own business and shut her mouth, storming upstairs just as they were about to leave for school.

'All you did was ask her if she'd remembered her gym kit!' Leila exclaimed with theatrical despair. 'Mummy, you are going to tell her off now, aren't you? She's being extremely naughty and disrespecting you!'

'I know,' Catherine had said, putting her hand on Leila's

shoulder and looking up the stairs. 'But she's a bit upset at the moment and cross with me . . .'

''Cos you won't let Daddy move back in?' Leila said matter-of-factly, crossing her arms.

'Yes,' Catherine looked at her younger daughter with some concern. 'How do you know, poppet?'

'Because Ellie told me and because I know anyway,' Leila said with a shrug. 'I wish Daddy would come back too. Ellie says he loves you and he loves us, but you don't love him, and you probably don't love us very much either otherwise you'd let him move back in.'

'Oh, Leila,' Catherine said, kneeling to hug the five-year-old tightly. 'You know that I love you two so much, don't you?'

Leila looked at her mother with her father's hazel eyes.

'I know that, Mummy,' she said. 'I told Ellie that you love us about a million otherwise you'd really kill us if you knew about the toffees under Ellie's bed, but you do know and you haven't killed us, so you must love us. Plus, mums must always love their children, even when they are bad, a bit like God always loves us even if we let him down, which we do quite a bit.'

Catherine put the palm of her hand on the heart-shaped curve of Leila's face.

'You are completely right.'

'Well, then,' Leila said, 'I don't know what all the fuss is about. I told Ellie I love you and Daddy about a million and her about four to five hundred, and we all love each other as much as we can and that's that.'

'And what did Ellie say?' Catherine asked her gently.

'Well, she said I was a stupid little baby and didn't understand anything,' Leila replied with a cheerful shrug.

'You are not a stupid little baby,' Catherine told her. 'You are a very clever, wonderful girl.'

'I know,' Leila said. 'God gave me an extra big brain. So are you going to shout at Ellie now? I think you have to shout at her, Mummy, or she'll become a *monster*. I can come and watch, if you like.'

'I'm not going to shout at her,' Catherine said. 'But I'll go and talk to her and fetch her down, otherwise we'll be late for school.'

'Good luck, Mummy,' Leila said, holding a hand out for Catherine to shake. 'May the love of Christ be with you.'

'Thanks,' Catherine said as she advanced up the narrow stairwell. 'I think I'm going to need him.'

And she hadn't been wrong. Eloise had kicked and screamed, flounced and shouted all the way to school. It was so unusual, so out of the ordinary for Catherine to be at odds with either of her children, that she felt at a loss to know what to do, and she wished that just for once she would be able to give them exactly what they wanted instead of only ever being able to offer them cut-price solutions and an imperfect bargain-basement life.

This time, like too many times before, she couldn't make their dreams come true.

Jimmy peered out from the hatch to his boat and looked up at the rain. It was slicing down in thick sheets, colliding with the tin roof of the boat with a violent clatter.

He looked back at the girls, who were wrapped as one in his duvets, sitting on the bed-cum-seat, cowering from the leaky roof.

'We'll try again in a minute,' Jimmy repeated. His mother had been out when they arrived in Aylesbury on Friday evening. After mooring the boat they waited for a break in the weather until it became apparent that no break was going to come, and Leila said she thought they'd be drier outside anyway. With no umbrellas, they ran the two hundred yards or so from the towpath to his mother's house and Jimmy knocked on the door, but no one answered.

After a few moments he knocked again, and again, and then he went round the back and peered though the french windows. The living room was silent and dark. Sensing his daughters' expectancy, Jimmy kneeled down and peered through the letterbox: the hallway light was on. But that could mean anything. His mother had always lived by the conviction that burglars would never rob a house with a hallway light on, on the off chance that the entire family plus a guard dog might be convening on the landing.

Shepherding the girls under the meagre protection of the porch, Jimmy phoned both her home (although Leila had pointed out if she was in to answer it they wouldn't have been standing outside in the rain) and mobile number several times. Then Eloise noticed a milk bottle with a note sticking out of the top of it.

It was written in his mother's fat, loose handwriting, the ink faded and bleeding into the paper where the rain had reached it. It read, 'No milk for two weeks, please.'

Jimmy stared at the note and got an uneasy feeling in the pit of his stomach. Mum never missed her chance to see the girls, and in the winter Jimmy always brought them here when it was his weekend. He didn't like them spending the night in his boat at all, but especially not in this weather. He hated them having to see past the romance and fun of how he lived to the damp cold reality.

Jimmy recalled the last conversation he'd had with his mum when he'd phoned to give her the dates they'd be visiting in March.

'Now that first weekend I won't be back from Spain till Saturday morning, OK? So bring them on Saturday at about eleven. It'll be lovely to see their little faces and I'll bring them back some presents.'

'OK,' Jimmy had said, or something like that.

'Did you get that?' his mum had persisted. 'Bring them Saturday morning? Write it down, James. You know what you're like.'

'I don't need to write it down,' Jimmy now remembered saying testily. 'I'm not an idiot, Mum.'

As if he needed any further proof of his general inadequacy, it was official: he was an idiot.

He had forgotten that his mum wasn't going to be back until Saturday morning; probably from the moment he had put the phone down on her until this very second, that piece of vital information had floated out of his head. Jimmy looked at his girls huddled in the porch and did his best to hide his frustration from them. If he'd remembered that his mum wasn't due back until tomorrow morning then he could have told Catherine, she would have let him pick up the girls dry and warm and happy then, and maybe he would have had one more night to stand between her and the next part of her life, the part that was not going to include him.

At a loss over what to do, he'd taken the girls to McDonald's, where they had sat over three Happy Meals (Jimmy didn't have quite enough cash for anything else) until the early evening crowd thinned out and the late evening collections of angry-looking boys and bored-looking girls began to fill it up. At that point even Jimmy, who was noted for being hip with the kids, thought the girls probably didn't need to hear language quite so Anglo-Saxon. By the time they got back to the boat it was almost ten and he could see his girls were cold and damp and miserable, even though they were trying their best to look as if they were having a good time, especially Eloise, who was determined to prove that nothing her father did could ever be wrong.

Jimmy made them hot chocolate and they huddled together around the stove, singing Meat Loaf numbers until finally sleep overtook first Leila and then Eloise. Jimmy was still kicking himself when he drifted off at last, and finally the three of them slept sitting up, huddled like birds in a nest.

The rain hadn't stopped all night. It was just after six, when a hint of grey daylight was struggling to appear through the sodden gloom, that Jimmy woke up. He'd been phoning his mother's mobile on and off ever since, though he knew she wouldn't turn it on until she got back into the house. She always said she didn't want to be a slave to it, because it was only for emergencies and she didn't want to run the battery down. She never had quite grasped the mobile part of a mobile phone.

'Try again,' Eloise whined miserably, nodding at Jimmy's phone. 'It must be past eleven now and I want to be warm, Daddy.'

'We've had lovely time,' Leila said consolingly. 'It's just we can't feel our noses now. It's a bit like when Jesus spent forty days and nights in the desert. Only cold.' She sank her chin into the neck of her coat, which she had worn all night, adding, 'I love you, Daddy,' just before the lower half of her face disappeared completely.

Jimmy bit the inside of his mouth and pressed the redial on his phone.

As his mother answered he knew at least one thing for certain. He was *never* going to hear the end of this.

'Look at my girls,' Pam said as she put another plate of toast in front of the children, who were bathed and changed into the brand-new and largely pink outfits that she had bought them in duty free. 'Pretty as a picture.'

Pam was always buying her granddaughters things, pretty things, nice things. The things their mother didn't seem to give two hoots about. Her gifts and outfits went home with them, but since she never saw them wear anything she'd ever given them again, she wouldn't put it past that woman to sell them on.

'I've missed you,' she said, hugging first one and then the other, and then adjusting the bow in Leila's hair.

'We missed you too, Nana Pam,' Leila said, with feeling. 'Especially when we were freezing like ice cubes and penguins.'

'Hmph . . .' Pam caught her son's look and bit her tongue. 'Well, if your daddy didn't love that leaky old boat so much . . .'

'I'm like a pirate, girls,' Jimmy said, mustering himself now that he had his own plate of toast, not to mention some dry old clothes that his mum still kept in his wardrobe, and which were only marginally too tight for him now. 'I sail the high seas looking for adventure.'

'You sail the canal, you mean,' Leila said.

'And you don't even sail it 'cos you haven't got a sail,' Eloise added.

Jimmy sipped his tea and said nothing. Sometimes he felt like he was the best father in the history of fathers. Like last night – yes, he'd got his daughters cold and wet, and with nowhere decent to sleep because of his own stupidity, but when he and the girls had been singing 'Bat Out of Hell' and he realised they knew all the words, at that moment he was officially the coolest father in the world. But then the real world came crashing in and he'd acknowledged that a comprehensive knowledge of the Meat Loaf catalogue was not what an eight- and five-year-old really needed from their father. When Eloise looked at him the way she just had, he felt inconsequential. Like someone his daughter had to endure in their lives because of the inconvenience of having him as a father. He knew they didn't think or feel like that, at least not consciously, but somehow that made him feel worse because they didn't know any different. They didn't know exactly how much he'd stuffed up their little lives. And worse than that, just now Eloise was blaming the whole sorry mess on Catherine.

This wasn't what he had planned when he'd first met Catherine twelve years ago. He'd planned to marry her, yes, about twelve minutes after he'd met her. And after half an hour he wanted to have children with her. But not like this. He'd never seen his future panning out like this.

'Well, it's chucking it down out there,' Leila said, making everyone laugh. 'What are we going to do, Nana? Not another puzzle of kittens, please – I'm bored of puzzles of kittens.'

'How about shopping?' Pam suggested, which always got a roar of approval from the consumerism-starved girls. Their mother wouldn't like it, which was principally why Pam did.

'Ooh, yes, can I get some nail varnish?' Leila asked her, her hands clasped to her face in excitement. 'I really need some.'

'I'd like some new bobbles, please, Nana,' Eloise added. 'Some of those floaty sparkly ones with the stars and hearts on that the girls who go to ballet class wear.'

'OK. Well, you go and wash your hands and brush your hair and we'll set off in a few minutes.' Pam smiled at the girls scrambling up the stairs, climbing over each other in a race to the summit.

'Why don't they go to ballet class?' she asked Jimmy. 'Doesn't she approve of ballet?'

'It's expensive, and money's tight,' Jimmy said.

Pam spent several silent moments clearly trying to hold back the words that threatened. She failed.

'All night in that . . . that . . . *boat*,' she huffed at Jimmy, keeping her voice low so that only he would hear her disapproval. 'That's no way for two girls their age to live.'

'It was one night,' Jimmy sighed.

'It's no way for a man of *your* age to live,' Pam added, her voice tight with frustration. 'It's a wonder you're not dead of pneumonia.'

'It's temporary,' Jimmy said. 'I sent off a new demo to record and publishing companies last week. It's the best material I've ever written. It'll get picked up, you'll see.'

Pam sniffed dismissively. 'Two years ago that boat was temporary. It's been two years since you and Catherine separated and you're still stuck living on that leaky old boat, still in the same situation as you were the day you left her. Why don't you divorce her, James? At least then you can split your assets. It's not right. Half that house is yours.'

Jimmy looked at his mum and took a painful breath.

'All of that house is Leila and Eloise's; it's their *home*. It's about the one steady thing they've got. Even if we did get the divorce I wouldn't have them move out. They need stability, Mum. It's not their fault that me and Catherine didn't work out.'

'No, well, if you'd listened to me and never married her in the first place –'

'Then there would be no Leila or Ellie – would you want that?' Jimmy asked her wearily. If he had a pound for every time he and Pam had had this identical conversation then he'd be living in one of those penthouses in the new warehouse conversion they were building across the canal from his boat. But his mum never tired of saying it. She never tired of being right.

'You need to get a flat of your own,' she told him. 'Start afresh, face up to reality. Honestly, James, you've lived your life in limbo since you were seventeen years old. When are you going to grow up? Get a *proper* job, a teaching qualification like we've talked about. They'll take anyone these days. I'd help you. You could live here while you went back to college.'

'No, that is not who I am,' Jimmy said, gesturing down at himself. '*This* is who I am. I'm a musician, a song writer – a *guitarist*. *This* is my life. I'm not going to get a qualification or a "proper job", as you call it. I *love* what I do, Mum. I'm going to keep on doing it until I get my break or I die, whichever comes first, and if either one of those things happens while I'm living on a rotting old boat then so be it. But what I'm not going to do is give up. You don't give up your passion.'

Pam sat back in her chair so that one chin tucked into another.

'Is that why you've never divorced her?' she asked him, as he knew she would.

'I cheated on *her*, I left *her*,' Jimmy repeated painfully. 'I was the one who broke the marriage up. I did it. The reason we haven't got the divorce settled is for the girls. The girls aren't ready to deal with it yet.'

'Are you sure it's the girls who aren't ready?' Pam asked him, sighing heavily. 'I don't know what your father would have said.' Jimmy looked sideways at his mother.

'He'd support me,' he said quietly. 'Because he always told me to follow my dream and not let myself get trapped in a life that didn't belong to me like he . . .' Jimmy trailed off. His dad had died of bowel cancer when Jimmy was seventeen, something that neither he nor his mother had ever quite recovered from. 'Dad always told me to give it my best shot, never give up. Don't be a quitter, son – that's what he said.'

'Well, he should have said, quit while you're ahead, James. Look, if everyone who ever wanted to be a pop star made it then you wouldn't be able to walk out your front door without bumping into them. Wanting something to happen is not enough to make it happen. You can chase your dreams when you're thirteen or twenty-three, but you're *thirty*-three now. It's time you grew up.' Pam leaned forward so the girls wouldn't hear her. 'James, you've got two smashing girls. Wouldn't you like to give them what they want – a few bobbles and some nail varnish, a couple of ballet lessons? It's not that much to ask.'

'I . . .' Jimmy had been about to launch his usual defence when suddenly all his strength left him and he reached out across the table and gripped his mother's hand. Pam looked up, startled.

'What is it, son?' she asked.

'I still love her, Mum,' he said. 'I love her and I'm going to lose her. After everything I did, two years after we split up, and I've only just realised it. I thought I could go on pretending that everything was fine between us, but I can't. I'm going to lose her and there's nothing I can do about it now.'

Pam watched him for a moment, her lipsticked lips pressed into a thin line, and then she covered his wrist with her free hand.

'There's more out there for you, James, a whole world of nice decent women who'll treat you the way you deserve to be treated. Who'll appreciate you like she never has. Look at that lovely Sally Mitchell from the bingo. She's a lovely girl, steady, does a lovely roast. I could invite her for lunch tomorrow.'

'No, Mum,' Jim said sadly. 'It doesn't matter how nice Sally Mitchell is, or how many other women there are out there who'd be good for me. It's her I love, it's her I want. It will always be her.'

'You know I don't think she is good enough for you,' Pam said, catching hold of Jimmy's hand when he tried to withdraw it from her. 'But I must say, I'm surprised at you, James Ashley.'

'What? Why?' Jimmy asked.

'You're the boy who spent his entire adult life chasing after one dream and never giving up. You had good A levels. You could have gone to university, could have a good job now doing something in an office with a pension plan. But no, not my Jimmy. My Jimmy never said, "It's no good, I'm never going to make it. I think I'll chuck it all in and become an accountant," worst luck. You never give up, Jimmy, you never do. And yet here you are telling me you're giving her up without even the ghost of fight. Now, after all these years of devoting yourself to her and your children, you're rolling over and playing dead while she does as she pleases. That's not my Jimmy.'

'What are you saying?' Jimmy asked warily, looking sideways at her.

'She's the mother of your children, and I suppose a good one judging on how those angels have turned out, despite the clothes she puts them in. And you say you've only just realised now. But I don't think that's true, James. I think the light went out of you when you walked out on her and I've been waiting for it to come back on but it hasn't, so . . . so just think – what would your father say? What did he say when he was encouraging you to learn the guitar?' Pam asked him.

Jimmy looked puzzled for a moment, and then his face cleared.

'He'd say, give it your best shot, never give up, don't be a quitter. If he was here now he'd tell me I've got to fight for her, go back to Farmington and tell her how I feel, tell her how she feels and why we were meant to be together. Why we were never meant to be apart. Tell her she can't make any choices about what to do next until she knows that I still love her and that I always have. That's what he'd tell me.' Jimmy sat up a little straighter and squared his shoulders. 'That's what he'd say, wouldn't he, Mum? He'd tell me to give it one more shot to make sure that I knew, absolutely knew, that I had done my best.'

Pam nodded, pursing her lips.

'He talked a lot of rubbish, your father,' she said, but she squeezed his hand as she said it.

Chapter Nineteen

'Oh my God, look at the face on you,' Kirsty said when she opened the door to Alison. She quickly glanced over Alison's shoulder and then dragged her indoors, slamming the door behind her.

'What was that all about?' Alison asked, smoothing herself down as she slipped off her coat.

'What was what all about?' Kirsty looked perplexed, as if she always greeted her visitors by hurling them into the living room. She looked Alison up and down, admiring her straight knee-length claret cord skirt, worn with soft light brown leather heeled boots and topped off with a tightly fitting cream cashmere sweater. 'Is that your standard reunion with an estranged friend outfit? I'm just asking because it doesn't seem to provide the option for a cat fight. You'd never get the blood out of that sweater.'

'Ha, ha,' Alison said mirthlessly. 'Don't wind me up, Kirsty. I don't care how much this sweater costs, the way I'm feeling . . .' Alison clenched her fists and actually growled.

'What's up?' Kirsty asked her, hurriedly pouring Alison a large glass of white wine.

'When we moved here, back when I still thought we could salvage *something* from the wreckage of our marriage, Marc agreed that Friday afternoons would be family time. The one day of the week when we could guarantee that we would all sit down together and eat as a family. I knew it wouldn't ever happen and it hasn't. Yesterday Dominic turned up and went ballistic, just wound Marc up until he blew his top and they both walked out. The girls were there. They got so upset that Gemma asked me if Marc and I were going to divorce.' Alison looked unhappily at Kirsty. 'I couldn't bear to see her any more upset, so I said no, and I meant it. I thought, I don't care about anything except making my children happy. Oh, I know Dominic wanted me to leave him, but that's just because he's fifteen and angry. I thought I could talk him round, explain things to him like an adult. And Marc has seemed so *altered* since I told him how I felt, as if he is really affected. And I thought maybe this is it, maybe this is enough to get him to really commit to us. I told myself that it didn't matter that I didn't love him at the moment because in a few months or years I'd love him again. You see those old couples, don't you, couples who've been married for about a hundred years, and you think, there is no way they have loved each other for all that time. At some point they must have hated each other's guts. But then they come to a point where they can just rub along. And for the girls' sakes, for all our sakes, I thought I could do that too.'

'OK,' Kirsty said slowly, looking at the door. 'Far be it from me to judge your insane reasoning, but what's changed and made you so cross?'

'I found out he went round to see Cathy. I knew he would. I knew he wouldn't be able to resist it. But I hoped that he hadn't because then there might still have been a chance for us. After everything he's done to me I was still hoping for one last chance! I'm so stupid! But finding that out rather overshadowed all of his tears and declarations of remorse.'

'Oh, *that*.' Kirsty rolled her eyes. 'That was nothing, it wasn't even a kiss. It was barely a bit of hand-holding. It was all very repressed, all very *Brief Encounter*. Besides, Jimmy walked in at the last minute and broke it up.'

'You knew?' Alison exclaimed, finishing her drink and pouring herself another one from the bottle that Kirsty had left on the mantelpiece. 'And you didn't tell me?'

Kirsty pursed her lips, looking at her watch as she folded her arms.

'Right, now listen, she'll be here in a minute so let's get this straight. First of all, I'm doing you a favour here that you begged me to do even though I've only known you five minutes. And secondly, no, I didn't tell you but neither have I told her that you offered to have sex with her husband. So can it with the condemnations, lady. I am not part of your Jacobean tragedy.'

'Oh,' Alison said, her crossness stalling and stuttering to a standstill. 'Well, OK then.'

'And if Catherine not kissing Marc is enough for you to doubt your genius master plan to remain locked for ever in a sham marriage then maybe she actually did you a favour.'

'Oh, I don't know,' Alison said a little sheepishly. 'I heard that a lot of women are perfectly happy in sham marriages. They have the money, the status, sex with their personal trainers on tap . . .'

'Don't talk to me about sex with personal trainers,' Kirsty said crossly. 'Now let's get this evening back on track and concentrate on what it's really about. Getting you and Catherine talking again.

'OK,' Alison glanced nervously at the door.

'Good, well, I'm nothing if not a good hostess. So help me microwave these curries.'

*

'I must admit,' Alison said as she vigorously stabbed the film of one of the dishes, 'I was surprised that she agreed to meet me quite so easily. What on earth did you say to her to get her to agree just like that?'

'Nothing,' Kirsty said, studiously reading the back of a packet of microwavable rice as if it held the secret to eternal life.

'Nothing?' Alison stopped stabbing, her fork hovering in mid-air.

'Well, obviously she doesn't know you're going to be here!' Kirsty exclaimed impatiently. 'She would never have agreed to come then! No, this way is best, like ripping a plaster off a wound quickly. She'll get here, she'll be shocked and angry, possibly violent. And then we'll all have a glass of wine and laugh about it.' Kirsty bit her lip. 'Hopefully.'

Alison put down the fork. 'I'm going home,' she said blankly, heading for the front door.

Kirsty stood in her way. 'No you're not. You're the wound I've got to rip the plaster off.' There was a sharp rap at the front door. 'And besides, she's here now. Don't worry, this is Catherine. As far as I know she's never hit anyone. Not since she decked that tart that slept with her husband.'

'Hi!' Catherine chimed as Kirsty opened the front door, determined to relax and enjoy the evening, even if she couldn't stop thinking about Eloise. She handed Kirsty a bottle of sparkling rosé wine. 'Do I ever need a drink. I hate it when the girls aren't around, even if Eloise hates me. All I've done all day is pace around and think about . . .'

Catherine tried to step past Kirsty and into the living room but Kirsty blocked her way. Catherine laughed and then frowned.

'What's going on?' she asked sternly. 'Don't tell me you've

gone and ditched me for Sam? Have you got him in there naked on the rug?'

Kirsty stood on her tiptoes as Catherine peered over her head.

'Now look,' Kirsty said, 'don't get cross or say anything . . . *loud*. Try to remember that I'm your friend and I love you and believe it or not I listen to you. And so the only reason I've told this tiny little white lie is because I honestly thought that this was a really good idea, the perfect opportunity to banish all the demons and start afresh.'

'What have you done?' Catherine asked her, snatching back the bottle of wine on impulse.

Taking a breath, Kirsty stood aside and let Catherine in.

Alison was standing by the fireplace, clutching onto her glass of wine for dear life.

'Hi, Cathy,' she said. 'Fancy meeting you here.'

'I'm going home,' Catherine said, turning on her heel, but Kirsty stood with her back against the closed front door.

'Normally it's men I have to prevent from leaving,' she joked for Alison's benefit before lowering her voice. 'No, you're not leaving. Remember what you said to me? Remember that you said that when you saw her you didn't hate her like you thought you would, that you even missed her a bit? Remember?'

'I know, but I'm not ready for this, and you know I'm not ready, and that's why you didn't tell me.'

'I know you. I know you'd never be ready. Just like you'll never be ready to divorce Jimmy unless someone makes you. Well, now you have to be ready. Just give her a chance, see how it goes. Wouldn't it be nice to just clear this whole thing up once and for all and forget about it?'

'Look, I'll leave,' Alison said, cutting into their whispered conversation.

'Oh, for goodness' sake, will everybody stop trying to leave before I start to take offence!' Kirsty stared hard at Catherine, who returned the look with one that said, 'I'll get you later for this.'

'No,' Catherine said, backing away from the door and turning to face Alison. 'No, don't go. We're here now and Kirsty's microwave curries are famous for miles around.'

'Good,' Kirsty said efficiently. 'Well, dinner will be ready in approximately forty-five seconds so let me take that bottle and your coat, and why don't you two sit down and talk amongst yourselves?' She paused. 'Do you want it directly on your plates or in the plastic container? Only it saves on washing-up that way.'

She waited as Catherine and Alison eyed each other warily.

'Oh, what the hell, it's a special occasion. I'll put it on plates. You two can wash up.'

'I didn't know,' Alison said, 'that you didn't know. I wouldn't have come if I'd realised she'd set us up. I thought you were happy to come. I was really pleased.'

'That's Kirsty for you,' Catherine said. 'Full of idiotic plans.'

'It's weird seeing you after all of this time,' Alison said tentatively. 'You look great. I can see why my husband tried to kiss you.' Catherine's mouth dropped open and she looked over her shoulder towards the kitchen. 'No, no, Kirsty didn't tell me and neither did he. I just found out. I'm not going to get upset about it now. I just thought that as we're here, on a new page, we might as well get everything out in the open.'

'I'm sorry,' Catherine said, with a shrug that hinted she wasn't that sorry.

Alison raised her eyebrows. 'Well, don't be too sorry. I offered to have sex with your husband.' She tilted her head, adding a touch sharply, 'Sorry about *that*.'

'Did he accept?' Catherine asked her, surprised by the tension she felt in her chest.

'No, he turned me down flat. I never could get him to fancy me. All those years I used to follow him around . . . do you remember? He's still a fox.'

'I know,' Catherine replied defensively, even though, to be quite honest, she hadn't dwelled on her husband's attractiveness for quite some time.

'So how's it going in here?' Kirsty asked brightly as she came in with plates of steaming and largely orange food, adding proudly, 'I chopped that coriander.'

'Awkwardly,' Catherine said, shooting her friend a look that Kirsty studiously ignored.

'Drink some more and that will sort *that* out,' Kirsty said, opening another bottle of wine. 'Now come on, dinner is served, and I haven't slaved over this for, well, minutes, just for it to get spoiled.'

There was silence as Kirsty refilled Catherine's wine glass for the third time, watching her neighbour push a bit of irradiated chicken round her plate with a distinct lack of enthusiasm.

As she topped up Alison's glass, Alison emptied it almost immediately.

'It seems to be taking you two a lot of wine to loosen up,' Kirsty observed, looking at the empty bottle. 'At this rate I'll have to go to the offy.'

Neither of her guests replied.

'OK,' Kirsty said. 'The way I look at it we can do one of two things here. Either we could treat this as a sort of therapy session. You two could air all of your grievances, talk about the sense of loss, the betrayal. You know, purge yourselves of all the bitterness and recriminations, hurl insults and accusations, make each other cry, and blah, blah, blah, *or* . . .'

'Or what?' Catherine asked.

'Go home?' Alison added, hopefully, her eyes meeting Catherine's briefly as for the first time in fifteen years they had something in common.

'I've told you. Not an option,' Kirsty said quite sternly, before erupting into a smile once again. '*Or* we can make my house Switzerland. We can pretend we don't know anything about stealing husbands, abandoning friends, inappropriate passes and all of that sordid business you married types get up to, and just hang out and try to have a laugh. Tonight you are on neutral territory and from now on we shall not talk about anything to do with either of you. Here we shall talk woman to woman, friend to friend, and only of the truly important issues in today's world.'

'Which are?' Catherine asked.

'Me and how I can get Sam to like me, of course!' Kirsty replied. 'You two men-stealers must have a few tips on that between you. So drink up, we've got a lot of planning to do, and I always find the drunker I am, the better my plans get.'

Kirsty put her palms on the table and looked around her. 'Talking of which, where did I put that bottle of tequila?'

'I'm not sure this is a good plan,' Catherine said, screwing up her eyes as she sucked a wedge of lemon and then downed another shot of tequila.

'Don't be crazy, it's a genius plan,' Alison countered. 'How could it possibly go wrong?'

Catherine wagged an unsteady finger at Alison. 'You would say that. You're the girl who thought it would be a good idea to smuggle vodka into school in Coke bottles.'

'I don't know why you're complaining. I took the fall for that one,' Alison said, turning to Kirsty. 'Three days' suspension I got, when she was just as drunk as me, only when

I'm drunk I get all loud and hilarious, and when she's drunk she gets all quiet and sullen so no one could tell the difference.'

'I didn't even know the vodka was in the Coke . . .' Catherine began.

Kirsty topped up their shot glasses. 'OK, let's recap the plan. We go round to Sam's flat and then what?'

'That's as far as the plan got,' Alison said, downing her shot.

'That's why it's a terrible plan,' Catherine said, her eyes watering as she downed her shot. 'Going round to a man's flat at past . . . one in the morning to spy on him qualifies as stalking, not wooing.'

'She's right,' Kirsty said. 'I can't just turn up there and peer in through his windows to look at him. That would be wrong. Also, he lives on the second floor so it would be dangerous too. When we're there I'll tell him I love him and then . . . then he'll know.'

'Perfect,' Alison said.

'You are insane,' Catherine said, leaning forwards on her elbows so that her nose was mere millimetres from Kirsty's.

'I told you,' Alison said, tipping her chair back at a dangerously obtuse angle. 'Sullen and morose, every time. She's not a happy drunk.'

'I am not sullen,' Catherine protested, swinging her head in Alison's direction. 'I'm a very funny drunk. And anyway, it's better than being a slutty drunk . . .'

'*Anyway*,' Kirsty said, slapping her palm down on the table, 'Catherine, you should be pleased. You're always telling me I shouldn't try and play games with him, that the whole ignoring him thing wouldn't work. Well, *now* I'm listening to you. *Now* I'm going to talk to him. Woman to woman. Man to man. Man to woman to . . . whatever. I'm following your advice so actually this is *your* plan that you're dissing.'

Catherine shook her head and began to stand up.

'The pair of you are mentals and I'm not coming,' she said, swaying forward and having to use the table to steady herself. 'I want no part of this madness!'

'Which is his flat?' Catherine hissed as the three women crouched in the somewhat thorny bushes outside the Longsdale House apartment block.

'It's either that one,' Kirsty said, pointing rather vaguely at three or four windows at once. 'Or that one. Or that one. Or that one.'

'The lights are on in that one,' Alison said, pointing at one set of illuminated windows. 'Let's try that.'

'Hang on!' Catherine held her palms up in the universal stop sign. 'What if it's not his flat?'

'Then we'll try another one, obviously,' Alison said.

'That's not a good idea,' Catherine frowned at her. 'I don't know why, I can't remember just at the moment. But it'll come back to me.'

'Yeah, yeah, yeah,' Alison said, making a 'w' with her fingers. 'What*ever*.'

While they squabbled Kirsty had got up and was kicking about on the ground before bending down rather unsteadily and picking up half a brick she'd found whilst lurking in the bushes.

'And what are you going to do with that?' Alison asked her. 'Brain him?'

'No, I'm going to chuck it at his window – you know, like they do in the films,' Kirsty replied, limbering up.

'That will go right through his window, you moron,' Catherine said. 'If it even is his window. Come on, let's find some stones, pebbles. If you're going to throw stones at a random window you might as well do it properly.'

'Swot,' Alison said under her breath as she joined in the search for pebbles, on her hands and knees.

'Bike,' Catherine replied, as she clawed through the dirt.

'Ladder,' Kirsty added.

'What?' Catherine and Alison asked her, both at once.

'Ladder. I could really do with a ladder,' Kirsty explained.

After a few minutes they had got together a handful of small stones for Kirsty to throw at the window that might or might not belong to Sam.

'Right, I'm ready,' Kirsty said, taking a deep breath. 'This is it, girls. Showtime.' She chucked the meagre handful with all her might and they peppered the soil about a foot and a half in front of her. 'Oh. That didn't go so well,' she said, looking confusedly at the floor.

The three women stood in silence for a moment, puzzled by the anticlimax.

'I know!' Alison shouted before she remembered that this was a stealth operation. 'Sing him a song.'

'Oooh, good idea,' Catherine said, before immediately checking her enthusiasm for the plan. 'Better than chucking bricks is what I mean. This whole thing is *mainly* a bad idea, but that particular part of it was a bit less bad than the rest.'

'What shall I sing him?' Kirsty asked them.

'Well, what's your song? What number sums up the precious moments that you've spent together?' Alison asked her.

Kirsty thought for a moment. 'His mobile phone did go off once during sex. Apart from that we haven't got a song, unless you count the combat training mega-mix workout at the gym. We used to take that class together.'

'Well . . . how does it go?' Alison encouraged her.

'Sort of Da, da, da DA DA, da da DA DA, DA! DA! DA!'

Catherine and Alison joined in with gusto, if not exactly any skill, and the three of them, leaning haphazardly against each other, sang at the tops of their voices.

Once they'd run out of puff they paused, looking up at the lit window, waiting for a response. None came.

''S not working,' Kirsty said, her shoulders drooping.

'Double bastard glazing,' Alison said. 'Keeps out singing, which in my opinion is an unforeseen drawback. No wonder romance is dead in the modern world.'

'We need to drink more,' Catherine suggested. 'If we drank more we'd have a better plan. I think I'm sobering up. For some reason I seem to have a terrible headache.'

'Wait!' Kirsty grabbed both of them and froze to the spot like a meerkat in the desert. The lights in the communal stairwell were coming on one floor at a time. Someone was coming down the stairs.

'Hide!' Catherine hissed, rugby-tackling the others into the bush just outside the door.

'I've broken a nail because of you!' Alison groaned miserably, wiping her muddy hand on her sweater. 'Bitch.'

'I wonder who's going out at this time of night,' Catherine said sombrely as they waited for the front door to open. 'Must be a drug addict. Only a drug addict would be out now.'

'Right, wait until whoever it is opens up and then rush the door,' Alison said.

'OK,' Kirsty said. 'Why?'

'Because then we'll be inside, of course,' Alison said. 'I bet the doors inside aren't double-glazed.

The three held their breath as the last set of lights switched on.

'Now!' Kirsty yelled, making one poor unsuspecting man jump out of his skin, gripping onto the door for dear life.

'Please don't hurt me, just take my wallet, plea— Kirsty, what the fuck are you doing here and why are you all covered in mud?' Sam eyed Catherine and Alison warily. 'Are you lot in some kind of coven?'

309

'Oh, do you live here?' Kirsty asked him. 'What a coincidence. We were just out on the town having a carefree devil-may-care girls' night out, like happy single women do, when Alison here lost her car keys and so we were looking for them.'

'Here?' Sam smiled at her. 'She lost her car keys here? What were you doing with your car here and . . . I'm not being funny, but I don't think any of you should be driving.'

'I know,' Alison said, tottering over to Sam, putting her arm around his neck and fluttering her lashes. 'Which is why it's your civic duty to make us all coffee.'

Sam laughed. 'I haven't got any milk,' he said. 'I was just off to the garage to get milk. I couldn't sleep.'

'That's OK,' Alison said in a husky voice. 'We like it strong and dark.'

'And bitter,' Kirsty added.

'And slutty,' Catherine piped up.

Sam rubbed his hand over the top of his head. 'I must be crazy but you'd better come in before you get arrested.'

'Oh God, I love you,' Kirsty gushed, before catching herself and saying, 'I mean, thanks ever so. Most kind.'

'Plus, you have a very nice arse,' Catherine said as she walked in. It took her the four flights of stairs to believe what had just come out of her mouth.

'Coffee was a bad idea,' Alison said to Catherine, peering down at her ruined sweater. 'Because now I'm starting to realise I'm in some strange man's flat, covered in mud, with a jackhammer going off in my brain.'

Catherine leaned her forehead against the cool of the window she was looking out of, and sipped her coffee. 'I don't think I've stayed up this late since . . . since Jimmy played this gig at the Marquee in London. It was supposed to be his break supporting some American band. We all got excited and

310

stayed out all night, watched the sun come up in Regent's Park. Nothing came of it, of course, but I think that was the last time I stayed out this late, before Eloise was born.' She paused and pinched her temple. 'My eyes hurt. Is it possible for eyeballs to explode?'

She shifted her attention to the kitchen where Kirsty was helping Sam with the instant coffee.

'Do you think they're talking in there or having sex?' she asked Alison blurrily. 'Based on previous occasions I'd say having sex.'

But to her surprise Kirsty walked out of the kitchen fully dressed, and sat on the couch nursing a mug of steaming coffee.

'I'm sorry about all this,' she said to Sam as he sat down precisely one cushion apart from her. 'We drank tequila and then they said we should come over and do stupid stuff.' She pointed at Catherine and Alison. 'They made me do it.'

'We did,' Alison said, winking at Catherine. 'We're evil, us.'

'It's the coven, you see,' Catherine said. 'It demands a sacrifice.'

'We all just wanted to see you, all of us together,' Kirsty attempted to explain. 'To, you know, see how you are and that. How's Sam? we wondered, and the next thing we knew we were here. That's tequila for you, because you know I'd . . . we'd never do anything so stalkery without the demon tequila.'

'You didn't have to do mud wrestling to get my attention,' Sam smiled. 'If you wanted to see me you should have rung the bell. I was up anyway. Like I said, I couldn't sleep.'

'*We* didn't know if you wanted to see *us*,' Kirsty said with heavy emphasis on the plural. '*We* thought you might be with some other slut.'

'Of course I wanted to see you,' Sam said, looking puzzled. 'You're the reason I can't sleep. I thought that you . . . lot . . . didn't want to see me. You haven't spoken to me since we spent the weekend together. I thought that you weren't interested any more and that you'd had your fun and moved on. It's been getting me down, actually, because I can't stop thinking about you, by which I mean just you and not those two other scary women you brought with you, no offence.'

'Ahhh,' Catherine and Alison chorused, catching each other's eye and giggling.

'What – pardon?' Kirsty asked him, rubbing her ear vigorously just in case she'd misheard.

'I like you, Kirsty, a lot,' Sam told her.

'But you left without saying goodbye or anything,' Kirsty said. 'You just went. I thought that was your way of telling me it was a one-off.'

'I had a run with a client,' Sam explained. 'Six a.m. every Monday, before he goes to work in the City, we run two miles further every week. He's training for the London Marathon. I left you a note on the pillow next to you.'

'Oh,' Kirsty said. 'I'm a very restless sleeper.'

'You didn't see it on the floor?' Sam asked her.

'There're a lot of things on my floor,' Kirsty said. 'Sort of hard to pick one thing out from another if you don't know what to look for.'

'Oh, so he's not a heartless philandering sex pest after all,' Alison cut in happily. 'Shame.'

'So,' Sam said. 'What do you want to do now?'

'Go to bed with you, please,' Kirsty replied instantly.

'And after that?' Sam smiled.

'I don't know, maybe breakfast and then more bed . . .?'

'No, I mean, do you want to go out with me? Be my . . . actual girlfriend?'

'Oh.' Kirsty looked thoughtful. 'OK then. Can we go to bed *now*?'

'A-hem,' Catherine coughed loudly. 'And what about us?'

'Well, you know the way home, don't you?' Kirsty said, unable to take her eyes off Sam.

'Actually, no,' Alison said. 'This block of flats wasn't even here last time I lived here. I have no idea where I am.'

Kirsty looked pleadingly at Catherine.

Catherine sighed.

'You can come back with me, I suppose,' she said. 'It will be morning soon, anyway.'

Kirsty got up and hugged both of the other women.

'You see this evening has gone exactly as I planned. It's gone perfectly. I so totally knew what I was doing. I never had a single doubt.'

'Of course you didn't,' Catherine said to Kirsty in a low voice as Alison made her way out of the flat and gingerly began the descent of the stairs. 'Just one more thing.'

'What's that?'

'I'll deal with you later,' Catherine promised.

'Like I care,' Kirsty said, and she slammed the flat door shut in her face.

Chapter Twenty

Catherine handed Alison a cup of tea, conscious of her old ex-friend looking round her tiny front room.

'Bit different from your place,' she said.

'Yes,' Alison admitted, taking the tea carefully as if she expected that at any second Catherine might throw it in her face. 'But if anything it's nicer – more homey. Marc picked out our house; sometimes it feels like a bit of a mausoleum. Sort of a fitting setting really for the death of our marriage.'

'Homey is one word for it,' Catherine said, glossing over Alison's reference to her marriage. 'Poky and tatty is another.'

The pair sipped their tea in silence for a few minutes, sitting at the small square oak table, the dry mud flaking on their hands, each trying to work out how to talk to the other, or even if either of them had anything to say.

'This is not at all how I imagined meeting you again would be,' Alison said suddenly, setting her mug down firmly and looking at Catherine. Catherine sat back in her chair and took a steadying breath. The moment to talk had finally come.

'Me neither,' she said. 'I could never have imagined on our first proper meeting after fifteen years we'd be high on tequila and trying to break into some strange man's flat. But that's Kirsty for you. She's got the brain of an eighteen-year-old inside the body of a thirty-year-old woman, although she would also insist she had the body of an eighteen-year-old if you asked her.'

'But haven't we all?' Alison asked her. 'I think I have, especially now. Especially in Farmington. I feel like I've been play-acting at being grown up for the last fifteen years, and now that I am actually a proper grown woman I don't want to play any more.'

Catherine looked at her. 'No,' she said simply, half shaking her head. 'I don't feel like that. I feel more comfortable in my own skin now than I ever did when I was teenager. It's taken me a long time to get here, but now I'm here I'm . . . strong.'

They watched each other for a moment. It was Alison who dropped her gaze first.

'I thought that when we, *if* we, saw each other again that there would be a lot more shouting and tears. And a lot more bitterness and recrimination,' Alison said.

'I don't really shout,' Catherine said. 'I hardly ever cry but I do still have some bitterness and recrimination. I do still feel . . . *angry*, Alison. I thought I didn't, but then we spent tonight together, and it was fun and I liked being with you.' She shrugged and glanced out of the window where the sunrise was bleeding into the sky. 'So now I'm angry, don't ask me why.'

'I was only seventeen,' Alison said quietly, offering a tentative excuse.

'So was I,' Catherine pointed out. 'I look back now at what I was doing, getting involved with some older strange man I met in a park, when I'd never even kissed a boy, never mind had sex with one. Letting him take me home, and take me to bed. I think about that and I can't believe that was me, that I did something so idiotic and dangerous. It makes me terrified for my daughters.' Catherine shook her head in disbelief. 'Marc told me on that first day that he would be no good for me but I didn't care. It was almost as if I *wanted* to be hurt by him, I *wanted* to have my heart broken because then I'd feel something that was mine and only mine. It was like living in a dream. But I always knew he would have hurt me anyway. All the signs were there if I'd known where or how to look for them. We never once talked about using contraception; he told me that if he was careful we wouldn't need it. He never spoke about a future beyond the summer holidays, about what would happen to our great love affair once his contract was finished and he had to move on. And he knew I was pregnant, Alison. The night he ran away with you he knew and he didn't look back once, didn't call, didn't write, didn't try to check what happened to me and his child. Not once.

'I got involved with a bad lot, as my mother said. And I think that maybe that's why I'm not angry with Marc. Because he never tried to hide who or what he was from me. He never put on an act, or made me promises he couldn't keep. Even when he said he loved me I knew instinctively that it was a temporary emotion, one that might even vanish the second I left his sight, and I wasn't too far wrong, was I? I was stupid enough and naïve enough to hope that he could be better than he was with me, but that was my fault and not his. So, rightly or wrongly, I'm not angry with him.'

Catherine paused, and Alison watched the muscles in her jaw tighten and her face tense. 'But *you* . . . since we were eight years old you'd spent almost every day telling me to trust you, to follow your lead, that I could rely on you because you were my best friend, my family, my hero. And then in one second?' Catherine snapped her fingers, making Alison start. 'All of that went up in smoke and you sacrificed our friendship, you sacrificed me to get what you wanted. I don't care if you were only seventeen and that we were both foolish girls caught up in a moment. What I *care* about is that, after everything, you left me. You left me all alone, too weak to be able to stand up for myself, because I'd never had to before. You always did it for me. I didn't know how to cope without you. I wasn't strong enough to stand up to my parents over the abortion. And if you'd have been there with me I would have been. So at the end of the day it's not that you slept with Marc behind my back. It's that you chose him over me. That's why I'm angry at you, and at me, and I know that it's not fair, but it's how I feel, even now after all this time. We had fun tonight, even if it was fuelled by tequila and Kirsty's neurosis. For a little while we felt close again and all I could think about was the last fifteen years I've had to go through without you.'

Gradually the morning sunlight seeped into the room, illuminating the condensation on the window, and creeping across the carpet, briefly turning it into a field of shimmering gold. Catherine stretched out her palms face down on the table and let the sun warm them.

'For a while,' Alison began hesitantly, 'for years, actually, I was so convinced that I'd done the right thing, for me *and* for you. I honestly believed that I'd rescued you from Marc, and him from his life, and had won myself the only man I could ever love in the process.' She glanced tentatively at Catherine's face, trying to read her expression, but her features were locked. So Alison took a breath and went on.

'It was horrible being away from home for those few weeks, truly awful. We stayed in hostel after hostel because we couldn't afford any better, places that stank, were crawling with vermin and where you couldn't leave anything lying around because the second you turned your back it would be gone. Every night I'd cry, but when Marc was asleep because I didn't want him to know. I wanted to come back home so badly, have a bath, sleep in a clean bed, have my mum cook me tea. Those first couple of weeks were hard, but even though I wanted to go home and I missed Mum, I never once considered actually going because I was so convinced that I'd done the right thing. I thought I loved him – that's what I told myself – it was love, pure and simple. But it was more than that. I was jealous of you, Catherine, and angry that you, the plain quiet mouse, had got him when it should have been me. I didn't want you to have him so I took him, without realising what I was getting myself into. And then when I found out I was pregnant and I realised it was real life and not some little girl's game I was terrified. I knew I couldn't let him go. I knew I had to say anything, do anything to make him come with me. I knew he felt lonely, that he missed having a proper family. I knew that not because he told me, but because you had. Because you were the one that really knew him. So I used that to make him choose me. I told him I'd be his family, I'd look after him. But what I really meant was that I needed him to look after me. I didn't tell him about the baby until after he left with me. I tricked him into going with me and I manipulated him into staying. Or at least I thought I did. Looking back now I don't think he would have stayed with me if it hadn't suited him, no matter what I said.

'Eventually Marc got some casual work in a car dealership, washing the cars, cleaning up, and they let him watch them work, teaching him a few things. Once we got the cash together we rented this little bedsit in Camden. This one room, with a shitty little electric hob that didn't get hot and a fridge that didn't get cold. After about a month at the garage Marc told me that they agreed to apprentice him and help him go to college. He was so pleased with himself, so proud. And I looked at him and I thought, he feels like that because of me, because he's doing all of that for me, and I think that's when the jealousy and fear began to drain away and I realised that if I could hang on to him now, even though I'd won him so

318

unfairly, then I would be able to love him and he would be able to love me. After about six weeks Dad found us. He'd been looking all that time, apparently, poor Dad, every day and all night, walking the streets, trying to spot me. Someone at one of the hostels we'd stayed in gave him our address.

'He and Marc had a fight, a proper fist fight. You should've seen me, Cathy. I was on Marc's back, trying to drag him off my dad, begging him not to hurt him. But when I finally got in between them I told Dad to go home alone. It was the hardest thing I've ever done, I missed him and Mum so much and I'd have given anything for a hug from him. But I couldn't go home because by then I loved Marc and I was crazy about him. I just couldn't get enough of him. I was always thirsty and hungry for him, always starving for his attention. He never left my side during those first couple of months, except when he was working. He never once suggested that I go back home, or get off his back, but he *was* distant, just a little bit removed from me. He was thinking of you, I expect, but I didn't know that then, or want to know it.

'He worked and worked and worked until finally he and I and our lives began to knit together. We felt close; *I* felt close to *him*. The years after Dominic was born were the happiest years with him. When we didn't have much but we had enough and he was proud of himself, felt good about himself because he was improving our lives day by day, taking care of his son, and then after a few years his daughter too. If he was seeing other women back then, I didn't know about it. Or I didn't want to know about it. I was so happy.'

Alison paused. 'I didn't think about you much then. I blocked you out of my memory, cut you out of my life. And if you did ever cross my mind I told myself I'd done what was best and I'd look around at our flat, at Dom and Gemma and at how happy Marc and I were, and I'd tell myself,

319

there's the proof, there is the proof that I was right to do what I did.

'It was while I was pregnant with Amy that I found out about the first woman – the first one I was aware of, anyway.' Alison took a breath and rubbed her hands over her face. Catherine noticed that her fingers were trembling as she rested them back on the table.

'It was a nursery nurse, from Gemma's nursery. I couldn't believe it when I found out because Marc never picked Gemma up from nursery except for this one time when I'd been so tired with the pregnancy that I'd begged him to leave work early and do it for me. And then a few days after that I began to notice that this girl – Lou, her name was – who'd always been so polite and friendly, began acting all off with me, and while once she would happily chat about Gemma with me, now would barely speak a word. I didn't know what I'd done to upset her. She was only a young girl of about nineteen but you know, when you're pregnant you become sensitive about everything. I was really worried about it. I even mentioned it to Marc and he told me it was my hormones playing up again. We even laughed about it.

'Then one day after dropping Gemma off I asked Lou if everything was all right. I told her I was sorry if I'd offended her in some way and that maybe I was just being stupid and pregnant but if I had I hoped she'd forgive me. She burst into tears and she told me right there in the reception at the nursery. She told me she'd been seeing Marc and she hated herself because she knew he had two kids and another on the way, but she couldn't help it, she loved him . . .' Alison trailed off into silence and Catherine waited, impassive, for her to go on.

Perhaps almost a minute passed before Catherine prompted her. 'What happened?' she asked.

'I took Gemma out of nursery. I hadn't wanted her to go in the first place. It was Marc's idea. He thought I'd need a break from both the kids during my pregnancy. And I waited until Marc came home that night and I said to him very politely that if he didn't stop seeing Lou at the nursery I would be leaving with both of his children. He wasn't shocked or horrified that I'd discovered him, just . . . regretful. He apologised, said it wouldn't happen again and that was that. Looking back, I can't believe how calm I was. How ready I was for the whole incident to be over and for me to not have to think about it again, to go on as before. I think I was more upset about Lou being off with me than about her sleeping with Marc. Probably I had been expecting him to stray sooner or later. I'd prepared myself to accept it. And I had a baby on the way, I was in my twenties with three kids and I'd never had a job. I couldn't think of a job I could do. Being on my own just wasn't an option.'

'But that wasn't the last time?' Catherine asked.

'No.' Alison shrugged. 'There were four more that I know of after that. The last time was at Christmas. One of his salesmen's wives came up to me at the Christmas party and said, "Look, Alison, I don't want to do this to you, but it's not right. Everyone knows what he's doing except you. He's with her right now." And she told me he was with his PA in the office.' Alison's laugh was mirthless. 'The thing was, his PA was my next-door neighbour, a woman of about my age. *I'd* got her the job with him because she wanted something part time now her children were at school. We used to go to Pilates together on a Thursday morning. And the salesman's wife was right: this time Marc had been extra careful that *I* shouldn't find out. But everybody else knew. All the mums at school, the families along our street, the people at the dealership, even Dominic. It was as if my whole life was colluding to keep Marc's secret for him. For the first time in ages I hadn't seen it coming and that's why I think it hit me, hit us, so hard. The love and passion I had for him had begun ebbing away long before that night. But I think I used up the last little bit I had right then.' Alison turned her face to the window, her features fading in the glare of the sun. She closed her eyes briefly and then turned back to Catherine. 'I look at him now and really try to feel something, but I don't, not a thing. And the funny part, the really hilarious bit is that one minute he's crying his eyes out over me telling him I don't love him, and the very next . . . he's coming round to pick up where he left off with you.'

'It's hard when someone has cheated on you,' Catherine said, her features still implacable. 'I know that. I sympathise. But if I'm honest there's a bit of me right now that's saying, "Serves you right." It's not a bit of me I like very much but it's there. And there's no point in me pretending not to feel how I do. Otherwise we'd never get anywhere.'

'Fair enough,' Alison said, pausing for a second. 'It was just after Christmas that I started wondering if I'd made a terrible mistake. I started to think that instead of fixing things, making them right, I'd run off with your life and you'd accidentally ended up with mine. I began to think that that was why Marc and I never really fitted properly, not even when we were happy, and when Marc moved us back here and I found out that you were married to Jimmy Ashley – *my* Jimmy Ashley – it seemed even more possible. I let myself think that the reason you and Jimmy weren't together was for the same reason that Marc and I couldn't be happy. Because we had each other's lives.'

'Really,' Catherine said, without emotion.

'I know, it sounds deluded and I was a bit. I was looking for meaning and symbols where there weren't any. The truth is when I left with Marc I was too young to know what I was doing to me, to my parents and most of all to you. I thought I was in love, and I was if being in love means being jealous and obsessed and competitive.' Impulsively she picked up Catherine's sun-warmed hand, holding on to it when Catherine tried to pull it away.

'Please, listen,' Alison pleaded. She felt Catherine's hand relax in hers. 'I did the wrong thing. I should never have slept with him behind your back or run away with him. But I realise now, it wasn't your life I stole. It was mine. It was the ten more years I could have had with you of messing around like we did last night, having fun, being free, being young. I should have grown up with you. Instead I tried to grow up alone, overnight, and I failed.

'I'm sorry, Catherine, I'm sorry for everything I did, and if I thought there was any way that you and I could be even just polite to each other in the playground I'd feel so much better. I'd feel so much stronger. Even if that's all that we can manage – what do you think?'

Catherine considered, pursing her lips.

'I don't know, Alison,' she said slowly, withdrawing her hand from Alison's. 'You sitting here in front of me and knowing where you are again makes me feel – I don't know – sort of completed, but at the same time I just can't get my head round that you and I being friends again should be that easy. It doesn't seem right.'

'Do you remember that time when we were about nine that we fell out and the whole of our class fell out along with us? I mean, you were either on Cathy's side or you were on Alison's. You got all the nerds and I got all the cool kids, remember?'

'I remember,' Catherine said. 'It was horrible. I used to dread going to school. I can't even remember why we fell out.'

'Heather Hargreves invited you to her party and not me. I

got jealous and uppity and I took it out on you because Heather Hargreves was too scary. That's why we fell out,' Alison said. 'I could be a little cow even then.'

Catherine shrugged. 'How is this relevant?'

'I remember it so clearly, Cathy,' Alison told her. 'I remember how awfully sad I felt every single day and how empty. I was so angry with myself for falling out with you but I couldn't admit that I'd behaved stupidly. I couldn't bring myself to apologise. I'd see you in the playground hanging around with those other girls and all I wanted to do was to come over and say hi. I knew that all I had to do was to say hi and that we'd be friends again, just like that.'

'It took you long enough,' Catherine commented.

'I was waiting for you to do it first,' Alison said. 'But you were stronger than me. You stuck it out because you knew I was in the wrong. It seemed to go on for ever.'

'It was probably about a week, if that,' Catherine said.

'Do you remember how we made up?' Alison asked.

Catherine nodded, the ghost of a smile on her lips.

'We were in the gym, getting changed for PE. I sat down next to you on the bench and I said, "Hi, Cathy, I'm sorry." And you said, "That's OK", and that was it. In an instant we were best friends again. It was back to you and me against the world and I can still remember to this second the enormous relief that I felt in that moment. It was as easy as saying "hi" – that's all it took to make everything all right again. And I think I've been living with that sense of loss and panic all these years, waiting to see you and say hi and tell you that I'm sorry.' Alison paused as she studied Catherine's profile. 'What I'm trying to say is that if you want to get to know me again it doesn't have to be hard or painful. You can just decide to do it.'

Catherine was silent for a long time and then she turned to Alison, the morning sun igniting her hair.

'I'm going to have to insist that you don't sleep with my ex-husband,' she said. 'I know I don't have a right to insist it. But if you did, that would be it between us because I . . . I just wouldn't like it.'

'He turned me down pretty conclusively,' Alison said. 'I won't be asking him again.'

Catherine nodded once. 'One day, when you and I know each other properly, and when I . . . *if* I feel like I can trust you again I'll tell you about the abortion. I have to tell you about it, Alison, about everything that happened with my parents after you went and how I got up the courage to leave home and why it's taken me years to be able to feel good about myself again. I'll have to tell you about it even though it will be painful and difficult. And I'll blame you for some of what happened, which I know isn't fair because you were only a seventeen-year-old girl and you weren't responsible for me, but I will anyway, and I think you'll need to accept that.'

'OK,' Alison said steadily. 'I'll be ready.'

'I've missed you,' Catherine said, and suddenly tears sprang into her eyes. 'I've missed you a lot.'

'Me too!' Alison said, and then briefly, clumsily, the two women reached across the table and hugged each other very hard.

And then both of them laughed, the tension in the room deflating in an instant like a popped balloon, sucking fifteen years of time out with it.

'Your face, when Kirsty picked up that brick,' Alison said with a giggle.

'And your singing,' Catherine retorted. 'Thank God those windows were double-glazed otherwise we'd have been arrested for noise pollution.' They chuckled again.

'Well, I'd better go. Marc will want to go into the dealership, I expect,' Alison said. 'It's going to wind him up

325

something rotten that I was out with you all night. It will make him competitive, you know; he'll want you to like him more than me.'

Catherine raised her brows, and rubbed the back of her aching neck.

'Well, if you're going to promise not to sleep with my husband, I think I can manage to return the favour.'

'No, don't,' Alison said, making Catherine's head snap up in surprise.

'Pardon?' she asked.

'I'm not saying sleep with him, if you don't want to. But as much as I hope I could do something with our marriage I know now that I can't. All I can do is try to find the best way to end it for all of us, the children especially. When Marc brought us back here part of the reason was to try and find that ideal version of himself that he's never quite been able to pin down since the summer he met you. Maybe that man exists, maybe he doesn't. But I'd like him to find out if he does and I think maybe he needs you to help him with that. So if you want to sleep with him, then I won't mind.'

'Right,' Catherine said. 'I don't know what to say.'

'Don't say anything,' Alison said. 'So I'd like to have your girls over for tea. Maybe next Wednesday?'

'They'd love that,' Catherine said slowly. She half smiled at Alison. 'I'm sorry, this all feels a bit surreal.'

'I know,' Alison said. 'It's cool, isn't it? And maybe you and I could have a coffee sometimes . . . or even go out for a drink, maybe with Kirsty too?'

'If she's not too loved up to notice us,' Catherine said. 'That would be good.'

'OK then,' Alison said, picking up her coat and pausing for a second to look down at her mud-smeared clothes. 'Well, goodbye then.'

'Goodbye,' Catherine said as Alison headed for the door, then added, 'Hang on a minute.'

'What?' Alison turned and smiled at her.

'Are you sure you don't want to climb out of a window?' Catherine asked.

Chapter Twenty-one

'This has got to be the first properly sunny morning we've had in months,' Jimmy said as he steered the boat back down the canal towards Farmington. 'You can even feel the warmth on your face. Maybe spring's on its way at last, hey, girls?'

'Maybe,' Leila said, sitting at his feet, happily chalking a masterpiece depiction of Jesus and a lot of angels in heaven, having tea with God, in God's car, on the painted door of the boat.

Eloise sat opposite him on the little bench at the helm of the boat, her arms crossed, her face turned away from him, looking at the canal bank as it slowly drifted by.

'Did you have a good weekend, Ellie?' he asked her. 'I mean, after the bit where we all nearly froze to death.'

'Course I did,' Eloise said, smiling at him. 'I liked going to the multiplex with you and Leila and Nana Pam. I love this . . .' She put her hand on her new sparkling hot-pink and silver scarf that Jimmy's mother had bought her, and which clashed violently with her hair. 'And even the cold and rainy night on the boat was fun, because we were with you. I just wish I didn't have to go home, that's all. I'd rather spend a hundred cold and rainy nights on the boat than go home to *her*.'

'I wouldn't, so don't try and make me,' Leila scoffed, as she drew.

Jimmy sighed. Eloise had been making digs about her mother all weekend, just the odd word here and there, and of course his mother had loved it, but it had upset both him and Leila, who at one point had punched Eloise hard in the arm, causing a full-blown fight to break out, Leila launching herself onto her sister, her arms flailing wildly.

'Tell her to stop it!' Leila had protested when Jimmy lifted her bodily off, copping a few punches as he did so. 'She is not being kind!'

'Well?' Eloise had exclaimed when Jimmy tried to talk to her. '*She* is not being fair to us! What the stupid little baby doesn't understand is that it's Mum's fault we're not together any more.'

'I AM NOT A STUPID LITTLE BABY!' Leila had screamed at the top of her voice, tearing herself out of Jimmy's arms and launching herself at Eloise again. Jimmy had had to keep them in separate rooms for half an hour after that until the pair of them had calmed down.

Jimmy had known that if he'd tried to talk to Eloise then, when she was angry, she would react just like Catherine did when she was angry, by getting even more angry. In the past, before the ladies' loos in The Goat, Jimmy had known to wait until Catherine was mellow before trying to talk to her about anything. Eloise was sulky now, but at least she was chilled. And that meant she might actually listen to him.

'Look, you can't be angry at your mum, Ellie,' he said. 'Your mum didn't make us break up.'

'She did,' Ellie said. '*I* remember it. She got really, really cross, and threw you and all your stuff onto the street. And me and her were crying and crying, but she still did it, even though she could see that we were crying because of what she was doing. She made you go and she won't let you come back again, even though you are sorry. She said you only ever had one chance and you blew it.'

Jimmy thought for a moment, realising that if his daughter was right about that then he was in an even bigger mess than he'd first thought because if Catherine wouldn't give him another chance, and there was every possibility that she wouldn't, he'd be heartbroken. And although he'd been heartbroken since the day he left, he hadn't known it until a few days ago so it hadn't, until now, seemed nearly such a desolate prospect.

'She threw me out because I'd done something really, *really* bad,' Jimmy said. 'Mummy's never told you what I did because she doesn't want you to hate *me*, but if I hadn't done the really, *really* bad thing – then who knows? We might all still be together now.'

'What did you do?' Leila asked him, looking up from her drawing. 'Stealing? Lying? Worship a false idol? Did you covet thy neighbour's wife?'

Jimmy swallowed. When he'd started this talk he hadn't planned far enough ahead to know quite how to answer that question. He basically hadn't planned further ahead than the first three words he'd spoken out loud. He really needed to start thinking these things through a little bit more.

'Do you know what covet means?' he asked both the girls.

'No,' Leila said.

'Not sure,' Eloise mumbled.

'Well, that's what I did. I coveted my neighbour's wife.'

Leila screwed up her face in an expression of disgust. 'What, Mrs Beesley? But she's got a beard, Daddy!'

'No, not my actual neighbour's wife,' Jimmy corrected her hastily, desperately wondering if he was doing the right thing talking to them like this or if this conversation was destined to come back and haunt him. 'Not *anybody's* wife, actually; she wasn't married. But I did covet another lady, a lady that wasn't as beautiful or as wonderful or as important to me as your mummy is, but I did it anyway because I was stupid and confused. And your mum found out I was coveting her and she got really, *really* upset. So she told me to covet off.'

'Huh?' Eloise said.

'Nothing,' Jimmy answered. 'Anyway, the point is that I don't blame her at all. I deserved it.'

'You liked another lady apart from Mummy?' Leila asked him, frowning deeply. 'That's wrong, Daddy, because you are married.'

'I know, and the funny thing is that I didn't even really like the other lady,' Jimmy said. 'I certainly didn't love her the way I love, loved, your mum. But I coveted her and I was stupid, which, you'll find as you grow up, most boys are.'

'I know that already,' Eloise said, rolling her eyes.

'Me too,' Leila said. 'And stinky.'

'OK, well, that's good, I think,' Jimmy replied. 'But the point is that the break-up was my fault. I risked everything I had over the chance to feel free and young and footloose again,' Jimmy said. 'But the funny thing is that ever since I've actually been free and footloose all I've felt is lonely and sad, and as if something is missing in my life. And the thing that's missing is the thing I had to begin with. All of you.'

'But you've still got us!' Leila said. 'Even if you did covet that lady, which is a bad sin. But we forgive you because we love you.'

'I don't forgive you,' Eloise said. 'I hate both of you now,' but she spoke without any venom in her voice, her bottom lip protruding like it used to when she was much younger.

'Grown-ups are often a bit rubbish,' Jimmy said. 'They are a lot more rubbish than kids, because at least kids always know what they want. And they know what's good and what's bad and most of the time they stick to it. Sometimes grown-ups forget all of those things and they stuff up.' He paused and grinned at his daughter. 'Do you really hate me, Ellie?'

'No,' Ellie said sulkily.

'And do you really hate Mummy?' Jimmy asked her. 'Especially now you know the truth?'

'Well, she could let you come back now you're sorry, couldn't she?' Eloise asked him. 'If she wanted to.'

'She could,' Jimmy said, feeling his chest tighten with hope. 'But if she doesn't want me to then we still can't be cross with her, OK? Not ever. She loves you two. She'd do anything for you. The pair of you are her sunshine.'

Jimmy looked up at the faultless blue sky. 'You make her feel like spring is on its way even when it's a rainy and cold day. So don't be hard on her any more, OK? I know you don't want to be.'

'I have felt bad about it, actually,' Eloise said. 'Poor Mummy. It wasn't like me at all to be so mean to her.'

'That's what I said,' Leila said, chalking with enthusiasm. 'Turn the other cheek, I said.' She looked up.

'Right then,' Jimmy said, taking a deep breath and feeling the nerves of what he was planning to do when he got back fizzing in his gut. 'Full steam ahead!'

'Don't be silly, Daddy,' Leila said, returning to her drawing. 'We don't have any steam.'

The house was quiet when Jimmy let himself and the girls in through the back door. The living room was still and quiet, dust spiralling in the still air where the sunlight streamed in through the windows. Jimmy looked around. There were two cold cups of tea on the table. Two cups: someone had been round. Probably Kirsty, he reasoned, but still he stared hard at the cups for a moment as if he might be able to determine some masculine aura around one of them. Realising what he was doing, Jimmy blinked and shook his head briefly: this was not him. He had never been, as Lennon put it, a jealous guy. And now was not the time to start.

'Cat!' he called out. 'Cat? Babe? We're back.'

'Mum!' Eloise and Leila shouted at once. 'Mummy! Mum! We're here!'

They heard a creak of floorboard upstairs as somebody got out of bed and Jimmy composed himself, methodically shutting down every single image of Catherine's long white limbs entangled in Marc's hairy dark ones, which appeared to him on each heartbeat as he heard the sound of footsteps on the stairs. He fully expected his wife to appear, hair tousled, wrapped in a sheet and sleepy from an endless sex marathon.

He'd never been so glad to see her looking so terrible.

'Hello.' Catherine yawned, appearing in her pyjamas, rubbing her eyes, with what little make-up she wore ingrained into the skin. She mustered a weary smile. 'Hello, girls,' she said, holding her arms out. The girls ran to her and hugged her hard. 'Oh what a lovely hug.' Catherine sat down with a bump on the carpet and then toppled onto her back, a daughter in either arm. Jimmy smiled at the three of them giggling helplessly on the carpet.

'You look terrible, Mummy,' Leila said, peering at Catherine through the ropes of hair that lay across her face.

'Thank you, darling,' Catherine said. 'I feel pretty awful. How was Nana Pam?'

'She was great,' Leila said. 'We went to the multiplex and McDonald's, and Nana Pam bought us loads of lovely things and best of all at Nana's house it was warm so our noses and toes didn't turn blue like –'

'They would have done if we were Arctic explorers,' Jimmy interjected hastily, not keen to lie to Catherine but quite keen not to see that lovely lazy smile disappear from her face quite yet.

'Yes,' Eloise added. 'That's right. We were playing Arctic explorers at Nana Pam's house, in the warm and not in the cold at all.'

'Sounds lovely,' Catherine said, smiling up at Jimmy. 'I haven't had much sleep so I'm a bit . . . you know, thingy.'

'Good night?' Jimmy asked her hesitantly.

'Weird night,' Catherine chuckled, 'but a good one. Kirsty set me up on a blind date with . . . Alison.'

'Really?' Jimmy crouched down on the carpet, feeling rather left out being the only one of them who was perpendicular. 'What was that like?' he asked, wishing very much he could lean over and kiss that smile.

'Tense, bitchy, and in the end sort of good,' Catherine said. 'And I *think*, I actually think, we might be able to co-exist, at the very least. Maybe even be friends again. I don't know if it's because I'm tired or if it's because of Alison but I feel lighter, suddenly. Like I could float away.' She hugged the two girls to her. 'But we didn't get in until six this morning so . . .' The word evolved into a self-explanatory yawn.

'Is that why you are in your pyjamas, Mummy?' Eloise asked, leaning up on one elbow to peer at her mother's face. 'Were you in bed at four o'clock in the afternoon?'

''Fraid so,' Catherine said, closing her eyes.

'Well, I think that's cool,' Jimmy said. 'Living it up, having a good time, remembering you're still young and beautiful . . . it's all good, so why not?'

Catherine screwed up her shut eyes. 'Because it hurts,' she moaned.

'Well, if you like,' Jimmy suggested hesitantly, 'if you're OK to watch the girls for a bit, I'll pop back to the boat, sort a few bits and bobs out and then I can come back and cook dinner, if you want. I mean, I don't have to. But as you're feeling rough, I could. If you liked, but not if you don't, but . . .'

'Would you?' Catherine asked him, opening one eye. '*Could* you?'

'Course I can. I don't just live on ready meals and Pot Noodles when I'm on my own, you know,' Jimmy lied happily. 'I can do a roast. Stick a chicken in an oven – how hard can it be?'

'Then thank you, Jimmy,' Catherine said, opening both eyes to smile at him. 'You're my hero.'

Jimmy looked at her lying there, flanked either side by their daughters, and he knew that if he sat on that carpet for one more second the sight would bring him to tears.

'Right then,' he said, jumping up in one agile move that his back would pay for later. 'I'll be back in an hour.'

Catherine flopped her head left to look at one daughter and then right to look at the other. 'You are going to Gemma and Amy's for tea next Wednesday,' she told them, wincing as they cheered at the news. Leila kissed her on one cheek and then, after a second of hesitation, Eloise kissed her on the other.

'Mummy.' The elder girl propped herself up on one elbow.

'Yes, darling?' Catherine said, smiling at her.

'I haven't been kind to you very much, about you and Daddy. I thought that it was your fault, but Daddy explained it to me, about how he made you sad and angry even though he loved you and that really grown-ups are stupid a lot of the time, especially him, so don't blame you for it. So I'm sorry. I love you.'

'I love you too,' Catherine said, feeling tears spring into her eyes that somehow made the morning seem all the more bright and clear. 'You feel very sad, don't you, about me and Daddy?' She looked at Leila. 'You both do.'

The girls nodded but did not speak.

'It is sad, and I am so sorry,' Catherine told them, looking at each in turn. 'And I am so sorry that it happened to you. When I married your daddy and we had you, we never, *ever* planned that this would happen, that we wouldn't always be together, all of us. But sometimes life has a way of sweeping you off course when you are not looking, and turning things upside down. It makes you feel cross and sad, and it takes a while to get used to the fact that nothing is going to be the same any more. So I'm sorry, I'm so sorry you have to feel sad because of me and Daddy getting swept off course. But, you know, we both love you so much and we will always look after you, even if Daddy lives in a boat and we live here. We will always be a family.'

She hugged the girls close to her and kissed each one on the forehead.

'I expect God is proud of you, Mum,' Leila said into her hair. 'Because you are trying very hard, and God loves a trier, Mrs Woodruff says.'

'Glad to hear it,' Catherine said.

'And, Mummy,' Eloise said. 'I'm sorry I was horrible to you.'

'You don't have to be sorry,' Catherine said. 'I know you didn't mean it.'

'Mummy . . .' Leila said after a moment or two. 'I was never horrible to you at all, was I? Do I get a treat?'

'I think we all deserve one,' Catherine said, pretending to look thoughtful. 'How about we all . . . watch *Beauty and the Beast* until Daddy gets back with the food?'

She covered her ears to protect her pounding head from the cheers, but the meagre shelter of her hands was not nearly enough.

Chapter Twenty-two

Alison took a long time to get back home because she didn't want to face Marc and, besides, she knew what would happen the moment she saw him. Her phone had run out of charge at some time in the night so she was spared any demanding or angry messages he might have left her. He'd want to know all about her night with Catherine and she didn't want to tell him. The time she'd spent with her old friend had gone better than she could have imagined and this morning she felt for the first time in a long while as if some unnamed disjointed part of her life had clicked back into place. Last night was purely hers and she didn't want to share it with Marc, so after she had left Catherine's, as tired and as nauseous as she was feeling, she did for the first time what she had either neglected or had been unable to do since she had arrived back in Farmington. She went for a walk in her heeled tan boots and she visited all of their old places.

At last Alison felt as if she had been handed a passport to her past.

Her first port of call was the tree in Butts Meadow; they used to climb and hide out in its canopy for hours, telling stories and jokes, reading comics and, later, magazines. Alison was delighted to see that the tree was still there, its branches bare now and braced for spring. She stood at the foot of its trunk and looked up into its tightly laced branches. It was there as a nine-year-old that Alison had persuaded Catherine to wind the hands on her watch back one hour so they could have some more time to finish their game. The following Monday at school Catherine had shown Alison the bruises on her legs she had suffered for the extra hour.

Then Alison walked through the near-silent town to the coffee shop, 'Annie's Kitchen' as it used to be called. Now it was a PC repair shop, and Alison pressed her nose against the window and peered through, trying to imagine how it used to be.

It was in Annie's Kitchen that they'd tasted their first cappuccinos, aged twelve, and where Alison had made them come back every single day until they got a taste for its bitter sweetness and could tell the other girls with all honesty that they were bunking off PE to go for a coffee. Thanks to Alison, Annie's Kitchen had become the hot spot for schoolchildren for several years.

Taking a step back, Alison looked at her reflection, wan and transparent in the glass, and she wondered how long the café had lasted in Farmington after she left, how long it had taken for change to overcome it so that all that remained of that hot and crowded landscape of her childhood existed only in her memory. It was then, with her head pounding and her mouth parched, that she retraced her walk to her son's school on the hill, the school that had once been hers and Cathy's.

She felt the heels of her boots sink into the churned mud and grass as she crossed the playing field to find the copse at the back of the school, backing on to a paddock of horses. This had once been, and still was, judging by the butts that littered the muddy floor, the smokers' den. It was here Cathy would sit and smile and listen while Alison and the other girls smoked like troupers but did not inhale.

Once when they had been alone Alison tried to explain to Cathy that all you had to do to fit in and look cool was to hold the smoke in your mouth and then blow it out again, tapping the ash off the end of your cigarette as often as possible so that it would burn down quicker. Eventually she had managed to get Cathy to try it, but all that had happened was that Cathy had accidentally inhaled and thrown up all over her feet just as the other girls arrived.

Alison sat down on the same low branch of a tree in the copse that she always used to and that somewhere under all the moss and mould must still bear both her and Cathy's names, carved rather inexpertly with a knife nicked from the canteen, and looked out across the field that glittered fiercely as the sun strove to evaporate the morning dew.

Even on that night when she had left Farmington with Marc she'd always told herself that she was Cathy's saviour, her crusader and her hero. Was the true sum of their friendship that she was always getting Cathy in trouble for being late, encouraging her to skip school, even trying to get her hooked on smoking? Not to mention breaking her heart. Alison had always thought that she was the strong one, the one that Cathy needed, but now she realised that not only was that no longer true, it had never been true.

The girl she had been sixteen years ago, Alison the hip kid, the sexy girl, the one who was in with the in crowd and fighting off the boys, had always needed Catherine to keep her anchored to the ground. And it was the moment, the very second, that she had chosen to let go of her friend that her life had begun, ever so slowly at first, to spin out of control. But with each revolution had come a fractional increase in speed, like the earth spinning on its axis so fast that you don't even notice it. So fast that Alison didn't notice until finally her world spun off its fixing point and she was floating free, flaying around in freefall without a clue how to land safely.

Cathy had always been the strong one, she'd always been the brave one, and if Alison was honest she'd always been the beautiful one too. All Alison had ever managed to do was to burn a little brighter than Cathy for a short while, to burn so angrily that she put her friend in the shade. Now though, Alison's light was, if not out entirely, then almost extinguished.

And here she was, in this town that Marc had brought her back to. Here with her children and one hundred promises she could not keep.

As Alison sat there, the sun beginning to warm the sky, she understood that now she had to be strong, she had to stand on her two feet alone for the first time in her life. Because now there was only her, and no one else to blame if she got it all wrong.

At eight o'clock Alison headed back to the gym where she showered and changed into the workout gear she kept in her locker, and rang home to speak to her daughters from a payphone in reception. But the home phone was engaged, probably knocked off the hook at one of its many extensions, and it went straight to voice mail.

'Hi, guys. I stayed at Cathy's last night. Sorry I didn't call but it was late before I decided to stay over. I'll be home in a little while. See you then!' Alison hung up the phone, knowing that the message would languish undiscovered until someone picked up the phone to make a call, which on a Sunday might not be for hours. She could have used her last twenty-pence piece to dial Marc's mobile, she supposed. But then it would be him and only him that answered the phone and she still wasn't ready to talk to him without the buffer zone her children provided, keeping things even and calm between them.

Alison left the gym and was on her way home when she saw a train rumbling into the station. The impulse to be anywhere except at home with Marc overtook her and she caught the next train to town, where she walked and shopped and ate a quiet lunch until she knew she could not put off returning home any longer. Once or twice she glanced at her dead phone, the screen silent and dark, and wondered what messages might wait for her locked inside it. Perhaps there were none. Maybe Marc was either too angry or not angry enough to phone her and ask her where she was.

Alison didn't know which situation was preferable.

It was just after four that she finally arrived home, hesitating with her key in the lock, suddenly aware that she had no idea at all how to proceed with her life, and that for some reason she felt guilty. She felt as if she'd been seeing someone behind his back, and she supposed that in a way she had.

But before Alison could turn the key, Marc opened the door. His clothes were crumpled and his face was heavy with dark stubble.

'Where have you been?' he demanded, his body barring her entrance to the house.

'Don't start,' she said, ducking under his arm and heading for the stairs. 'I've been out, Marc. I stayed out with Kirsty and Cathy last night and today I just needed some time to myself. And I'm sorry if you actually had to spend some time with your children instead of breezing in and out of their lives in five minutes flat, but frankly you are such a hypocrite. I left a message on the answer phone at least. How many times have you never bothered coming home without ringing?'

Alison had begun to race up the stairs when Marc's words stopped her in her tracks.

'Dominic went out last night and he hasn't come home since,' Marc shouted at her. 'I called you, I left you message after message. Where were you?'

Alison turned on her heel and looked at him.

'My phone went flat. What do you mean, he hasn't come home? Is he with friends? What do you *mean*?' she asked him urgently.

'You went out,' Marc began. 'I was cooking the girls their tea when he came in. He'd obviously been drinking and he reeked of smoke. He said a few things, swore in front of the girls. So I said a few things and . . . it got out of hand.'

'Got out of hand?' Alison asked him, her voice tense. 'Marc? Did you hit him?'

'Did I . . .?' Marc looked stricken. 'No, Alison, I did not hit our son. He just makes me so furious, but I'd *never* hit him. I said a few things I shouldn't have, but he . . . he makes me so mad. I don't understand him, I don't know him any more.'

Marc shook his head, as if these details were irrelevant. 'He stormed off and I haven't seen him since. I tried his mobile. It's off. I've tried you a hundred times – where *were* you?'

'I needed some time to myself,' Alison said, biting back the anger she felt at Marc's implied accusation because she knew he was worried. 'Well, have you looked for him?'

She turned and walked slowly down the stairs, each descending step drawing her nearer to the fear she was beginning to feel for Dominic.

'I tried, but I don't know any of his friends,' Marc said as she approached him. 'I don't where he goes, I don't know anything about him. I put the girls in the car last night and again this morning and we drove around the school, and a few other places but we couldn't see him. I don't know where he is. I didn't know what to do without you. I didn't know what to tell the girls. I told them you were at a sleepover. Amy cried for you.'

'I didn't know, I thought everything would be fine here. Look, I'm sure Dom is fine,' Alison said, for her benefit as much as Marc's. 'He'll be at Ciara's or maybe with one of the boys from Rock Club. He can take care of himself, and this is Farmington.'

'You don't seem very worried,' Marc said, blame touching his voice.

'Of course I'm worried, Marc, he's my son,' Alison snapped. 'I asked you to look after them for one night – *one* night – and still you couldn't be the parent, could you? You had to rise to him. No wonder he thinks you don't love him.'

'Mama!' Amy shrieked, crashing down the stairs closely followed by her sister, hitting Alison's legs with full force and buckling them so that she had to sit down on the bottom stair. 'Where *were* you, Mama? Dom's gone away and we don't know where he is or where you were. Were you with him?'

'No, I was having a sleepover with my friend, with Leila and Eloise's mum, remember? I didn't know Dom was gone until just now.'

'Daddy didn't know where to find him,' Gemma told her. 'We thought of everywhere we could look but he isn't anywhere.'

'Mama?' Amy's voice was low, her eyes huge as she wound her arms around Alison's neck. 'Is Dominic dead, like the teenagers on the news? Is he shot?'

'Of course not, of course he isn't. He'll be fine, I promise you.'

She felt the weight of Marc's stare on her and when she looked up at him, his whole body was clenched with anxiety.

'You stay with them,' he told her. 'I'll take the car out again and have a proper look. Do you know any of his friends' numbers?'

'No, but Ciara told us her surname; I'll look in the book. I'll try all the numbers under that name. If I can find her maybe she can tell me some people he might be with if he's not with her . . .'

'What?' Marc asked her.

Carefully Alison kissed first Amy and then Gemma on the cheeks. 'Would you girls go and make Mummy a sandwich? I'm ever so hungry.'

'I can do that easily,' Gemma said.

'I'll help, though,' Amy said, and the pair trotted off to the kitchen, reassured for the time being.

'What if he's run away, Marc?' Alison asked her husband once her daughters were out of earshot. 'Gone back up to London? We might never find him then, not if he's gone back up there.'

Marc took her in his arms and held her for a moment.

'Come on, you were right the first time: he'll be fine,' he said. 'He'll be holed up somewhere playing silly buggers and hoping like hell that he's causing all of the fuss and grief that he is. I'll go out, you ring round. He'll turn up.'

'OK,' Alison said, feeling suddenly awkward in his embrace.

'You know that you and I are a good team,' Marc said, holding her a little tighter for a second.

Alison disengaged herself from his grasp. 'Just find him, Marc,' she said. 'And when you do, don't be too hard on him. Once upon a time you and he used to be such good friends. Don't throw that away too.'

Jimmy was determined to be prepared as he climbed back on board his boat.

No more starting a conversation without thinking it through. Like the conversation he'd had with the girls on the boat earlier. Like when Donna Clarke asked him to go to the ladies' loos with her even though he knew his wife was somewhere round the corner and he'd said yes. No more not thinking anything through.

The best thing in life that had ever happened to him, apart from his daughters, had been the one thing he'd put all of his forethought and planning strategies into. And that was getting Catherine to marry him. It had taken him ten months to get her to agree, ten months to persuade himself that one day she would have to love him as much as he loved her, otherwise she wouldn't always look and be so happy when she was with him. Every single day he'd offer her another little bit of carefully gleaned proof that he was the man for her, until she dropped the last of her guards and defences and let him love her the way he knew he could, for ever. For ten months she'd resisted him and then one morning as he'd been proposing to her between kissing each one of her toes, she said yes.

Or more precisely, 'Yes, yes, OK! Yes! Just stop it, *please*!'

'Yes what?' Jimmy had said, sitting up at the end of the bed, his heart in his mouth.

'Yes, I will marry you, you idiot.'

'Why?' Jimmy had asked, crawling along the bed and stretching out next to her.

'Because you won't shut up about it,' Catherine had retorted, pulling the sheet over her breasts, 'and I'm tired of lying to my mother about where I am.'

'Your mother doesn't know you have a lover?' Jimmy asked her playfully, enjoying the illicit implications of the word.

'No she doesn't,' Catherine told him, her smile dimming. 'I need to get out, I need to be myself and when I'm with you that's who I am. You let me be completely me and you still seem to like me, so yes, I will marry you, Jimmy. You're the best thing in my life.'

'That's the most romantic thing you've ever said to me,' Jimmy said, grinning from ear to ear.

Laughing with pure happiness Jimmy had pulled her into his arms and kissed as much of her as he could before she squirmed away, rolling herself up in the sheet.

'I love you so much too,' he'd told her, intent on revealing those lovely breasts again.

'I know,' she'd laughed as he pulled her back close to him. 'And knowing that makes me the happiest I've ever been.'

Twelve years ago months of careful planning and persistence had got him his wife in the end. And that was exactly what he needed now to get her back. Because when Jimmy thought of him and Catherine then, laughing and happy, entangled in that sheet, he knew he loved her just as much now as he ever did. No, he loved her more because after everything they'd been through she still had the strength and generosity not to hate his guts for it. She was the most amazing person he was ever likely to know, and even if she was never able to love him back in the same way, he had to try to make her see that he was still the man for her. He had to be able to know that at least he had tried.

So now he was going to think through from about a million different angles how he was going to tell Catherine he still loved her and persuade her to give him a second chance. He was going to be prepared for any eventuality. Every single one of them. He was going into this like a barrister: sharp-witted, determined to win and impossible to distract . . .

Jimmy paused. A plume of smoke seemed to be rising from the other side of the bushes that edged the towpath. He inhaled deeply. He'd know that smell anywhere.

Lightly Jimmy hopped off the edge of the boat and crept across the towpath.

'Gotcha,' he said as he jumped round to the other side of the bush. He stopped when he realised who the huddled figure was.

'Dom?' he said, looking at the crumpled teen, bundled in a parka, his hand trembling as he attempted to relight the joint that must have gone out almost the moment it was lit.

'Have you been out here all night, mate?' Jimmy asked with some concern.

'I couldn't stay at home,' Dom said. 'Mum wasn't there and Dad . . . I hate him. I really hate him. I couldn't take his bullshit any longer, acting like he can tell me what to do. So I walked out. I hung out with my mates for a while but then they all went home, so I came down here to see if you were in. But your boat wasn't there, so I got a bottle of cider and waited. I must have fallen asleep. I'm fucking frozen. Good job I've got some gear to warm me up.'

'Get up,' Jimmy said, holding out an arm and hauling the boy to his feet. 'And that muck isn't gear, it's weed, if it's that. It's probably oregano that some arsehole's sold you. Either way it's muck, so come on, I'll make you a warm drink and you can tell me why you'd rather freeze your nuts off out here than go home.'

With what might have been relief on his face Dominic pocketed the joint and followed Jimmy into the boat.

'I can't go home,' he said as he watched Jimmy stoke the stove. 'I can't go home because I hate him and every time I look at him I get filled up with this . . . *massive* anger and I just want to punch him. I tried to punch him before, but he just grabbed my fist and laughed at me. Told me he could beat me to a pulp if he wanted. Well, maybe he could now, but not for ever. You wait, one day I'll show him . . .'

Jimmy put the kettle on the stove and sat down opposite Dom.

'I thought you might be cool, if I came here,' Dom said blearily. 'Because after all it's your life he's ruining, not only mine. So I thought I'd come here. But you weren't in.'

Perplexed Jimmy got up again and poured boiling water on a tea bag, sloshing in the last of his milk and setting the mug down in front of Dom, whose face wrinkled with distaste as he took a sip. 'Got any sugar?' he asked

Jimmy spooned first one, then a second and a third spoonful into the mug until Dom stopped nodding.

'I am cool about you coming over,' Jimmy told him. 'I'm just sorry that I wasn't here for you, man.'

'Whatever,' Dom said, cupping his hand around the mug of warm tea, letting its steam bathe his chilled face. 'It's no big deal. I was all right on my own.'

'You stayed out all night and your mum will be going spare,' Jimmy said.

'She won't,' Dominic said. 'She went out with *her*, Dad's latest tart. My mum actually went round to her house to play nice with her.'

'With who?' Jimmy asked.

'I'm sorry, Mr Ashley, but my dad's been seeing your wife,' Dominic told him. He thought for a moment. 'I'm sorry I called your wife a tart,' he added. 'But she is.'

'He hasn't,' Jimmy said flatly. 'Your dad hasn't been seeing my wife.'

'I saw him this one time last week, I saw them together,' Dom protested. 'I don't know about other times. But I know my dad – there'll be other times.'

'I know about that, Dom,' Jimmy said, nodding. 'It was nothing, just two old friends catching up. Nothing was going on, I swear to you.' Perhaps it was wrong to lie to the boy. After all, something had been about to go on, but in the end it hadn't. And Jimmy didn't want Dom getting angry over something that hadn't happened. It seemed as if he had enough real stuff to try to deal with as it was.

'Maybe not this time,' Dominic said with a shrug. 'But if he wants it, it will happen. He's done it before, loads of times. He's an evil bastard, he bloody is.'

'I know,' Jimmy said mildly.

'It's like he lives in this world where he's perfect, where he's king and he expects everyone else to fall into place around him.

'Yeah?' Jimmy said. '*Arsehole*.'

'And he never looks at me, he never listens to *me*. The only time he sees me is when he's so angry that he practically wants to hit me.'

'You're right, that doesn't sound like good parenting at all to me,' Jimmy said. 'What a fucker.'

'He's scum,' Dominic agreed. 'I hate him. I wish he was dead, I wish he was dead, I do!' The next breath that Dominic drew in was a ragged one that caught in his throat with the threat of tears.

Diplomatically, Jimmy looked out of the window for a moment or two while the boy composed himself.

'Why aren't you disagreeing with me?' Dom asked him after a while. 'When I say stuff like that at home Mum always says, "No, you don't hate him, Dom, you don't wish he was dead, you don't feel that way." But I *do*, I *do* feel that way. I feel it so much that sometimes I think I might stop breathing because it fills my chest up. I thought it was your job to tell me that I don't feel the way I do; I thought that's what you lot did.'

'So is that why you came here then? Is that what you wanted to hear?' Jimmy asked him. Dominic shook his head, sinking his chin on his chest. 'Look, I believe that you feel that way. The question is, why, and what to do about it?'

'Why?' Dom's head snapped up. 'Because of the way he treats Mum, because he's a fucking hypocrite, playing at happy families with us while he's off fucking everything that

349

moves behind our backs. And because . . . because it's never me, it's never *me* he's pleased to see when he gets in, or *me* he sits down and talks to. He hasn't listened to me play my guitar for over a year, or asked me how school's going since we moved to this dump. When I was brought home by the pigs *then* he looked at me. Or that time I beat up Joe Clayton over what he was saying about Mum. He had something to say to me then. The only time he's got any time for me is when I've done something wrong.'

'So actually you kind of miss him then,' Jimmy said mildly. 'You're not so much hating him as missing him and feeling angry that he doesn't seem to miss you.'

'No, that's wrong – I don't . . .' Dominic began to protest, then stopped to consider. 'Nothing's felt right for so long,' he said at last. 'When I was a little kid, Gemma's age, a bit older, he'd take me down the park every Sunday to play footy. Sometimes he'd let me go to work with him. Sit in the cars and pretend to drive them. He helped me buy my first guitar. Not just any piece of crap but a Rickenbacker. He used to tell me he was proud of me, that he believed in me. I thought the sun shone out of his frigging arse. Then I found out about him and the other women. And he knew that I knew, that I saw him for what he really was. Not a hero, not my dad, but just some lecherous old creep that put fucking before his family. His hasn't looked or talked to me since, not really. He hasn't got the guts.'

'Listen,' Jimmy said, 'I'm not saying you don't feel angry or that you don't hate him, I can see both of those things are true just by looking at you. But you know what? You don't get either of those emotions without love. If you didn't love your dad, then you wouldn't be bothered what he did or how he treated you. He'd be nothing to you.'

'I hate him,' Dominic repeated, his voice low.

Jimmy thought for a moment. 'A couple of years ago I thought I hated my life. I felt trapped by it. Somehow me, the rock god, the superstar in waiting, had got into his thirties with a wife, two little kids and a mortgage I could hardly pay. I woke up one day and I thought, what happened to my dreams? When did I forget to make them happen? I had no money to speak of, and not much prospect of getting any. I found myself thinking that if I hadn't got married and spent so much of my life trying to get this woman to love me I'd have been free to really go for my dream, to make the band happen, to get discovered, get out of this dump, as you call it, really live life, live out my dreams because I'd always been so sure that was what the future held for me. A stadium full of seventy thousand people shouting my name. Not struggling week in and week out just to get by.

'So I started to get angry, not loud and shouty angry but just everyday, whenever I looked at my beautiful girls and my incredible wife I'd feel a little bit more angry and I'd wonder what my life would be like without them. It was so settled, the same day after day, and I felt as if my guts were being hollowed out with a spoon. I couldn't stand it.'

'What's this got to do with my dad?' Dominic asked him bleakly.

Jimmy had to think for a moment or two; he couldn't remember.

'You'll see,' he said, hoping he looked wise and sagacious. 'So one night I'm at this gig at The Goat – it's a pub in the town. Cat's there and so are all our mates. It was usually a good gig, loads of people, good atmosphere, but I was restless, angry. We were having a break and I looked round for Cat but I couldn't see her so I went to get another drink, trying to drown the anger. I was by the bar when this woman Donna Clarke came up to me, told me she fancied me, told me she

351

wanted to . . .' Jimmy looked at fifteen-year-old Dom, 'get off with me. And for a split second, I thought that getting off with her was what I wanted. I thought that would make me happy, that would make me free. And I was right. I went off with this woman and Cat caught me and her together. She set me free, all right. She booted me out that night.'

'Are you saying that's why Dad does it, because he feels trapped by Mum and by us?' Dominic asked him unhappily, his voice sharpened with anger.

'No! No,' Jimmy said hastily. 'No, I'm not saying that. I don't know why your dad does what he does, but I do know that him and me are about as different as two blokes can get, which isn't to say that I'm better than him, just really, really different. What I'm saying is when I saw the look on Cat's face when she realised what was happening . . . the first thing I saw was shock and then, for about a split second, hurt and then . . .' Jimmy blew out a breath of air and whistled, 'anger. My God was she ever angry with me. She grabbed me by the hair and smacked me one right in the eye. Donna Clarke ran off before Cat could do the same to her. She was so angry because I'd betrayed her trust, you see, and because . . . I'd made her trust me, and on that night for the first time ever I could see in her face that she loved me. Her anger and pain showed me her love. But I saw it too late.

'All of my stuff went out of the house window. All my vinyl ended in pieces on the concrete. All my shirts and even my Donnington eighty-nine T-shirt, limited edition, shredded. I'd be standing there outside the house, shouting and screaming, and the girls would be crying, begging us to stop, but we couldn't . . . not for the longest time.'

'But if you were bored, trapped, if you didn't want to be with her any more, why did it matter?' Dom asked him.

Jimmy sighed. 'That's what I've been trying to tell you. It

352

was only when I saw how angry she was that I realised she loved me, fiercely and deeply, even if those few minutes were the first time she felt that way. And at that exact same moment, the moment when I finally knew that she loved me as much as I loved her, I lost her. Her anger was like the last flare of a lit match. When it went out, her love went out too. It was burned out.'

Jimmy was silent for a moment as he looked into the stove.

'I don't get what this has got to do with me,' Dominic said after a while.

'I'm saying you and your dad make each other angry. Which means that you and your dad love each other. Now I'm not saying that he's perfect. In actual fact, I think he's a bit of a tosser. But I don't doubt that he loves you. And as for you, well, pulling stunts like sleeping out all night on your own is a pretty low thing to do. It's attention-seeking, the kind of thing little toddler girls do, not axe-men, not gods of rock. We are men of the guitar, Dom; we have our standards. But if you are willing to do something so stupid and dangerous to get his attention then you must still care about what he thinks of you. You must still love him.'

'Shit,' Dom said, after a while. 'Mum'll be doing her nut in.'

'Your dad will be doing his nut too,' Jimmy said, unable to resist a little smile. 'You'll have dropped him properly in it.'

'Good,' Dominic said gruffly.

'Look,' Jimmy said, 'I had a dad once. He died when I wasn't much older than you. Can't say I argued with him, or hated him like you do yours. Me and my dad got along pretty well. He was always on my side, always knew what to do about everything. He was a decent bloke, straight up – no complications. I miss him, Dom. I miss him and I wish he was here now to sort me out. I know you hate your dad right now, but if you give him a chance, in a few weeks, a few months or even a few years, the two of you will grow together again and you'll be friends. And when you are you'll be so glad you've got him, Dom. Unless he is a total dickhead, that is, but my dad told me everyone's got at least one redeeming quality, so I think we still have reason to be optimistic he isn't a completely lost cause.'

'I might . . .' Dom blinked heavily and then got up, 'I might go outside for a bit, get some air.'

'You've got your mobile on you?' Jimmy asked him. Jimmy held out his hand. 'Give it to me. I'll phone your mum. If you're lucky they'll be so glad to see you back in one piece they won't kill you. And when you get a chance, talk to your dad. Say to him, "Hey, Dad, I'd love to talk to you." Pretty much any dad is better than no dad at all.

'Oh, and Dom?' Jimmy held out his hand again. 'Give me that spliff, mate. It's going in the canal.'

However, when Jimmy had tried 'Mum' on Dominic's phone it went straight to answer phone. His thumb hovered over the dial for a second or two before he took a breath and pressed 'Dad' instead. Marc arrived, after a brief and terse conversation, only a few minutes later to pick Dom up.

As soon as Dom, who had been sitting on the roof of the boat, saw him, he scrambled over the top of the boat and shut himself inside.

Jimmy sighed and glanced at his watch. He'd told Catherine he would be back in a couple of hours with his precious chicken, which was even now languishing in his fridge, even though it was quite often colder outside the fridge than in it. It was now two and a half hours since he'd seen her and he hadn't spent one minute of it working out how to tell her that he loved her and wanted her back. He was fairly sure that his pastoral duties as one of the boy's extracurricular tutors shouldn't have to extend to chatting with the man who was currently intent on seducing his wife, but the boy clearly needed a go-between here, someone to smooth the water for him. And besides, Jimmy was a man of principle, and one of those principles, taught to him by his father, was never to judge a book by its cover. Despite everything he'd heard, everything Cat, Alison and Dom had told him, *he* didn't know Marc personally, and so he wouldn't judge him. Just because the circumstantial evidence made him out to be a complete wanker, it didn't mean that he actually was.

'He turned up about half an hour ago,' Jimmy said, as Marc approached the boat. 'He just needed someone to talk to, I think.'

'Half an hour ago?' Marc snapped at him. 'We've been going out of our minds and you've known where he is for half an hour?'

Jimmy took a breath, 'Yeah, you're right, I probably should have phoned you straight away, but I don't have your number and the kid was skittish. I think if I'd said to him, give me your phone, I'm calling your parents, he would have legged it and then we wouldn't have known where he was again.'

'You should have just made him give you his phone number!' Marc told him. 'Why didn't you?'

Jimmy paused, thrown for a second by the question.

'Anyway, he's back now so that's good, isn't it?' Jimmy stated firmly, trying very hard not to judge Marc.

'Yes, it is,' Marc said, glancing at the closed boat doors. 'If I can get him to come out.' Jimmy saw the look on the other man's face. Somewhere behind that square jaw and stubble he was nervous.

'He's pissed off with you,' Jimmy said conversationally, looking up at the sky. His chicken was supposed to have been in Catherine's oven a good half-hour ago.

'Thanks, I had gathered that much,' Marc said bitterly. But he didn't make a move to go into the boat to fetch his son out.

'What are you scared of?' Jimmy asked him.

'What?' Marc looked at Jimmy. 'What do you mean, what am I scared of?'

'Well, why aren't you going in there all guns blazing, hauling him out and whacking him round the ear? That's what he expects you to do. You do know that he thinks you only ever notice him if you're fucked off with him?'

Marc shook his head. 'That's just not true . . . I spend a lot of time with him, or at least I would do if he wanted me to. But he doesn't. He's made up his mind about me, and the conclusion he's come to is that I'm a pretty low kind of person. I know what he thinks of me. So I try and stay out of his way. I try not to let his wind-ups get to me. If I let him get under my skin I lose it with him. I don't mean to, because I love the boy. And I know I don't have any right to get angry with him, but I do. I can't reach him now. Even if I wanted to.'

'Bollocks,' Jimmy said simply.

'I beg your pardon?' Marc asked.

'Listen, you're not talking to a chick now,' Jimmy said. 'Don't try all your touchy-feely "nobody understands me" crap out on *me*. You and me are both men. We know the score. You've been busy, you've been busy with work and quite possibly women other than your wife, maybe even mine. You're caught up in your own mid-life crisis, having a drama and wondering how you ended up with a beautiful wife and three lovely kids – that's something that confuses me too, as it goes – and you're so involved in you that you haven't got time for the boy. Your little girls are cute and adoring, and so you give them your attention when you're there. But he,' Jimmy hooked his thumb towards the boat, 'he sees right through you, and he's angry and prickly and frankly a bit stinky, and

356

on your long list of priorities that mainly reads "me, me, me, me" you've put him at the bottom of it.'

Marc stared at him with those black eyes that seemed to turn sensible women to jelly, and Jimmy wondered how much it would hurt when the other man punched him. But Marc didn't move a muscle.

'Is this about me and your ex-wife?' he asked Jimmy.

'There is no you and my wife, and she's still my wife. We are still married. Listen to yourself, man. You're here to pick up your son, your fifteen-year-old son who has been gone all night, who slept rough, and you're trying to score points off of me because you fancy my wife. I think I got it spot on when I listed your priorities: "you, you, you."'

Marc dropped his head and shoulders for a moment before looking back up at Jimmy.

'I don't know what to say to him,' he confessed. 'He used to think I was a god, that I was the bee's knees. And I loved that, you know. I never had a dad myself, but I thought, this is what it's all about: father and son. I let him down. The *one* thing I can't let myself mess up is what I have with my children. I never had that, not having had a dad. I *need* to get this right somehow, but I keep getting it wrong.'

'That's parenting,' Jimmy said. 'You try your best but sometimes you let them down. I think the trick is to keep picking them up again and to not let them think even for one second that you don't care about them more than anything else in the world. Even if they are fifteen, stink of stale smoke and swear like a bastard. He's a good kid, your son. He's funny and smart. He's got real musical talent. He loves his mum and his sisters. You can be that father to him, the father he used to look up to as a god, if you try. You'd be amazed at how great it would make you feel. I know what it's like to be without a dad too. It's shit. Don't make him go through that. Because, after all, you're the parent. It's up to you to make the first moves. If you spend all your time waiting for him to forgive you, you'll never work things out. But if you ask him to forgive you then he will because he loves you. And if you do then you have to be certain that you will never ever let him down again, because you can only ever ask someone to forgive you once and mean it.'

Jimmy let his own words sink in for minute. That was it. That was what he had to say to Cat. In the aftermath of the ladies' loos in The Goat, in all the yelling and the fury, he'd never once asked her to forgive him. Not even over the last few months when they'd finally clicked back into some sort of friendship again. They never talked about that night. They talked about the consequences of it and how to deal with them the best way for the children, but they never talked about why it happened. And Jimmy had never once told her that he was sorry, and that he regretted those few minutes more than anything else in his life. She didn't know he was sorry. She didn't know that he was desperate for her to forgive him, because until recently he hadn't understood it himself and because he'd never asked her to. Maybe she would be able to love him again and maybe she wouldn't, but Jimmy knew he had to tell her how sorry he was for that night. He owed her an apology.

'Maybe you're right,' Marc said, cutting into his thoughts. 'But things are difficult at home. Our lives are changing and he's going to blame me for that. If Alison leaves me he's going to blame me for that and if she stays then he's going to blame me for that too so . . .'

'So what's the point of trying?' Jimmy asked him.

Marc shrugged. 'Everyone thinks I'm a terrible person,' he said. 'Sometimes it's just easy to go along with them.'

'Look, I don't know you and what I do know of you doesn't

exactly put you in the running for a Nobel Peace Prize or anything,' Jimmy said, 'but I can see you love your kids. This is your opportunity to be a good person, a great dad. Go for it.'

'Thank you.' Marc looked at him, 'I will, I will go for it. Look, about Catherine . . .'

'Don't talk to me about Catherine,' Jimmy said. 'Don't say a word about her, not now when I'm doing my best not to judge you.'

'I still have feelings for her,' Marc said. 'And I think she still has feelings for me. And I think both of us need to discover what they are and if they mean anything.'

Jimmy focused very hard for the twenty or so seconds it took him to stop wanting to punch Marc.

'Take your son home,' he said. 'I'm going to cook dinner for my wife.'

Chapter Twenty-three

When Jimmy came back down the stairs after settling the girls in bed he found Catherine lying on her back on the sofa, a cushion over her face.

'Dinner wasn't that bad, was it?' he asked her, a smile in his voice.

'No,' she said, her voice a little muffled by the cushion. 'Actually it was really nice, even if nine at night is a bit late to be giving a five- and an eight-year-old their tea.'

'Yeah, I'm sorry about that,' Jimmy said. 'That was one big mother of a chicken. Who knew they took so long to cook?'

He waited, standing at the bottom of the stairs. It was normally round about now that Catherine would ask him if he fancied a glass of wine before he went home and he invariably said yes. But tonight, of all nights, the night when he had a speech and declarations to make, she just lay there like a wet rag on the sofa, a cushion covering her face.

'I'm too tired to go to bed,' she half groaned, half giggled.

'I could take you up if you like?' Jimmy offered. 'Like I did the night we moved in, do you remember?'

Catherine laughed and batted the cushion off her face so that it tumbled to the floor.

'Yes, I remember. I bumped my head about four times and you put your back out for a week! I don't think it's quite come to that yet.' Wearily she pushed herself into a sitting position, rubbing the palms of her hands over her face.

'I'd ask you to stay for a bit but I think I've got to go to sleep now, Jim – before I pass out.'

'OK,' Jimmy said, covering both his disappointment and relief, because his stomach was churning so violently just at that moment, he wasn't sure that he could have gone through with it anyway. 'Whatever you say.'

'Will you pull me up?' Catherine held out both of her hands to him and, taking them, Jimmy pulled her to her feet a little more robustly than he planned so that she collided with his chest. For a second they were nose to nose. Jimmy caught his breath as she stood so close to him. On the other hand, he didn't think he could wake up another morning on that boat without having told her how he felt.

'I love you,' he said suddenly, dropping the three words into the room like an anvil. Catherine stared at him for a second, her green eyes as clear as glass, and then laughed.

'Me too, you idiot,' she said, and she wrapped her arms around him and hugged him tightly. For a moment, for about two seconds, as his arms enclosed her waist and he felt her warmth crushed against his ribcage, Jimmy marvelled that it could be that easy, that to turn his life round completely was as simple as telling her he loved her. And then he felt Catherine tense in his arms and, putting the palms of her hands on his chest, she pushed him away from her a few inches so she could look in his face again.

'God, Jimmy, your heart is pounding,' she said, her smile faltering as her hand rested on his chest.

'Because I love you,' he said quietly. 'Like I said, I love you. And standing this close to the woman you love does tend to make a man's heart pound a little.'

'Yeah, but you didn't mean that you *love* me, did you? You

mean you're fond of me. You care for me, in the same way that I care for you.'

'Actually, I fully *love* you,' Jimmy said, his voice dropping almost to a whisper. 'I always have. I didn't want to admit it after we split up. I wanted to forget I loved you because it seemed so bloody pointless. But love is love and there it is. I can't do anything to stop it. It was the night Marc and Alison came back, and you were so upset and confused I realised I'd do anything to stop you feeling that way, because I still love you. I love you, Cat.' He took a deep breath. 'And I wanted to ask you if –'

Catherine broke their embrace, pushing herself away from him, taking three steps backwards and sitting down heavily on the sofa he'd just helped her up from.

'Jimmy, don't.' She shook her head. 'Don't say it. I'm tired.'

'I know,' Jimmy said impulsively, kneeling at her feet. 'I know you're tired and I know I probably shouldn't say any of this now, but I have to because I can't go on hanging around you all day every day without you knowing how I feel. And if I go now then the cat will only be half out of the bag and you won't be able to sleep anyway, worrying about whether or not I've gone off my rocker. You don't have to say anything, decide *anything*. Just please let me tell you how I feel.'

Catherine dropped her head in her hands, but she did not say no. Jimmy watched her for a second, her hair flowing over her fingers like water. This was it, he told himself. This was his moment.

'When I had sex in the loo with Donna Clarke at The Goat I made a mistake,' Jimmy said, watching Catherine's fingers tighten in her hair. 'Not just because I had sex with her, although that was a massive, *massive* mistake. I made that mistake because I thought I didn't want our marriage any

362

more. I thought I was worn out with loving you. I thought I wanted to be young and free and single and alive again. Billy had drunk himself to death and I didn't want to go the same way as him; I didn't want to have the hopelessness he had at the end, that sense of losing something he'd never even had.

'I thought about the gigs the band got, the weddings and parties, and I thought about the tutoring I did and how you and I managed just about from hand to mouth, week to week and month to month, and I thought this isn't it, this isn't *my* life. It can't be, because sooner or later I'm going to end up dead like Billy or Dad, and I won't have lived *my* life. Touring Japan and bedding groupies, that was the life I was supposed to have. I was angry with Billy for giving up the way he did, I was angry at myself for failing and I blamed that on you for not bloody delivering something you never once promised. For not loving me. And I've never told you how sorry I am about that. So now I'm telling you. I'm sorry, Cat, because while I was with you I had the best life I could have ever hoped for. I had everything that a low-achieving bum of a musician like me didn't deserve, and everything Billy did but couldn't have. But I couldn't see it. And I'm asking you to forgive me for what I did, for what I threw away, and to say that you'll give me another chance because I promise you I won't let you down ever again.'

Slowly Catherine lifted her head, raking her hair off her face with her fingers. All trace of colour had drained from her cheeks and her expression was taut.

'I . . . I don't know what you want me to do,' she said. 'I don't know why you are saying all of this to me now, *now*, Jimmy, when things are finally at peace between us. Is it because of Marc? Is it because suddenly he's back on the scene and you've decided to get protective of me? Jimmy, this is typical you. You think you love me but you don't, not really. You care about me, you're worried about what I might do, and you love your children and you'd like them to be happy. You're thirty-three and the band isn't taking off, maybe it never will do. You're feeling low, and maybe all of those things muddled up inside you make you think that you love me, but you don't. This is just a phase. It will pass.'

'It won't pass,' Jimmy said urgently. 'Yes, it is all of those things you said, but it's more than that. I can't stand to see you unhappy. I can't stand seeing you and not being able to touch you. When I make you smile I feel like the king of the world, like I am someone important, and when I piss you off I want to punch myself in the face.'

'Jimmy, stop it,' Catherine pleaded with him urgently. 'Don't say all this, don't make things difficult between us again. You and me being together that way is in the past. Finally, *finally* I can deal with that. I can accept it. We've made peace for us and for the children. I don't want to rake it up again, Jimmy. I don't want to –'

'But don't you see, you don't *have* to accept it,' Jimmy said, grabbing her hands in his. 'You don't have to. Because I love you and I think that finally you could love me if only you'd let yourself. We can be together again. After all, we're still married. I could move back in tomorrow and it would be as if the last two years had never happened.'

Sharply Catherine pulled her hands out of his.

'The last two years happened, Jimmy,' she said, an edge of anger flashing on the blade of her voice. 'Donna Clarke in the ladies' loos *happened*. Me trying to get used to the idea that the man who *begged* me from one month to the next for almost a whole year to marry him, who *promised* me that he loved me and he would never let me down, and kept on promising until I believed him, just ripped all of those promises and that marriage to shreds and in a matter of minutes, *happened*.' Catherine stopped, catching the rise in her voice, and closed her eyes for a second as she steadied herself. 'You say you still love me, but I don't think you do. And even if you did, even if you were as stupid and as arrogant as to think that after everything you've put me and your children through, you can just waltz back in here and pick up where you left off, well, I don't love you. I got over you, Jimmy. It *happened*.'

Jimmy didn't move, he didn't breathe. He felt caught in that moment, afraid to break it because the very next second and every second that would ever follow it seemed pointless to him if she didn't feel the same way.

'We get on OK, don't we?' Catherine asked him, levelling her voice. 'I like you being around. The girls need you around. So please let's just both go to bed and forget we ever had this conversation. Let's wake up in the morning, you on the boat and me here with our daughters, and carry on as if nothing has happened. Please, Jimmy.'

'I can't do that,' Jimmy said, standing slowly. 'I can't because I've said it now, it's out there, and I can't hide it or lie about it any more. I can't go back to the way things were before tonight.' He paused, looking around him as if he didn't recognise where he was any more. 'Look, I knew you might not feel the same, I knew that maybe I had got it wrong but for a few seconds when I was holding you just then it felt so right, so perfect, Cat. And I thought . . . I thought I could sense you felt the same way.'

'But you didn't sense that,' Catherine said doggedly. 'I don't feel that way about you.'

'Right.' Jimmy stood up straight and squared his shoulders, his voice taut and distant when he said, 'I think I'll catch the late train up to town. See my mates about that session work, after all. You've got the situation covered here. And besides, I could really do with the money and you never know what it might lead to.'

'Jimmy, don't,' Catherine stood up. 'Don't go because of this. Please.'

'You're not being fair to me, Cat,' Jimmy said. 'You don't want me, but you want me to stay. And I can't live like that any more. I can't hang around and be your friend and your babysitter, because I need more. So I have to go for a bit. Tell the girls I'll call them and I'll see them soon, but right now I have to go.' He paused. 'I can't be around you now.'

'Please, Jimmy, don't go like this –' Catherine began.

'Don't!' Jimmy raised his voice, making Catherine start a little. 'Don't ask me to stay if you don't feel the same. It's not fair. You must see that.'

Catherine reached out a hesitant hand and touched his face. 'Take care up there,' she said.

'You know me,' Jimmy said, with a twist of a smile. 'It's London that had better take care.' He leaned forward and kissed her just barely on the cheek. 'I'll see you.'

'See you,' Catherine said, standing perfectly still in the middle of the room.

Softly, slowly Jimmy closed the front door behind him so as not to wake the girls. He headed for the boat. He should just about have enough time to pick up his guitar and catch the late train into town.

After that he had no idea what he was going to do.

Alison sat down opposite Marc at the table and waited for him to say something. When he had arrived back with Dominic, the boy had run upstairs and slammed his bedroom door shut, and Marc had gone into the kitchen, opened a bottle of beer, which he had not taken a sip from, and sat at the kitchen table. That was three hours ago.

Alison had stood looking up the stairs towards Dom's room and then back at the kitchen towards Marc. After a moment's thought she'd started up the stairs and as she reached the top Amy's door opened, spilling a wedge of rose-tinted lamplight onto the landing.

'Is he back, Mummy?' Gemma asked her as she and her sister appeared in the doorway. They must have been in there together, listening, waiting to hear something. Alison had been so frantic phoning all of Dom's friends that she hadn't given them a thought until Dom was back. Now she kneeled and held her arms out to them.

'Yes,' Alison said, as she gathered up her girls. 'He's back and he's absolutely fine. Hey, listen, I'll make you some tea soon. What would you like as a Sunday treat? Beans on toast with Marmite, followed by chocolate ice cream?'

'Can we see him?' Amy asked her, padding towards Dominic's bedroom door at the end of the corridor.

'Of course you can,' Alison said, a lot less certain about Dominic's state of mind than she sounded.

The three of them stood outside his door and Alison knocked.

'Dom? It's Mum, Gemma and Amy,' she called out, careful to alert him to the presence of his sisters. 'Can we come in?'

A moment passed and then Dominic opened the door.

'I was going to have a shower,' he said, with a rueful smile. 'I smell a bit. Of countryside. It's rank.'

He and Alison looked at each other across the top of the girls' heads.

'I'm sorry, Mum,' Dom said.

'We missed you!' Amy said, before Alison could speak, running into him so hard that he staggered back a couple of paces. Dominic was soon engulfed by both sisters.

'Daddy took us out looking for you in the car in the dark,' Gemma told him. 'It was scary, but we didn't find you.'

'Daddy said you would be fine, but we were worried. And

I said you should have had the stranger danger class at school,' Amy said, 'like me.'

'Dad was really worried,' Gemma told Dom carefully. 'He stayed up all night waiting for you. We tried to, but we fell asleep.'

'Lightweights,' Dom said, ruffling their hair. 'I'm sorry, Gems. I'm sorry, Muffin, OK?'

'You do rather stink actually,' Gemma said, wrinkling up her nose fastidiously.

'You do. You stink of smelly socks and cow poo!' Amy said giggling, as Dominic tickled her.

'Right then,' Alison said. 'I think we'd better let your brother have his shower, don't you?' She bundled the girls out of the room. 'Go down and think about what you want for tea. I'll be down in a minute.'

'OK, Mummy!' the girls called as they raced down the stairs.

'You look like shit,' Dominic said. 'Were you up all night too?'

'Actually,' Alison started slowly, 'I stayed with a friend last night. I didn't know you'd gone until this afternoon because my phone had gone dead. But if I had known I would have been up all night worrying myself sick, just like your father was. What were you thinking, Dom? Were you trying to punish him by putting yourself in danger?'

'Mum, don't start defending him,' Dominic said wearily, sitting down heavily on his bed.

'I'm not defending him. I'm just asking you to think about what you did, about how bloody stupid you were.'

'Mr Ashley reckons I hate Dad so much because I love him,' Dom said, picking up his towel.

Alison thought for a moment. She had been both intrigued and relieved when she found out that the first adult Dom had gone to was Jimmy. He'd only known him properly for a few weeks and yet he felt he could turn to him about his father. It was good that there was someone in his life he felt that way about, but it broke her heart that it wasn't Marc.

'Maybe he's right about that,' she suggested tentatively.

'I thought Dad was going to bollock me, rip me to shreds when he picked me up but he didn't say anything, not a word,' Dom said. 'It was like I was invisible.'

'Maybe he doesn't know what to say,' Alison said, 'or how to say it.'

She took a step closer to her son and put her hands on his shoulders, chasing his constantly averting gaze until she finally made eye contact with him.

'You're fifteen, Dom,' she said. 'I know you feel like you're invincible but anything could have happened to you out there, anything.'

'I know,' Dom said. 'I didn't mean to sleep rough all night. It was shit and freezing fucking cold. I was going to ask Mr Ashley if I could stay with him, but his boat wasn't there.'

'You could have been mugged, beaten up . . . murdered, even,' Alison said, feeling her voice vibrate like a drum. 'Don't ever do that again, not ever. I probably should have come home last night, I should have been there for you. But I promise you from now on I always will be, so no matter how angry you feel or how hurt, never *ever* run away from me like that again. Promise me? I couldn't stand for anything to happen to you.'

'I won't do it again,' Dominic said, dropping his head. 'I don't know how you ran away for good when you were seventeen, Mum. It was bloody horrible.'

'It was bloody horrible for me too,' Alison said. 'But I had your dad and he looked after me.'

'Are you really going to stay with Dad?' Dom asked.

Alison was silent for a long moment. 'I need to talk to your dad before I talk to anyone else about that, OK? But I'm going to need you a lot over the next few weeks, Dom. I'm going to need you to support me and the girls, OK?'

'I will,' he promised her, dipping his head, mumbling a barely audible, 'Love you, Mum' into his T-shirt.

'So what do you want to do now?' Alison asked him. 'Do you want to talk about it? Tell me what happened yesterday with you and Dad? What it was like out there all night?'

'Honestly?' Dom said, looking back up at her, his eyes filling with tears. 'I want to cry.'

The girls had eaten Sunday tea, a feast of sausage and beans, around Marc, chattering away to him while he sat with that same flat and warm bottle of beer at the table, nodding and smiling. He wasn't the same as he usually was when he was with them, revelling in their attention. He was reserved and withdrawn. Alison thought he seemed almost bruised.

Still touched by guilt that she had been absent last night she bathed both the girls together and spent an extra long time reading them each their favourite story, making sure that each one was tucked in their separate rooms, night-lights on and favourite toys tucked under arms. As she brushed Gemma's hair back from her forehead and kissed the top of her nose, Gemma put her hand on her wrist.

'Love you, Mummy,' she said.

'I love you too, darling,' Alison replied.

Next she walked along the corridor to Dominic's room where he was lying in his bed in a T-shirt and jogging bottoms, his iPod plugs in his ears, strumming the tune he was listening to on his guitar. He sat up when he saw Alison was there, pulling the earpieces out.

'You must be starving,' Alison said. 'Why don't you come down and I'll make you something. I've got sausages.'

'Is he down there?' Dominic asked her. Alison thought about her husband sitting at the kitchen table.

'Yes,' she said. 'He's been sitting downstairs thinking since you got back. I think he's waiting to talk to you – and I mean talk, not shout. Come down and eat with us. Please, Dom.'

Dominic hesitated. 'OK,' he said eventually, steeling himself to his decision by squaring his shoulders and brushing his hair off his face. 'I'll be down in a minute.'

'Thank you,' Alison said.

Just as she was leaving Dominic's room, she noticed Amy's door being pushed closed again. Wondering if she'd got up to go to the loo, Alison carefully pushed Amy's door open to check she was OK.

She found that both her daughters were curled up together in the same bed.

'She can't sleep without me,' Gemma explained, sitting up.

'I can't, Mama,' Amy told her. 'Please can she stay?'

'Otherwise she won't sleep and it's school tomorrow,' Gemma said. 'I can sleep fine on my own, but you know what Amy's like. She'll only worry. Besides, I don't mind looking after her, Mummy.'

Alison crossed the room and pulled the cover across both of them, tucking them in.

'Of course you can stay here,' she said, kissing both of them again. 'And, if you like, tomorrow we can move both your beds into one room so you don't have such a squash and a squeeze.'

'Thank you, Mummy,' Gemma and Amy said together.

'Girls,' Alison started, 'I'm sorry that everything is so up and down at the moment. It will settle down one way or another soon, I promise you.'

'We know, Mummy,' Amy said on a yawn. 'We know.'

When Alison got downstairs Dom was already in the

kitchen hovering around the fridge in his bare feet and jogging bottoms. Marc was still sitting at the table, the two of them ignoring each other as if they were standing in parallel universes where the other one simply did not exist.

'Right then,' Alison said, determined to draw their realities together, 'sausages and beans all round because I can't be bothered to make anything more demanding than that.' She glanced at Dom. 'Sit down.'

Warily Dominic sat down at the table at the furthest possible position from Marc. Marc did not look at him.

'Do you want another beer?' Alison asked him, hoping to break his silence. 'That one's sat there for hours.'

Marc looked up at her, 'No,' he said. 'I'm fine really.'

As Alison set the food down in front of them and also sat down, she prepared herself; even hoped for another silent meal. This strange shuttered version of her husband sitting just to her right was better at least than the shouting and threatening one that had emerged recently. It seemed to Alison that both Marc and Dom appeared surprised by what last night had turned into for both of them. And perhaps that was a good thing. Perhaps silent reflection was exactly what they needed.

But Alison had not finished chewing her first mouthful when Marc spoke.

'Dom,' he said, looking at his son at last and making the boy start. 'I shouldn't have shouted at you the way I did last night. And I shouldn't have threatened you like I did on Friday. I'm sorry.'

Dom stared at his plate, holding his knife and fork in each hand as if he were afraid to move.

'I haven't got an excuse or even a good reason really,' Marc continued. 'I never had a dad. I never knew who he was or what he was like, don't have a single memory of him. Not even

372

a photo. I hardly knew my mum either, to be honest. She was out of my life by the time I was three. I know that you know all of this, I know I've told you a hundred times how I pulled myself up by my boot strings and created myself from nothing. But that's not the truth, is it? I didn't come out of nothing. Probably somewhere out there still are the man and the woman that made me. And I suppose I might take after them, I don't know. Like I don't know sometimes how to be a dad, especially now. Especially now that you are becoming a young man yourself. It was easier when you were little, when you thought I was the best thing since sliced bread. But now you know that I'm not perfect. You've judged me and I failed you, Dom, and I'm sorry but I love you, son, and somehow I'm going to put this right between us. I think I'm going to need your help, though.'

Alison found that she was holding her breath as Dominic looked across the table at Marc. 'And what about what you've done to Mum?' Dominic asked him. 'Are you sorry about that too?'

'Dom, your dad's said sorry –' Alison began, trying to head off another confrontation before it ignited.

'No, it's OK,' Marc said, holding his hand up to stop her. 'It's a fair question. And the answer is that of course I'm sorry. I'm always sorry. The truth is I've always wanted to be better than I am, and until now I've always failed. I'm a far from perfect husband, a far from perfect father, a far from perfect man. But I am so proud of you and the decent, caring, principled boy you've become, despite me. I think I need to try and live up to your standards.'

'Are you going to tell us that you'll try and change?' Dominic asked him, a hint of sarcastic serration in his tone.

'No, I'm not saying I'm going to change,' Marc said. 'I've said that too many times and it hasn't worked. I'm saying I'm going to do what I *know* that I can, which is to be a good father to you and your sisters, and I want you to remember that I will always be around for you, no matter what happens between me and Mum. I want you to remember that because I'm going to move out. Find a place of my own. You can all stay here if you want, or sell it and buy somewhere new. It's up to you. But I want you all to understand that I'm not moving out because I don't love you. I'm moving out because I do. I wanted to tell you two first. I'll explain it to the girls in the morning. I hope you will both be there to help me with that.'

As Marc spoke Alison felt ice-cold panic grip her heart and squeeze it, and a sense of dizzying unreality, as if she were watching this next turn her life was taking playing out before her on a movie screen.

This was it: the moment she had seen coming for months, possibly years, and yet had never quite believed would arrive, and he had chosen to make it happen, he had found the courage. He was really going. After all of this time he was going to leave her to stand alone in the world, and even if this had been the very thing she knew had to happen, hearing him say it shocked and terrified her.

'Are you leaving for ever?' Dominic asked him stiffly, two red blotches standing out on his otherwise pallid cheeks.

Marc looked at Alison and picked up her hand. 'I think so,' he said.

Alison returned his gaze and for the first time in a long while she felt close to him.

With a single nod Dominic stood up and held out his hand.

'I'm sorry about yesterday too, Dad,' he said. 'I behaved like a kid.'

As Marc let go of Alison's hand in order to stand up and shake his son's, Dom added, 'And for what it's worth, when I was a little kid and thought you were the best dad in the world that wasn't because I was little and didn't know any better. It was because you *were* the best dad in the world. And . . . I'm glad you're my dad because I think you will still be a great dad. I think you and me will be OK.'

Dominic looked at Alison, nipping at his lip.

'I might go up now,' he said. Alison, still unable to speak, nodded.

Dominic picked up his still-full plate. 'I might take this with me,' he added apologetically.

Alison was surprised to hear herself laugh. 'Go on then,' she told him. 'Just this once.'

When Dom had gone Alison got up from the table and found an opened bottle of wine in the fridge. Her hand shook as she poured herself and then Marc a glass.

'I don't know about you,' she said, setting the drink down in front of him, 'but I could do with a drink.' Marc mustered a smile for her and held the wine glass by its stem.

'I don't know what to say, Marc,' Alison said eventually. 'Or how to act. I don't think that what you've just told me has sunk in yet. I can't believe this is happening now, that after more than fifteen years we're splitting up.'

'Pretty good going, I'd say,' Marc said. 'Considering we'd only known each other five minutes when we got together. Considering that, I'd say fifteen years and three kids is pretty good going.'

'We've grown up together,' Alison said. 'I've always had you, always relied on you. Even when you weren't very reliable I could always rely on you. I'm thirty-two and I've never had a job, never had to pay my own bills. God, I'm a spoiled bitch.'

'I'll still be around,' Marc said. 'I'm not leaving the town. I'll still be building the business. I'll see the kids as much as I can and you too, if you'll let me. You don't have to get a job if you don't want to, or even pay your bills. I can still take care of all that.'

'No.' Alison smiled but shook her head. 'It's about time I learned how to be independent. You should keep contributing towards the children but not to me.' She laughed and took another sip of wine. 'I can't believe that we're sitting here talking about the end of our marriage like this. Where are the tears and the screaming?'

'I think there's been enough of that recently, don't you?' Marc said.

Alison nodded and the two were silent for a minute longer.

'This is going to be hard on the girls,' Alison said.

'Yes,' Marc said. 'It will be.'

'Do you think,' Alison felt panic surge through her like a current again, 'that we should just keep things as they are after all? Just until the girls are older, maybe until they're at uni . . .? I mean, we rub along OK, don't we, you and me? We understand each other now, and I'm . . . I'm frightened.'

Marc shook his head and covered her hand with his own. 'Jimmy Ashley told me today that you can only ever ask somebody to forgive you once, because once is the only time they might actually do it and mean it. But if you ask them a second or a third or a fourth time, no matter what they say they can't ever really wipe the slate clean again because they know now that you won't change. You know I won't be the sort of husband you deserve, and now I think I know it. I love you but I'm tired of hurting you and if I stay I know that sooner or later that will happen again. I don't want to do that any more.'

'Jimmy Ashley was the one that made your mind up to leave?' Alison asked. 'That's ironic.'

'Is it?'

376

'Long story. Funny that after fifteen years and three kids there's still so much you don't know about me and so much I don't know about you.'

'How did it go with you and Cathy?' Marc asked her suddenly, as if he had just remembered something about himself that Alison didn't know.

'It went well,' she said. 'We talked, we told each other . . . everything.'

'Ah,' Marc said. 'I'm sorry about that.'

'Marc,' Alison said carefully, 'do you honestly think there is still something there between you and Cathy? I mean something real? Because if you don't, don't go after her, please. Don't get her caught up in everything that's happening between us again. She doesn't deserve it.'

'There's something there,' Marc said, and Alison was surprised by how much the revelation stung her. 'I don't know if it's real but there's something, something that would be hard to leave alone.'

'Just be careful with her, please,' Alison said. 'Don't treat her like you treated the others.'

'I won't,' Marc promised her.

'Right,' Alison said. She looked at the kitchen clock, it was barely ten p.m. 'What shall we do now?' she asked him.

'Let's go to bed,' Marc said. 'And if you don't mind . . . can I sleep in bed with you tonight? It's just that . . . you're my best friend, Al. You're the person I want to hold now this is happening to me.'

Alison nodded and held out her hand. 'Me too,' she said. 'Me too.'

Chapter Twenty-four

'Do you think you can sprain your vagina?' Kirsty asked Catherine and Alison as they met for lunch on Monday. 'Do you think it's possible that too much sex in too many positions can actually make you pull an internal muscle – let's call it the love muscle – because I'm telling you I've had so much incredible sex this weekend I think I might actually have sprained my vagina. I might have made medical history, because you know what, it is actually true. Sex is better when you're in love with someone, isn't it?'

Catherine ignored her tuna salad sandwich and Alison sipped her coffee.

'God, I thought the whole point of you two making up is that the world would be a happier lighter place, ceasefires would be called across international war zones, mammals on the verge of extinction would start mating again, the ozone layer would repair itself overnight. If I'd known you were both going to be so miserable I wouldn't have bothered getting you back together again, let alone asking you to meet for lunch. What is the point of me being blissfully happy and in love if I can't share it?'

Catherine looked at her. 'I think that being blissfully happy and in love is sort of the point.'

Kirsty raised a brow. 'If you say so.'

She looked from Alison to Catherine. 'OK, I give in. Go on, tell me what the problems are and make it snappy because I want to talk about me and Sam and the sex we're having again before I have to go back to work, although if I'm lucky I probably could have sex in the storage cupboard with Sam if I got back before my two o'clock so . . .'

'Jimmy told me he loved me, that he wanted to get back with me and then he went to London,' Catherine blurted out.

'No wonder he wouldn't sleep with me,' Alison said.

'According to Jimmy, he's always been in love with me,' Catherine said bleakly.

'Interesting,' Kirsty said on a yawn, wincing as both women looked daggers at her. 'Well, the fact that he's in love with you and wants to get back together with you is old news. I could have told you *that* months ago. The part where he gets on a train and goes to London is a bit confusing. How does he think that's going to help?'

'He doesn't,' Catherine said. When Kirsty looked perplexed she went on, 'Well, of course I'm not going to get back with him, am I?'

'Aren't you?' Kirsty asked.

'Of course I'm not!' Catherine exclaimed. 'I told him that I didn't love him. I told him that we weren't going to get back together. And he looked really, really sad and said he was going to London to find work.'

'And let me guess, now you're feeling really, really sad?' Kirsty asked her.

'What if I am? I don't want things to be bad between us, do I?' Catherine snapped at her. 'He's the father of my children . . .'

'The love of your life,' Kirsty mumbled.

'He's not,' Catherine protested. 'I told him, I took long enough to get over him. But I did. Our relationship is finished and that's that.'

'OK,' Kirsty said, more than a little sceptically. 'If you say so. What about you, Alison? Why are you in such a mope?'

'Marc is moving out of the house at the end of the week,' she said. 'We're appointing solicitors. We're doing it, we're getting a divorce.'

'I'm sorry,' Catherine said, reaching over the table.

'Me too,' Alison said, biting down hard on her lip. 'It's so stupid, I keep crying. It's me that wanted it. It's me that doesn't love him any more and it's him that's a selfish unfaithful pig, so why am I *crying*?'

'Because it's the end of a part of your life,' Catherine told her. 'A part of your life that when you started it you believed would always be wonderful, and would always be happy. And when you have to face up to the fact that that isn't going to happen any more it's sad and makes you want to cry.'

'Bloody hell,' Kirsty said. 'You two are really bringing me down here.' She turned to Alison. 'Look, you're doing the right thing. You've just got to tough it out now because things will sort themselves out. You might even end up being best friends like Catherine and Jimmy, although that degree of closeness can lead to confusion for some ex-spouses, particularly the less intelligent ones like Jimmy.'

'He is not less intelligent,' Catherine said indignantly. 'He's one of the cleverest, most brilliant and sensitive men I know, the ignorant pig.'

'Is he?' Kirsty said mildly. 'You should marry him then – oh, no, wait, you already have.'

'He was brilliant with Dominic,' Alison said, and when it became clear that neither Catherine nor Kirsty knew anything about Dominic she filled them in on his disappearance and how Jimmy talked him into going back. 'He even said something to Marc. Something that made him decide to leave.'

'Now that's what I call marriage counselling,' Kirsty said. 'It was probably, "Hey, mate, fancy coming on the pull?"'

'What did he say to him?' Catherine asked Alison, studiously ignoring Kirsty.

'He said that you can only ever ask someone to forgive you once and if you do you have to really mean it and never let them down again. And if you don't think you can do that you shouldn't ask them. Marc said he couldn't ask me to forgive him again because he knew I wouldn't be able to do it.'

Catherine stared at her tuna and salad sandwich. 'He's such a bastard.'

'Who, Marc?' Kirsty asked.

'No, Jimmy. Jimmy is such a bastard,' Catherine said furiously. 'I was happy with him, I trusted him – it nearly killed me to let myself do that after . . . well, after you know what. But I did it. And then he had sex with Donna Clarke in the ladies' loos in The Goat. Now he's saying that he still loves me, that he still wants me and he's going around rescuing teenage boys and giving the kind of advice that finally makes men leave their wives and he's doing it all too late. Two years too late. And that makes him a selfish, fucking bastard. And I hate him. I hate him because I can't love him now. It's too late.'

'Have you ever thought,' Alison said, laying each word down ever so carefully, 'that the reason you feel so angry towards him is because you do still have feelings for him?'

'No,' Catherine said firmly.

'OK then,' Alison said, catching Kirsty's eye.

'Come on, ladies, snap out of it,' Kirsty said, banging her fists on the table so hard it made the two old ladies at the next table send her disapproving glances. 'Let's summarise. You,' she said, pointing at Catherine. 'The man you say you don't love has just cleared off to London for a few days. What's the big deal? There is no big deal, that's what.' Kirsty shifted her attention to Alison. 'And as for you, your no-good cheating husband, who you don't love anyway, has finally packed his bags, leaving you in the nice house with every chance of a great big fat divorce settlement. We shouldn't be moping, we should be celebrating! I know, let's go out tonight. Let's go to The Goat. I hear there's a great new band playing and every chance of some toilet action if you play your cards right.'

Catherine and Alison looked at each other across the table.

'Well, I suppose I've got free babysitting until the end of the week,' Alison said. 'I should probably make the most of it.'

'And I'm sure Mrs Beesley would babysit if I asked her,' Catherine said, a little less certainly.

'Great,' Kirsty said. 'Let's tear this town up. Monday night in Farmington, rock on. Two bitter single chicks and their blissfully happy friend – how can we fail to have a great time?' Kirsty flashed her best smile at the outraged old ladies. 'Now can we get back to talking about me and my vagina?'

'Mummy, what are you doing?' Eloise asked Catherine as she hovered in front of the mirror that hung over the fireplace, her nose about an inch from its surface.

'Applying eyeliner,' Catherine told her. 'The trouble is, I don't know how people do it because as soon as I get this sharpened pencil anywhere near my eyes I want to screw them up, so I can't see what I'm doing. I don't understand eyeliner. It's not natural. Why would anyone ever want to wear it?'

'You are trying to wear it,' Eloise observed, tilting her head to one side as she watched her mother jabbing at her eye. 'Trying quite hard, and you never normally wear eyeliner, especially not green eyeliner.'

Catherine put the pencil down on the mantelpiece and looked at Eloise.

'On the way back to work from lunch today I brought a magazine. I thought spring is here, it's a new start, a fresh beginning, I'll give myself a spring clean . . .'

'Are you dirty, Mummy?' Leila asked her as she stomped down the stairs in a pair of Nana Pam's special clear plastic high heels that set off her Dalmatian pyjamas particularly well.

'No, not that sort of a clean,' Catherine said, looking rather perplexed at the magazine article she had open and balancing precariously on top of the TV so that she could refer to it while attempting eyeliner in the mirror. 'Give Your Make-Up a Spring Clean and Put a Spring in Your Step!' it yelled at her, the headline feeling more like a set of orders than a suggestion.

Catherine never normally bought magazines, especially not women's magazines, because she supposed, perhaps a little loftily, that on some level she didn't consider herself to be that kind of woman, concerned with earthly things such as shoes and make-up and . . . hairdos. But in the last couple of weeks her life had changed completely. Old wounds had closed and healed over, final breaks between herself and the past had been made at last and she felt as if she should be a new woman. Somehow the tentative renewal of her friendship with Alison had helped her see her life from a new perspective, as though through a fresh pair of eyes. She hadn't realised until she had told Jimmy point blank that she was over what had happened between then, that it didn't hurt her at all any more. And seeing Alison again now, as an adult, a mother with her own problems almost engulfing her, made Catherine realise she couldn't blame either the woman she now knew or the seventeen-year-old Alison had once been for what had happened to her back then. She couldn't even blame Marc because all that happened to her was the same set of wrong turns and bad choices that had beset almost every seventeen-year-old girl since the dawn of time, mistakes that had to be made and owned in order for her to become a whole person, a grown-up woman. Just recently everyone had been telling her how strong she was but it was only now that Catherine believed it. She would always mourn the loss of the baby that she never knew, always regret that she couldn't have been close to her parents, but whereas once she thought those two things defined her, now she realised that although they were a part of her, they did not represent her whole. Finally, at the age of thirty-two, Catherine was ready to become herself.

The only trouble was she wasn't entirely sure how to go about it.

And when she walked past WH Smith and saw the headline on a magazine that shouted out 'Ten Steps To a New You!' she picked it up and bought it, because it seemed a good place to start, and after a quick scan of the article so did eyeliner.

'When I say a clean, darling,' she told Leila, who had found her Dalmatian ears headband behind a cushion on the sofa and had shoved it unthinkingly on her head at a rather rakish angle, 'I mean more like . . . well, a makeover.'

'A makeover?' Eloise perked up. 'I can make you over, Mummy. I know all about makeovers. I've got makeover Barbie, plus Nana Pam makes us over all the time.'

'Yes,' Leila said. 'From Orphan Annie to Little Princesses,' she said as if she were remembering a direct quote, which she no doubt was. 'Nana Pam said we could always look beautiful if only you put in some effort. Is that what you want to do to yourself, Mummy, put in some effort?'

'Like Isabelle Jackman's mum?' Eloise asked her. 'She always puts in effort and she's . . .' Eloise trailed off thoughtfully.

'You could have coloured steaks in your hair,' Leila said, her eyes widening in awe. 'And glittery eye shadow, Mummy. I've got some of that!' Leila was poised to race upstairs and retrieve it.

'No, no, not that kind of makeover either,' Catherine said hastily, as she envisioned her youngest child tearing her room apart in a bid to locate all of their secret cosmetics stash. 'Apart from perhaps a bit of eyeliner. More than changing how I look I mean just trying to be a bit different, maybe doing things I wouldn't normally do, being a bit more adventurous and impulsive.'

'What's impulsive?' Leila asked her begrudgingly, clearly disappointed that she was not going to get to apply the glittery eye shadow.

'Doing things without thinking,' Catherine said.

'Like buying eyeliner?' Leila asked her dubiously.

'Well, yes,' Catherine said, looking at the offending pencil and putting it back in her capacious but barely filled make-up bag.

'But why?' Leila asked.

Catherine blinked at her. 'Because, you know, it's spring, new plants, new . . . lambs everywhere, new me.'

'I like the old you,' Leila said. 'I like the you that's you, Mummy, only I don't mind if we give up eating so many vegetables and maybe eat more cake. Is cake impulsive? Anyway, Jesus loves you if you wear eyeliner or not.' Leila thought for a moment. 'He might actually prefer if you didn't wear it, though, especially if it's green.'

'What I'm trying to explain to you,' Catherine started again, well aware that it was more herself she was trying to enlighten than her persistently curious five-year-old, 'is that I'm not changing into a different person, I'm more sort of becoming more like me than I am already. Sort of Mummy, but more so.'

'Mummy but more vegetables so?' Leila asked her.

'No, I just mean that from now on I might wear eyeliner sometimes and perhaps the odd skirt . . .'

385

'That is an odd skirt,' Leila said, looking at Catherine's knees.

'And go out for drinks on a Monday night,' Eloise said.

Catherine turned to her.

'Yes, you don't mind me going out, do you?'

'Isabelle Jackman's mum started putting on eyeliner and wearing skirts and going out for drinks,' Eloise said in a tone of foreboding that made Leila widen her eyes. 'And now she's got a boyfriend with a beard. Is that what you're doing, Mummy, looking for a boyfriend?'

'Mummy!' Leila looked scandalised and Catherine wondered how her cack-handed attempts to apply eyeliner had come to this.

'No, I am not looking for a boyfriend. I am trying out eyeliner. It's not the same thing at all, Eloise. I mean, look at Kirsty, she always looks nice and . . . bad example. The thing is, a person can decide to change how they look for other reasons than to get a boyfriend so you don't have to worry about that at all, ever, OK? I promise.'

'Mummy,' Eloise's tone was slightly chiding, 'you shouldn't promise that. One day you might want to have a boyfriend, just like Isabelle Jackman's mummy, and Daddy might want to have a proper girlfriend that he likes.'

Catherine tried to imagine herself with some unknown unnamed absurdly titled 'boy' friend, and for some reason all she could picture was a beard. Was that really what this was about, buying a magazine and some eyeliner? Were these her first few tentative steps to trying to meet someone again? She tried to imagine herself out there, like Kirsty had been for so many months, getting involved with opticians, amongst others, dating and dancing and flirting and chatting, all because of the faint possibility that it might deliver her into the arms of a man who could make her happy. But she found it impossible to imagine. To even comprehend spending time with a man who wasn't Jimmy – apart from that near-kiss with Marc, which she was determined not to think about at all – and thinking about Jimmy with a proper girlfriend made her feel cross. She put the image out of her head and decided that she wasn't ready for eyeliner of any shade.

'Perhaps you're right,' Catherine said. 'I think I'll stay in tonight after all.'

'Hooray!' Leila yelled.

Eloise put her hand on Catherine's shoulder and looked at her with that unnerving green-eyed stare. 'I'm ever so proud of you, Mummy,' she said.

Catherine smiled, and put an arm around Eloise.

'Are you, darling? I'm glad.' She considered leaving it at that but the temptation to fish was just too great. 'Why?'

'Because even when grown-up things are happening to you, you remember to love us,' Eloise said. 'And because you know when not to wear green eyeliner.'

'Not coming?' Kirsty groaned, leaning against the door with her arms crossed. 'But it's *arranged*. Alison is coming and this is important. It's phase two of my plan to reunite you two. We've got over the hard bit, we've had an intermediate coffee, now you need to get drunk together again and reaffirm your fledgeling bond.'

'You see, I don't think inebriation is necessary to get to know a person,' Catherine said. 'Unlike you I haven't based all of my relationships on the consumption of alcohol.'

'Ouch,' Kirsty said. 'And anyway, it's not true. Not with Sam. When we went round there the other night he was stone-cold sober.'

'Yes, *he* was,' Catherine replied, raising a brow. 'Look, it's been a big weekend, a massive one, seeing Alison again, drinking tequila, things finally coming to a head with Jimmy. I need time to readjust and get used to the life I have now. At the moment it doesn't seem real.'

'But you and Jimmy were over two years ago,' Kirsty said. 'How much readjusting do you need?'

'Yes, but back then we were over because he cheated on me and I was devastated, and now we're over because I told him we are and now he's devastated, which makes me feel . . .'

'Devastated too?' Kirsty chanced.

'Sad,' Catherine said, nodding.

'Well, you are sad,' Kirsty said. 'I won't argue with that. Come on, come down The Goat and celebrate your freedom that you clearly so desperately want.'

Catherine pursed her lips. 'Another time, but maybe not at The Goat.'

'But you just said you're over The Goat. Come on,' Kirsty encouraged her. 'It's been two years – what could be more symbolic of your moving on?'

'Eyeliner,' Catherine said. 'And I'm not ready for that either.'

'What in God's name are you talking about?' Kirsty asked her, peering at her. 'Did you eat the worm in the tequila bottle? Because you don't seem like someone who's just found her best friend and ditched her deadweight husband at all.'

'Just go out and have a nice time with Alison and cheer her up,' Catherine said. 'I really want to stay at home tonight and readjust. That's what I want. I'm doing what I want.'

'God, you're selfish,' Kirsty said. 'I was hoping to sneak off with Sam after half an hour or so. Now I'll have to keep an eye on her all night.'

'Ah, well,' Catherine said with a cheery smile as she closed the door on Kirsty, 'that's what friends are for!'

Chapter Twenty-five

'So Marc was OK with you going out on the town after you finally split?' Kirsty asked Alison as she led her into the music bar at The Goat. It was a small space and packed to the rafters with the Monday night crowd who always turned up for the live music. 'He didn't expect you to observe a period of mourning, like Catherine seems to think she has to?'

'He wasn't there,' Alison said, having to speak louder as the band struck up. 'He didn't come back from the office before I left. I thought about phoning him but then I thought, what if he's flat hunting or talking to a solicitor or knocking off his secretary? And somehow it doesn't seem right for me to ask him to come home so that I can go out. Technically I could have left Dominic in charge but after his recent escapades I think he needs someone to be in charge of him. So I asked the neighbour instead. She lent me her au pair, German girl. Very no-nonsense.'

'How generous,' Kirsty said loudly, as she waved a ten-pound note at the barman and grinned at him. 'I hope one day I'll be rich enough to lend other human beings to people.'

'You know what I mean,' Alison said. 'Anyway, I don't think I'm going to be rich enough to be borrowing them from people for very long. A three-bedroom semi and some kind of job is what my future holds.' She smiled and took a gin and tonic from Kirsty, and they made their way through the crowd to the side of the room where they could get a good view of the whole place.

'So tell me,' Alison said, leaning close to Kirsty so that she could hear her, 'I haven't been on the pull in fifteen years. What do you do these days?'

Kirsty laughed. 'I see you don't have to go through a period of readjustment, like some people.'

'The last sixteen years of my life have been about readjusting,' Alison said. 'And probably the next sixteen will be too, but now I want to have some fun.'

'Well, first of all you scan the room, look for someone you fancy,' Kirsty instructed her, 'and then you catch his eye, make sure he knows you are checking him out, and then you go over there and flirt.'

'You make it sound like falling off a log,' Alison said sceptically.

'Well, it is usually a lot easier if you are so drunk that if you were standing on a log you would fall off it,' Kirsty replied. 'To be fair, a lot of people think that when a girl gets to a certain age she should start to be a little more reserved and a little less naked. But I say fuck 'em. Now see anything you like?'

Alison trawled the busy room until through a gap in the crowd she glimpsed the back of a man's head, long hair pulled back into a ponytail, a battered leather jacket on the back of his chair. He looked exactly like Jimmy Ashley from behind. He was the only person in the room who wasn't facing the small stage.

'OK,' she said, target identified. 'What next?'

'Make eye contact,' Kirsty said, looking in the opposite direction for her boyfriend.

'He's got his back to me,' Alison said. Kirsty looked at her.

'You've decided you fancy someone from the back of their head?' she asked. 'You're not fussy, are you?'

'I'm only practising,' Alison said.

'OK, well, go over to where he is standing and make eye contact,' Kirsty ordered her.

'You mean just go over and stand in front of him and stare at him until he looks at me? He'll think I'm a nutter.'

'You asked me how to pull, not how to become a secret agent,' Kirsty said. 'Go on.'

Alison looked at the back of the man's head. This seemed like a very odd place to come for a quiet drink.

'What if he's a serial killer?' she said.

'Perfect, then he won't be too needy,' Kirsty said, her face lighting up as Sam walked in the door. 'Now off you go. I'm not buying you another drink until you report back. Think of it as rehabilitation.'

Alison observed the look on Kirsty's face as Sam crossed the room and kissed her. She wondered if she would ever feel that way about anyone again, or if anyone would ever feel that way about her. Well, every journey started with a single step, even if in this case it was in all likelihood a very ill-advised one. Alison took a breath and began to make her way through the crowd towards the back of the man's head.

If I get all this way and he turns out to be a woman . . . she thought to herself as she approached, getting through the thickest part of the crowd and emerging in the near-empty seating area that was strewn with jackets and coats, and where only one person was sitting. Not quite sure how to position herself in order to make eye contact with him (or change her mind and hurriedly make her exit), Alison walked over to the juke box in the corner and pressed a few buttons, realising a little too late that nobody in their right mind would play a juke box when a live band was currently perforating her eardrums. She took a deep breath and turned round, hoping that the man looked a little bit like Jimmy Ashley.

Which was why she had mixed feelings when she found out he actually was Jimmy Ashley.

'You are not supposed to be here,' Alison said, just as the band took a break and the room filled with cheering and applause. Jimmy did not look up from his beer mat.

Taking another steadying breath, Alison went and sat opposite him. After a second or two he looked up.

'Oh, hi,' he said miserably. 'Great band, right? Really good, really . . . young.'

'Why are you here?' Alison asked him. 'Catherine said you'd gone to London.'

'I did, got there last night. There was no session work, but a mate tipped me off about something else and I went to an audition this morning.' Jimmy sighed. 'I got the job.'

'Jimmy, that's fantastic,' Alison said, reaching out and impulsively covering his hand with her own.

'It's with this gothic rock band my mate knows,' Jimmy said desolately. 'Their guitarist accidentally cut off his thumb during a fake satanic ritual. They picked it up and managed to sew it back on but he'll be out for weeks and they've got a tour coming up. The stuff they play is pretty basic, so I picked it up quick. They said with some black eyeliner and hair dye I'd be perfect. Oh, yeah, and I've got to straighten my hair too, because apparently the minions of hell don't have a natural curl.'

'Wow, that is exciting,' Alison said, struggling to keep up her enthusiasm when his misery was like a huge gaping chasm that sucked all the joy from the room. 'What are they called?'

'Skull Incursion,' Jimmy said dolefully. 'Shit name.'

'I've heard of them!' Alison said excitedly. 'Dom likes them . . . they're *awful*.'

'I know,' Jimmy said. 'But it's not for ever. Just while they are touring and this guy's thumb-graft takes. But it's good money and eight weeks' work while they're on tour.'

'On tour,' Alison said, 'with a band. That's cool, right?'

'In Croatia,' Jimmy added. 'Skull Incursion are big in Croatia.'

'Oh,' Alison said, desperately wishing she had ordered another drink before she came over here. 'I hear it's lovely out there in the spring.'

'Well, it probably is, but Skull Incursion don't play in direct sunlight. It contravenes vampire health and safety in the workplace regulations. Anyway, the flight leaves at five o'clock in the morning.'

'Tomorrow?' Alison looked at her watch. 'Then why are you here?'

'I came to say goodbye to Cat and the girls,' Jimmy said. 'Couldn't just go without saying goodbye to them.'

Alison looked at her watch. 'OK, so why are you in the pub?'

'I thought I'd revisit the scene of my downfall, first,' Jimmy said. 'The place where I fucked up so badly that one day I'd be taking a nocturnal tour with a bunch of faux vampires. I had a couple of pints and now . . . now I don't think I can see her. She'll just be all beautiful and amazing and not in love with me, and when I tell her I'm going away for eight weeks she'll be really supportive and pleased for me and I don't want her to be. I want her to fling her arms around me and say, don't go, Jim, don't go because I love you and I can't live without you no matter how well you get paid for dyeing your hair black and wearing a pair of fangs.'

Alison couldn't help but smile at him. He was even sexy when he was being all miserable over another woman.

'Jimmy, just go and see her,' she told him. 'If you don't you'll regret it.'

393

'There's hours yet. Buy me a drink first,' Jimmy said, looking at her directly for the first time, which made Alison sit back a little in her chair.

'OK then,' she said slowly as Jimmy watched her. 'I will. Back in a minute.'

'Two Jack Daniel's and Coke, please,' Alison shouted across the bar as the band began their second set.

Kirsty appeared at her side and clapped her on the back. 'I must say I didn't think you'd actually go through with it,' she said admiringly in Alison's ear as she picked up a drink. 'Thanks for this. I don't normally drink whiskey but –'

'Ah, that's not for you,' Alison said. 'It's for the man I pulled, who is not a man, but Jimmy Ashley. He's here in Farmington incognito and he needs someone to talk to before he goes round to see Cathy.'

Kirsty narrowed her eyes. 'Are you going to offer him sex again?'

'No, I am not,' Alison stated firmly. 'Even if I do really fancy him, and I'm fairly sure he'd go for it because he's depressed and confused and a bit drunk. But I do have some standards, and taking advantage of a vulnerable man for his body is not one of them. Besides, I ruled him out when Cathy and I called a truce. I'm not going to make that mistake again.'

'Hmm,' Kirsty said, scrutinising Alison for a moment. 'Well, if it wasn't for the fact that my gorgeous and incredibly well-hung boyfriend wants to take me home I'd come with you, but as it is, I'd much rather be snogging him than listening to Jimmy go on about how rubbish he is. Will you be OK if we shoot off?'

Alison looked over at where Jimmy was sitting, waggling both his empty glass and eyebrows at her in a decidedly come-hither way.

'Yes,' she said firmly.

'Are you sure?' Kirsty asked. 'You could come with us now; we'll walk you home.'

'No, you go,' Alison said. 'I can handle him. I can do this for Catherine. After all, I'm a grown-up now.'

Catherine looked at the TV screen and sipped her wine. Sometimes she wished that things hadn't been left so awkwardly between her and Jimmy. Then at least she could give him a call and find out how he was doing; ask him if he'd found a place to stay, got anyone to give him some food, that sort of thing.

Then she kicked herself hard.

He was a grown man, he could cope in the world on his own without her to worry about him. In fact, the very last thing he'd want would be her worrying about him. The trouble was, over the last twelve years she'd got into the habit of caring about him. It would be a hard habit to get out of. It unsettled her that he hadn't phoned to say good night to the girls, something he always did when he was away. It was probably nothing to worry about. Either he was working in some studio and couldn't get out in time to phone or . . . well, there was always the possibility that he was dead in an alleyway somewhere because there were very few things that would keep him from saying good night to his daughters and death was one of them. Catherine was determined not to worry about that, however. She was determined not to think about Jimmy, full stop. The only trouble was the more she thought about ways to not think about him the more she thought about him. Turning her brain off was much harder than she thought it should be.

Eloise had been right, even if she hadn't known it. Going out today, buying eyeliner and magazines of all things – Catherine supposed she was trying to transform herself into the kind of woman that might attract a very tall man who liked redheads. She had been trying to find her feet again and part of that balancing act was feeling good about herself, feeling sexy and even sexual. For two years she'd shut that part of herself away as she'd concentrated on healing herself and keeping her children happy. It had got almost to the point where she didn't think she cared if she never had sex again. Then Marc walked back into her life and nearly kissed her and that part of her hadn't slowly roused so much as rudely awakened. Eyeliner was Catherine's body's way of saying she was ready for a man in her life again. But even if her body was, she wasn't sure if she was.

She and Jimmy had taken a long time to get to know each other's body. They had taken it very slowly, inch by inch over several weeks before they finally went to bed, and then, even though it was still awkward and embarrassing, it didn't matter because they were already so close, and so bonded. With him Catherine hadn't felt self-conscious about her long white body, and boyish figure. With him she'd felt womanly, she'd felt beautiful. It had hurt her so badly when she discovered that she was not enough for Jimmy; it had hurt her even though she had no right to feel that way. How long could she have realistically expected him to go on running on empty in their marriage? Why had she felt it was OK for her to allow him to live that way? The anguish of finding him with another woman had ripped her to shreds, even if she knew that she had been just as responsible as Jimmy was, for driving him into Donna Clarke's arms. Jimmy had done what he wanted to with Donna Clarke, but Catherine had made him want it.

The relief she felt now was that the pain of that discovery had ebbed away to nothing at last. That finally after two years she could look him in the eye and smile and be close to him again, because that sense of completeness she had known when she was with him had been hard to live without . . . Catherine metaphorically kicked herself again, only harder this time.

These warm feelings and thoughts she was having about Jimmy weren't real. They were a confused muddle caused by simply caring about him as a friend, and the fear of being without him, of having to stand on her own two feet like she claimed she wanted but was really terrified of doing. They were feelings that she had to get over, feelings that were simply a reaction to truly being without him for the first time, like when you take off a warm coat and you feel the chill of the winter. She had to keep reminding herself that these feelings weren't real, that they were just illusions, mirages that would fade soon enough, because it would be so wrong not to let someone go just because you felt half naked without them. And she had to let Jimmy go now because, despite everything she had said to him before he left for London, Catherine knew their marriage had failed because she couldn't love him enough. To bring him back to her side now with more false hope and half-baked promises would be too cruel. It was so much less than he deserved.

Catherine kicked herself really hard again and then gave herself a metaphorical slap for good measure. The reason she was thinking about Jimmy so much wasn't because she loved him, it was because she didn't love him. Her brain knew that, but her heart hadn't quite been able to believe it yet.

Just then there was a knock at the front door. Catherine looked at her watch. It was late. Gone ten. It had to be Jimmy. He was the only one who would show up at this hour and he hadn't called because he was on his way back from London. He probably hadn't come to the back door because, after the way they'd parted, he felt that formal was the way to go.

It was only when Catherine reached the front door that she

realised she'd run to answer it. But that was OK. It was OK to be pleased to see him so long as she didn't give him any kind of false hope because that simply wouldn't be fair. She took a breath and composed her smile before she opened the door.

But it wasn't Jimmy at the door.

'Marc,' Catherine said. 'What are you doing here?'

'I wasn't in the neighbourhood,' Marc said, holding up a bottle of wine, 'so I thought I'd make quite a long detour and drop by.'

'I'm supposed to be out,' Catherine said. 'With your wife.'

'Really?' Marc said, his smile faltering fractionally. 'She didn't tell me. She's avoiding me at the moment. We're avoiding each other. It's awkward, the end of a relationship when one of you hasn't exactly left yet and neither of you especially hates the other one. It's like sharing a house with someone you don't know very well. She's trying to be kind to me even though I don't deserve it. We haven't told the girls yet. We were supposed to do it today but they were so happy this morning, getting ready for school. It just goes to show what our marriage had come to. Their parents are barely speaking and they don't notice the difference.'

'They notice,' Catherine assured him. 'They always notice.'

She looked at Marc standing on the doorstep in his coat, clutching a bottle of wine, for a second longer. Asking him in had implications. But Catherine didn't have a choice. She had to ask him in.

She had to know.

'It's like a film,' Jimmy said, downing his third Jack Daniel's and Coke since Alison had sat down with him. 'A bad film. Boy meets girl, boy loses girl, boy ends up in Croatia. Where's the happy ending, hey? My film's going to be a flop at the box office. Story of my life really.'

'There's always a happy ending,' Alison tried to reassure him. 'It just might not be the one you expected.'

Jimmy looked up at her again, making her tummy do a backflip. She wished he would stop doing that. One minute he'd be all maudlin and pathetic, still cute, but quite easy to cope with, and then she'd say or do something and he'd get this look in his eyes, like she imagined a particularly disillusioned wolf might have when it was sizing up a nice lamb because steak was off the menu. And when he looked at her that way she got the distinct impression that this evening could go a whole different way if only she would let it.

'Maybe you're right,' he said, leaning forward a little bit, looking at her as if he were preparing for a bite. 'Maybe I'm not in love with her at all and what I need is for someone to show me.'

'Actually, I think you are in love with her,' Alison squeaked nervously as Jimmy focused his attention fully on her, placing one hand on her knee. 'I think you're crazy about her.'

'I like *you*,' Jimmy said, patting her knee. 'You've got pretty hair and a very nice cleavage in that top.'

For one or two simultaneously mortifying and electrifying moments Alison endured Jimmy staring at her breasts.

'Got a lot of buttons, that top,' he added. 'I like a challenge.'

'What I think you need,' Alison said, 'is a nice cup of coffee and some focus. You have to go and see her, Jimmy. You have to tell her you're going. Give her a chance to ask you to stay.'

'I don't know why she fell out with you, because you are lovely,' Jimmy said. 'Apart from the whole sleeping with her boyfriend and then running off to abandon her with her psycho parents thing, and even then everyone makes mistakes. Even her, even Catherine. I bet you that right now she's somewhere making a mistake, a really big terrible mistake.

Yeah, and then who's she going to come running to, huh? Huh? Not me, because I'll be in Croatia playing my guitar in a coffin. Oh God, I love her.'

'Right,' Alison said. 'Well, if this is the attitude you are going to take then maybe Croatia is a good idea.'

'How do you work that out?' Jimmy asked her, looking bemused. 'Are you drunk?'

'No, well, yes, a bit,' Alison admitted. 'But what I mean is, you've given up at the first hurdle. You told her you love her and she's told you she doesn't love you and now you're all drunk and on the next flight to Croatia. That doesn't strike me as really loving someone. I think if you really loved her you'd stay and fight for her.'

'She doesn't want me to fight for her,' Jimmy said, frowning deeply. 'I'm doing what she wants because I love her. The funny thing is, all my life I thought that this, touring with a band, playing a gig every night to thousands of people, was my ultimate dream. And it's not any more. Yeah, I want to play and write and be in a band and earn a bit more cash. But I want to do it here, in my home town, with my girls, so I can kiss them all good night every night, all three of them. Why does God do that? Why does he move the goalposts just when you've finally scored? Well, I'll show him. I've just signed up with the other side.'

'Right, I've had enough of this,' Alison said. 'If you're not going to go and see her then stop whining and just go to Croatia. It helps a lot not seeing the person you have unreciprocated feelings for, and if you manage to stay away from them for long enough the feelings wear off quite a lot. Sometimes even totally. It's when they keep popping up at inopportune moments it gets a bit tricky . . .' Alison trailed off as she looked into Jimmy's hazel eyes. 'And there would be no chance of Catherine popping up in Croatia, would there, so if

400

you haven't got the guts to go and see her then shut up and get on the train.'

'Can't,' Jimmy said. 'Can't go without saying goodbye because, first of all she is the mother of my children, second of all she is my best friend, and third of all I bloody love her, I do.'

'Go and see her, Jimmy,' Alison said.

'Or,' Jimmy said, 'I could just take my mind off things with someone else. Someone sexy and friendly and smiley, with a nice buttony top . . .'

'I think,' Alison said carefully, 'I might just nip to the ladies. Look, wait here. When I come back I'll get you a coffee and you can pop round to Catherine's before she goes to bed.'

'You're very sensible,' Jimmy said as Alison stood up. 'You never used to be so sensible when you were Catherine's friend in your tight tops and little skirts.'

'I thought you said you never noticed me,' Alison said.

'I only said that because I was afraid you were going to make a pass at me. I would have to have been blind never to have noticed you,' Jimmy said, leaning rather far back in his chair so that it rocked dangerously.

Alison couldn't help but beam, and then Jimmy crashed backwards in his chair.

'Get up,' Alison ordered him as she helped him, glad that the din of the music had covered the commotion. 'When I get back I'll bring you a coffee.'

Once she got into the relative safety of the ladies' loos, Alison splashed some cool water on her heated cheeks and looked at her damp face framed in the mirror.

Jimmy Ashley had noticed her when she was seventeen, he had admired her in her tight tops and little skirts. And who knew, perhaps . . . perhaps if she had never found out about Catherine's secret boyfriend, perhaps while Cathy was busy with Marc, Jimmy Ashley would have finally noticed how much she fancied him and put down his guitar long enough to ask her out. Alison closed her eyes and tried to imagine what it would have been like to be Jimmy Ashley's girlfriend back then, holding hands with him in the cinema, being the girl he sang to at gigs, kissing him like crazy on her parents' doorstep. Would he have stayed with her for a couple of weeks or months, or maybe, just maybe, if she hadn't left town and he hadn't fallen for Catherine, maybe he would have always stayed in love with her? Maybe if she'd never known Marc they'd still be together now . . . except they weren't together now and she had met Marc, and Jimmy Ashley was in love with Cathy.

Alison shook her head and patted her cheeks. If only he wasn't so hot. Even when he was drunk and miserable he was gorgeous. Even when he was clearly only sizing her up because he was desperately in love with Cathy and only wanted some-one to take his mind off that, to stop him from taking any positive action, he made her knees tremble. Even though Jimmy Ashley was only flirting with her because he was drunk and in love with another woman, she couldn't help but like it, a lot.

Reapplying her lip gloss, Alison wiped away traces of eye-liner that had run around her lower lids with the edges of her thumb. She tossed her hair back over her shoulders and straightened her shoulders. This was her chance to show Cathy that she could be a good friend to her, even one of her best friends again. Jimmy needed to remind Cathy exactly what their relationship used to be like, and even though Alison had no idea what that was exactly, from the way she felt when Jimmy looked at her she could hazard a pretty good guess. She knew exactly what he had to do to bring Cathy to her senses. And even if Cathy never knew that she'd given up the chance to get off with Jimmy Ashley for her, it wouldn't matter because Alison would know. And she'd know that she'd done the right thing.

It was then that she looked back up at the mirror and saw Jimmy reflected in it too.

'You and me, babe,' Jimmy whispered in her ear, his arm encircling her waist. 'How about it?'

'So,' Catherine said, handing Marc a glass of wine, 'how are things?'

'Difficult,' Marc said. 'But I can't complain. I've brought it all on myself. I've got to start looking for a place to live but I can't quite bring myself to do it.'

'Oh? Where do you think you might look?' Catherine asked him, desperate to make small talk, as if trivial conversation might fill in all the gaps between them and stop him from coming any nearer her. 'Kirsty's boyfriend lives in this quite nice place up by the golf course, really excellent double glazing . . .'

'I don't care really,' Marc said. 'I don't care where I live.'

'Oh, well, it's good that you're flexible. They say often when people are looking for property they have expectations that are far too high.'

'You do know why I came here, don't you?' Marc asked her. He put down his glass of wine; Catherine looked at it. She held on to hers as if it were a talisman that might protect her from what she knew was coming next.

'For a bit of a chat?' she said.

'Because the last time I was here we were interrupted,' Marc said.

'Oh, right, that.' Catherine heard herself laugh, conscious that mirth was the last thing she was feeling.

'I think,' Marc said, leaning over and taking her glass out of her hands, 'that I was just about to kiss you.'

'Um, well,' Catherine said, backing away, 'you were, but in the meantime I've been having a think and I wonder if really you kissing me is the most sensible thing for either of us to do because . . .'

And then his mouth covered hers and whatever she had been about to say was lost, engulfed by his kiss.

'Foxy lady,' Jimmy muttered as he pushed Alison back against the tiled wall of the cubicle, forcing the door shut behind him and locking it. He kissed the curve of her neck, his hands in her hair, as his tongue flickered in her cleavage. 'You are a very sexy woman,' he told her.

'Oh God,' Alison sighed, trying to find the will to push him away. 'Jimmy.'

'Baby,' Jimmy said, running his hands over her shoulders and cupping a breast in each hand, 'need to get this top off, too many buttons, might have to rip it.'

'Jimmy, wait,' Alison said, planting the palms of her hands firmly on his chest and levering a few inches of space between their bodies.

'What's wrong?' Jimmy asked, looking around at the cubicle as if he'd only just realised where he was. 'You're right, not here. How about out the back? It's cold but I'll warm you up . . .'

'Jimmy!' Alison protested, looking down at Jimmy's hands, one of which still encased a bosom. She forced herself to concentrate. 'Don't treat me like this, Jimmy. I'm trying to be a friend to you and to Catherine. Don't use me like this because you know how much I like you. It's not fair.' She rather awkwardly removed Jimmy's hand from her chest and held his wrists down at her sides. 'You know you are a really great guy, and if you and Catherine were properly split up, and you didn't still really love her, and she didn't still probably love you, then I'd do it with you right here. I'd take my top off for you anywhere, and I wouldn't care because I bloody fancy you a lot. I always have.'

'So we're good to go then,' Jimmy said, smiling and dipping his head forward to kiss her.

'No, we are not,' Alison said, turning her head at the last moment so that his lips grazed her ear. 'I know you're drunk, Jimmy, but didn't you just hear what I said? Think about what you're doing; think about why you are doing it and how bad it is going to make you feel if it happens.'

Jimmy took the one step back that the cubicle allowed and blinked at her. Without warning he sat down on the toilet and dropped his head in his hands.

'OK,' Alison said, feeling chilled now that the heat of his body was no longer pressed against hers. 'A little less despair and misery would have been tactful.'

After a moment's more hesitation Alison pulled her top back into place and crouched down in front of him. She put her hand on his shoulder and felt it shaking.

'I'm sorry,' Jimmy told her, struggling to control his voice. 'You're a nice person. You must think I'm a pig . . . I *am* a pig.'

'You're not,' Alison said. 'You're just drunk and really, really stupid.'

Jimmy covered his face with his hands and Alison crouched there with him, holding his shoulder until finally the trembling stopped. Jimmy's face remained covered by his hands.

'I'm going outside,' Alison said. 'I'll ask the barman to make you a coffee. Then I'll walk you round to Catherine's and you can tell her you're going to Croatia. And I think I've got an idea that might make her sit up and think.'

'Really?' Jimmy said eventually. 'Look, I know I'm drunk as a bastard but I'm sorry for behaving so badly. Catherine's got a good friend in you.'

'She has,' Alison said as she straightened up with quite some difficulty. 'It's great, isn't it?'

The moment that Catherine closed her eyes it was summer again and she could feel the heat of the sun radiate off his body as he pressed her back into the cushions that yielded beneath her like the soft long grass in the park. She felt the warm breeze caress her skin as his fingers deftly unbuttoned her shirt and ran lightly over her breasts, and she was powerless in his arms. More than that, she was seventeen again, fresh and new, with no idea what would happen next, and as long as she was in his arms, she didn't care.

His stubble grazed against the skin of her neck as his kisses travelled lower, and Catherine knew that if she kept her eyes closed it would always be summer, that summer long ago when, for a few precious moments, her life had shone like other people's always seemed to. Then she felt Marc's hand on her breasts, his teeth on her nipples and she heard him groan. Opening her eyes just a little she saw his dark head, his tawny complexion contrasting starkly against her own alabaster skin and suddenly it wasn't summer any more. Catherine wasn't in that park, basking in the warmth of the sunlight, she was half naked on the sofa in her living room, her children asleep upstairs and letting a man she barely knew now, had barely known then, and still had no reason to like or trust, undress her.

Catherine realised that she didn't want to be that powerless seventeen-year-old any more because her life had shone brighter since after she knew Marc than it had ever done when she was with him.

'Stop, please,' she said, stilling his hand and easing herself out from underneath him.

His hair ruffled, Marc smiled at her. 'I'm sorry,' he said,

sitting up a little. 'I'm going too fast. I wasn't prepared for how much I wanted you. There's still something between us, isn't there, Catherine? Still something really strong.'

'Yes,' Catherine said, quickly buttoning up her shirt, her fingers fumbling the fastening as Marc watched her.

'It's OK,' he said. 'I could unbutton that shirt all day long. All night long too.'

'Marc,' Catherine said steadily, 'there is something between us but it's not real. It's the past. It's a moment in time where we both were once. A moment that meant a lot to us then, a time we've both often wished we could revisit but I think maybe that's only because our lives now aren't going the way we want them to, not because we still have feelings for each other. It's summer fifteen years ago that's between us, and all the heat and passion we felt then. But it's not real, Marc. How can we feel anything real for each other when we don't know each other at all?'

Catherine could feel the heat in Marc's eyes as he looked at her. 'Maybe you're right but does it have to matter?' he asked her.

'What do you mean?' Catherine asked him, wide-eyed. 'Of course it matters. We don't feel anything for each other. I don't love you, Marc.'

For second Marc looked stung, but then his expression became still and thoughtful.

'I loved you once, a long time ago, but I don't suppose I love you now. I don't see how I can when I still love Alison,' Marc said, looking up at Catherine. 'I still want you, though, more than anything. Loving her isn't enough to stop me from wanting you.'

He leaned forward again to kiss her but Catherine stood up.

'If you love Alison then why do you do this? Why have you tried so hard to see me again if it wasn't because you thought that being with me again was somehow going to save you? You said you moved your whole family back to Farmington to find me when the only woman that can save you is the one you can't be faithful to.'

'I do this, I say all of this, because . . .' Marc sighed, 'because I wanted to have sex with you again. You're a very desirable woman. And because that time we had together back then, when you were seventeen, *was* special to me. It was a time when I kidded myself I could be just like any other man out there, happy and content. But even that memory is a deceit. After all, it wasn't so special that I didn't sleep with someone behind your back. Not so special that I didn't leave town with a girl who I didn't know was pregnant because I guessed that you were. Catherine, a lot of the time I like to think that I'm misunderstood, that my nonexistent childhood scarred me and made me into the kind of man I am. Sometimes I like to think that if only I'd met the right person, stayed with the right person, then I could be a decent man, the man I pretend to be. But I think it's time I stopped pretending to myself as well as everybody else. I'm the man who, loving his wife as much as he does, still pursues other women, including you, because at the end of the day that's what you are to me, Catherine. Even you, that wonderful golden memory I've treasured all this time, is just another woman. And even though I know it's wrong, right now I don't care, because I want you and I think you want me.'

As Catherine looked at Marc, the intervening fifteen years since she had last kissed him settled quietly on his shoulders and he looked his age. Why Marc saying everything that she already knew upset her quite so much she couldn't quite put her finger on, except that once she had carried his baby and cried for them both when they were taken from her. And because when she'd told Jimmy to leave, it was the thought in

408

the back of her mind of kissing Marc that had partly spurred her on to end it, because she had to end it properly with Jimmy before she could explore any feelings she had for Marc. To discover so quickly that she didn't have any was quite a blow.

'I think you should go,' she said.

Marc drank the remainder of his glass of wine in one and stood up.

'That's a shame,' he said. 'I'd thought we could both help each other through this period of transition.'

'That's just it,' Catherine said. 'For me this *is* a period of transition. For you it's your life: this is what your life will always be, moving from one woman you don't love to the next. I don't want to be one of them.'

Marc nodded and shrugged on his coat.

'Funny,' he said, 'how people are always so keen to tell me how to live my life. It used to be Alison, then it was my son, then it was your *husband* and now it's you. You're all the same.'

'It's not the same,' Catherine said. 'Alison, Dominic, and even Jimmy try to help you because they care. Because they want the people that love you to have a chance to be able to keep on loving you. But I don't care. I really don't care what you do next, Marc.'

'You feel pretty good saying that to me, don't you?' Marc said with a hint of a smile.

Catherine thought for moment and smiled at him.

'Damn right,' she said.

'Hello, darling,' Marc said to his wife as she appeared at the end of the path, with Jimmy, whose shoulders were hunched against the chill of the evening, despite the pint or so of hot coffee that was swilling around inside him.

'Hello, dear,' Alison said, taking his appearance completely in her stride. 'Pleasant evening?'

Marc hesitated and looked at Jimmy.

'Your wife despises me,' he said. 'She wouldn't have a bar of me. So at least you know that.'

Jimmy nodded and stood up straight. He looked down at the rectangle of light where Catherine was standing in the doorway.

'You are supposed to be in London,' Catherine said.

'I know, but I needed to tell you something work-related,' Jimmy said. 'Don't worry, I'm not here to declare my undying love to you again. I got the message.'

'Come in, Jimmy,' Catherine said. 'It's good to see you.'

Both Alison and Marc looked back at the smile on Catherine's face as she let Jimmy in and closed the door behind him, narrowing the rectangle of light into oblivion. The pair of them stood at the end of the path, looking at the shut door.

'So you didn't score then?' Alison asked her husband.

'Nope, did you?' Marc asked her, catching the wistful look on her face.

'No,' Alison said. 'If there's one thing I've learned it's that you can't stand in the way of your best friend and true love.'

'And when did you learn that?' Marc asked her. 'Fifteen years ago this summer?'

'No,' Alison said. 'Just about an hour ago, as it happens.'

Marc nodded. 'Can I walk you home?' he asked her.

Alison shook her head. 'No, I think I'll stick around for a bit longer in case I'm needed. If you could go back, though, that would be good. Next door's au pair will be wondering where I've got to.'

'Leave her to me,' Marc said.

*

'Croatia! On tour!' Catherine exclaimed. 'Well . . . I mean, *wow*, Jimmy, that's great news! Of course we'll miss you but you must go. Eight weeks isn't for ever. The girls and I will manage. They can always phone you and email. You do know how to use email, don't you?'

'I'll learn,' Jimmy said without enthusiasm.

'Well, then,' Catherine said. 'Well done.' She hugged him briefly and as she released him she briskly rubbed his upper arms. 'Well done, you.'

'Thanks,' Jimmy said, looking at her. 'On tour at last with a fairly famous band. Dreams do come true.'

'Yes they do,' Catherine said, furious with herself that it was such an effort to be happy for him because, after all, it was because of her that he was leaving, because of her that he couldn't stay. She could at least try to give him a good send-off.

'So can I go up and see the girls? I know it's late and a school night but . . .'

'Go,' Catherine said. 'Go and wake them up. It's more important they see you.'

Catherine sat on the top stair and listened as Jimmy talked to the girls, his voice low, theirs high and questioning.

'How long is eight weeks?' Leila asked him. 'How many sleeps is it? Is it longer away than Christmas?'

'No, darling,' Jimmy told her. 'I'll be back by the summer in time for your birthday. And it's not many sleeps. It's about . . . well, it's a few sleeps.'

'Is Croatia nice, Daddy?' Eloise asked him. 'Are the people kind?'

'Croatian people are the nicest people you could hope to meet and it's a lovely country, with mountains and a seaside and lots of sunny weather,' Jimmy said. 'Not that I'll be seeing any, what with me being a creature of the night and all.'

'Like an owl?' Leila asked.

'Pretty much,' Jimmy said.

'I don't think I want you to go,' Leila said eventually, her voice very small. 'I think I'll miss you too much, Daddy.'

'I'll miss you both too, darling,' Jimmy said. 'So much. But I sort of think I have to go.'

There was a long silence and when Catherine peeped through the crack in the door she could see the three of them hugging each other desperately. As she watched them together it was as if the sun was already rising in the room.

'OK now,' Jimmy said eventually. 'You two had better get back to sleep. I'll speak to you really soon and Mummy said I can even send emails to you somehow, I don't know how. Magic, I expect. The time will fly by and when I get back I'll have about a million presents for each of you.'

'OK, Daddy,' Leila said sleepily. 'I'll pray for you. Love you, Daddy.'

'And me, Daddy,' Eloise added. 'I love you too.'

'Love you too, love all of you too,' Jimmy said. 'See you later.'

Catherine had crept back downstairs before he came out of his children's bedroom. When he did emerge he stood outside the closed door for quite some time, waiting until he could hear their breathing steady and slow as they drifted back to sleep.

'Right then,' Catherine said. 'Got your passport? Because it would be awful if you got there and didn't have your passport and had to come home again.'

'Yep,' Jimmy said. 'I picked it up from the boat earlier, so no danger of that happening.'

'Is it in date?' Catherine asked him.

'Amazingly enough,' Jimmy chuckled. 'I had to renew it

when we went to Spain with the kids and Mum, do you remember? That was the last holiday we had . . . Anyway, yes, it's in date.'

'Travel insurance?' Catherine reminded him. 'You need travel insurance. Can't travel without it.'

'The band takes care of that. They need it, what with all the guillotines and swords. Turns out the undead are very safety conscious.'

'And you're all packed?' Catherine said, aware that she was starting to sound like an overprotective parent.

'Two pairs of jeans, my jacket, a shirt and a T-shirt,' Jimmy said. 'If I'm careful I won't have to do any laundry.'

They smiled at each other and then, as they remembered what was happening, their smiles quickly faded.

'Is there anything else you want to say to me?' Jimmy said after a moment.

Catherine looked at him for a long time and thought of about one thousand things she wanted to say to him but didn't think she could, because she wasn't exactly sure why she wanted to say them, and they were all things that had to be said for exactly the right reasons.

'No,' she said.

'OK then,' he said. 'I think I'll go.'

'There probably won't be a train for ages this time of night,' Catherine said. 'Why don't you wait here for a bit longer?'

'Anything in particular you want to say to me in that half-hour?' Jimmy asked her.

Slowly Catherine shook her head.

'Then I have to go now,' he said.

'Right then,' Catherine said.

'After I've done this,' Jimmy told her.

And then, quite without warning, he took her in his arms and kissed her. Not on the cheeks or quickly on the lips like he sometimes did. He kissed her properly, deeply, thoroughly and passionately, his arms pulling her body into his as if for those few brief moments he might absorb her right inside of him. And just as Catherine found herself kissing him back he broke the embrace and walked out of the back door.

'Jimmy, wait . . .' But before she could say anything else he was gone.

Chapter Twenty-six

Catherine felt as if she should be dreaming, as if she should be having one of those dreams where you absolutely know you've got to be somewhere doing something that is completely vital but you can't remember what it is, and the more you try to get there and the more you try to remember what it is, the more you realise you are never going to make it. She felt like she should be having one of those dreams only she was wide awake. All at once she was completely wide awake.

At the quiet knock on the back door she flew out of her chair, scrambling for her keys to unlock it.

'You came . . . Alison,' Catherine said, her face falling. 'Jimmy's gone to Croatia. He's gone.'

'I know. That's why I've come,' Alison said. She smiled. 'I was going to climb in through the window for old times' sake, but I thought that might push you over the edge.'

'You know that he's gone to Croatia?' Catherine asked.

'Yes, he told me in the pub. How do you feel about that?'

'How do I feel?' Catherine repeated, a little dazed. 'Oh, well, I'm pleased for him, of course. And he certainly needs the money for a deposit on a flat.'

'Catherine,' Alison said, inviting herself in because Catherine clearly wasn't going to, 'he's not here now. No one is here except you and me. So tell me, how do you *really* feel?'

415

'I want him to come back and stay here and not go to Croatia,' Catherine said desperately, leaning against the work-top. 'I don't want him to go, but it's not fair, is it? What right have I got to hold him back just because I don't want him to leave? I haven't got any right, have I?'

'No,' Alison said. 'Unless you happen to love him, for example? Because if you do then he has the right to know, you know.'

Catherine stared at her open-mouthed, as if she had, just that moment, been frozen in time.

'How can I tell him one minute that I don't love him and then, just as his big dream is about to come true, tell him that actually now he's about to leave me I might love him after all? I can't stand in the way of his dream again. He hated me for that before and he'll hate me for it again.'

'He won't hate you for telling him the thing he most wants to hear,' Alison said.

'But I'm over him,' Catherine protested. 'I don't care about Donna Clarke in The Goat any more. If I think about it, I don't feel anything at all.'

'That means you are over *that*,' Alison said. 'Not that you are over him. That means you have forgiven him, that you know that it didn't mean anything to him to be with her, and that if he had you again he wouldn't ever, ever need anyone else. That means that you two have a chance to be together without any shadows of the past hanging over you, no bitterness or unfinished business. That means you should get your coat on and run after him right now. Because you love him and you finally have a chance to be happy.'

Catherine looked at her. 'Why are you helping me?'

Alison smiled. 'Because you are my best friend. Look, his train is leaving in ten minutes so it's decision time. If you want to go I'll wait with Leila and Eloise till you get back.'

Catherine hesitated for a moment and then she grabbed her coat and ran.

Her chest heaved and her lungs screamed as they filled with the cold night air, and for the first time in her life Catherine wished that her legs were longer and that she was even lighter and thinner than she was, so that she could run just a little faster to find her husband.

And then suddenly Catherine stopped, her chest heaving as she gulped at the damp night air.

'What am I doing?' she asked herself. 'What if it goes wrong? What if I don't love him after all? What if he doesn't love me? What if me chasing after him now is one big terrible mistake?'

She stood frozen to the spot and she heard the blood pounding in her ears, the chill of the air against her skin, the water from the pavements soaking through her slippers, and in that one gloriously uncomfortable moment she felt utterly alive, as if all the energy in the world was for that briefest of times flowing solely through her. And Catherine knew she could only feel that way because she loved Jimmy. If loving him was a risk then this time, finally, it was one she was brave enough to take.

As she skidded into the station she heard the rumble of the London train above her head, pulling into the platform.

'Jimmy, wait!' she yelled, her voice echoing down the empty underpass. 'Wait!'

As she approached the steps that led up to the platform she slipped in a puddle and lost her footing for a moment, falling to her knees for a few precious seconds. As she finally plummeted onto the platform the train had already screeched to a halt.

'Jimmy!' Catherine looked up and down the length of the platform. It was empty. 'Jimmy!' she called again.

Just then the alarm sounded as the doors were about to close. Making a split-second decision, Catherine leaped on board.

The carriage was completely empty except for one boy in a hooded top, his head lolled against the window, his mouth open as he snored. For a split second Catherine wondered if Jimmy had got on the train at all, and then she realised that of course he had. He hadn't believed that he had any choice. Catherine had to find him and she didn't have much time because in a few minutes the train would stop once more and then there would be no more stops until London.

He wasn't in the second or third carriage that she stalked through, her long coat flapping around her, her slippers slapping on the carriage floor. But he was in the fourth one, staring bleakly out of the window, looking pale and tired.

'Jimmy,' she said as she arrived in front of him, sitting down with a sway and a bump.

Jimmy looked at her.

'I'm still a little bit drunk,' he said. 'Are you actually there or am I hallucinating?'

'Jimmy, I'm so stupid,' Catherine began, the words tumbling out. 'And I know I don't have the right to ask you this but, please, can I talk to you?'

'Why?' Jimmy asked her, frowning. 'What more is there to say?'

Catherine looked in the window at her own translucent reflection. Now was the time to make her courage stick. Jimmy crossed his arms and raised an eyebrow. She took a breath and looked him in the eye.

'Because I love you, I love you. I've only ever really loved you. Even when I hated you I loved you, even when I didn't love you I loved you and I can't lose you now that I've come to my senses. I've wasted twelve years not letting you know how much you are loved and I don't want to waste another single second. I couldn't let you go without telling you that when you come back from Croatia, if you want, me and the girls will be waiting for you. Waiting for you to come home to be with us again as a family. And I'm really sorry to rush you but if you do want that you have to tell me right now because I've got to get off this train when it gets to the next stop, which is in about twenty seconds.'

'Well, that's typical. You get two years to make your mind up and I get twenty seconds.' Jimmy looked at her, a tiny smile lighting his mouth. 'What was it that brought you to your senses? Come on, tell me. Was it that kiss? That was one hell of a kiss, wasn't it?'

'Yes, it was,' Catherine said, allowing herself to smile back. 'It certainly was.'

'I don't have to go,' Jimmy said, leaning across and catching her hands. 'Tell you what, I won't go. I'll come with you now. I want to, Cat, because all that stuff you just said – it's made me pretty much the happiest man alive on this planet.'

'Oh, I want you to come back but you can't,' Catherine told him, briefly pressing her cheek to the back of his hand. 'You have to go – this is your big break! Go on tour and have fun, be brilliant and enjoy it, Jimmy. Because I'll be waiting for you when you get back and anyway, missing you will be almost nice now that I know it won't be for ever.'

'They'll be the longest eight weeks of my life.' Jimmy pulled her close to him and kissed her as the train pulled into the next station.

'This is the happiest goodbye I've ever had,' Catherine told him, her fingers entwined in his as she stood up.

'This isn't a goodbye,' Jimmy said, kissing her hand before he let it go. 'This is the beginning.'

As the train pulled out of the station Catherine Ashley

stood on the platform for a very long time, trying to understand exactly how her life had just changed. And then
something occurred to her.

She had absolutely no idea how she was going to get home.

'Thank you,' Catherine said to Alison as they sipped tea and
watched the sunrise together for the second time. 'And thanks
for lending me the money to pay for that cab. I don't think any
of this would have happened tonight if it hadn't been for you.'

'It's my pleasure,' Alison said. 'Are you sad that he's gone
for eight weeks?'

'I'm happy because I know that at last, maybe for the first
time, I've made him happy. And anyway, I've got the rest of
my life to enjoy with him,' Catherine said, smiling fondly.
'Besides, I enjoy spending sunrise with you. It's becoming a
regular thing.'

'Did you ever think we'd be like this again?' Alison asked
her. 'Friends, I mean?'

Catherine shook her head. 'No. No, I never dreamed that
we would be friends again but now that we are I can't imagine
a time when we won't be.'

'And to think now our daughters are friends like we once
were. Do you remember how we used to talk about that, how
we said we'd always be together for all of our lives, how our
children would be friends and we'd always have each other?'

'We were almost right,' Catherine said. 'In the scheme of
things it hasn't been that long that we've been apart. And now
the girls have found each other I suppose we'll be together a
lot more.' She smiled at Alison. 'It's good to have you back,
Alison.'

'You don't know how glad that makes me feel, hearing you
say that,' Alison said, her voice catching a little as she turned
her face away from Catherine.

They sat in silence for a few minutes longer and then Catherine put her arm around Alison.

'Are you OK?' Catherine asked her friend.

Alison looked into the rising sun so that the light drenched her face, and smiled.

'I'm going to be,' she said. 'I've got a funny feeling that I'm going to be.'

The Accidental Mother

Rowan Coleman

Sophie Mills has worked her Manolo Blahniks off to reach the near-top of her profession. And she's very happy with her priorities in life – her job, her neurotic cat Artemis and her passion for shoes. After all, relationships only get in the way. And as for children? She hasn't even begun to think about them yet. Until one day an unexpected visitor brings news of a strange inheritance and Sophie is suddenly, out of the blue, in sole charge of two children under the age of six. But motherhood can't be all that hard, can it?

Within twenty-four hours, her make-up is smeared all over the bathroom, Artemis has taken up residence on top of her wardrobe, and Sophie is in despair. And all her unconventional mother can suggest is Dr Roberts' *Complete Dog Training and Care Manual*.

Determined to rise to the challenge, Sophie soon realises that she'll need more than a business plan to cope with all this . . .

Praise for Rowan Coleman

'A witty, wonderful, warm-hearted read' *Company*

'Touching and thought-provoking' *B*

arrow books